Shallow Waters

HORROR FLASH FICTION ANTHOLOGY

SPECIAL PAPERBACK EDITION

Edited by Joe Mynhardt

Published by Crystal Lake Publishing
Tales from The Darkest Depths

Website: www.crystallakepub.com

WELCOME
TO ANOTHER

CRYSTAL LAKE PUBLISHING
CREATION

Table of Contents

INTRODUCTION

Eleven eBooks and now a massive paperback edition barely touches the surface of what the Shallow Waters series means to me and so many authors and readers.

What started out as a small flash fiction contest on the Crystal Lake Patreon page, quickly grew into quite a popular monthly event. We posted the finalists on our Patreon where our patrons would read and vote for their favorites, with a winner announced at the end of every month. This contest has always been free to enter, but payment is offered to the top three stories, as well as a publication in an upcoming Shallow Waters eBook volume. A lot of those winners and popular finalists are included in the book you're currently holding. Take note that, since these authors are scattered all over the world, you'll see some of these stories with US and others with UK spelling.

Over the years the contest has evolved even more, and the winner now has the option of hosting an upcoming contest by selecting a theme and choosing the top fifteen to twenty finalists (for extra remuneration, of course). It's a great way to see how things work behind the publishing curtain.

This might be the last Shallow Waters volume, but we're not nearly done yet. I'm happy to say that a new anthology series (featuring future Shallow Waters contest winners) will take its place. All top three stories will be published along with short stories by invited authors who've caught our eye.

Whether you're an author or a dedicated reader, if you find a sense of belonging and friendship in the stories ahead, be sure to visit Crystal Lake Entertainment on Patreon. We hope to see you there!

Joe Mynhardt
28 August, 2023

Closure on a Bed of Nails

Chad Lutzke

It was the only cactus that still blossomed flowers. That was the landmark, the bouquet of ghost-white petals. Without them, the cactus stood amongst the others like a field of conforming soldiers. Spiked and juniper green. At its foot, feet bheeneath the soil, the bones of his lover. A gentle, beautiful woman who taught him to see beauty in the most mundane of things. Even the desert. He liked to think it was her who sprouted the flowers, reminding him of the beauty still found in an empty world. Reminding him of her, of their engagement that ended early by sickness, then death.

But the flowers had long ceased serving their purpose. They were no longer a beautiful sight among the bland. Now they were a prick in his heel, a thorn in his side. A still photo of cancer that haunted him daily. That ivory blemish in a bone-dry sea. A scar outside his home, across the road, catching his eye and taking his breath. The cursed things glowed against the green-fingered sandscape.

Remember the time we...

The blank could be filled with countless memories, each of them worthy of remembrance. But when would the healing come? Where was the closure he was promised? The flowers seemed to mock him now.

She's buried here with us. We have her now, they'd say as he left for work, as he came home.

Guilt clawed at him for his disdain toward the blooming. How could he hate the thing she'd sent in her place?

One final time the blemish caught his eye. This needed to end. The healing had to begin. He retrieved the ax, headed across the road and through the field of cacti. The sun massaged his naked back, the wind his scalp.

He had stood there more times than he cared to remember, wetting the ground with a leaking face, overtaken with grief. And here he stood again, for the last time.

"I love you too much," he said, fingering the soft, white petals. Like baby's hair and avian down.

The horrible beauty. The damned reminder.

He plucked a single flower from its nest, anticipating a scream. Not from her, but from himself. He placed the flower in his pocket and gripped the ax, then swung the blade at the base of the plant. And this time there was a scream. His throat burned with the shriek as he swung again and again. His screams raced across the desert, warning the tendrilled orchard that the healing must begin.

His face straining, he swung again and again. The desert ate the sound, consumed it like rainfall. Another swing and the cactus tipped. It would never give birth again.

The man dropped the ax and threw himself atop the spiny plant, its quills sinking into his flesh. A punishment for his closure. A horizontal crucifixion. He bled on the green, decorating the cactus. Christmas colors on a bed of barren earth.

As he hugged the plant, its spines digging deep, he begged for forgiveness, pleaded with her to understand. And as if an understanding had been made, it began to rain. As though God himself wept for the grieving.

A thousand stings carried the grief away and with a groan like thunder, the man rolled off his bed of nails and sobbed, the rain cooling his tiny wounds. For ten minutes it rained, washing away the sin of letting go. Then with ax in hand and a pocketful of memories, he walked home.

The box which held her ring still sat on his chest of drawers. He placed the flower in the box and closed it with a snap--a merciless loop of sound.

Deep into a drawer the box was placed, where he could be reminded by choice, not as an intruding violation on an otherwise peaceful day. It would be at his own will he would open the box and gaze at the flower, spinning the reel of memories. His choice only.

But he never looked again.

Chad Lutzke's short fiction can be found in several dozen magazines and anthologies, and some of his books include: Of Foster Homes & Flies, Stirring the Sheets, Skullface Boy, The Pale White, Three-Smile Mile, *and* The Neon Owl *series. Lutzke's work has been praised by authors Jack Ketchum, Richard Chizmar, Joe R. Lansdale, Stephen Graham Jones, Tim Waggoner, and his own mother. He can be found lurking the internet at www.chadlutzke.com.*

The Silence of the Sirens

Loren Rhoads

Throughout her time in Prague, Alondra had contemplated a visit to Kafka's grave. He understood futility like no one else. She came out of the subway station to find herself across the street from a towering white gate. She gathered the fur coat more closely around herself and trudged across the slush-piled street.

She thought she had the graveyard to herself. Many of the stones were polished black marble, engraved with the blessing hands or the Star of David. Too many of them bore birthdates followed by a hyphen and then the names Auschwitz, Dachau, Bergen-Belsen.

As Alondra kicked through the crystallized snowdrifts, her thoughts circled back to Victor in England. Tears prickled her eyes. She wiped them away before they froze and blinded her.

For forty days, she had not interacted with another human being. Abstaining from sex had been easy in this city where she knew no one but her landlord and the thief who'd procured the equipment for her Work. Perhaps *that* was where the fault lay: her failure had been insufficient bribery to purchase Emperor Rudolf's treasures to stock her lab. The taint of theft could have corrupted her results. She could blame her desperation and haste that the universal solvent had not transmuted.

If John Dee's furnace in the collection of the British Museum had been reparable, she wouldn't have sunk to theft. If she'd had any options at all...but Victor's life was almost over. Time was too short for anything but desperate measures.

She gazed at Kafka's pink granite obelisk. Buried with his mother and hated father: how that must rankle in whatever afterlife the author had flown to. She wondered if she was doomed to be buried alongside her own blood kin.

Somewhere in the winter graveyard, a man shouted. "*Kam jdete?*"

Alondra turned. An elderly man shuffled through the snow toward her. She realized he must have shouted at her several times.

"Are you crazy?" he demanded in Czech. That much she understood. Her landlord often screamed it through her locked door.

She wondered where Victor's grave would be, who would chase her away from it.

The graveyard's caretaker harangued her, shivering and rubbing his hands. Eventually, Alondra grasped that he meant it was too cold for any sane person to wander the graveyard. He paused, clearly expecting an apology. Alondra opened her mouth, but her voice—after forty days of silence—refused to oblige. Even if she'd spoken his language, there was no arguing with Czechs. She gestured she was mute.

Disgusted, the caretaker shook his head and waved her toward the exit. He had clearly decided she was deaf, too.

Pain blossomed in her chest, jagged and cold. Suddenly, she had to run. Encumbered by the heavy fur coat, Alondra bolted out of the cemetery, away from the dead, dodging traffic as she crossed the road, fleeing down into the metro station. She paid her fare and found herself, swaying, on the edge of the platform, breathing the sharp scent of electricity and steel.

People stared at her—the crazed redhead in the expensive fur coat. In the Malá Strana, below the old castle, women were wealthy and fashionable. They looked at her coat with measuring eyes, craving their own. Out here in the suburbs, the coat represented blessings that the fall of Communism never bestowed. Alondra wondered if someone would stop her from jumping if only to salvage her coat.

A light appeared in the tunnel, stabbing through the shadows as it grew nearer. To her own surprise, Alondra stepped away from the platform's edge and watched the train arrive. She could not kill herself. Her death would hasten Victor's, take away a pillar that supported his will to live. As long as he knew she existed somewhere in the world, he wouldn't give up. She wouldn't destroy him by hurtling herself prematurely into the maw of death.

After he was gone...well, she made herself no promises.

Loren Rhoads' *Alondra stories have appeared in the books* Best New Horror #27, Strange California, Fright Mare: Women Write Horror, Sins of the Sirens, The Haunted Mansion Project: Year One, *and* nEvermore: Tales of Murder, Mystery, and the Macabre. *They're collected in kindle format on Amazon. Learn more at lorenrhoads.com.*

It's Me, Not You

Jonathan Winn

His fentanyl dreams thick, her beloved slept.

Hours ago, they'd met. Tousled hair, lop-sided grin, his greasy paws clutching a wrench, he'd poked his head into her driver's side window. "A squeak, huh," he repeated as she sipped her morning double shot raspberry mocha. By lunch, here, in the house they now shared, his calloused palms smearing her dimpled flesh black, she'd given herself to him. By dinner, his eyes closing half-way through the mashed potatoes, she knew he was The One.

By nightfall she was hoisting her snoring Goliath, his muscled limbs heavy and useless, up eleven stairs to the attic.

Now she sat near, watching him.

They'd left before, the other Ones. Half a dozen, at least. Or so it seemed. Disappearing before she woke or slipping out the door while she showered, the scribbled apologies propped on her pillow as soothing as alcohol on an open cut. The lie of those inevitable four words—"It's me, not you"—soon sharpening the dull ache of perpetual abandonment into a bone-white blade of dangerous calm.

But this beloved—locked behind the thick bars of a Rottweiler-tough kennel, arms duct-taped to his sides, his mouth silenced, his thighs webbed tight with a second roll of metallic gray—would stay.

That band of gold taunting her from his left hand would not.

But despite the tugging and pulling, twisting and nudging, the ring wouldn't budge. The metal too small or his finger too thick, this single-paycheck remnant of his past mocked her with its stubborn refusal to yield.

Until it did. Clattering to the floor, her gardening shears slicing flesh and cracking bone, it surrendered as her Adonis dreamt. Then, moving quick, a red-hot iron cauterizing the seeping torrent into blackened calm, she swaddled the orphaned knuckle in gauze.

And, just like that, her beloved was no longer betrothed.

She stretched. Dawn crept 'round the heavy drapes, the dark giving way to a soft, dusty glow. He'd be waking soon.

She was ready.

Earlier, while the stars still shone, while he still slept and bled and dreamt, and his bandage was still the panicked shout of bright red and not the harmless

Pepto-pink it'd become, she'd ducked downstairs to slip into one of her wedding day-white dresses. The first thing he'd see in this, his new life, would be of her in innocent, virginal white on their wedding day.

And soon, kneeling before him, his one and only, a woman no longer wandering life as a desperate, hopeless spinster but as someone loved and adored and desired, they'd begin again. She'd learn his favorite foods. His favorite music. She'd be his heart, his soul, his voice. His whole, wide world. In time, she'd learn his most basic needs and most private desires.

She'd learn his last name.

Their days would be spent together, she decided, the lock unlocked and the door of the kennel creaking open, her hands coaxing the battered work boots from her sleeping Adonis' large feet.

He'd never slip out when she was in the shower. Or tip-toe through starlight to escape. That she was sure of. It'd be impossible. "We're soul mates," she said, the words the barest of whispers as she rolled the socks down his calves and over his heels.

"Twin flames." She reached behind for the knife. His bare foot rested in front of her, the sweaty sole nestled against her knee. "We're destined." The blade rested on his ankle.

His eyes were open now. He blinked slow, once, twice, his mind, his body, his thoughts, reason, fear still lost in an opioid haze. She smiled, shushing him quiet and still.

"With you, I'll never be alone," she then said as his eyes closed and the first cut sliced deep.

Jonathan Winn *is a screenwriter and author of almost a dozen books including* Eidolon Avenue: The First Feast *("a great read...powerful and jarring,"* Cemetery Dance)*, Martuk...the Holy (A Highlight of the Year, 2012 Papyrus Independent Fiction Awards) and* The Martuk Series, Vol. 1, A Collection of Short Fiction.

Motel 8

Francesca Maria

Camellia needs a good night's sleep like a junky needs a fix. A two hundred mile stretch of nothing forces her to keep driving on the gray potholed roads from Texas to California. Her eyelids droop, carrying the extra weight of her weariness. A pink neon beacon of hope a hundred yards up the highway draws her in like a fly to a bug zapper on a warm summer night.

A lone motel isolated on an acre of dry dirt looms through Camellia's windshield. Camellia doesn't notice the lot is empty as she pulls her car under the overhang that reads OFFICE. The single level structure reminds Camellia of the countless strip malls she's passed along her route. The white trim of the flat roof hangs over the building just enough to create shadows on the doors and yet not enough to keep out rain, should it come. Camellia sees paint chipping away at the dark brown exterior. A dead rat blocks the office door.

A bald, middle-aged man with a face that has been punched more times than most pushes the protesting screen door and leers at Camellia. He kicks the rat into the dried bushes across the driveway.

"Need a room? Fifty dollars. Cash only." He fiddles with something in his teeth with a sausage finger. The sucking that follows makes Camellia's insides somersault. She eyes her car. Sensing her hesitation, "There ain't nuthin' else for seventy-five miles. Motel 8 is the last place on the map." Camellia sees his pants are unbuttoned and pink flesh pokes out of the opening.

Her car, too full to sleep in, packed with all the remnants of a life she's escaping, is not an option.

"Do you have a clean, quiet room?" She immediately feels stupid as the words leave her mouth. His Cheshire grin doesn't reassure her.

"The room at the end, number one-twelve, hasn't been used in over a month and is as clean as a baby's bottom." A laugh-cough escapes through his open mouth. Something wiggles in his teeth.

"I guess... I guess I'll take it." Reaching into her wallet she pulls out a hundred and gives it to him. He grabs the bill greedily and retreats back into the office. After several long minutes the P.T. Barnum specimen comes back through the creaky screen door which slams loudly behind him. He hands her the key. She waits. He ogles.

"My change?"

"Oh, I'll be keeping that as a deposit, in case you know, you make a mess. You'll get it in the morning when you check out." Turning his back toward her, "Have a good night now and don't let the bedbugs bite! Ha, ha, ha! Just kiddin'. Just a little motel humor for ya. Our bedbugs don't bite, ha ha ha!" Slam. The screen door closes leaving Camellia alone under the overhang.

Key in hand, she hurries back into her car and locks the door for the short drive to her room. If she wasn't afraid of falling asleep on the road she'd be driving away from this god-awful place.

Pulling up to the shit-brown door with faded white trim, Camellia hears the sound of her dead momma's voice echoing in her skull, "Camellia, we just gotta make do." A common mantra tattooed into her DNA at an early age.

"Well, Momma, I'll try." Her voice sounds weak and cracked. Something low to the ground shuffles behind her. She can't see it in the dim light and hurries to fit the key into the hole. The door is so lightweight it swings out of her grasp and bangs against the back wall.

The smell of mothballs, stale smoke, and urine infests her senses. Memories of coming home to her daddy, sitting in the dark, drunk, and itching for a fight, invade Camellia. She clutches the Zippo in her pocket she stole from him. She half expects to see him sitting on the bed when she flips on the light. Empty.

The room is worse on the inside than on the outside. The burnt orange walls scream Seventies porno and the once plush carpet is an indistinguishable green, yellow and orange swirl. It squishes under her feet as she moves toward the bed. A velvet picture of a blond child, with an enormous head and weeping giant pools for eyes holding a sagging stuffed puppy, stares back at her.

She has to pee. She's had to pee since about an hour before she spotted the Motel 8 sign. Her feet feel like they're walking on wet sponges as she traverses to the miniscule bathroom. She flips the switch and hears the low buzz of fluorescent lights as they struggle to illuminate through a rusted plastic cover. She squints through clenched eyes as she lifts the toilet lid, saying a few prayers to whoever's listening that it's not as gross as the rest of the room. Blessed relief. White and clean, unsoiled by man or vermin.

Washing up, Camellia inspects the blotchy mirror above the sink. It's bolted haphazardly to the wall, no doubt repurposed from a truck stop or gas station. A scraping sound like keys on glass pierces from behind the mirror. Movement in the bottom right corner of the reflection startles her awake. She must be hallucinating from the lack of sleep. She'd driven fourteen hours straight to get as far away from Curtis as fast as possible. She sees familiar yellow-green-purple marks forming on her biceps.

Furry charcoal legs, attached to a nondescript host, scurry across the bottom of the mirror. Camellia turns and sees only the nauseating carpet behind her. *Just keep it together. A few hours of sleep then I'll be out of this hellhole.* The thought leaves her feeling strained.

Retrieving her purse and overnight bag from the car uses the last of her strength. She plummets onto the polyester bedspread, with the same sick color scheme as the carpet, and collapses.

Camellia sleeps, but does not rest. She's drowning in a current of cold abyss, gasping for air as her lungs struggle in her dreamscape. Milky foam seeps into her mouth as it skims the water's surface. Tiny hands pull her under. Hairy pats tickle her face as she tries to break free.

A noiseless scream escapes her lips as she wakes. Camellia coughs violently, finding her breath. She cannot raise her head. A sea of black spiders crawl over every inch of her exposed skin. They are pinning her down with an elaborate crisscross web. One skitters into her mouth as she gasps. The weight of a thousand legs crushes her as they pile onto each other, multiplying before her eyes.

The door opens. The Teeth Sucker waddles over, sticks his puffy head over Camellia's and laughs. Spit escapes his mouth and splashes onto her forehead.

"I told ya, miss, our bugs don't bite...hee hee hee...they suck!" At that last word, thousands of needles penetrate her pores. Her body succumbs to a rhythmic jerking as the infestation sucks her blood in unison.

The light in her eyes fades as the motel manager undresses and pulls down on a skin tag under his chin. A thin obsidian zipper turns into a V revealing gray matted fur. Two dish-size eyes, wet and glistening, appear behind the chest followed by a row of smaller eyes below the belly button.

The skin suit falls on the green-yellow-orange carpet with a moist slap. The monster shakes the mucus off like a dog after a bath. The smell of rotten meat and sewage permeates what little air she can still breathe.

No.

She did not escape her tormentor to fall into the hands of another.

No.

She will not die like this.

Finding her fingers, she squirms, reaching inside her pants pocket. She flips open the Zippo. Fire ignites the flammable web, freeing her from its hold and scattering its creators. The giant spider creature moves on top of her.

She has been in this position before. She knows what to do.

Camellia slams her knee into the belly of the beast with every ounce of strength she has. It recoils just long enough for her to light its underside. She kicks it again and again. Payback for every kick she's received. Every punch, every burn, every form of torture she endured comes out in a mix of fury and fire as she pummels the beast. Until it's over.

The mini-spiders retreat into the carpet while their progenitor lies belly up, twitching.

Camellia wipes the sweat from her brow, grabs her bags and keys and lights the polyester bedspread on fire. The room goes up in a *whoosh*. She turns and looks at the room as she makes her exit. "Never again." The door slams behind her as smoke billows out the shit-brown door with white trim.

Francesca Maria writes dark fiction surrounded by cats near the Pacific Ocean. She is the creator of the Black Cat Chronicles, a true horror comic book series narrated by a mystical black cat. Her short story collection They Hide: Short Stories to Tell in the Dark *from Brigid Gate Press debuted as an Amazon #1 Best Seller. Her short stories and essays can be found in various anthologies and publications including Crystal Lake Publishing's Shallow Waters,* Death's Garden Revisited *and* Under the Stairs. *You can find her at francescamaria.com.*

Christmas at 19b

Karen Bayly

Walter Proctor cared for his tenants. Inside the apartment building, the lights turned on at sunset and off at 11:45 pm. Air temperature he maintained at 18 degrees Celsius and 50 percent humidity. And although those who lived at 19b Harrowgate Way were disinclined to let the world into their humble abodes, the blinds were in working condition. Walter's tenants required privacy, and being a considerate landlord, he fulfilled their needs.

Now, Christmas was almost upon them. Walter adored this time of year. His own residence at 19a Harrowgate Way currently gleamed with all the trimmings. An evergreen wreath graced the Victorian oak door. A pine tree, with needles so luxurious each branch was a bottle brush of green, occupied pride of place in the mullioned window on the ground floor. He'd spent hours on its decoration; now the tree stood festooned with luscious strands of red, silver, and gold tinsel, twenty-five glimmering silvery bells, twenty-eight shiny golden balls, and a rosy-cheeked angel on top.

He had also draped fairy lights from the upstairs balcony at 19a and from the rooftop of 19b. Anything to get into the Christmas spirit. Locals described the place as spooky, and although people staying away in droves suited him, Walter didn't want a reputation as a Scrooge.

He whistled 'God Rest Ye Merry Gentlemen' as he descended the stairs into his basement workshop. He opened the cold room, wheeled out his soon-to-be new resident, and drew back the sheet covering her face. No matter how many times he gazed at her delicate features, a small sigh of joy escaped his lips. Her driver's license said she was Miss Amber Preston. She was such a beautiful young woman, so full of laughter and life that he'd experienced a small twinge of sorrow when he'd thrust the stiletto into her heart. Yet death was necessary to save her from the ravages of time. With him, she'd be gorgeous forever, treasured and revered. He was proud of the unique—if unsanctioned—service he offered.

As he dressed in his personal protective gear, he hummed a medley of tunes from his favourite musical, 'Sweeney Todd'. He certainly didn't possess Mister Todd's revenge issues, but the character excited him, put him in the mood for his blood-letting duties.

The next task was to mix his own custom brand of embalming fluid. He was proud of his formula which he called *Proctor's Preservation Potion*. The standard embalming fluid was a product of modern science and had no pizazz. While he'd studied the contemporary methods of embalming, he preferred the techniques of the old masters, such as da Vinci, Hunter, and Baillie, who all used Venice turpentine and oil of lavender. However, his greatest inspiration came from Ruysch, whose recipe required clotted pig blood, Berlin Blue, and mercury oxide. He adopted a similar concoction, substituting human blood for the porcine variety. Miss Preston's embalming fluid would contain the blood of Mister Tambin, and thus she would be a part of Walter's select group, even before her debut.

Gently, he slid the sheet from Miss Amber's beautiful body. He made an incision near her collarbone to access the carotid artery and jugular vein. Into the carotid, he inserted the embalming machine's arterial tubes, one directed toward her heart, the other toward her head. Next, he inserted forceps into the jugular vein to facilitate blood drainage. The machine pumped his embalming fluid into the artery, which forced the blood out of her jugular vein. This he captured in glass flagons, which he stored for the next tenant.

Using a soapy sponge, Walter massaged her body with vigorous strokes to assist drainage and distribute the embalming fluid. Not one millimetre of her would fall prey to his enemy, Decay. He beamed as her tissue firmed and blushed under his touch. Then, he caressed her extremities to encourage the preserving fluid into her elegant fingers and toes.

A wise woman once told him a surprise death trapped a person's soul in its fleshy prison, only to be released when the body decayed or burnt, or through the intoning of hymns. Because of this, Walter always killed his tenants before they comprehended their imminent demise, and he had mastered the art of circumventing post-mortem ravages. He warbled 'Silent Night' as a further preventative measure and hoped Miss Amber found his serenade freeing. Years ago, he'd received compliments about his rich baritone voice.

Finally, he raised his charge's hand to his moist lips and kissed her palm.

"I love you, dear one."

The long, hollow, metal trocar glinted in the lamplight as he positioned it above her belly. Deftly, he slid the tube into her abdomen. He sang louder as he vacuumed up the fluids remaining in her belly, making space for yet more embalming fluid. Soon she would be ready to meet her neighbours at the Yuletide costume party he'd arranged for her debut.

The others waited in Flat 6 at 19b, keen to meet their new member. Mister Tom Andrews dressed as Santa Claus, a role he took on every Christmas. Usually, Miss Jennifer Johns played Missus Claus, but in the interest of equal opportunity, Walter gave the role to Miss Yasmina Nadoo this year. Miss Johns was not the type to be peeved, and instead graciously accepted the role of Head Elf. The others dressed as elves or reindeer, except for Mister Jake Tambin, who agreed to a Christmas tree costume.

Miss Amber would attend dressed as a saucy elf in a short skating skirt with a pom-pom trim. The other ladies might be jealous, but it would pass. To be an exemplary landlord meant shaking things up occasionally, otherwise, 19b would be a boring place to live. Sometimes the parties there roared hot and heavy, but not at Christmas. No, those shenanigans were best kept for New Year's Eve and other holidays.

He closed the trocar-made incision with a small plastic button on which was written 'Loved by Walter.' He washed her once more, this time in a luxurious body wash redolent of apples and cinnamon, and covered her skin in a matching scented lotion.

The grandfather clock upstairs struck 8:30 pm. Party time. He'd laid out Amber's clothes on the bed in her new flat—number 5 at 19b. Walter wheeled her from his workshop to the basement of 19b, into the service elevator then up to the third floor. He grinned at the light creeping out from under the door of Flat 6. They were having a splendid time inside.

Within minutes, Miss Amber Preston was ready for her grand entrance. Adorned with makeup, she posed on a wheeled chair, red velvet skating skirt demure but sexy, legs crossed to reveal a flash of tempting thigh, cute green and red jacket showing off her slender waist and plump cleavage. Walter was so proud of her.

He wheeled her round to number 6 and threw open the door. Seven faces greeted him, sightless eyes warm with affection, mummified lips blessing his name. He parked the lovely new girl next to Mister Jake, who appeared especially happy—and why wouldn't he be? Miss Amber was everything a man could desire.

"Now, you be a gentleman, Mister Jake. No fast moves," Walter said, waggling a precautionary finger. Then he winked. "At least, not today."

Walter's mother had proclaimed he'd never have a family. Mean old cow. He wondered if she'd rotted away to nothingness yet. It was better than she deserved. Anyway, he proved her wrong. He had a genuine family now, and they loved him more than she ever did.

Choking back his emotions, he raised a glass of eggnog. "Merry Christmas, one and all."

Everyone smiled at 19b.

Karen Bayly is a writer, software tester, and author of two books: Fortitude *and* Tesato's Code. *Her short stories and poems have appeared in Yellow Mama Webzine, Black Petals Magazine, and Every Day Fiction, and anthologies from Black Beacon Books Black Hare Press, and Crystal Lake Publishing. She lives in Sydney, Australia, with two cats, a guitar, and a ukulele.*

The Naughty List

Tom Deady

Billy was on the Naughty List. Billy was *always* on the Naughty List. He just couldn't resist putting thumbtacks on kids' seats at school or melting crayons on the old radiators in the classrooms, filling the air with that acrid, waxy smell until Mrs. Jensen was forced to open the windows. *Mischievous*, Principal Billings had told his parents the one time he'd been caught putting a whoopie cushion on Mrs. Jensen's chair. Billings had looked like he was trying not to smile. Mrs. Jensen had just looked mad. Yes, he was on the Naughty List, all right. At the very top. And that's where he intended to stay.

It was Christmas Eve and he sat in the living room staring at the fireplace. His stocking hung limply as if knowing it would never be filled. There was no plate of cookies for Santa. No glass of milk. No carrots for the reindeer. His gaze shifted to the Christmas tree, listing in its stand like the drunk who put it there, half decorated and unlit. Under the tree, no brightly wrapped gifts lay for him to prod and shake. Only dead pine needles and an empty liquor bottle and the jumble of light cords.

Billy never meant any harm while planning his pranks, not at first anyway, he just thought they were funny. Most of his classmates seemed to think so, too. Well, not the ones pulling thumbtacks out of their butts, but everyone else. Lately, he'd started pulling more pranks at home even though his parents most definitely did not find them funny. Ever since his dad lost his job at the mill, things at home had changed. His parents didn't seem to find *anything* funny. All they did was drink and yell at each other. Unless they happened to notice Billy, then they yelled at him. Or worse.

While Billy had never been a huge fan of school, it had become a refuge from his home life. From the yelling and hitting and...the other stuff. When Christmas vacation had started, it had put his stomach in double knots. Home all day, *every* day, with his parents. No homework to keep his mind occupied during the long evenings when his mother and father spoke in angry, slurred, swear-laden voices. When they were loose with their tongues and their fists and their cigarettes. His pranks were the only thing he had to keep him sane.

The first day he'd waited for his mother to take her "nap"—at least that's what she called it after drinking in front of game shows all afternoon—then emptied his father's bottle. He knew his father would blame her, how could he not when Billy had placed it on the floor next to his snoring mother? The fight had been glorious to listen to, one of the worst ever. Then he'd heard the bed springs squeaking and animal-like noises and knew they were making up. That prank had failed. He'd thought maybe his father would kill her for drinking his booze.

The next day he'd broken open a firecracker he had left over from the summer and tapped out the gunpowder onto a piece of paper. Next, he'd snuck a pack of his father's cigarettes and carefully tore a small hole in one and poured in the gunpowder, resealing it as best he could. Knowing his father, he wouldn't notice. Most of the time the package was so crumpled from being in his pocket that the cigarettes were bent at odd, comical angles. He wasn't sure what to expect when his father lit the lucky cigarette. He'd watched his father all day, getting a cuff in the ear at one point for being so fucking nosy.

When the time came, the result was a little disappointing. When the butt burned to where the gunpowder was, it flared and hissed wildly for a second. That was all. But the timing had been good—it had happened just as his father was talking a long drag. His father's eyes had bulged, and he'd tossed the cigarette to the floor with a childish squeal. Then he'd just picked it up, looked at it with confusion written all over his face, and kept smoking. Billy had bitten down on his tongue to stifle a giggle when he'd heard that sissy-like scream, but he'd secretly been hoping his father's face might burn off. He wondered if he could somehow disguise a whole firecracker as a cigarette...

That night, his parents had been eying him suspiciously. He thought for a split-second he might be caught. Then he dismissed the idea. He only got caught when he *wanted* to get caught, like the time with the whoopie cushion. He couldn't explain how or why he always managed to get away with things, but he always did. What he had planned for Christmas morning was going to be his magnum opus. He'd learned that phrase from Mrs. Jensen and stored it in his memory bank. He liked the sound of it. Liked the power of its meaning. He stood, glancing around the room at his handiwork, then went to bed.

The next morning, he woke at dawn, not to run downstairs and tear the paper off his presents—that was for normal kids with normal parents—his present would come by his own hands. He wanted to make sure everything was ready.

He sat on the couch drinking a mug of hot chocolate piled with whipped cream. He'd put a Christmas album on the turntable and had the sound up loud enough to wake his parents. A roaring fire crackled and popped, warming the room. He heard them shuffling down the stairs and grumbling in their gruff

23

hangover voices. He was filled with excitement, placing his mug on the coffee table in front of him, not wanting to miss a thing.

His parents paused in the doorway, staring at Billy. He stared back, grinning. His father's hair stuck up in the back and his mother's face was still puffy with sleep. Both wore bewildered expressions that made them look as dumb as Billy knew they were.

"Come in, Mother. Father. It's Christmas Day."

His parents looked at him. It was his mother that showed the first hint of fear in her eyes. His father was too busy letting his rage boil over.

"Plug in the lights, Mother," he said, still grinning gleefully. "Let's make this a Christmas to remember."

His mother moved toward the tree, shaking off her husband's hand as he tried in vain to hold her back.

"Son—"

"No!" Billy screamed. "Don't you call me that." He pulled his fiery gaze away from his father, watching as his mother plugged the extension cord into the outlet. The Christmas tree lit in a rainbow of colors for a second, then every light on the tree exploded simultaneously. The sound was like music to Billy. Better than the old man on the stereo crooning about God and stars and angels. Sparks flew everywhere and the smell of burning plastic filled the air. But that wasn't the best part.

Billy's mother was dancing and jigging, her hair standing straight from her head as electricity flowed through her. Blood ran from her nose first, then from her ears and eyes as well. Eventually a circuit breaker tripped, cutting off the music with a scratch of the needle across the record, and she collapsed to the floor, smoke rising from her body. The smell of burning flesh filled the room. The Christmas tree had also caught fire and was burning wildly.

Billy glared at his father. He was still staring at what was left of his wife before he turned, pulled by Billy's simmering rage.

"Son— I mean, Billy—"

Billy stood and reached under the couch cushions, turning toward his father. He held the axe he'd found in the basement when his father had locked him down there the week before. It was old and splintery, and the blade was rusty, but Billy thought it would do the job.

He swung low, aiming to make his father's escape impossible. The blade sunk into the meaty part of his father's calf before striking bone. His father screamed as he collapsed to the ground grabbing for his leg. Billy had to yank hard to get the axe out of the bone. Then he raised it and began chopping.

The noise was wet and squishy at first, sending bright streams of blood arcing through the smokey air. When the blade found bone, it sounded like chopping wood. Billy's father screamed and writhed, his eyes finally finding his son's.

"Billy..."

There was no mercy to be found.

When the screams died down and the blood stopped squirting, Billy collapsed onto the couch, muscles spent. He watched the flames from the Christmas tree spread. Sirens sounded in the distance. Billy smiled and picked up his mug.

Tom Deady's first novel, Haven, won the 2016 Bram Stoker Award for Superior Achievement in a First Novel. He has since published several novels, novellas, a short story collection, and the first book in his YA horror series. He has a Master's Degree in English and Creative Writing and is a member of both the Horror Writers Association and the New England Horror Writers Association.

Tunnels

Tom Over

The experiments had begun by accident, or rather, because of an event that had been out of his control. This was after his mother had passed away, and he now lived alone in the house. The rambling old Victorian residence she had raised him in. He spent his time indoors, didn't go outside much; rarely mixed with other people. He'd worked at a supermarket while his mother was alive, in the warehouse out back—away from the public, as his employers had wished it. But now that he had his inheritance, he saw little point in working at all.

The rare occasions he did go outside were mainly just to buy groceries. It was during one such infrequent trip that the event occurred. He'd been returning home from the supermarket, a different supermarket to the one he'd previously worked at, when he noticed two unsavoury looking characters approaching him. Both wore dark hoodies and skulked in a manner that was unnervingly purposeful.

It wasn't until he jammed his free hand into his pocket that he realised the pocket still contained his mother's gold pendant; a chipped heirloom he'd been examining earlier in the day and had forgotten to put back in its box. Panicked, he seized the antique and, with scarcely a second thought, shoved it into his mouth. It scratched and bit on its way down his throat, but he was glad of his quick resolve because the pair had indeed planned to rob him. They made off with his wallet, but he didn't care. His most valuable possession was far beyond their reach.

It took several days for the pendant to pass through him. When eventually it emerged, something wasn't quite right. Once he'd cleaned it up, his suspicion was confirmed—the pendant was no longer cracked as it had been. Not only was it structurally restored, but its surface, now free of all nicks and abrasions, gleamed flawlessly like the day it was made. His astonishment was such that

26

he had to sit down. He remained that way, quietly contemplative, for a very long time, unable to comprehend the thing he kept turning over in his hands. He inspected the pendant with a magnifying glass, but no matter how long he studied it, he could not begin to rationalise why it looked the way it did.

He wondered if his mother were somehow watching, puzzling over this mystery along with him, trying possibly to communicate the answer. On her death bed, she'd ruminated deliriously about the light at the end of tunnels, and whether or not she herself might experience it. Now, scrutinising this improbable object, he pondered whether his dead mother had attained that fabled luminosity, and with it some unknowable cosmic influence.

The next day, still mystified, he came to a decision. He needed to know if what had taken place was just some freak occurrence, or a scientifically replicable phenomenon. Something that could be tested, measured. The first trial he reasoned to keep simple.

He fasted all morning and then, in the afternoon, selected a penny from the bottom of his money jar. It was a very old coin, scuffed and darkened with age. Before placing it on his tongue, he opened up a notebook and recorded the coin's date, imperfections and colour tone.

Within a couple days he passed the coin. But even before washing it, he could identify the change. Beneath the crust of excrement, the burnished sheen of the penny was startling. Its glossy surface was so pristine as to appear newly minted. He supposed his insides may have cleaned the coin, his stomach acid possibly dissolving its aged outer layer. But that didn't explain its uncanny, factory-fresh condition. Of the visible scratches and blemishes he'd observed prior to swallowing, not a single one remained.

Despite predicting this outcome, he was no less bemused by it. He noted his findings and decided to sleep on the results. He ate a minimal amount of food in preparation for the next experiment.

Upon rising the next morning, he went about looking around the house for small objects that were both broken and digestible. Not finding anything appropriate in the lounge, he went upstairs to peruse his mother's vanity dresser. Surveying its many trinkets, he reached past her urn to probe inside her jewellery chest. In it he found a small quartz pocket watch that had belonged to his grandfather. The watch had stopped working years ago, whilst its owner was still alive, and had remained that way ever since. He picked up a diminutive crystal egg which contained his mother's wedding ring. He unscrewed the egg at its middle and examined the contents. Seeing that the ring was missing two of its gemstones, he pocketed it before replacing the egg back in the chest.

When he had five precious objects in varying states of disrepair, he lined them all up on the dining room table. Sitting down with a glass of water and his log book, he set about recording the defects of each individual article. When he was satisfied, he took a preliminary sip of water, and then commenced the experiment.

Within a couple days, four items had emerged. All were in immaculate condition. Each a profoundly strange dissident of entropy, except for his grandfather's timepiece, which now ticked off the seconds with atomic precision. The fifth object, his mother's ring, did not reappear. Considering this a minor setback, he decided to push on with his research.

He'd originally planned to sell the restored goods, but now, more intrigued than ever, a new compulsion took hold of him. He wanted to push the experiments further, explore the limit of what his body could do.

The next day he went out into the grounds of the house and approached a tree in which he knew there to be a nest. He listened for signs of life and, soon enough, heard the faint sounds of cheeping. He looked around on the grass for a suitable stone.

Minutes later he returned to the house with his hands cupped in a ball, and went straight to his mother's bedroom. Eventually he came back downstairs and proceeded to arrange a selection of things on the dining room table. He seated himself before them and regarded each one in turn—his log book, a shot glass half full of olive oil, and his mother's crystal egg, with the starling chick nestled inside it. A row of tiny pits lined the circumference of the egg; these he believed might act as breathing holes for the bird. But if there was no oxygen to be had where the chick was going, it wasn't something that particularly concerned him. The results were all that mattered. After recording the necessary data, he knocked back the shot of oil and then inserted the ovoid capsule down his throat.

When the egg came back into the world it was not without a struggle. He ingested many laxatives and rocked on the toilet bowl for half a day. Upon emerging, hot tears exploded in his eyes. He rubbed them dry, and when he saw the object, he rubbed them some more. Nothing about what he was looking at made sense. He gently shook the egg, rattling the smaller egg that was inside it. He felt an intense compulsion to know what was inside the new egg. He took it to the kitchen and cracked it over the sink, half expecting his mother's ring to spill out. But it didn't. Just a partially formed bird foetus slid grimly towards the plughole.

With his mind irrevocably blown, he pored over his findings. Following days of analysis he arrived at a staggering conclusion, and for many more deliberated on its possible consequence. Finally, his decision was made. He fasted for a day and a night in preparation for his pinnacle experiment.

The next morning, at the dining room table, no items were laid before him other than a solitary glass of water. He unscrewed the cap of his mother's urn and emptied it into the liquid. Swilling the solution around the glass, he placed it back on the table and allowed it to dissolve. He curled his hands in his lap and exhaled deeply. Eyes closed. A full minute seemed to pass before he finally opened them. He picked up the glass and drank, slaking his ultimate curiosity.

A week went by and nothing happened. He became convinced that nothing would, and so returned to his studies. Whilst preparing a meal one evening, he felt a sharp bowel movement and rushed to the bathroom. As he went to sit down his abdomen bucked and he crumpled to the floor. He writhed in agony, clutching his torso. The pain was so great that he may have blacked out. When he returned to his senses he was screaming. His screams got louder until he could taste blood in his throat, and then, like some lupine creature of the night, he howled as a jet of black blood sprayed across the tiles. His whole body jerked with violent convulsions. A sickening tear filled the room and he glanced down between his legs. His vision swam but he remained conscious long enough to see a human hand erupt out of his body. Slick with viscera, it clenched and flexed in the pallid light. A ring glinted wetly on the hand's third finger, all of its gemstones now present.

Tom Over is the 2x Splatterpunk and Wonderland Awards-nominated author of The Comfort Zone and Other Safe Spaces, his first book of short fiction. Stories of his have featured in anthologies by PS Publishing, Aphotic Realm, Hybrid Sequence Media and mostly recently 11:11 Press's Children of the New Flesh: The Early Work and Pervasive Influence of David Cronenberg.

Rats Scratched in the Linen Cupboard

Dani Brown

Rats scratched in the linen cupboard. Waiting for a nurse to come in the morning and let them out. The corridor glowed with the strange buzz of fluorescent lights on their last hour.

Children slept in beds, waiting for death to take them in the night, waiting to be allowed home with medicine and instructions to follow to stay alive. Marcy's boots dropped dirt on the dusty tiles and her zippers sang with the Song of Death. A bucket of slime spread tendrils of rotten decay up the walls. No nurses lurked in the station. No new admissions in the middle of the night.

Eggs suspended in slime caught the light of the dying fluorescents. Each one fertilised with a baby with bright blue eyes and tentacles in place of limbs. Marcy's boots picked them up and carried them a few paces before they squashed in a repeat of where she had been only four seconds before.

Rats scratched in the linen cupboard and climbed Marcy's boots to perch on her shoulder. She opened the door and stepped out onto the dimly lit corridor. The bucket of slime tipped over. The floor decayed. A baby with tentacles instead of limbs and Donnie's bright blue eyes screamed at her. A rat bit her finger and pulled a waxed black thread holding her hand together.

The Tentacle Queen stepped out from the shadows, her form concealed behind latex. The monster projected onto the walls. She held a stopwatch.

"Time's up."

Rats scratched in the linen cupboard. Marcy's legs swelled together. Her shaking hand pulled the door open leaving behind a layer of skin. A child's long forgotten doll stared at her with its cotton insides leaking into the puddle of slime. Marcy pulled the door shut. Tears cut down her cheeks flaying the skin.

Rats scratched in the linen cupboard. Marcy's tears dragged off chunks of flesh. Her hands rested in a pile of dead flies. She lifted them to feel the wall to the door handle, dragging waxed black threads with her movement. The flies buzzed into life.

She opened the door and stepped into the dusty corridor. The fluorescents gave a final high pitch hum and flicker. Strange pink light cut across the floor, distorted through the dirty windows. Her swollen thighs protested with each step forward. Fluids leaked from vagina to anus and saturated her trousers. Each echo of her footsteps brought fresh pain. She couldn't go forward.

Rats scratched in the linen cupboard. Dead flies waited on the floor. Donnie's face shimmered from a photograph hanging from the shelf, hidden behind a filter and photomanipulation. Her thigh split open, spilling more fluid into her trousers. She grabbed the door handle and let the flies and rats out ahead of her. She didn't make it any further.

Rats scratched in the linen cupboard. Faint pink light highlighted the slime oozing under the door. Marcy pushed herself to her elbows and rolled over.

She reached high, tearing her seams, to open the door and drag herself into the corridor.

Children cowered behind the closed doors lining the wall opposite the dirty windows. The forgotten doll lies with its insides dissolved in slime. Kord stepped before her, arms pointed to the sky. *Powered by a jet, baby.* A cassette tape rewound. *Powered by a jet, baby.* The rats urged Marcy through. Only a hologram projected onto bottled fog and distorted by pink lights through the dirty windows. Dead flies on the floor buzzed to life as she pulled herself along the dust.

Rats scratched in the linen cupboard. Marcy's head banged in a 56 second drum loop caught on repeat. Kord pounded behind the rotten wood. Flies buzzed into life and rats opened the door. Kord was gone. Marcy dragged herself along the corridor.

The sound of children's laughter bounced off the crumbling walls and plaster fell from the ceiling. She raised her hands to shield her pounding head. Honey with a taint oozed down the walls and swallowed the puddles of slime. Urged forward by the rats. Their fur eaten by moths.

A toddler with tentacles instead of limbs and Donnie's bright blue eyes dropped a contact lens in Marcy's path and screamed until it passed out beneath the pink lights distorted through the dirty windows. Marcy manoeuvred her body around the tentacles with protests from her swollen legs. She left a trail of fluids behind. A feast for the flies. Sharp pains gripped her shoulder blades.

Rats scratched in the linen cupboard. The door ajar with Marcy's hand blocking the way. A puddle of her own fluids showed her reflection. Deformed wings stood out from her shoulders. She flapped but couldn't fly without feathers.

"Sir says you need to get up now and move to the end of the corridor."

A child slapped her with a tentacle. Donnie's picture stolen and printed from social media landed in front of her face as the child faded away. Marcy dragged herself along the floor lubricated by her own fluids.

A door opened. A teenage girl lingered in a doorframe. Hooks instead of hands caught the distorted pink light. Donnie's same blue eyes, enhanced with contacts, stared at her. The door for the next room opened on another teenage girl with hooks for hands. Her shaking dislodged dust and plaster. Marcy raised her hand and the ceiling oozed with honey, picking up the taint from the corridor and neon light.

The rats pulled her when she couldn't drag herself any further, cutting a fresh path in the dust with her fluids. Forever watched by the two teenage girls with hooks instead of hands. They stepped into the corridor and held each other as Marcy opened the door.

Dirt fell onto the dusty tiles from beneath the Forest of the Dead. Marcy touched it with her fingers held together by waxed black threads and it began to sing. The only way out was up. She would have to dig.

Suitably labelled "The Queen of Filth", extremist author **Dani Brown**'s *style of dark and twisted writing and deeply disturbing stories has amassed a worrying sized cult following featuring horrifying tales such as "56 Seconds", "Sparky the Spunky Robot" and the hugely popular "Ketamine Addicted Pandas."*

One Parent Survives

Wil Dalton

The fire pup clamps onto a loose strand of toilet paper and runs for the kitchen. The mummy spins and moans, collapses in slow-motion, and rolls under the coffee table. I yell at my daughter to be kind to her brother.

"He's a fire hazard," she says.

God, I hate *Paw Patrol*.

The doorbell rings. The kids scream and run in circles. My other daughter, Maddie, the unicorn princess, started that relaxing tradition earlier in the evening, before the sun set.

"Angela!" I shout over "Monster Mash" (the Kidz Bop version).

"Can you give out the candy? It's in the pumpkin bag by the door."

Buzz Lightyear crashes into my shin. He looks up, points his finger at my chest, and squeals, "Pew, pew, pew!"

"Hey, Eddie. Andrew's in the playroom."

I need another drink.

"Jen," I say, "Did we get any not-pumpkin beer?"

A tall cowboy grabs my shoulder.

It's Donnie's dad. "Nice costume," he says. "You won't believe what they're doing on the radio. You should switch to KISS-FM."

No way. I wasn't going to risk hearing "Thriller" again.

Jen lets in a clown and a priest and their three kids, all cats.

A dinosaur pulls down the fake spider web by the door.

"Marcia!" I shout. "Can you redirect Connie?"

"They're playing some kind of *War of the Worlds* gag, but super local," Donnie's dad continues. "They keep broadcasting updates about this escaped mental patient. Hook for a hand. Trail of dead trick-or-treaters. It's fucking riveting."

"Watch the language," I say, not because I care as much as I don't want Jen hearing.

Lately, she's throwing an intense protect-the-kids punch. Helmets on scooters. No YouTube. Organic berries. I keep getting compliments on my costume because I'm wearing one of her dresses. I had a $400 Darth Vader costume ready to go, but she worried not being able to see my face would frighten Maddie's friends.

Not sure why she let Thomas in wearing a head-to-toe white sheet. Our invites clearly said no monsters. He lives next door. Easy-changing distance.

Whatever. I'm not bitter. It's not like hearing how helpful it is to have the work-from-home Thomas available if Jen needs to run a quick errand during Maddie's naptime has got me hating the guy. I'm glad they're friends.

Fucker.

The oven beeps. Donnie's dad follows me into the kitchen. I wish I remembered his name.

I pull out the brownies and the twins, Suzy and Julie (I never know which is which), pull on my dress.

"Give me, give me, give me," they say.

I scan the room for their mother.

The ghost glides in from the hallway. He left the bathroom door open.

"Hey, Thomas! We want to keep all the doors shut. Keep the kids contained."

He ignores me. Like somehow he can see through his sheet, but can't hear. Whatever.

Fucker.

A siren blares down our street.

"Sounds like the high school kids are having fun," Marcia says.

"Nice," Donnie's dad says, pointing at her T-shirt.

It reads, "This what a disappointed feminist looks like."

"You don't get to say 'nice' like that," she says to him.

To me, she says, "That's the fifth cop sirening past tonight."

Donnie's dad says, "I heard pranks are out of control this year because of TikTok."

There's a loud crash from the playroom. I'm not worried. The babysitter we hired to guide the kid games is in there. A crying banana runs into the living room. His astronaut tells him if he wants friends, he needs to be friendly and to go back and share.

The ghost sits alone on the couch. Jen thought that Thomas would appreciate meeting our parent friends, but he's kept to himself all night. I guess he feels he can't relate. He is the only adult here without a kid.

35

The doorbell rings.

A caterpillar has peed her pants.

Jen puts her arm around me. "I'm thinking hosting a Halloween party was a mistake."

"Safer inside," I say. "I hope Maddie sleeps through the night."

About a month ago, our youngest started having nightmares after I let her watch a cartoon with ninja trains. Our hope was by hosting a party we could protect her from seeing the shambling zombies and fanged vampires roaming outside.

A scream from the playroom causes the priest to sprint away from the group of parents chatting around the dining room table.

"Where'd you put the big knife?" Jen says. "I want to cut the brownies."

"Should be in the drawer."

Donnie's dad says, "It's crazy how we can distinguish our kids' screams. You got your play-cry, your scared-cry, your hurt-cry, your better-call-the-doctor-cry..."

"It's not here," Jen says.

"Look again." I tap my bottle against Donnie's dad's bottle and say, "To our kids' unique screams. May they always be recognizable. Happy Halloween."

My beer is cold and refreshingly not pumpkin. There had been one Märzen-style in the back of the refrigerator, left over from our Oktoberfest dinner with the Ahmadis.

The ghost stands up abruptly from the couch and nearly knocks me down as he barrels past. I spill my drink down the front of my dress.

"Dammit, Thomas," I say at the back of the ghost, now pushing its way into the playroom.

"Watch your mouth," Jen says.

"What'd I do?" Thomas says from the dining room table. He's laughing at something Eddie's mom said. He's wearing a skull and crossbones pirate hat, an eye patch, and a make-up mustache.

Fucker.

I hear a loud gasp from the playroom and what sounds like a jack-o-lantern being thrown against the wall and, maybe, milk spilling? And then? An unsettling absence of noise. The sudden quiet is more alarming than the relentless chaos that preceded it. It's the sound of a breath being held after a boo-boo, of little limbs tensing before a fall, of tender eyes clenching before seeing something truly terrifying.

I drop my beer and every parent runs for the playroom.

Wil Dalton is an AmeriCorps*NCCC and Peace Corps (Bulgaria) alum. He earned his MS in Student Affairs and worked several years in residence life. He currently parents three beautiful children. You can find him at wildalton.substack.com.

Don't Eat the Candy

Matt Bliss

She tells me as we stand on the porch—*don't eat the candy.* Jess grips my arm and holds me with a piercing stare.

I nod and adjust the mask to better line up the almond eyeholes with my own. Her face is different tonight. It's not the silly pointed hat sitting above it, or the black cloak lined with a snarl of lace that wraps her—*it's her eyes.* Hard and shimmering like two polished stones.

The door opens suddenly and a tall man wearing a wolf mask stands in the opening. "Jess," he says in the calming cadence of a therapist. "Happy Halloween. This must be the one you told me about. Come on in. Come in." He stands aside as Jess steps in, tugging at my hand to follow.

The house is casket dark and pungent like black licorice. I hear a cacophony of voices and laughter beyond the foyer, and the man in the wolf mask guides us toward the sound.

"So wonderful for you to join us," the man says, taking short, careful steps through the darkened hall. "The others will be quite thrilled to see you here."

Jess grips me tighter.

Don't eat the candy, I remember her words.

"Jess has come to every Halloween party for the last three years. It's terrific to finally meet her partner."

He opens the double doors ahead of me, then steps into the large room adorned with chandeliers and candlelight. Men and women cluster throughout the space, each wearing elaborate costumes and sipping from tall champagne flutes.

Jess turns to me and smiles. I smile back, but doubt she can see it under the mask.

A sound rings out, dinner chimes, and I turn to see a short man knocking a mallet against the instrument in hand. He plays it again, *high note—low note—middle note.*

The group moves to a seemingly endless mahogany table at the back of the room and seat themselves around it. I pick the seat next to Jess, three chairs from the head, and look to her for assurance. She smiles and nods, but her eyes still look like granite.

A man dressed as a revolutionary soldier stands at the head and clears his throat. "Tonight," he says in a booming voice, "is Halloween. We celebrate yet again. Another party with my distinguished friends and guests. And," his head swivels from left to right, "as with every Hallows Eve, we shall drink, and eat, and dance to celebrate life...by looking toward death."

Someone slams a fist on the table and cheers in agreement.

Jess looks at me to gauge my reaction.

Already my pulse is racing.

"But tonight," the man at the head continues, "we have a *special* guest." He gestures a hand toward me, and all eyes follow.

The room goes silent. I can feel their gaze upon me as I look from one costumed person to the next. My heart pounds too loud—they can hear it, I know they can.

"We have a tradition here," the man continues. He hunches over the table, pressing his icy face in my direction. "The newest member *always* gets the first piece of candy."

The man in the wolf mask appears like a ship through fog. He lowers a covered platter to the table in front of me. I see my panic in the warped reflection of its polished silver surface. Then I see the faces, the masks, all staring at me.

Don't eat the candy.

"Only *after*," the man continues, waving his splayed fingers over the room, "the *proper* party will begin."

Wolf Mask squeezes the cover with a gloved hand, and lifts it, revealing a bone-white plate on a gleaming silver tray. At its center is a small, *harmless looking* chocolate square.

I swallow the lump in my throat and scan the surrounding faces. They lean closer, watching with hungry eyes. Waiting with eager smiles.

Don't eat the candy.

"I shouldn't," I say and turn toward Jess. Her face is impassive, and her eyes...*still hard as stone.*

"Go ahead," the man says with a smile that flickers like candlelight. "Take a bite."

My heart thumps faster. I feel my mask twitch with each hurried beat. "I don't think I—"

"Eat it!" someone yells, cutting me off.

Sweat builds behind my mask and drips hot like mercury. They lean closer, watching. Waiting. I remember what she told me, *Don't eat the candy,* but the faces around me demand it. They scream behind the eyeless holes of masks. "Eat it!" they yell, yet Jess doesn't speak.

She turns away and, in one smooth movement, I raise the candy to my mouth underneath the mask and place it on my tongue.

The room claps and howls wildly, rising to their feet in the excitement.

Jess smiles. It's a smile I don't recognize.

I move my tongue left and place the candy between my teeth. I exhale a shaking breath and clench down on the piece.

Something moves inside me. It hums inside my gut, and I freeze. A sound—*a bass note*—rising through my throat and rattling inside my teeth.

The others, Jess included, move away from the table and line themselves in the center of the room. Wolf Mask grabs my chair and turns me to face them. They all watch with poised stares.

I bite again.

This time, something escapes from my lips. *More sound*, moving across my lips like a bow across tensioned strings. It vibrates the air around me with heavenly music—*high note—low note—middle note*. I stop, gasping around clenched teeth, and the sound stops, too.

The others move with the sound. One-step to the left, turning, until stopping with the silence.

I shift in my chair, feeling the sugary sweetness between my teeth, watching the mass of people frozen mid-step before me.

Wolf Mask slides his gloved hand over my face and works my jaw up and down.

The sound escapes my lips again.

Bass, violin, piano—all streaming from my mouth like a scream I cannot contain. Thumping in the rhythm of each bite. *One—two—three,* the people before me dance to its beat. They move as one. Stepping and turning with the tempo. Swinging costumed bodies with each measure, floating with the ease of marionettes.

A smile slides over my lips.

Wolf Mask disappears in the crowd as I chew faster. The music speeds up with the chewing. They all step and turn quicker. Moving through choreographed patterns as the volume builds inside my head.

Faster, louder, the song grows and builds toward a crescendo.

They flip, turn, and kick faster in a blur of movement. The sound rises until it's roaring inside my head. Screaming from within me. *High note—low note—middle note.* It becomes unbearable, screeching in my ears at deafening volume. I can't take anymore—the sound, the ringing in my head—yet I can't stop. I grip the sides of my chair when suddenly, the song ends with a clanging splash of cymbals.

The people before me drop to the floor. They lay rag-doll limp, motionless, and though I wait, none seem to move.

I stand and step toward Jess, eyeing her dark cloak in a rumpled heap before me. I kneel to her side, but I already know something's wrong—*the smell.*

The air tastes old and fetid, filling my nostrils with its wrongness. I roll Jess toward me too easily, *she's too light,* and then I see her. Her skin now taut over skeletal remains. Her lips, desiccated and shriveled, curled back around exposed teeth and jaw. Where Jess just stood, only a corpse remains, wearing her clothes and staring at me from two polished stones pressed into her skull.

I peddle backward, catching a heel on another. I look down at more shriveled remains inside a costume that only moments ago held a man.

All of them... Rotten flesh and spindly bones, staring blankly from the gleaming eyes of smooth granite.

I turn and run, and try to scream, but only music pours out. Bass, strings, piano—all playing to the tune of my cries as I sprint into the night. Over the melody that escapes from my lips, I hear words hiss out from cadaverous teeth.

Don't eat the candy.

Matt Bliss *is a construction worker turned speculative fiction writer from Las*

Vegas, Nevada. His short fiction has appeared in MetaStellar, Cosmic Horror Monthly, and Diabolical Plots among other published and forthcoming works. You can find more of Matt's works at flow.page/mattbliss.

Gently Used

Jonah Buck

I stood in the middle of the lot, near a giant, inflatable gorilla. I must have been gawping at the merchandise because a salesman sidled up to me.

The kid looked like he'd just graduated, and his face was fighting a war of attrition with acne. The acne was winning.

"It's time for Big Mike's annual April sale. We're overflowing with deals on selected inventory. Be sure to check out our Dealer's Choice item. We'd have to be crazy to have such low prices," he rattled off a spiel that he'd no doubt memorized from a notecard.

"Give me the skinny on the Dealer's Choice." We started walking to another section of the lot.

"The Dealer's Choice is a Model DT-10, with a sleek, metallic finish and upholstered interior. The previous owner was Big Mike's very own grandmother. Last used on a drive to the church, this luxurious DT-10 has minimal wear and tear. It's a steal at any price."

"Little old lady only used it once. Never heard that before." What turnip truck did he think I just fell off of?

The salesman was unfazed. He had a pitch to get through. If he lost his place now, he might have to start over.

"Perfect for you, your spouse, or up to three children, the roomy interior is stylish and comfortable. Big Mike guarantees you'll love the mahogany accents. The exterior's sleek, timeless lines make the Model DT-10 a classic, and the scratch-resistant finish ensures that your purchase will remain in perfect condition. The Model DT-10 can handle any terrain, from mud to rocks."

"What're your pricing options?"

"With our Dealer's Choice item, we'll take no money down and no interest for twelve months."

"Mind opening it up? I wanna check the interior."

The salesman produced a key, and the door popped open. I took a good, long gander.

"There's some scratch marks on the interior upholstery. That knock the price down any further?"

"Interested in buying? We should go to my office."

I started to follow him past the Big Mike's Gently Used Coffins sign toward the showroom.

Jonah Buck wanted to study eldritch knowledge and commune with pale, furtive creatures of darkness, so he went to law school in Oregon. His interests include history, paleontology, professional stage magic, and exotic poultry. He is the author of several novels, including Carrion Safari *and* Substratum.

The Water Tower Ghost

Darryl Foster

A faceless boy stood in the shadow of the town's old abandoned water tower. Lisa stared at the apparition from the sidewalk with a white-knuckled grip on her school books. A grave whisper—*help me*—drifted through her head. Lisa's throat constricted. Adrenaline coursed. She tossed her math book at the boy and ran for home.

"The boy really scared me." Lisa hugged her dad.

"I don't want you going that way to school anymore."

"Because of the ghost-boy?"

"Yes."

"Do you know the water tower ghost story?"

"I do, and it's not for children."

"Dad, I'm almost eleven. You've got to tell me. Please!"

"Okay."

"Yes!"

"The story of the water tower ghost goes back decades." Lisa's father made ghostly gestures and his voice turned spooky. "They say the bones of a drowned boy lie at the bottom—"

"Dad." Lisa crossed her arms. "Chill the drama."

"Okay, no more drama." Her father's face resolved to an unsettled and dark expression. "Here's the story. There were two brothers: twelve-year-old Peter and eight-year-old Danny. Peter had tormented Danny all his life. One day Peter lured Danny up the rickety steel staircase that curled around the old water tower's red-brick wall. On top, in the middle of the tower's planked roof, was a metal lid. Peter had opened it, unveiling a black abyss of deep water. He dared Danny to dive in, but Danny had backed away. Annoyed, Peter grabbed his brother, hauled him to the roof edge and threatened to toss him off the tower.

Danny screamed his submission and so Peter schlepped his brother back to the hole and said, 'Get in.' Frightened and enraged Danny broke free and pushed his older brother into the water. Despite Peter's cries for help, Danny closed the lid and bawled until the splashing and pleas stopped—"

"Dad, stop. That's horrible! Danny killed his brother!"

"I told you this wasn't a story for children." Lisa's father smirked, and somewhere in the back of his mind a spider skittered through a tangled cobweb of old memories—*and I don't miss my brother.*

Darryl Foster *is a Canadian writer. His story* "Red Silk" *won an online competition in the Writer's Arena and his story* "Crude Lake" *appeared in the horror anthology,* Fearless Fathoms: Tales of Aquatic Terror, Volume II. *Darryl can be found camping with his family in the woods north of Toronto.*

Standing Tall

Kenneth W. Cain

Wicked creatures frequent our homeland. Long ago, they came here to hunt, but soon they began to wield larger weapons and grew more violent. They developed a boldness, and some even took to living among us.

At first, we heard only rumors of their evil deeds, passed along like whispers in the wind. By the time the truth revealed itself, I could only watch as they dismembered so many of my kind. They took my mother's life when I was still young, cutting her to pieces right before my eyes. Afterward, they left a small piece of her behind as a reminder of her fate. For many years, I watched her rot. And I wondered: If I could have done something, would I have?

Today, when they emerge from the mist, I count at least a dozen, shouting at one another, laughing and joking. They commence with the massacre of a dear friend. Her screams went unheard by her tormentors, barely audible above the roar of their weapons. Two more are slaughtered before nightfall, leaving me to stare at parts of their bodies left behind like refuse. Still, I'm incapable of action. That is, until their weapons turn on me.

I should feel terrified, yet I am not.

Out of nowhere, I experience a sharp pain. Their buzzing weapons cut deeper. Every second, they take a little more, and I feel myself slipping away. But, lunacy offers a certain peace.

Weakened by their onslaught, my collapse imminent, somehow, I stand tall. My friends look saddened, but it's then I know what I must do.

When I teeter, I throw myself sideways, bending and twisting my body. Pain shoots through me like a lightning bolt as I strike the ground with a loud *whomp*. Even in my wavering state, I manage to heave myself forward hard enough to snap one of my branches. This causes me to roll right over a handful of the men and women, their tiny bodies squishing beneath me. Listening to their screams gladdens me, as does the feeling of them squirming to a still beneath me.

Calm washes over me as I finally leave this world.

Kenneth W. Cain *is the author of over one hundred short stories and thirteen novels/novellas, as well as a handful each of nonfiction pieces, books for children, and poems. Cain has edited ten anthologies, and is editor-in-chief at Crystal Lake: Torrid Waters. He is an Active member of the HWA and a Full member of the SFWA. His full publishing history is available on his website at kennethwcain.c om.*

Makes Three

Michael Harris Cohen & Mark Allan Gunnells

I was washing the dinner dishes when I first noticed it, a burn mark on the wall, near the power socket. We'd just moved in and daily, it seemed, found flaws we'd missed in our home-buying euphoria.

On closer inspection, I discovered it wasn't a burn at all but a small patch of mold. A vague shape, fat on one end and tapering at the other.

Black Mold?

A prickle of worry followed. The stuff is supposed to be toxic—memory loss, respiratory issues, a litany of health nightmares. I took a deep breath, then remembered reading that vinegar was a good, natural mold-cleaning method.

I mixed some in a bucket of hot water, donned rubber gloves, and started scrubbing. It came away easily and, honestly, it didn't seem much like mold at all. Five minutes of scouring cleared it.

Upstairs in bed, Beth was snuggled in with a murder mystery. I told her about the spot.

"Did you clean it?" she asked without looking up from the pages.

"Yeah, think I got it all."

"Good job. Now hop under the magic quilt with me."

She finally looked up, putting her book on the nightstand. She had that look, a look she hadn't dared much of late, not since I'd lost the baby.

I was about to tell her I was too tired, that the move had exhausted me, that my new anti-depressant made me feel off, not quite in my body. But I imagined her response, a huff of annoyance as she re-grabbed her book. We'd go to bed suffocating under a blanket of freighted silence. It wasn't hard to read the future based on the past year.

New house, new start, I told myself. I smiled and undressed. I crawled in next to her and we wrapped each other like strands in a rope.

After, I spooned her in that way she likes when she falls asleep. I closed my eyes but couldn't go under. I kept seeing that tapering mark.

• • • • ● • ● • ● • •

It reappeared the next night. This time Beth noticed it. She came into the living room with a bowl of popcorn and what I called her "irked mom" face.

"Hey, I thought you said you cleaned the mold."

"I did."

"Well, you didn't do a very good job."

I paused our film and went into the kitchen. The stain had grown into a basketball-sized blob. A chill zipped my spine. I told Beth to watch the movie without me and told myself I was being silly. *It's just mold*.

I repeated the cleaning from the night before, this time with bleach. Even after I could no longer see the mold, or whatever it was, I continued to scrub until I practically shredded the wallpaper.

• • • • ● • ● • ● • •

The next morning it was the size of a malformed bear, its too-big head lolling halfway up the wall. When I showed Beth the stain she just shrugged. She was late for work and distracted.

"You don't think this is seriously weird?" I asked.

She shrugged again. "It's like when you get toothpaste on your shirt. You wipe it off with a damp cloth and think you got it, but once it dries, it's still there."

"But it's growing," I said.

"We'll paint over it. Whatever. I've got to get to work."

Had she leaned into the last word? It was an old fight—me: still unemployed, maybe unemployable. Her: unhappy in her job. But I had other concerns, bigger than our top-ten arguments about work and money.

I stared from the mold to my wife, unable to understand how Beth didn't feel the same, wondering if I was "frazzling," as she called it. When I looked at it, I felt the disorientation one experiences seeing something unnatural: A two-headed calf. Siamese twins.

"I'm calling someone," I said, my tone more defensive than I'd wanted.

Beth rolled her eyes, grabbed her keys and kissed me. She chuckled. "Go ahead. Call a *mold*man."

But I wasn't laughing. Not at all.

• • • ● • ● • ● • •

I led the mold-removal guy to the spot. He loped to his van, then returned armored in coveralls, thick gloves, and a fancy-looking respirator. I flashed on how I'd only worn thin rubber gloves for protection. When I asked about the mask he spoke one muffled word, though it ping-ponged in my head: "Spores."

He examined the wall. The mark had split since this morning. It was two blobs now, joined by a thin thread of splotches

He pulled the mask off. "Well, it's not black mold."

"Thank god for that."

"But it's spreading *and* I've never seen this kind before. You got shitty ventilation. Come spring you'll have mold colonies all over, wherever there's moisture. That's what it feeds on. Moisture. Gotta do a full remediation."

"Sounds expensive."

"It's not cheap. We'd have to biocide it, then spray it with encapsulant and—"

"Is there a cheaper solution?"

He grinned, teeth crooked and amber-colored. "You could burn down your house." He waited for a laugh that didn't come, then shrugged. "Or maybe just the biocide."

Seventy-five dollars and an hour of scrubbing later, the mold was gone again.

· · · · ● · ● · ● · ·

Two days later it was back. Now split into three. Two elongated blobs with a smaller one between them. Beth still didn't worry. Not one bit. She said we'd paint over it. She said it was "sort of pretty." Our own Jackson Pollock.

Though I saw something else. Clearer each day.

· · · · ● · ● · ● · ·

I didn't bother to clean it anymore. While Beth was at work, I sat cross-legged on the floor and watched the shapes grow and define. Familiar shapes. If I watched closely enough, I could see the spots swell and spread in little dots of grey. *Colonies,* the mold man had called them, spitting spores in ultra-slow motion.

Spores.

· · · · ● · ● · ● · ·

Beth told me she'd always had the mark on the back of her neck. "You called it my 'beauty button'. Remember?"

I nodded and forced a smile, because I didn't remember or believe her. Not at all.

The next day I found the marks on my leg. Black speckles in wobbly circles. Quarter-sized.

I didn't hear Beth when she came home or when she knocked on the bathroom door. She found me in the tub, naked, furiously scrubbing the marks with bleach and steel wool, the water beneath my pruning skin as pink as Rosé.

"What the fuck, Sarah? What the *fuck*?"

I didn't look up. Didn't say a word. Just scrubbed and scrubbed, wiping the skin away, shredding my flesh like the wallpaper, as she leaped to the tub and wrenched my hand from my leg.

"I am not going through this whole self-harm shit again. I'm just *not*!" Her face was enflamed and tear-streaked. She hurled the steel wool against the wall and slammed her way out of the bathroom.

Later, I apologized. I cried. I told her I was losing it. "Frazzling."

I promised I'd go back to therapy. We hugged and then she cried. I asked her if she wanted tea with rum, our old comfort drink. She sniffled and squeezed my hand. "That'd be nice," she said.

I'd made up my mind in the bathtub what I had to do. Because I knew what those three shapes in the kitchen were. What they were becoming.

The mold-man had said this was something he'd never seen, and we'd been inhaling its spores. They were inside us, growing. *Colonizing*. Beth would say I was losing it. *Frazzling. Unraveling*, again. But I knew it, felt it, even if she couldn't.

• • • ● • ● • ● • •

Beth snored heavily, just like she always did after taking an Ambien. I'd stirred two into her tea. I stood over her on the bed. I wondered what she dreamed as I trickled gasoline onto our magic quilt, the one we'd made from patches of old clothes. Punk T-shirts, faded jeans, even swatches from what we'd worn on our first date. Did she dream of me? Had it colonized her dreams, too?

51

What has more moisture than a human? It didn't matter if we moved out. It was in us, becoming us. Or we were becoming it. Three figures on the kitchen wall. *Beth and me and baby makes three.*

I dumped the rest of the gas over my head, stinging my eyes and nostrils. It was cold though I'd expected it to be warm. I don't know why. I crawled into bed next to her. I put my nose to her hair to drink in the smell of her, but all I smelled was the gasoline.

I whispered in Beth's ear, told her the why and the what of the mold. I told her I loved her. I reached across her for the lighter on her nightstand. I was as calm and clearheaded as I've ever been. My thumb rolled the flint wheel as my other arm clenched her, as I spooned my wife, my love, as tight as I could.

Mark Allan Gunnells loves to tell stories. He has since he was a kid, penning one-page tales that were Twilight Zone *knockoffs. He likes to think he has gotten a little better since then. He loves reader feedback, and above all, he loves telling stories.*

Michael Harris Cohen has published stories in Conjunctions, The Dark Magazine, Pseudopod, Apparition Lit. and numerous anthologies. He's won F(r)iction's short story contest, judged by Mercedes M. Yardley, The Modern Grimmoire Literary Prize, as well as Mixer Publishing's Sex, Violence and Satire prize, judged by Stephen Graham Jones, which was published as his first collection, The Eyes. *His most recent collection,* Effects Vary, *came out last year from Cemetery Gates. He lives in Sofia, Bulgaria with his wife and daughters, and teaches creative writing and literature at the American University in Bulgaria. Find him online at Michaelharriscohen.net.*

The End of the War

Joseph Mulak

It's almost over.

The war between humans and zombies that has raged for as long as I can remember is at its end. The last of them is a mere three feet in front of me, writhing in pain. I can end this now and the world can be at peace.

I take a step toward it and stop. I want to savor the moment, bask in my victory. I shouldn't take pleasure in my enemy's suffering, but I do. We have been murdered relentlessly by these things for years. Even my earliest memories are of survival. Run. Hide. Repeat. We've felt nothing but fear and helplessness as we were hunted and killed without understanding why. Now, it seems, the tables have turned.

The creature struggles to get up, but can't. It wants to get away, struggles to get to its feet but it's at my mercy. I can take as much time to enjoy this as I want.

Another step. It turns its head to look at me. It's afraid. I've only known them to show relentlessness and a lack of mercy. Now I know they feel fear and the revelation is somehow satisfying.

A third step. I'm close enough to look into its eyes and it looks back at me, ceasing its struggles long enough to use its eyes to plead with me. It can't speak, so it uses facial expressions to beg for mercy.

But I do not intend to show mercy.

I intend to make this thing suffer like its kind has done to us.

I take the final step and I am close enough to end it. But I don't. Not yet. It's not a danger to me. Not anymore. I don't have to worry about it attacking me. Its injuries are too severe.

I crouch down, slow and deliberate. I want it to know its end is coming. I want the realization to sink in and add to its suffering.

I open my mouth and lower my head and, in a satisfying moment, the human race comes to an end.

Joseph Mulak is the author of Devil Music, Ashes to Ashes, and Haunted Whispers. He lives and writes in North Bay, Ontario, with his wife Alicia and has five children and three grandchildren. You can visit him at www.josephmulak.com.

To Stop Further Slaughter

Raymond Gates

Josh sat at the worn melamine table in his kitchen, naked save for an old pair of boxers which looked oversized on his slender frame. One hand held a cigarette, now mostly ash. The other, a Phillips screwdriver. The glow of a neon sign outside his window kept the pre-dawn darkness away. The faint drone of his refrigerator seemed to add to the silence rather than interrupt it, a tenuous lifeline from the void.

"You have to kill her, you know."

Josh closed his eyes and willed Mark to go away.

"You saw what she did. You can't let that happen again."

"It wasn't my fault," Josh said softly.

"No one's blaming you." Mark was always the voice of reason. The one he turned to when everything turned to shit.

"But she will do it again, and you're the only one that can stop her."

Josh looked at the cigarette as if noticing it for the first time. He let the ash fall to the floor and then took a long, satisfying drag.

"I don't think ya got the sack ta do it," Jesse said in his bullying baritone. "'Sides, she might be a little bat-shit crazy, but hey! Who isn't?" Josh's neck hairs rose as Jesse chuckled.

"She's a murderer!" Mark's anger was evident. "No, she's much worse than that. She's a monster."

Josh exhaled in a steady cloud.

"Murderer." The word tasted foul on Josh's lips. He stared at his hands. The blood caked on them looked black in this light.

"Please, Josh," Mark said. "Before she comes back."

"Yeah, c'arn Josh," Jesse added. "I dare ya."

For a moment he did nothing, then with a shake of his head, he flicked the cigarette butt across the room, and brought the screwdriver up to the inside corner of his eye. The cool metal stung the sensitive tissue.

Josh slammed the heel of his hand as hard as he could against the screwdriver's handle. There was a sharp crack as the blade penetrated his skull.

He worked the screwdriver in a circular fashion until the voices were silenced.

Raymond Gates is an Aboriginal Australian writer currently residing in Wisconsin, USA, whose childhood crush on everything dark and disturbing evolved into an adult love affair with horror and dark fiction. He has published many short stories and is working on his first novel. Learn more at: http://www.raymondgates.com.

The Comb

Theresa Derwin

Sarah was my bestie.

We'd grown up together, played games together, played jokes on each other, played jokes on our big sisters.

At Hallowe'en, every year as far back as I can remember, Sarah's parents held a party for us at the house with the green door.

I was fourteen and Sarah was twelve the year we saw *her*.

I followed my sister, Trisha, into the back garden. Sarah and her family were stoking the campfire they'd built as our sisters wrapped us up in our plastic witch costumes, pinning our pointed black hats to our hair.

"Go on!" Sarah yelled, and I spun around the roaring fire, dipping behind large orange flames.

Huffing out a breath, I stumbled, stopping near the old wooden table laden with cakes, pumpkin pie, and homemade lemonade.

"Dad, can we do the apple bobbing now?" Sarah asked, face flush with excitement.

We were having a blast, ignoring our family, eventually collapsing in a heap by the old, lurid green back door.

It smelled of mildew.

Sarah's parents owned two houses, but they only opened this one once a year—at Hallowe'en.

I didn't know why, though I know that house always gave me the heeby jeebies. And it wasn't just me; Sarah's family never lived in that second house and it was always empty. Apart from the voices.

I thought I could hear those voices now, whispering in my ear, "Come on—"

"Come on," Sarah said, grasping my hand and standing up, "let's explore."

"I don't know," I whined, more than a little afraid.

"Come on," Sarah pleaded this time, and I relented.

The heavy green door groaned as it opened onto a dusty hallway—old, cracked tiles on the floor echoing fear with every footstep.

The smell made us gag: mold, cat wee, and...something else.

It almost smelled like rotten eggs.

And it was cold.

More than cold.

A chill breeze played with my long hair, like fingers twirling it, and in the breeze I could hear a voice whisper "yessss," a sibilant plea. It seemed to slither between my shoulder blades.

I shuddered as we walked through the long corridor, dodging cobwebs, the otherwise silent house...eerie.

Then Sarah began to sing, voice lilting, rising along with the crackle of the flames we could still hear from outside.

"She dances round the fire,

The flames are leaping higher

Her comb, it dances too,

Its sights are set on you."

I spun around, gasping. "Where'd ya learn that?"

"Sive taught it to me," Sarah said and then she laughed, making ants crawl up my spine.

"Don't know her," I mumbled, then, "Who is she?"

"Shh, come on."

Sarah headed up the old staircase, floorboards creaking underneath us as we climbed, each footstep sounding a death knell. I could've sworn I heard her say, "She's calling us."

When I reached the top I stopped to catch my breath, cold air escaping from my lips in a cloud, like when it snowed outside.

It was too cold.

"Dad used to tell us creepy stories about the banshees in Ireland," I told her, delaying the moment we went farther. "Women who combed their hair and counted; one, two, three, and on, until they reached a hundred."

And when they reached that number, they would throw the comb with a blood-curdling scream.

I shuddered as Sarah led the way to the back bedroom, opening the door like a tomb opening in a graveyard.

And whoever the comb was aimed at...next morning, they'd be dead.

I trembled at the memory of it, even as Sarah continued to sing, her hushed voice reminding me of those legends.

"Who is she, then?" I asked. The ash from the earlier fire coiled in my throat—a snake tightening its grasp.

Sarah stopped too, and looked at me with a mischievous, secretive smile.

"You can't tell," she breathed.

"Promise," I answered, leaning in closer to her, thinking of all the secrets we shared.

"Okay," she said, glancing furtively left and right, "That woman in the window told me."

"What?" I asked.

Sarah smiles eerily, and I wondered if she were just trying to spook me.

Then we heard it.

Thump.

Thump.

Thump.

The thudding of my heart drowned out all other sound.

Sarah was grinning.

With a horrible cackle, the girl I'd once thought of as my best friend raised her arm, pointing at that darkened window and the shadow woman in grey rags who stood there.

Slowly, her movements awkward, the woman turned round to look at us.

Heart still thumping in my chest, I stared at her, frozen in my fear, watched as the shadow walked towards us, gaining substance, a gnarled, wooden comb held in one pale hand. Her stringy, dark hair obscured her features as she pushed the comb through it.

"She dances round the fire," whispered Sarah's voice behind me.

Pure terror clawed at my insides, turning them cold, as I watched the skeletal hand raise the comb up high.

Dead eyes, black as oil, stared straight at me.

Her putrid mouth opened wide and she let loose a high-pitched screech, high enough to shatter glass.

I couldn't move.

This was it—I could feel it in my bones. I was about to die, and my best friend had led me here with a smile on her face.

I watched, frozen with fear, as she threw the comb...

• • • ● ● ● ● ● • •

First, there was a black fog.

Then nothing.

The next moment I was standing looking out of the back bedroom window, watching my sister in the garden with Sarah and her family.

And another figure, that had drifted away into the night.

I was cold as death.

Before I knew it, I took the gnarled wooden comb that had found its way to my hand, brushing my tangled hair.

And started to sing.

Theresa Derwin writes Horror, dark comedy and Romantasy. She has just achieved her MA degree in Creative Writing. She is the 2019 HWA Mary Shelley Scholarship recipient. She has over sixty anthology acceptances, including a story titled "Shift Left for Love" in Brigid's Gate Press' Weretales which made Ellen Datlow's 2021 recommend long list. She has published four collections and edited ten anthologies. Her forthcoming books include God's Vengeance from Crystal Lake Publishing.

Follow her on IG @theresa.derwinauthor

Website in progress.

Puzzle Pieces

Armand Rosamilia

Yesterday the piano, buried in the living room, mocked me.

I'd been restacking the *New York Times* from 1982 through 1983 when I heard it, plain as day. Three feet from the cache of pink flamingos I'd rescued from behind the JC Penney store. Just to the left of the six foot stack of takeout trays I'd mean meaning to sort by color.

One thin twang of a piano string, just loud enough I heard it.

I knew it wasn't a rat or a mouse. I had three hundred and fifty seven traps inside the house and checked them every hour on the hour.

Between counting and recounting my collection of Ziploc bags.

My ex-wife said I was a hoarder, as if she had any clue how great my work here was. As if she knew what needed to be done.

She was always cleaning up after me, trying to throw my valuable possessions away. She didn't understand what was happening.

Life was a puzzle and I was collecting all of the important pieces. Years ago we'd gone to McDonalds and there were game pieces and a game board to win prizes. She never understood my fascination with collecting all of them, even if they were expired.

In the bathroom, underneath the neat pile of women's bedroom slippers, was a cardboard box with all of my pieces collected so far. Thirteen thousand eight hundred and six.

This morning the piano, still underneath sixty-two boxes of expired Kraft macaroni and cheese, mocked me for the second time.

I swore it wouldn't do it again.

Every few months the nosy neighbors would call the police because some of my collection would have to be stored outside my home for a few weeks while I reconfigured each room.

The police would talk down to me, patronize what my life's work was, and tell me to clean up the sixteen gas masks and ninety-seven picture frames or the stack of sixty White Castle number thirteen placards. The bicycles, the tricycles, and the motorcycle parts, as well.

Once, to calm down a particularly young and pushy officer of the law, I'd taken him on a tour of the house. When he saw how empty my bedroom was, my inner sanctuary, with only a box spring and mattress on the floor and nothing else, he'd smiled. Shook his head. Left without another word.

I didn't collect junk. Only things that mattered. My only vice was the single television in the living room, perched on eight long boxes of Superman comic books, four high and two wide.

On Saturday night I'd watch John Walsh and take note of the FBI's Most Wanted, hoping I'd seen one of them at the grocery store or the flea market. Maybe the junkyard, where my ex-wife had had her terrible accident and left me with her life insurance, the house and the savings from when her parents had died.

It allowed me to quit my job. Focus exclusively on my work and figure out the pattern.

My sole purpose in life was hidden in the patterns on the floor. In the stack of aspirin bottles, stacked six feet three inches so far, or the five hundred and eighteen packs of playing cards in another stack next to the aspirin bottles.

In the seven hundred and thirty copies of Stephen King novels. I'd never read them and I never would. Not my taste. But it is part of the puzzle.

Just now the piano mocked me again.

I carefully dug through boxes of old 45 records, mostly Elvis, and neatly folded piles of bathrobes, until I came to the piano.

Instead of growing silent, which I thought would happen, it let out another two very low noises, barely audible. I'd heard it because I was listening.

The hallway closet contained what I was looking for, so I moved items carefully like the sixty two umbrellas, still wrapped in plastic, and the three cigar

Indians. The closet door opened with a groan, as if it knew what was going to happen, and I selected the perfect choice from the nineteen leaning against the closet wall.

It was the same one I'd used on my ex-wife in the junkyard when she'd mocked me for wasting my time and money on what she called junk.

Come to think of it, the piano was hers as well, a gift from her parents when we moved into the house.

I used the ax to chop into the piano, and it screamed. White and black keys shot through the air, trying to take out my eye, and the piano wire flailed, seeking to grip my hand and pull me into its bowels.

I fought the piano for what must've been hours, until it was no more. A pile of wooden shards and bent piano wires, crushed keys and dust.

Somehow it had gotten the best of me, though, and when the wire tightened around my neck, tied to the ax, I closed my eyes and hoped this was what it had all been for.

Armand Rosamilia writes horror, crime thriller, contemporary fiction and a bunch of other genres. He loves baseball and reading. He loves talking in third person. He's also a podcaster with both Arm Cast Podcast and The Mando Method Podcast. He runs Project Entertainment Network. Find him on all social media. https://armandrosamilia.com.

Stupid Girl

Michael Patrick Hicks

Her headlights cut through the black velvet of night, the only source of illumination on this stretch of US 72. There were no streetlights, no traffic lights, not even any other drivers on this long and lonely road.

Heather had been driving for hours and the last signs of civilization—a small town called Grayling—were nearly an hour in the rearview mirror. She was more than an hour away from Traverse City, a northern Michigan tourist hotspot that sat in the webbing between pinky and ring finger of the mitten state. Although the weather was warm, it was still off-season for the tourists and she looked forward to taking in sparsely crowded beaches, vineyards, and the various restaurants lining Front Street. Even more, she looked forward to doing these things alone.

Mark had been out of her life for the better part of two months, but this morning made it official. The divorce was final, the paperwork signed and agreed upon. Finally. Even the circlet of pale skin where her wedding ring had once sat was tanned over. This trip north was her surprise gift to herself.

Fuck you, Mark!

She turned on the radio, needing a blast of music to keep awake. She'd gotten a late start on her spontaneous road trip and it was nearing midnight. She hadn't bothered to call work, but she'd get up early enough to call in sick, then go back to sleep. After that, it was a book on the hotel beach and whatever drinks the outdoor bar was slinging. After a minute of cycling through the local FM stations, Garbage's "Stupid Girl" flooded her speakers.

You certainly were stupid, girl, she thought ruefully. Shirley Manson sang on about wasting all you had and selling yourself lies, and Heather couldn't disagree. The song wasn't a perfect match for her marriage, but close enough.

She tapped her fingers on the wheel, her eyes flicking between the mirrors and windshield. The woods on either side of this two-lane stretch of highway were home to all kinds of wild animals, she knew, and the last thing she needed was a deer running out in front of her. She tried to stay aware of what was around her, even if she couldn't fully see into the darkness beyond the conical beams of light. Hell, she could barely make out the trees she knew were there.

A flash of movement caught her attention, her head snapping toward a pair of glowing eyes at the edge of the road just as the Escape crested the top of the one of the many hills that rolled under 72. And then it was gone, quick as it came. She turned back to the road, eyes forward and—

"Shit!"

She slammed on the brakes, white flashing light filling the cabin of her SUV. Her tires squealed loudly against the asphalt as she cranked the wheel, the front of the vehicle pulling onto the rumble strip.

Another vehicle was pulled halfway off the road, its back end jutting into the street with its hazard lights on. She kept her foot on the brake as she fought to calm down, adrenaline pumping through her. The car was empty, the driver's side door open, but no signs of the driver anywhere.

She looked on either side of the road, waiting for the glow of lights from another driver, somebody who could help. A minute passed. Then two. Nothing. Her fingers found the cold metal of the door handle.

What are you doing?

What if somebody's hurt?

You can't just stop here and get out! Who knows what's going on?

You should call the police!

A sensible suggestion, if she hadn't forgotten her phone. Her trip north was so impulsive she hadn't bothered to pack any clothes and had forgotten her cell at home. She'd grabbed her keys, wallet, and nothing else. *Stupid girl.*

Her door opened with a sharp squeal and in the quiet night air rocks crunched like gunshots beneath her shoes. She slowly walked to the other car, looking between it and the woods that stood revealed in its headlights. She reached the door and stopped, drawing in a shocked breath. A dark arc of liquid stained the road less than a foot away from the deserted car, leading toward the trees. Her throat clicked as she swallowed.

"Help." The word came weakly from somewhere beyond the headlight's reach. A man's voice. "Please," he said, struggling.

She couldn't see him, but she stepped forward, slowly, cautiously. Whatever exhaustion she'd felt was absent now.

"Where are you? Are you hurt?" Stupid question, she thought. The way he sounded, she'd be surprised if he *wasn't* hurt.

The leaves and grass at her feet were slick, and as she stepped farther into the woods she could hear the panicked cries of an animal.

He hit a deer, she thought, understanding now. Hit it and was dragging it into the woods.

Something moved in the dark and she could just barely make out...a pod, maybe? A cocoon? Swaying from a pine tree's branch ten feet overhead. As her eyes followed the contours of that strange shape, she saw the deer within, kicking its legs and whinnying. Blood ran in sheets down the structure, raining onto grass below. And there was the man. Most of him. Gore burbled from between his wet lips and her mind struggled to make sense of the mess of torn flesh and scattered organs. His tongue pushed out as his single remaining eye fell upon her.

Deeper in the shadows, something large moved toward her. Multi-limbed, almost spider-like, but the configuration was all wrong. More like a praying mantis, but with more and bigger arms. And teeth. So many teeth, like the maw of a leatherback turtle. She saw hundreds of teeth encircling the inside of its mouth as it reached toward her.

She screamed, and she cursed herself for not staying in the car.

Stupid girl.

Michael Patrick Hicks *is the author of several horror books, including* The Resurrectionists, Broken Shells: A Subterranean Horror Novella, *and* Mass Hysteria. *His debut novel,* Convergence, *was an Amazon Breakthrough Novel Award Finalist in science fiction. He lives in Michigan with his wife and two children. Find out more about his work at https://michaelpatrickhicks.substack.com/.*

Ghosts of the Wood

Tim Meyer

Ashen columns of dead wood stood before her, naked and pale, a graveyard amongst the otherwise vibrant sea of towering pines and sweet birches. Petals of stiff, curled leaves carpeted the dirt, and as she moved through this palace of lost souls, everything that used to be alive crunched and cracked beneath her feet. A mile in every direction lay endless stretches of healthy greenery, but here, in this place, the blaze had ripped through and claimed many lives, had stolen the soul from the tight-knit community that had called this slice of nature their home.

Oh, how the town in the woods had burned on that terrible day. Though the deadly tragedy had happened many moons ago, one could still smell the smoke and flames, the sizzled, burnt flesh of its victims. The air was forever tainted here. On days that presented strong earthly currents, the woodsmoke smell was strong. But the rotten stench of charred flesh was always stronger. Even the softest zephyr brought stomach-churning odors. The bravest of travelers wouldn't dare cross the threshold into the barren section of the vast forest, as the collective stink of scorched wood and over-roasted meat persuaded them down alternate paths.

But this traveler was different. She was a woman of the wood. She was a force, had been a part of the secluded community since its conception, a "founding father" if you will.

Founding Mother, she thought, her lips curling as her bare feet stamped the trees' crisp clippings. The smoky veil that had dropped over the world filled her body with certain vigor. An energy, ancient and rooted in the heart of the wood, pulsed through her. The sensation brought sweet dreams of success, visions of a world where they no longer had to hide in the shadows of the forest, no longer confined to this dead space in the center of so much life. This dynamic power trickled through her veins, as it had in the many generations before her.

"Ghosts of the Wood," she announced, once she had stepped into the center of the circle, the black spot where the Great Burn had started to terminate all living things. "I gather before you today because we have a job to do."

Shadows began to form behind the wrinkled grey bark. The edges of her vision showed movement, slightly at first, but as she spoke to the stray spirits, they became more comfortable. More aware that she was an ally, not an enemy they needed to haunt, send home with stories of ghosts and dead things that whispered dreadful expressions as they traveled through the Dim Place.

"I've spent many years in the city of the living, pretending to be one of them. I return to you today because the time has come to rightfully claim what is ours. The living shall pay for what they've done to us.

"They shall burn."

From behind the assembly of deadwood, shadows formed definitive shapes. The Founding Mother watched as a man, his flesh tattered, crusty, and burnt tar-black, stepped away from his sanctuary behind a lifeless pine. A woman carrying a still child, both covered in sooty smears, approached from the misty atmosphere, limping every step of the way. Children gathered on a fallen trunk, their hopeful faces tuning their ears to promises of revenge and merciless victories. In a matter of minutes, The Founding Mother had her audience, a hundred strong, all ready to act upon her command.

"They called us witches and we burned for it," she said, her infectious grin spreading, conquering the lower half of her face. "Now it's time to show them how we are alive, more so now than ever. Bow your heads and pray to the Gods of the Wood, and may they give us the strength to carry out our destiny."

They hummed their prayers.

"Now gather your wood," Mother said. "The time has come to start *our* fire."

Tim Meyer *dwells in a dark cave near the Jersey Shore. He's an author, hus-*

band, father, podcast host, blogger, coffee connoisseur, beer enthusiast, and explorer of worlds. He writes horror, mysteries, science fiction, and thrillers, although he prefers to blur genres and let the stories fall where they may.

Memory Lane

Red Lagoe

A baby's laugh played on repeat when Victor pressed the button. She giggled, then rocketed to a high pitched coo, and back down to a stuttering laugh—like a song. A recording of Hayden's voice was locked into the yellow cover of a photo album, pages empty beyond eleven months.

Victor pressed the button again. *Giggle-coo-laugh.*

Again...

Around the edge of the plastic button, years of wear rubbed the cover bare.

He sipped from a mug and wished it were gin, but he gave that up years ago, right after he lost her to that damn drunk driver.

Victor pressed it again, but the recording slowed.

Again. It deepened and dragged. The giggle-coo saddened into a slow, manly drawl, and then the battery quit for good.

He pressed it again. Nothing.

Again... Silence.

A desperate finger pressed harder and harder, but Hayden couldn't talk to him anymore.

Victor rocked, head clamped between his hands, squeezing tufts of hair through his fingers.

"Victor," his wife Elena's voice rang. "Take these. It'll help." She pushed two small pills in front of him.

He swatted them away and they flung to the floor.

"Victor!"

He folded over in his chair and crumpled to the floor under the table, with Hayden's photo album against his chest.

"I need her back," he whispered. "Please. I need to hear her voice. Please. Please..."

He swayed in the painful silence.

Hidden beneath the draped shelter of a tablecloth, Victor prayed. "I'll give anything," he whispered, "just to hear her voice."

Guttural moans of despair spilled from his core. Saliva strung between his lips. Victor begged for help from Heaven, or from Hell, or from whomever would listen.

Something nudged his knee, and when he opened his eyes, a girl, no more than ten years old, pushed a blue photo album, much like his own, into his leg.

Victor scrambled backward up against the table leg, but she tilted her head and smiled.

"You can hear her laugh again if you take this." Her scrawny arms swam in a gray jersey as she held the album out for Victor.

He hesitated. "Who are you?" Her eyes were like Elena's—warm and kind, heavy lashes.

"Press the button," she said.

Victor reached for the book and pushed on the round plastic button.

Giggle-coo-laugh.

His shoulders relaxed with the glorious sound of Hayden's laugh.

As Victor tried to grab it, the young girl pulled it back. "This photo album is not just what *was*, but it's also what could have been."

"What do you mean?"

She opened the book.

Twelve Months: A birthday photo shoot with a big number one. Balloons. A picture of his daughter with cake and frosting smeared all over her face.

Victor's weeping turned to laughter. "There's another button," he said.

The girl in the gray jersey nodded with a grin. "Press it."

I yuv you, Dada.—the recording played.

Breath stole, Victor gaped at the impossible. He reached to turn the page, but the girl pulled the book away.

"There's a price," she said.

What price would he have to pay for such a gift? "Is it...my soul?" he asked.

"Don't be silly," she laughed. "You'll know the price when the time comes."

"Anything. I don't care." He grabbed at the book and the girl released it to him.

He flipped to the next page.

Two Years Old: Hayden wore a yellow raincoat, toddling through the zoo.

Victor released an ecstatic breath and smiled, but when he looked up, the young girl in gray was gone.

Next, a picture of her riding a carnival ride—a big blue turtle—and next to it, a button.

Weeeee! This is fun! Her laugh intoxicating.

Victor turned to the next page. Blank.

The next—blank.

Another page with nothing in it.

"What the hell?" Victor snapped. He turned blank pages until finally a photo.

Seven Years Old: A Halloween Costume—face painted green. A button.

Why can't you go trick-or-treating with me, Daddy?

"I wish I could," Victor whispered.

Then let's go.

"I can't" he cried.

You're always gone.

"Why?" he asked.

Mom says it's because you drink too much. She responded.

Silence followed. He tried pressing it again. *Why can't you go trick or treating with me daddy?*

Victor turned the page.

Ten Years Old. She's in a gray jersey—kind, warm eyes like her mother's. The girl who was under the table minutes ago smiles in a school photo. Beneath, an obituary.

And a button.

I don't want to go anywhere with you, Dad.

No you're not fine.

Then the sound of a revving engine. Peeling tires. Screaming. A squeal. Crash—metal on metal.

He bursts from under the table. The illusion of his home and wife peeled away to bright white walls. Nurses, patients. Surrounded by figures in blue scrubs, Victor thrashed as they restrained him.

The drunken, faded memory of strapping his eleven-month-old-daughter into the car seat.

A prick in his left arm, and his vision blurred.

• • • ● ●• ● •● • •

"Good morning, Victor," Elena's voice woke him, but it was not her. A nurse stood beside him. "Take these. It'll make you feel better." She set a cup of pills on his bed stand.

He swallowed them and picked up the yellow photo album. "Where's the blue album?"

"You only have that one, far as I know," the nurse said as she left the room.

Victor opened the album and flipped through all of Hayden's baby photos, right up until eleven months. Then nothing.

He closed the book and pressed the button on the outside cover—it worked, but the message changed.

I don't want to go anywhere with you, Dad.

He pressed it again, *I don't want to go anywhere with you, Dad.*

With each push of the button, his precious Hayden's voice spoke to him.

I don't want to go anywhere with you, Dad.

Again...

Again...

Red Lagoe *is the author of* Impulses of a Necrotic Heart *and* In Excess of Dark *(DarkLit Press 2024). In 2022, she launched Death Knell Press with an anthology she curated and edited herself,* Nightmare Sky. *Find more of Red's work at www.redlagoe.com.*

Judgment Call

Erica Ruppert

When that bitch took off her shoes, I knew this was no fight I could win.

Her bare feet flexed on the cracked pavement, those long, knotty toes getting a grip, and she leaned forward, tight, just waiting to spring. Her skin looked like old yellow wax under the dirty lights in the parking lot. I couldn't see her eyes for the shadows, but she smiled at me, slow, with strings of spit in her teeth. Those teeth were too long in her face. Her mouth was too big. It wasn't right. I turned and ran.

I didn't get far before I fell, and as I rolled over she was standing there, right at my hip, to let me know she could. She kicked me in the ribs hard but let me get up, let me keep running as a tease until I tired myself out, let me stumble down the empty street with piss down my leg like that rabid dog Atticus Finch put down. I wasn't going to end any better.

I should never have started with her. It was stupid, thinking anyone that oblivious wasn't setting something up. She raised all the flags like she was going down a list, out alone so late, parking so far from the last open store in the mall, playing with her phone as she strolled across the empty parking lot on loud platform heels.

I bit, anyway. It was a mistake.

When I grabbed her shoulder I felt hard muscle slip under her skin, and she spun out from under me. She crouched like a cat, ready for me to make a move. She wasn't big, but I fell back. There was something wrong with her face, with the way her mouth moved. Like she had too many teeth. Like her jaw had unhinged. I swear she snarled. Maybe it was a laugh, but it was thick like a smoker's cough and nothing funny in it. Not for me.

That's when she took off her fancy shoes. To run better on panther feet.

Now I'm hiding at the back of an all-night convenience store. She paced me the whole way, claws scraping pavement, showed me her long wet teeth and never said a word. She let me make it inside and veered off down the alley, out of the light. Now I've been staring at the soda case for way too long. The reflection lets me see if anyone else comes in.

She didn't go far. She's not done with me yet. I can tell that the weasel-faced clerk is thinking about calling the cops. That would be good. I'll argue, they'll rough me up a little and take me in. They could keep me till morning, maybe.

I slip a bottle of soda into my pocket. I make sure the clerk sees it. This might be my best shot.

She's still playing. I don't know where she is, now.

But I know she can smell me.

Erica Ruppert, HWA, SFWA. lives in northern New Jersey with her husband and too many cats. Her short stories have appeared in magazines including Vastarien, Lamplight, and Nightmare, on podcasts including PodCastle, and in multiple anthologies. Her debut collection, Imago and Other Transformations, *was released by Trepidatio Publishing in March 2023. When she is not writing, she runs, bakes, and gardens with more enthusiasm than skill.*

Paid in Full

Roberta Codemo

I design hauntings. Chances are if you've watched any of those ghost hunting shows on television, you've seen samples of my work. It's a lucrative business.

My team and I had just finished a job for a small town in Illinois. I'd gotten a call from the president of the Shoal Creek city council asking for our services. Like a lot of worn-out towns with empty coffers, they were looking for something different to attract the tourists. They'd chosen a cemetery on the north edge of town. Local teens had been telling stories about it for years and had reported seeing lights and the figure of a young girl wandering the grounds.

It was a simple matter to rig the site. As a bonus, I even called in my team of investigators to shoot a video. We planted a few stories in the media and everyone was happy. It wouldn't take long for word of a new "haunting" to get out and for what I call paranormal tourists to start showing up with money to spend.

I left behind two members of my team to oversee the site for the next six months and work with the locals to troubleshoot any problems and the rest of us headed to Springfield where we'd been invited to speak at a local paranormal convention that upcoming weekend. When we left, everything was working fine.

So I didn't understand the phone call I got tonight from Tim. Seems like ever since we'd left, there'd been several deaths reported on the Nokomis Road that runs by the cemetery. The most recent one was an elderly couple driving back from their daughter's house in Peoria who'd used that stretch of road as a shortcut to get home. They never made it. Their car was found crumpled in a ditch.

It's close to 11 p.m. when I flip on my blinker and turn off Route 127 onto the Nokomis Road. The three-quarter moon lies low in the sky and the air is thick with humidity. I have the windows down and Ellis Paul on the CD player.

The Nokomis Road unspools flat and straight ahead of me empty of traffic. Nothing but cornfields on either side with the occasional farmhouse tucked away down a side road. I glance in the rearview mirror and stare into the face of a stereotypical blond-haired, blue-eyed young girl. She's wearing a floral print sundress and her hair is tied back in a blue ribbon.

I don't believe in ghosts. As long as I've been in this business, I've grown jaded. So my first thought is who's messing with my set up. This wasn't part of the package we created. Moving hauntings are expensive to create and this town didn't have those kinds of bucks. Hell, I'd wondered how they'd scraped up the money to hire us to begin with but that wasn't my concern as long as the check was good.

She smiles and places her hands on my shoulders. Goosebumps pop up on my bare skin and my spine grows an icicle. Something doesn't feel quite right about this whole thing.

I wrench my gaze away from the rearview mirror and glance at the road, a knot of dread sitting in the pit of my stomach that something is going to rise up out of the road in front of me and hit me head-on. Nonsense. I shake my head.

She giggles and her hands tighten on my shoulders. The steering wheel twists under my hands. I slam on the brakes and wrench the wheel to the left before the vehicle ends up in the ditch alongside the road. The side road leading back to the cemetery is coming up on my left.

There's a car pulled over off the side of the road up ahead. I slow and pull up behind it and shut off the engine. Tim is slouched against the side of the car, hands jammed in his pockets, a cigarette dangling from a corner of his mouth. His long blond hair is pulled back in a ponytail.

"Kat," he says, when I walk up. He drops the cigarette on the ground and crushes it out with his booted foot. He looks back at my SUV, sees the girl watching him, and swallows hard.

"What's going on?" I lean against the car beside him, arms folded across my chest.

"I'm from here originally."

I glance at him. He pulls a battered pack of cigarettes out of his pocket, fumbles one out and lights it, sucks in a lungful of smoke and lets it out.

"You've met my sister Carley." He nods in the direction of the girl.

He sucks in another lungful of smoke. "She was 13 when I killed her. I was driving too fast and lost control. My dad pulled some strings and got me off. I was 17."

He takes another drag on his cigarette before tossing it on the ground and crushing it out. He picks a gun up off the hood of his car.

"I destroyed everything," he says, looking down the road towards the cemetery. "We didn't want you turning her home into a tourist attraction. She didn't mean to kill anyone. She's sorry about the elderly couple. All she was trying to do was scare them." He turns the gun over in his hands.

"I've seen her every night since we got here," he says. Carley's standing in front of us. "She died right here 25 years ago tonight." She holds out her hand to Tim.

Before I can react, he shoves the gun in his mouth and pulls the trigger.

I wipe blood and bits of brain matter off my face and realize I'm crying. Carley and Tim are walking towards the cemetery. They stop and wave before fading.

I see a piece of paper tucked under the wiper blades. I pull it out and open it. It's a receipt dated today stamped "Paid In Full."

Roberta Codemo *is a freelance health journalist and horror writer. She lives in a small town in Illinois, population 1,200, with her black cat Coal. She cut her teeth on horror and has been writing and submitting work since she could hold a pencil in her hand. She still remembers the first line of dialogue she ever wrote: "Let's join Mrs. Jones in the delivery room as she's about to give birth." She likes to think she's gotten better since then. She always said she'd never write a horror novel until she wrote one that scared even her and is currently working on her first book. This is her first piece of published fiction that is loosely based on a true incident.*

A Table Set for One

Dani Brown

Burgers. Chips. Cola. Beer. Repeat until he's numb and his gastric band slips. His daughter died at the hands of his bride. Honey oozed down the wall and grease dripped from Donnie's fingers and beard. Another burger appeared. Orange orbs flickered around the table set for one. The miners held their lanterns high.

He didn't know where his bride had gone. She sent her wraiths to stand guard, lured from their resting place inside the tin mines. He took a bite of his burger and nearly lost a veneer. His daughter cried for her birth mother from inside the walls. He swallowed the bite down with beer and checked his teeth with his tongue. The miners lit up their eyes with their lanterns and made them glow red. They'd follow into his dreams if his bride didn't return before he fell asleep.

Grease ran down Donnie's wrist. The wooden chair creaked, and the miners hid behind their orange lights. Donnie ran his tongue along his flesh and sucked up the grease. His daughter cried from the wall.

A cockroach scuttled across his plate, highlighted in orange. His cottage lacked electricity. His daughter pulled the wires out behind the wall. A skewer came down and impaled the cockroach for the miner's tea. Even wraiths needed something to eat.

Donnie ate the rest of his burger and swallowed it down with cola while he waited for another to appear. He chewed the chips with his mouth open so he couldn't hear his daughter cry inside the wall and licked his fingers.

Honey oozed down the plaster and formed into her face. He looked away, into the orange orb hanging above his head. His bride should be back soon. The orange bulbs went out. The wraiths returned to the tin mines.

The door opened and blue neon light flickered. His bride threw him a greasy brown bag.

"I thought you might be hungry."

His daughter scratched from inside the wall and swallowed her tears. Her stepmother didn't like to hear her cry. She wanted to go home to her birth mother.

The flickering blue neon light circled Donnie as his bride came up behind and planted a kiss on top of his head.

"You're covered in grease," she said.

The necklace jangled around her neck, made with the finger bones of teenage girls killed the day before they turned fourteen. She went to her knees by Donnie's side, took his hand and sucked grease from his fingers.

"I can give you a new daughter. Keep eating your burgers and chips."

His bride moaned with his index finger in her mouth. She licked down to the knuckle and sucked. Her finger bone necklace began to sing. The flicker of blue neon light took on a steady hum. Donnie burped.

"I can't eat anymore. I think I might be sick."

"Finish your meal and then I'll give you a new daughter."

Burgers dropped out of the bottom of the brown bag, dissolved with grease. Donnie fell off his chair and his bride dropped his hand so he could crawl around on his knees and feed. She took off her necklace and used it as a whip.

"Eat."

He swallowed the last burger and was immediately sick. The finger bones became caught in the layer of fat hanging off his back. A face formed out of his sick. A baby girl. Donnie heaved and she started to cry.

"I said I'd give you a new daughter."

"Daddy, no, it is a trap."

His flesh and blood banged from the inside of the wall. His bride pulled her necklace from Donnie's back and sent her away. Donnie's eyes rolled back in his head and he fell.

"Don't listen to the voice inside the wall."

Neon blue flickered from around his bride's neck. She put her necklace on and cradled the baby born out of the contents of Donnie's stomach.

"She'll grow fast."

Donnie looked up from his place on the floor.

"I have a few calls to make. Sit up and take your daughter."

Her voice echoed around the cottage. The walls fell silent. His daughter was gone. Gagged and bound somewhere outside. Orange orbs filled the room as his bride left. Miners called out of the tin mines to guard Donnie, isolated in the cottage without electricity.

Honey oozed down the wall and the baby started to cry. She smelled like grease and Donnie heaved. The miners held their lanterns and the table was set for one with a selection of sliders and a heaving bowl of chips.

"Where's my beer? Where's my cola?"

The glasses appeared and a cockroach scuttled across the wooden table. It couldn't avoid the miner's skewer. His bride fed them too, so they'd keep coming back.

The baby in his arms blinked and wiped her mouth. His bride forgot to leave her a bottle. Donnie took a bite of the first slider and washed it down with cola. The baby in his arms grew an inch. Another slider and another inch. He couldn't stop himself from swallowing the third and finishing the pint of cola, despite the baby's abnormal growth spurt.

He looked down and she opened her mouth with her arms held up.

"Da-da."

Sliders filled his plate and Donnie ate. The baby crawled away and walked back as a teenage girl. His bride stumbled through the door and the miners went back to the tin mines with their orange lanterns held high.

Silhouetted in neon blue and a knife in her hand. Her necklace lost the song and Donnie's daughter cowered in the corner. He couldn't get up to save her with the mountain of sliders on his plate. The girl screamed as his bride chopped off her hands. Silenced with a slit to her throat, she dissolved into digested food. All except her fingers. His bride threw her on the compost heap.

They would repeat the ritual again next week. When her necklace lost its song and flicker of blue neon.

Suitably labelled "The Queen of Filth", extremist author **Dani Brown***'s style of dark and twisted writing and deeply disturbing stories has amassed a worrying sized cult following featuring horrifying tales such as* "56 Seconds," *"*Sparky the Spunky Robot,*" and the hugely popular* "Ketamine Addicted Pandas."

Mixed Marriage

David Bernard

Even facing the altar, I could sense her daddy behind me, his shotgun pointed squarely between my shoulders. And at this range, he couldn't miss. His Glorianne was getting her wedding no matter what. That joke about the farmer's daughter? Not so funny in reality.

The room grew quiet. I looked up. The minister's jaw had fallen off again. While he attempted to reattach it, I glanced at Glorianne. What smelled like embalming fluid was soaking through her gown and another maggot crawled out of her good eye. I think she tried to smile at me, but it was hard to tell since the decomp took out the right side of her face. I'd consider making a run for it, but I was pretty sure her daddy's trigger finger hadn't fallen off.

Nothing like a zombie outbreak to ruin a perfectly good one night stand.

David Bernard *is a native New Englander who hightailed it to South* *Florida as soon as he was informed that grown-ups can live anywhere they* *want, and that in spite of opinions to the contrary, he was considered to be an* *adult. His previous works include short stories in anthologies such as* Twice Upon an Apocalypse, Legacy of the Reanimator, *and* The Chromatic Court.

Starlight and Fairy Dust

Chloé Harper Gold

Lacey was made of starlight and fairy dust. I've been telling her this since she was still in the womb. From the moment of conception, I was more in love with her than anyone else before. I could feel her heart beat from deep within me, feel her tiniest shifts and kicks. I would lie awake for hours with my hands on my belly, enjoying the private thrill of our pulses syncing up. Lacey was born in December in the middle of a snowstorm. The nurses were all in awe of how her eyes were open and focused.

"You've got a remarkable little girl, Ms. Leeds," they said. I smiled my thanks. My daughter was remarkable. She was flawless. She was perfect.

Lacey hit all of her milestones early. She could sit up by herself at three months and was reading by three-and-a-half. My little girl was destined for greatness. I knew it and I made sure Lacey did, too. She was a smart girl and eager to push herself to be smarter. By the time she was six, she was reading whole chapter books by herself and asking me to take her to the library every week for more. She colored within the lines and went on to create her own masterpieces from scratch with charcoal pencils, pastels, and watercolors. She always got the highest grades in her classes at school and won the spelling bee three years in a row. When she was in the third grade, she scored the goal that made her soccer team win the finals. That year, she taught herself how to play piano.

My daughter is made of starlight and fairy dust. She's perfect and she always will be.

I told Lacey's teacher, Mrs. Marks, this during our parent-teacher conference. Lacey's in fifth grade now. Next year she would start middle school.

Mrs. Marks looked at me with an expression that I couldn't pin down.

"People are flawed, Ms. Leeds," she said. "Flaws make us human."

I shook my head and smiled. Not my daughter, I told her. My Lacey doesn't have flaws.

"Lacey will be starting a new school next year," she said. "She'll be joined by new kids coming from the other schools in the district. I'm not saying Lacey's not smart—"

"Lacey is the smartest student in this school," I said.

Mrs. Marks gave me tight smile. My heart quickened.

"There will be students who are just as smart as her," she said. "And some who are smarter. And better at sports. And more artistic."

I pressed my lips together. My head was pounding.

"And when she goes to high school, there will be even more kids to compete with," she continued. "The stakes will be raised then. Colleges are quite competitive. It's likely that Lacey won't be accepted into every Ivy or even every state school. By the time she's in high school, she might just have settled into the middle of the pack."

The middle of the pack. My mouth went bone dry. I lost nearly all sensation in my limbs. My scalp tingled.

"My daughter is not average," I said.

Mrs. Marks' smile widened, just enough to make it obvious she was enjoying this torment.

"Your daughter is not special," she said. "She will fail eventually. And it is up to you to support her when she does."

82

I left the conference and threw up in the bushes behind the school. Mrs. Marks' words echoed in my head the whole drive home. *She will fail. She will fail. She will fail.*

She was right, I realized with a stinging pang of clarity. Lacey was perfect now, but would she always be? Everyone fails eventually. Lacey's classmates certainly had, time and time again. They had to be used to it by now.

Lacey had never failed before. She had never felt the crushing blow of trying and not succeeding. Never experienced the bitter shame of knowing that someone had bested you, especially in an area where you had previously excelled. She had always been the best, the brightest, the most adaptable, and the quickest to learn a new skill. She had always been perfect. It was her lot in life and her cross to bear.

Failure would destroy her. My Lacey wouldn't know how to react or how to cope. She would be humiliated and spiral into a crisis of identity. If she wasn't perfect, then what was she? My daughter wasn't emotionally equipped to settle for being average.

She will fail. It's up to you to support her.

Truth be told, I wasn't sure if I could support her if she failed. After all, Lacey's failure would be a failure on my part, as well. I wouldn't know how to cope. We would fall apart together, mother and daughter, and latch onto each other as we fell into a pit of despair.

I wouldn't be able to support her when she failed. I could only prevent it from happening.

I made Lacey's favorite dinner that night—grilled cheese—and said that we could eat in front of the television for a special treat.

"It's a reward," I told her. "For all the great things Mrs. Marks told me about you."

We watched *Matilda* and ate in silence. I subtly looked around the living room to make sure the windows were shut and that both doors, the front and the one opening into the downstairs hallway, were tightly closed with the cracks at the bottom plugged with throw rugs. My daughter and I were safely sealed in the living room, enjoying the movie and our grilled cheeses. I put my plate down and lightly stroked Lacey's hair. I pushed away all thoughts of the gas leaking out of the oven and filling the room.

"You're made of starlight and fairy dust, Lacey-girl," I said. She smiled back at me one last time.

"You're perfect and you always will be."

Chloé Harper Gold is a lifelong devotee of all things spooky, macabre, and grotesque. Her most recent story, "Heartbeat," can be found in the premiere issue of Ghoulish Tales. Her other stories include "God Given Duty," "Snake Bite," and "Cradle to Grave" (Reanimated Writers Press' 100-Word Zombie Bites). Her short film Final Pickup *premiered at Screamfest LA in 2021 and has since played in several other film festivals including Chicago Horror Film Festival and Anti-Hero Fest. Chloé has also written for Nightmarish Conjurings, Dread Central, Horror Film Central, 71 Magazine, Honeysuckle Magazine, Adweek, High Times, and SuperRare.*

She lives in New York with her two cats, Nyx and Hecate, and can be found on Twitter (@yochlo13), Instagram (@yochlo13, @chloe_the_final_girl), and Tik-Tok (@chlo_ayyyy).

Meme

Michael Patrick Hicks

The Karma's A Bitch meme challenge was one of the hottest video fads to hit the internet a year or two back. It was actually based on another meme, a fan edit of the TV show *Riverdale*, in which the show's character Veronica utters the infamous phrase "Karma's a bitch." In the fan edit, Veronica is then shown in various outfits and styles through a series of quick cuts. The meme challenge borrows this editing style, with the people appearing one way, saying "Karma's a bitch," and then a quick cut to a radically different appearance. For instance, we'd see them in their pajamas one second, and then the next they're dressed in heavy make-up and leather, ready to conquer a nightclub. The meme challenge was big in China, but I don't think it ever caught on in the States. Not after the first murder, anyway.

The death of Mallory Rabben gained its own sort of notoriety and went viral for reasons far disconnected from a cult teen TV show. In her video, Mallory appears in her bedroom, lying in bed, wearing cozy looking fleece pajamas. Her mascara is streaked, her eyes puffy, and even in the dim lighting of her room you can see the jagged red lines in the twenty-year-old's sclera. You can't help but wonder why she had been crying, what had made her voice so fragile and broken as she said those three little words.

"Karma's a bitch." She sniffles, wipes at a tear, and then quickly pulls the covers up and over her face.

The flash of fabric serves as the single moment of continuity between Mallory Then and Mallory Now. It's like a magic trick, the way she transforms in that seamless instant of video manipulation. Even the scene itself has changed. The snow-white comforter falls and she's sitting now, bound to a chair by thick ropes, in front of a bare concrete wall. Duct tape seals her lips and winds around her head in a thick matte gray loop. An enigma dressed all in black stands behind her. You can see one black gloved hand grab a fistful of her shockingly red hair to pull her head back, exposing the long, narrow line of her neck. In an instant, a second black hand slashes across her throat and the bright overhead light glints off the large blade her killer holds.

All told, the video is exactly twelve seconds long. The recording ends on a grisly note as that first spray of blood ejects from her severed carotid. Twitter removed it, as did Facebook, Instagram, and even Reddit. You can still find it, though, if you look hard enough. Mallory Rabbens, and others, too.

There are currently three Karma's A Bitch murder clips floating around online, each posted roughly a month apart. Some internet armchair detectives have noted that the bedroom Mallory is first seen in, the one where she's crying in bed, looks eerily similar to the bedroom Gloria Gentry and Lisa Stevens were in. Both are even wearing cozy fleece pajamas, which they argue cannot be coincidental. The three girls do not look even remotely alike. They have different builds, different hair colors, and different eye colors. Visually, there's nothing connecting them. Yet they all appear in the same bedroom, and all are crying as they utter that singular phrase: "Karma's a bitch."

What are they crying about? What's going through their minds at that moment, before they pull the bed sheets over their heads? Do they know what's about to happen after the sheet falls? Is any of this even real, or is it all just an elaborate hoax? You can't help but wonder.

Maybe one day I'll tell you, or I'll let one of them tell you. But not today. I need to finish editing video number four.

Michael Patrick Hicks *is the author of several horror books, including* The Resurrectionists, Broken Shells: A Subterranean Horror Novella, *and* Mass Hysteria. *His debut novel,* Convergence, *was an Amazon Breakthrough Novel Award Finalist in science fiction. He lives in Michigan with his wife and two children. Find out more about his work at https://michaelpatrickhicks.substack.com/.*

As the Crow Flies

Kevin Lucia

1.

It's time. You've been pushed too far. Made a little crazy. Okay, more than a little. Maybe full-on psycho. Still. Life can't go on like this. You've tried, but you're tired. It's gotta stop. No more pain. Tonight, everything changes.

But there's not much time. Only a small window. Halloween. One chance to hurt those who've hurt you most. And you'll do it *right*.

Ease out of bed. Quiet and slow. Everyone's sleeping. No one celebrates Halloween in *this* house. Even so, you have to prepare, or tonight won't go right.

Kneel on the floor. Reach under the bed. Pull out that Ginsu knife you bought at Handy's Pawn and Thrift last week. Can't use one of Mom's knives. She'd notice it missing. This one's good enough. It sharpened up nice.

You straighten. Lay the blade flat against your palm. Press its edge into the meat. Don't want to break the skin, yet. Just feel the blade's kiss. Close those eyes, breathe deep. It's time. No one's going to hurt you again.

2.

You find her quickly. She always comes to the cliffs when upset. After what happened, who wouldn't be? You guys fooled around for hours in the back of her Camry. You did all the right things. Kissing, tonguing, squeezing, petting. But when it was time for lift-off...

No ignition.

Makes sense, now. After all those dark nights with HIM, she was the first *you* wanted. Easy to see how it was confusing. You worried it wouldn't be like you'd imagined. Worried it would just be another reminder of those grinding nights with HIM.

Plus, Angie and you have been friends since Junior Church. You've shared everything. Stories. Dreams. Nightmares. She's the only one who knows about HIM. How you're scared you'll never be normal because of HIM.

She offered, of course. So, you could see what it was like. And, even though it took her awhile to convince you, in the end it was easy. Let's be honest.

You love her.

Have forever. Her scarlet red hair, glimmering jade eyes and knock-out figure? C'mon. What's to think about?

But when your rocket didn't fire, Angie laughed. Called you "limp dick." Asked if she should've brought a bible. Is that what you need? Some Holy Rollin' Hellfire?

She laughed so hard she cried, because of course that's something else you share. HIM. He's been practicing his Holy Devotions on her for years.

So that's why she laughed and couldn't stop, until you backhanded her across the face. She stopped laughing, then. Real quick.

You ran. She screamed angry words which still cut you. That was weeks ago. You haven't spoken since. And you know, now. Things will never be the same. She's tried to call, but you haven't responded.

Until now.

The leaves and branches rustle. Angie walks along the cliff's edge, holding herself tight. Head bowed and shoulders quivering. Moonlight fires her hair red. As she paces along the edge, you glimpse her sobbing. Sure, she's upset. But does she care about you? No. Her messages only beg you not to tell HIM. She's more afraid of losing HIM than you.

Anger ripples through you. Makes you brush the branches. Its dry leaves rasp. Angie looks up, eyes narrowed. "W-who's there? Matt? Is that you? I swear...if you're spying on me, I'll..."

Hold still.

Angie turns away.

She never sees you coming. Bitter anger clogs your throat, so there are no words. All you can do is screech. You slash at her...

She spins.

Screams, eyes wide.

She back-peddles. Slips on gravel. For an instant her arms windmill...

She's gone with a *whoosh*. Seconds later a distant thud.

Then nothing.

3.

It doesn't take long to reach her. It's not far. "Near as the crow flies," like Grandpa used to say. She's in a twisted heap. Neck wrenched oddly. Her lips glimmer in the moonlight. She stares, eyes glassy.

Not how you wanted it. She deserved her pretty face slashed, eyeballs plucked out. Doesn't matter. It's done. Only one more.

HIM.

His fault. Things wouldn't be like this if it weren't for him.

You head home.

4.

HE comes into your room later, with his belt. That's how he likes it. Wrapped around your neck. It's very early. That's also how he likes it. Early, when it's quiet.

This morning he stops. Sees your open bedroom window, which you crept through earlier. The screen's gone. A light breeze curls the curtains. Next, he sees the altar in the corner. Black candles burnt to nubs. Between the candles, the remains of a crow.

When he sees your body sprawled before the candles in your chair, wrists slashed, he drops his belt. Good idea, facing the door when you cut. Looks like you're waiting for him. Your rigor-mortis grin shocks him so badly he doesn't see the leathery book open in your lap. Even if he did, he'd never understand. The knowledge contained within its pages is Ancient. Beyond mud-bound things like him. Beyond what you were.

With a flutter you streak from your hiding place in the rafters. You'll ruin his face. Pluck out his eyes. If you're lucky and fast, plunge your beak through his eyes into his brain.

He turns and shouts.

You screech.

He doesn't have a chance, because you're not that far away. Near as the crow flies...

Kevin Lucia is the eBook and trade paperback editor at Cemetery Dance Publications. His short fiction has been published in many venues, most notably with Neil Gaiman, Clive Barker, David Morell, Peter Straub, Bentley Little, and Robert McCammon. His first novel, The Horror at Pleasant Brook, *is forthcoming from Crystal Lake Publishing, October 2023.*

I Didn't Know What Love Was

Ben Lathrop

Nights make me lonely since Scott left. And February nights are the longest. Jogging helps me forget. That's how I ended up at the park. It's just a little playground really, tucked a few yards past the edge of the oil colored light of the street. I didn't see them at first, and then could only make out their silhouettes. A child sitting on the swings, and a man.

When I got closer, I could tell it was a little girl, maybe five or six years old. Skinny pink leggings poking out of a grey winter coat that was at least a size too big. One long sock with pink and white stripes, the other shorter with Hello

Kitty all over it. Both pulled up as high as they could go. I couldn't see her face under the adult-sized stocking cap that covered most of her head. The knit kind with a big puff ball on top that I can never tell if people wear ironically or not. This one had "Bengals" spelled out in orange yarn.

"Hi," I said. She didn't move.

"Hi," said the man. His hands were stuffed into the pockets of a hooded sweatshirt. "Can you say 'Hi,' Cass?" he said, bending down a little and looking at the girl. His ears were red from the cold. "Being bashful?" he asked her gently. "I'm sure she's nice."

He turned to me with a sheepish look. "Sorry." The girl hopped off the swings and ran over to the rickety looking merry-go-round, skidding to a stop in the frost covered wood chips and then gingerly stepping onto it. "I'm Jake," he said.

"Andi," I said, reaching my hand out to shake his. "Andrea, actually."

"Her name is Cassandra, but I just call her 'Cass' most of the time." The merry-go-round squeaked quietly as Cass rode in slow looping circles. Street-lights flashed off her eyes every time she came around. Jake put his hands back in his pockets and started shifting his weight back and forth from foot to foot.

"You look cold," I said.

"Yeah, well," he laughed a little. "Somebody forgot their hat at home so..."

Cass pulled the over-sized cap down a little farther with both hands and kicked at the ground to push the merry-go-round around again.

"Isn't *she* cold?" I hesitated.

"You'd think," he sighed. "But cold doesn't seem to bother her. And she gets so restless at night. The doctors said exercise was the best thing."

"I'm sorry. It's none of my business."

"No, it's ok," he said. "I know it must seem weird. It *is* weird." He kicked at the playground chips and paused to watch her swing around again. "I think she takes after her mom. She had a...well a condition, I guess. Hardly ever slept. No appetite for normal food. She...well, she passed when Cass was born."

91

"Oh, jeeze," I sputtered. "I'm so sorry, I..." he looked at my hand, which had somehow reached out to his arm, and then into my eyes.

"No, really," he said. "It's ok. That was a long time ago."

Cass dashed back to the swings. The frosted chains started to squeal with each kick of her little feet. "I know you're getting hungry, kiddo," Jake said. "Just be patient, ok?"

He kicked at the ground. I stood a little closer and we spent a little while coyly smiling at each other, talking about nothing in particular. "You'd think after a while I'd get better at talking to pretty girls," he said.

"You're doing ok so far," I said.

"That's good," he replied with a grin. "I don't really get many opportunities anymore."

"Oh, come on," I teased. "Handsome single dad with a cute daughter? Love story writes itself."

"Love story, sure," he chuckled politely. "I thought I loved her mom, but I didn't know what love was. Not til Cass... I'd do anything for her. Absolutely anything... Kids're innocent you know? I mean, anything that's wrong with them isn't their fault. It's yours. Your responsibility."

The squeaking had stopped. I turned to look and saw Cass motionless and staring at me from under that stupid floppy stocking cap. She slowly slid off the swings and slipped behind Jake and tugged at his sleeve. "I know sweetheart," he said, his voice catching a little. "Be patient."

I smiled as best I could and tried to think of an excuse to leave.

"She's hungry all the time now," he said. "She didn't really eat much as a baby... It was easy to feed her then. I just did it myself most nights..." He took a small step closer, and I started to take a small step back but he slid his arm around my back.

"Jake, no," I said. He pulled me closer, and whispered in my ear without meeting my eyes.

"I'm sorry."

It was just a little pinch. A paper cut. A nothing. And then I couldn't feel my arms or legs.

I could see the needle as Jake pulled it out of my neck. My heart started pounding and suddenly I was falling over. The impact of the frozen ground reverberated through my bones. "Help me!" I cried, but there was only a rasp, like dry leaves on concrete. The wood chips dragged tears down my face as Jake pulled me by my ankles behind the monkey bars.

The glare of the streetlight at his back transformed Jake into a black, man-shaped hole that took something from its pocket and clicked it open. Another shadow, smaller, hovered nearby impatiently. "Please." I barely made a sound, but the shadow heard me. She did not answer.

The metal was cold against the skin of my neck, but it gave way immediately to wet warmth. The little shadow drew close and gave me little kisses from her little mouth. Butterfly kisses. A kitten lapping milk.

"I love you, daddy," she said.

"I love you too, Sweetheart."

Ben Lathrop has written and taught on the history of cinema with a focus on the horror genre and cult audience behavior. He is a native Iowan, former television horror host and present librarian. He lives with his family in Cincinnati, Ohio.

The Talk

Lori Michelle

"I have something to tell you." She timidly placed her hands on the counter. "And please don't stop me before I am through, I need to tell you everything."

She didn't turn to look at him, expecting the inevitable backlash, but when none came, she took a breath and continued on. "I want out. I can't do this anymore."

She slightly cringed, anticipating a blow to the back of her head. She'd been slapped for much less, remembering the time she didn't take the cap off his beer correctly, or the nights she hadn't cooked his meat how he wanted. She peered out of the corner of her eyes to make sure he was still sitting there. She didn't want to look him full on, fearing another black eye. She could see his shadowy outline still sitting there at the kitchen table.

She closed her eyes and thought about all she had endured. She remembered the time she had mistakenly worn a T-shirt while house cleaning, and the subsequent punishment of spending the night in the dog cage. Or the time she had a migraine and he locked her outside to sleep in the cold.

She opened her eyes, inspecting her swollen bumpy hands. They were all crooked and gnarled from being broken so many times. The arthritis had already started but she dared not complain of the pain lest she should endure a new agony. Gathering strength, she made a mental note to wash her hands before finishing the preparation for dinner.

She looked out into space as she continued, waiting for his hands to start hurting her again. "I don't want to be your whipping girl anymore. I can't take the abuse any longer."

Tears started to drip down her face and she winced at the pain in her ribcage from where she had been kicked several times. All the years of her life she had given up just to be tortured. Why had she stayed? He had made her feel so worthless, like no one else would even look her way or need her. But the thought of living the next twenty years of her life afraid and in pain was too much for her to handle.

Taking as deep of a breath as she could, she finally turned to face him, his eyes wide open in shock. "I am done and I am leaving."

She took off the apron she was wearing, and meticulously wiped the blood which had settled on her hands. She set the apron on the counter gently and looked at him one more time, sitting there, quietly listening to her with the huge knife sticking out from his chest. The blood was running down his limp body and forming a pool at his feet, but she no longer cared. This wasn't her mess to clean up any longer. She was done.

"Goodbye." She turned and walked out the door.

Lori Michelle Booth is the co-owner of Ghoulish Books, the Ghoulish Bookstore and the hostess of the Ghoulish Book Festival in San Antonio. She is also one of the editors for Ghoulish Tales and Night Frights magazines. Lori formats books for several publishers and horror writers across the world. By day, she is publishing queen, but by night she is Mrs. Lori, dance teacher extraordinaire, where she teaches young minds the joy of a perfectly balanced pirouette. You can contact Lori by following one of the many links at https://linktr.ee/ghoulishbooks.

Sanctuary

David J. Rank

She writhed beneath a silent scream, skin blistering in the dawn light. The old priest found her on the stone steps outside the age-stained parish church. He dropped to his knees beside her. "Élise," the priest whispered.

"Fool! I hunted too long," she hissed, demonic tongue swelling and black.

The priest gagged as the stench of decay and flesh hissing into ash enveloped him. A remembered smell.

She reached for him. "Help me, Daniel. You remember—me," Curls of thin smoke snaked from her rupturing body, barely clothed in rotted rags, an ancient dress.

He had loved her once, as a young man—before her soul was ripped away. When he was known as Daniel. They thought love would nourish them forever and planned to wed. A lost lifetime ago they walked in a moon-lit field of flowers when a thing pale as a headstone, hideous as a maddened syphilitic attacked them.

The priest could not bear to watch her burn.

He lifted the vampire in his arms, cassock smeared with ashened flesh. Tears hissed into steam as they fell upon her. He hurried around the church to the rectory, his home, delivering his Élise—he could think of her only as his Élise—to the darkest corner of the basement. Rushing upstairs, he brought back blankets for her to lie on then carried buckets of fresh grave earth to comfort her.

"I will pray for you," the priest whispered, his voice catching on the words. As he watched, blisters and burns slowly heal. He brushed soiled tendrils of hair from her face.

That night long ago, the hideous thing flung him to the ground and carried away the shrieking Élise before his younger self could rise. His failure forever seared into his brain.

The priest continued to soothe her with soft words and gentle strokes upon her head, even though he knew the vampire, lost in the sleep of the dead, could not hear him or know he sat beside her. He wept.

· · · ● · ● · · ·

At day's end, the priest sat in his favorite chair, shadows thickening in the sparsely furnished room upstairs. He did not bother to light a lamp.

He thought of their time together, before that thing tore her away from him. Years he spent searching for his Élise in dark forests, in deep crags of the surrounding mountains, the ruins of long-abandoned villas and towns.

The day he found the hideous thing, curled like a babe in a dark crevice on a stone-strewn slope, the priest remembered his fury—no, his rage—at the sight of the thing, and his joy dragging the pale creature from its hole into the sunlight. He watched it burn and writhe and never forgot the stench. A stench he did not experience again until today.

For more years he searched for his Élise until grief and despair forced him to stop. Wanting solace and sleep unbroken by nightmares, he found his way to a seminary where he joined the brotherhood. Decades now, the priest buried himself in the care of his parishioners, their joys and sorrows, finding fulfillment in tending their needs. He almost forgot his Élise. Almost.

Footsteps ascended the basement stairs, entered the dark hallway behind him. "I must feed," she hissed, a shadow in the dying light of the priest's study.

"I know. I prayed for you all day."

"Did it comfort you, priest?"

"I hope it comforts your lost soul."

Slowly she circled the chair. "You could have killed me, left me on the steps to burn. Your hands clean."

The priest shook his head. "I could not. I still... I believe in my vows, the word of the Lord, 'Thou shalt not kill.' Even lost souls."

"You are a fool, but I thank you for that. I will feed."

"Better me than these poor people I serve."

The vampire's dance-like steps brought her closer to him. Dressed in tattered rags, even in her pale gauntness and distorted features she remained tempting—a memory of the girl he wanted to marry.

The priest looked into her black, deadened eyes. "Do you feel nothing anymore...for anyone?"

"I feel hunger. I can kill you or make you my bloodslave. Since you spared me, I will let you choose." She smiled. "That is fair, do you not think?"

The priest's hands trembled. He remembered their last night together, that young girl. For an instant he considered.

Mouth dry, he said, "I do not fear death. My Lord waits to embrace me."

She now stood behind him. Hands, cool as soil, rested on his shoulders. "Tell me, Daniel, is such virtue worth dying for?"

He gripped the chair to still his shaking hands. Her breath was cold on the beating artery beneath his jaw. "You do not frighten me. I pray for you, Élise. Lord, forgive her..."

She hesitated, breathed deeply his scent.

"Pray, priest," the vampire whispered above his neck. "If it comforts you."

"I still love you."

Black eyes gleaming, she fed.

Published author, editor, and recovering journalist, **David J. Rank** *is the founder and director of the nonprofit Novel Bookcamp educational programs since 2014. His 33 dark fiction short stories have been published in regional publications, online magazines, and five anthologies. A member of the Horror Writers Association and the Science Fiction and Fantasy Writers Association, he organized the HWA-Wisconsin (USA) Chapter in 2018.*

Dave also spies on things only found in deep shadows. www.facebook.com/davidjrankwriter, www.novelbookcamp.org.

That Which Makes Me Happiest

L. F. Falconer

Being overweight has never interfered with the pursuit of happiness in my life, but my mother views gluttony as a problem, one so malignant and blasphemous that she's forced me into rehab. In a place with a summer camp atmosphere, I am surrounded by counselors—those who attempt to prod my psyche, those who insist I get up and exercise, and those most dreadful of beasts who control my food intake—the dieticians. They are the worst. Stick people, these skinny, bland dieticians are little more than pretzels without any salt or even soft cheese to spread upon them to make them a bit more palatable. Tasteless pretzel rods who deign to deny me that which makes me happiest. Can they not understand the sheer joy of eating for the sake of eating? Can they not understand the force of food and its significance as a primal comfort, for what initially tempered the trauma of birth but Mother's milk?

Food. Its consumption is a rapture that rains down over my flesh like gravy. The very ecstasy, the power of eating, so like electric eels charging my feet, my hefty feet which spill over the tops of my shoes like plump, risen dough, propelling me into a cumbrous sprint through glorious corridors laden with mounds of roast beef and potatoes, lasagna, pumpernickel, meatballs, cakes and bacon and gooey cheese. The wild, euphoric moments of devouring, those pure moments of bliss that are mine and mine alone, to cherish, to revel in an homage to flavors and textures, to spice and sweetness, to tang and savory delights, thus driving away the drudgery of routine, responsibilities, duty, and mundanity, those soul-sucking vampires that haunt my lonely days.

Oh, but eating! The joy of eating unlocks my chains and buoys me upon the breasts of angels as I soar into the vaults of heaven, overcome with the purifying moments of gnashing and gnawing, of the chew, the swallow, of thick gobs of mastication chugging in bunches down my gullet, deep into the vast dark depths of my belly where it churns like butter in the bile of digestion.

These small, precious moments, these raptures are like the food of the gods, the ambrosia upon which I glut my soul with courage and strength which enables me to carry on, to withstand the dreary, empty days of life.

But here—oh, here the cupboards are bare. I am left destitute. Wanting. With nothing but these pretzel rods. These bland and puny pretzel rods.

They tried to deny me, but I choke them down without salt or cheese, one by one, their blood dribbling from my chin. They will never forbid me that which makes me happiest.

L.F. Falconer is a lifelong resident of Northern Nevada where she enjoys exploring ghost towns, gardening, and experimenting with new recipes in the kitchen. An indie author of dark fiction, she has published one collection of short stories and seven novels, earning various awards. Discover more at: www.lffalconer.com.

Driving On

Guy Medley

The man drove because there was nothing left to do now but drive. So, he drove. Next to him the woman sat in perfect silence, her face ruddy and sullen, tear-streaked, not so much as a plastic smile upon her trembling lips, afraid perhaps of what remained behind—of what lay yet ahead. The little girl in the back seat cried, the same as she had been since the trip began an eternity ago. Beside the girl, peacefully asleep in a bundled jacket despite the storm raging all around him, a baby boy. The man envied the baby the most, admired his lack of understanding.

He drove on, the apocalyptic fires consuming the world in the rear view, chasing them down like an out of control eighteen wheeler. There was no stopping for bathroom or burger breaks—for anything. How far could they make it? How long did they have left until the flames overtook them, swallowing them up whole? Before the car died—ran out of fuel, blew a tire, failed a curve—before it was finally just all over?

At first, he tried comforting the woman, the children, even himself, with rosy promises of 'It'll be okay' and 'We're going to make it.' But, eventually even he gave in to numbed silence, unable to admit to himself that they weren't going to be okay—that they were never going to make it.

Maybe it didn't matter anymore that they couldn't see it, weren't witness to the horrors his own eyes were as the hungry flames lapped at the bumper, the asphalt melting away practically beneath the road-worn tires, the very air outside the windows on verge of combusting and roasting them all alive. He told himself they saw none of it so that he could continue on—keep them moving forward for however much longer they could.

The skyglow filled the interior of the little car with fever red, while outside the trees and grass and deer and birds—all but cinders rising into the blistered sky, blotting out the sun to an insignificant pinprick.

The car shuddered, the gas petal pressed fully into the floorboard, gauges in the red as the road furiously struggled to maintain their course, to contain their trajectory into the blue, the car and its occupants maxed-out. The man drove on.

He dared not look at the fuel gauge, the mere thought of doing so—what he might see there—too terrifying. He drove on, through the stinging blur of sweat streaming into his eyes, and through the tears. He drove on.

The man drove on thinking maybe the woman and the girl and the sleeping baby boy—maybe they couldn't fully comprehend what loomed behind them, and that was a blessing, if but a small one, but he was certain that they could all somehow see what lay ahead for them, what was coming, and that thought, that realization, was destroying him more completely than any fire ever could. So, he did the only thing he could do. He drove on.

He drove on—

Guy Medley enjoys writing dark fiction for the amusement of his friends and family. He resides in the solitude of California's Mojave Desert, where the extreme heat has, undoubtedly, affected his mind.

Dichotomy

Jason Parent

Men scream as they die. The sound of my heart thumping in my chest drowns them out. I have not yet seen the enemy beyond outlines and shadows in the dark, their shapes monstrous, things children believe hide under their beds or in their closets, not creatures of true flesh and blood.

We're dying, and I don't even know where to aim. I hug my face against the dirt, low in the trench, rifle tight against my chest. The night above veils the carnage on the battlefield, an empty landscape between two civilizations. We know nothing of the Others or why we fight them. Just what we are told: that they are monsters, evil; that they must be killed so we might live.

My brother has fallen, so I need little reason to fight. Still, a tingling in my gut tells me this is all wrong, that we should keep to our side of the barren field and them to theirs, where both may live in peace and prosperity. But who am I to question my superiors; them, educated and wise beyond my years, me but a simple soldier knowing no more than a simple life filled with farming days and family nights? I am a fool to question them.

The stars above twinkle across a still plain, their tranquillity offering hope. They shine for all, even the Others. But they are too far away to hear our screams.

The enemy's banshee wails have my comrades shaking. My hands tremble as I hug my rifle closer. I see my face, white and ghastly, in the shine of my bayonet, wondering if tonight will be the night I die.

Our men are fleeing the front line, but our captain orders them back. Those who refuse are executed. With numbers dwindling, it'll soon be my squad's turn to march. Fingers fumble as I check and recheck my bayonet stud, bolt, and safety. *I am ready*, I lie to myself. I don't want to die.

A horn blows, our signal to move. I stand, but my weapon falls from my shaking hands. I suck in air, my breaths having come too fast and too short. I search inward for strength, the memory of my brother, the love of my family awaiting my return. It is not enough to steel myself for what is to come, but it will have to do. *Courage comes from hidden places*, I tell myself, chuckling awkwardly as if I could convince myself I'd find it.

Most of my squad has climbed over the lip. Cries of pain, death wails, come from everywhere. I pick up my weapon and dig my boots into the wall, climbing into hell before I lose my nerve. On unsteady legs, blinded by darkness, I charge. The enemy is in front of me, somewhere unseen.

Waiting.

The path before me is littered with the dead. I step over bodies, some of men I recognize: the baker from Danbury Street, an old schoolmate from my youth—people with wives and children, just like me, who will never share in their families' love again. Their faces are still, watching the stars as the stars watch them back, neither caring about those still alive on the ground.

I think to retreat, to run home and hide. But something inside me compels me forward. Whether it's fear of being slaughtered by my own comrades or of being labelled a coward by the ones I love, I do not know. Courage is the lesser of two evils. I must do this for my family, to protect them from the teeth and claws of monsters they'll never see, though being a husband and father seems more important than foreign sacrifice.

Even as I conjure the soapy smell of my daughter's hair all those times I cradled her in my arms, I step forward, closer to the enemy, the sight unseen. My boots squish in the blood of wasted heroes. Shots are fewer now. Screaming has been replaced by soft whimpering and prayers for help. I look to my left then to my right and see no one. Am I all that is left?

A massive shape, one of *them*, races toward me out of the black. I struggle to steady my rifle as I take aim, the enemy frightful, unnatural, instilling panic into my every nerve. My weapon shifts in my sweaty palms. I release my breath and close my eyes, the enemy's wails driving a spike of terror into my brain. Opening my eyes, I fire.

The shot goes wide, and my enemy lurches forward—smaller now, shadows and distance having played tricks on my eyes. I can almost see the beast, not much taller than me, but still with murder and wickedness in its soul.

It leaps. No time to aim and fire. I steady my arms, strengthened now by righteousness. I will deliver this evil from our world.

Seething and hissing, the monster strikes. Metal glints in its raised fist, a knife it means to plunge inside me. Its face is pale like death itself, contorted with rage—or perhaps, fear— horrible to behold. I crouch and spring upward, thrusting my bayonet into its gut. The blade falls from its hand as it slides down into mine, blood sputtering from its coughing mouth. Its weight is heavy in my arms. I flick my rifle to my side, tossing my enemy to the ground.

The beast sputters before gasping its final breath. I feel nothing as I check the horizon for others. The field has gone silent, and I am still alive.

Hesitantly, I crouch beside the slain creature, not wanting to see but needing to know whom or what I fight. Kneeling in the dirt, breath hitching in my throat, I see no monster at all but a man. His dead glass eyes, empty of soul, stare at the stars. I lean closer, his face familiar even in the dark night.

It looks like mine.

Jason Parent is an author of horror, thrillers, mysteries, science fiction and dark humor, though his many novels, novellas, and short stories tend to blur the boundaries between these genres and have earned him praise from both critics and fans of diverse genres alike. You can find Jason on Facebook, Twitter, and http://authorjasonparent.com/.

The Good Samaritan

L.F. Falconer

Half an hour south of Needles, I realize something's wrong. The gas gauge still reads full, but the car stalls and sputters to a halt. I wanted to reach the border by dawn, before anyone finds the body. Instead, I'm stranded out in the California desert on a pitch-black moonless night.

In desperation, I try to start the engine again. I don't dare call anyone—got to keep off any GPS tracking. It's too dark to venture out on foot and it'll be too damn hot come daylight.

I get out and kick the front tire, then lean back against the fender and light up a smoke. This is what I get for stealing a piece of shit Honda Civic. The tank registered full in Vegas and I should've suspected something was off when I reached Needles and the tank still registered full.

"Fuck!" I kick the front tire again, flicking my cigarette out into the road. In the distance headlights appear, disappear, then reappear, dipping through the hills of this two-lane back-country highway. I hope it's not a state trooper. I retrieve the tire iron from the trunk. It might need to get a little more blood on it tonight.

A distant coyote breaks the dead silence. I settle back inside the car, nestling the tire iron at my feet. Killing the headlights, I click the flashing hazard lights on.

Twenty minutes pass before a white utility van pulls over and parks on the opposite side of the road. Its headlights go dark. The driver doesn't make a move. Neither do I. We each wait, terribly, in the dark alone, while the amber hazard lights break the night between us.

A slow minute later, the van's door eases open. The driver steps out, briefly silhouetted against the brightness of the interior light until it's lost to darkness with the closure of the door. A tall, gaunt man crosses the road with a limp.

Guardedly, I step out of the Honda. "Hey, thanks for stopping."

"There is something about you which compelled me." His voice is self-assured, low and eloquent.

"Could it have been the pathetic appearance of a man foolish enough to let his car run out of gas in the middle of nowhere?"

"No," the man states. Within the flashing amber light, his face appears grotesquely misshapen. "That's not it."

I release a nervous chuckle. "Well, anyway, that's what happened. I'm Jay, by the way." Not my real name. Not knowing my name, this guy has a better chance of surviving here.

"And I am Lucien. Lucien Greyshire."

"Well, Lucien, you don't happen to have any gas you can give me, do you?"

He crosses the road to the rear of the van and opens the back door. In a moment he returns, bearing a three-gallon gas can. "I do have some fuel you can purchase."

"Uh...great. How much?"

"That depends upon your answer."

"What's the question?"

"What do you know about death, Ted?"

"It's Jay."

He shakes his head. "Ted."

Okay, this guy's really starting to creep me out. I step back toward the car. The tire iron rests on the floor. I don't know how he knows me, but I have to take him down.

"Death happens to us all someday," I tell him, grabbing the door handle.

"Occasionally, we die more than once. I died in a fire years ago, yet was brought back to life."

"Okay. Cool." I open the door.

"Do you know what it feels like to burn, Ted? To feel the heat melt the skin from your bones, leaving behind nothing but unquenchable, excruciating agony?"

His free hand thrusts forward. Pain jolts through my chest, zapping me from head to toe. I double over, quivering, nauseous, collapsing to the pavement. The copper Taser wires dangle from the barbs embedded in my chest.

Lucien steps closer. "I died and was brought back to life. However, not all of me returned. A portion of me still walks the other side, mingling with the spirits of Limbo. I can see one right now. Right above you. And she told me what you did, Ted. How you beat her and set her on fire while still alive. Her and the child she carried inside."

I yank at the barbs in my chest but he zaps me again. Writhing upon the ground, I feel the moisture splash down on me. I taste the gasoline.

Then I hear the match as it grates against the striker.

L.F. Falconer writes on the dark side, with award winners in both Fantasy and Horror. Her recurring character, Lucien Greyshire, made his debut appearance in Weirdbook Magazine # 36 *and was pleased to pop in for a quickie in these Shallow Waters. For more information, visit www.lffalconer.com.*

The Visitors

Mark Allan Gunnells

He saw the ship streak by overhead and land over the next rise. He had been standing out in the field, dreaming of a different life as he was prone to do, and instead of running back home, he ran toward the rise.

The ship was nestled into a natural depression in the land, humming softly. He stopped a few feet away, mesmerized. He knew many people believed in such things, visitors from other planets, but he'd never given much credence to the idea himself. Yet the evidence sat right in front of him, solid and undeniable.

With a *clunk* and a *whoosh*, a door opened in the side of the ship, falling slowly to create a ramp. As he watched, wide-eyed and his mouth forming a perfect ring, two creatures with bulbous heads and blank faces, bodies bulky and oddly shaped, climbed down the ramp, their movements stiff and awkward.

They spotted him and began to chitter in a rapid, harsh tongue that he could not decipher. He knew he should probably be afraid of them, flee from the area, call for help, but nothing about them exuded menace, and their clumsy lumbering seemed almost comical. There was no reason to believe they meant him harm.

He started toward them, and they reacted by scurrying back up the ramp, their chittering becoming higher-pitched and more strident. At first he was confused, but then he realized that *they* were afraid of *him*. These visitors who had travelled across space in an advanced craft, were afraid of little old him. Bizarre.

He held up his hands to indicate to them that he wasn't a threat, but they apparently viewed this as an aggressive gesture and one raised an odd metallic object that spat out a dart which stabbed into his chest. He felt an electrical current, his body spasmed, then he collapsed.

· • • ● • ● • • ·

Back on the ship, Roger removed his helmet and stared down at the alien creature strapped to the table. To his fellow astronaut, he said, "Wait until they get a load of this thing on earth."

Mark Allan Gunnells loves to tell stories. He has since he was a kid, penning one-page tales that were Twilight Zone knockoffs. He likes to think he has gotten a little better since then. He loves reader feedback, and above all he loves telling stories. He lives in Greer, SC, with his husband Craig A. Metcalf.

Twenty Reasons to Stay and One to Leave

Richard Thomas

(Originally published at *Metazen*. Nominated for a Pushcart Prize)

Because in the beginning it was the right thing to do, staying with her, comforting and holding her, while inside I was cold and numb, everything on the surface an act, just for her.

Because I couldn't go outside, trapped in the empty expanse of rooms that made me twitch, echoes of his voice under the eaves, and in the rafters.

Because she still hid razorblades all over the house.

Because I wasn't ready to bare myself to the world, willing to pour more salt into the wounds.

Because of the dolls and the way she held them to her bare breasts, the way she laughed and carried on, two dull orbs filling her sockets, lipstick on her face, hair done up, but the rest of her like marble, to go with her porcelain children that watched from his bed, defiling it, making a joke of it all.

Because at one point in our past she saved me from myself, the simple act of showing up. Lasagna filled my apartment with garlic and promise when all I could do was fall into a bottle.

Because I kept hoping he would walk in the door, backpack flung over his shoulder, eager to show me his homework, the worlds he had created with a handful of crayons.

Because it was my fault, the accident, and we both knew it.

Because if she was going to die a death of a thousand cuts, one of them wouldn't be mine.

Because tripping over a Matchbox car, I found myself hours later curled up in a ball, muttering and listening for his response.

Because she asked me to, and I hadn't learned to say no to her yet.

Because she wanted to live in any time but this time, jumping from one era to another, bonnets and hoop skirts, wigs and parasols, and I allowed it.

Because when I held her in the black void that was our bedroom, pressing my body up against hers, part of me believed I was a sponge, soaking up her pain. It was a fake voodoo, but it was all that I had.

Because I had no love left for anyone in the world.

Because I didn't want to go.

Because it was still my home, and not simply a house yet.

Because I wasn't done talking to my son, asking him for forgiveness.

Because I didn't believe that we were done, that our love had withered, collapsed and fallen into his casket, wrapping around his broken bones, covering his empty eyes.

Because I didn't hate her enough to leave.

Because I didn't love her enough to leave.

Because every time she looked at me, she saw him, our son, that generous boy, and it was another gut punch bending her over, another parting of her flesh, and I was one of the thousand, and my gift to her now was my echo.

Richard Thomas is the award-winning author of three novels, three short story collections, 150+ stories in print, and the editor of four anthologies. He has been nominated for the Bram Stoker, Shirley Jackson, and Thriller awards. Visit www.whatdoesnotkillme.com for more information.

The Knights of Cold Days

Dave Jeffery

Life is a series of happenings—events stitched together somehow making a kind of private sagacity. There are, however, situations and occurrences that dismay the soul. These are the bad things, the terrible things, the things that can ultimately break a mind, shattering it the way a tiled kitchen floor makes short work of a crystal wine glass.

Order is the first casualty as faith becomes collateral damage, the pieces of each tenet fracturing and fusing together to become one ruined mess. The quilt wrapped about me is my cocoon and underneath I am *changed*, the contained stink of a neglected body, a mind: twisted out to the point where there is *leakage,* a residue of torment.

I am abandonment personified. Acts and omissions have equal consequences when you're a single parent...

"I'm gone, Dad. Gone."

...*was* a single parent.

The bed is small, the covers emblazoned with a *Game of Thrones* motif, the duvet a cold comfort against despair. Deep down there is feeling, but it is smothered under the frost of detachment. I have closed myself off, locked myself in—the scene of the crime now a cinema where I can relive my failings in flashback, paying my dues via virtual reality on repeat.

This room, another time, where everything made sense. Teenage decor, posters and video game machines, shelves of books—the vestiges of contented solitude.

Or so I thought.

Walls aren't enough these days; assault comes through an Ethernet cable.

Felix wouldn't have hurt a fly, yet harmed himself from time to time. Tiny little scratches, a statement—pain's signature staking its claim on his young, pale flesh.

These were the signs, and I was so focused on the distractions of living, I missed them, perhaps worse, made excuses: the mid-term exams, the pressures of being young in an adult world.

My son has risen, the lofty position acquired by the Ethernet cable used to connect him with the world that took him. These days they call faceless tormentors 'trolls' but they are more than fabled monsters, they and their vile inflictions exist, cutting deep, poisoning self-esteem, corrupting self-worth. Anonymity is their armour in a one-sided onslaught against the defenceless.

I am sinking as well as lost. All I can see is my boy, suspended like a macabre marionette, and his hanging jaw, soundlessly screaming out his despair.

Felix looks like me, looks *at* me, and I cannot return the intense, glassy gaze. *I see you, but you don't see me*, his eyes say.

Life goes full circle, even in death. If I didn't get that, then it was written in the note on his closed MacBook.

Sloth is an edict, penance for my ignorance There are no more tears to shed, the account is clear. I wish to slip away, join my son in the *whatever*. The dull thumps from across the room tell me people are intent on challenging my stance on how this should end.

As they put through the door, gasps orchestrate their disbelief. Two fingers are at my neck and the voice on the air is tinged with relief.

"Alive," it says, "Still alive."

The duvet is removed, and my neglect is laid bare. Then comes the sound of someone retching, snuffed out by the clatter of a gurney, the crackle of high-vis jackets.

Gentle hands are upon me, lifting me clear. I've transformed, a miserable husk secured for transport to a place that gives care to those who no longer feel they deserve it.

For a moment there is blue sky and furrowed clouds, as though the heavens are frowning on my condition.

I'm hoisted into the back of the van, bleeps and clicks of equipment greeting me as I enter the domain of medicine. I am told I will soon see things differently, with more clarity. The voice holds conviction that I do not.

Soiled sheets become starched linen. Potions pumped via needle and plastic tube as good people do their best to strip me of the grey robes of anguish. On some level, I admire their ignorance.

Besides, how could they ever understand unless they endured the loss of a child, all too aware that those parents who survive do so behind a suit of armour, dragged down by its weight, dulled by its impregnable veneer.

We are the misplaced, suffering army in a war without end, destined to never know victory, never to find peace.

We are the knights of cold days.

Dave Jeffery is the author of 18 novels and novellas, two collections, and numerous short stories. His Necropolis Rising series and yeti adventure Frostbite *have both featured on the Amazon #1 bestseller list. His YA work features the Beatrice Beecham supernatural adventures. Jeffery is also the creator of the A Quiet Apocalypse series which has received worldwide critical acclaim. Actively involved in the Horror Writers Association (HWA), Jeffery is a mentor on the HWA Mentorship Scheme for which he was awarded Mentor of the Year in 2023, and he is also co-chair of the HWA Wellness Committee.*

Travel Bag

Bryan Miller

Everything went wrong—delayed flight, missed connection, a scrum at the luggage carousel, and on top of all that Scott forgot where he'd parked in the exhaust-fogged honeycomb of the parking garage, dragging his roller bag around three levels until he finally found the Honda. Then, on the drive home, his suitcase began to move.

Scott didn't notice at first. He was weary from five days on the road, his fifth travel week out of the last six. The succession of indistinguishable hotel rooms, a dozen variations of tiny soaps, guilty vending machine snacks in lieu of dinner, and the never-on-time airport shuttles had blurred his reality into one long sleepwalk. When the suitcase shifted in the backseat, he chalked it up to the motion of the car as he sped down the empty midnight interstate. Melissa and the twins would be asleep by now.

He was thinking about his boss, Steve Dixon—Steve Goddamn Dixon, who promised Scott his new position would only include "light travel"—when the suitcase jolted itself halfway out of the back bench seat.

Scott was certain for a final few weary seconds that he was hallucinating from exhaustion. Then it happened again, once, twice, three more times in rapid succession, like a TV magician struggling out of a straightjacket.

Then a sound came from the suitcase, muffled and panicked.

Scott eased his car to a stop on the shoulder of the road. He stared at the suitcase through the rear view mirror, which blinked orange-and-black in his hazard lights.

The suitcase rocked forward again, hard enough for it to tip partway onto the floorboards. At the same time it emitted a hoarse, squealing sound.

He sprang out of the car onto the concrete. After a few steadying breaths, he slowly opened the rear door. The suitcase wasn't bucking quite so hard now. It was trembling, with frantic, concerted energy.

The sudden bleat of his cell phone startled a shout out of him. The suitcase yelped back and wiggled all the way down onto the floorboard.

Scott checked his phone's display, expecting Melissa. He didn't recognize the number. Without taking his eyes off the suitcase, he answered.

"You have my luggage," a voice said on the other line. Calm, deep, a man's voice.

"Who is this?"

"And I have yours. You took mine from the luggage carousel by mistake."

Scott looked closer at the bag. It was almost identical to his, but for the little silver logo he hadn't noticed on the side. His luggage tag was blue; this one was red.

"I need my luggage returned immediately. But first you should know, most importantly: Do not open the suitcase."

At the sound of the conversation the suitcase began thrashing on the floorboards with nowhere to go, like a chicken that'd outgrown its impenetrable eggshell. The suitcase wasn't that big, though. You couldn't fit a whole person in there.

Could you? Scott wondered. Maybe if you *did something* to them.

"I'm calling the police," he said, and thumbed the call to an end. His hands trembled as he dialled 9-1-1.

Just before he could hit send, his screen flashed with another incoming call. The previous number.

"You don't want to call the police. And you certainly don't want to open that suitcase. It's my employer's luggage. He requires delivery immediately."

"I don't know who the hell you are, but—"

"I'll pick up the bag at your house. I'm pulling up there now."

"What?!"

"Scott Koski, 511 Gerard Street, Burnsville, Minnesota. It's with your phone number on your luggage tag."

Travel fatigue vanished. Scott's muscles burned with acidic energy. His heart raced. He pictured Melissa, asleep in their bed. Alone. Down the hall, the twins in their matching cribs.

"I swear to Christ if you so much as—"

"Hurry home, Scott. And remember. Do not. Open. The suitcase."

He slammed the back door, dropped into the driver's seat, pulled onto the road without looking. His foot flattened against the accelerator.

Behind him, the suitcase screeched and pounded itself against the back of the driver's seat. Scott took one hand off the wheel just long enough to crank up the radio; classic rock guitar blared so loud you could barely tell that whatever the hell was happening in the backseat was indeed happening.

Ten minutes later he pulled onto his silent street. There, parked in front of his mailbox, a man in a black suit and tie leaned against a shiny black Lincoln Navigator. As Scott sped toward him he could see the man was large, well over six feet, with broad shoulders and long arms like lumber chains. A suitcase nearly identical the one in the backseat huddled at the man's feet. Only this one wasn't shuddering and screaming.

Scott screeched into his own driveway.

"Mr. Koski," the big man said calmly, handing over Scott's heavy suitcase as though it were a bag of feathers. Scott dropped it onto the grass to stand between the man and his house's front door.

The man in the suit leaned into the backseat of the Honda. He rapped his thick fist twice against the thrashing suitcase. It fell silent, still. He lifted it, too, as though it weighed nothing, and carried it to the Navigator's trunk. The hatchback raised to reveal five more identical suitcases, all bumping and shaking and moaning. The man casually tossed the fifth suitcase among them.

"Good evening, Mr. Koski," he said. Then he eased into the driver's seat and drove slowly away.

Scott left his own travel bag on the lawn. He tottered unsteadily toward his front door, fingers struggling with his keys. Before he went upstairs to kiss the twins, to curl up next to Melissa, he made one more phone call. He only needed to leave a brief message.

"Steven? Scott. I quit."

It was so good, finally, to be home.

Bryan Miller is a writer and standup comedian living in Minneapolis. His horror and crime fiction has appeared on the Drabblecast, in Intrinsick Magazine and Crimson Streets, and the anthologies Hellfire Crossroads 7 *and* The Monsters We Forgot.

In the Desert, In the Night

Pedro Iniguez

The sun departed New Mexico and faded west, leaving the broad, sparse plains in darkness. Ashkii knelt beside the trunk of a yucca and parted a small swath of dry shrubbery with his hands. He placed two jugs of water underneath the yucca's shade and removed their caps. Across the way, the corrugated border fence separating Mexico and the U.S. swayed to a gentle breeze.

The desert wind ran through his long hair while he whispered a prayer. As he stood the jugs exploded, completely soaking his clothes. The delayed sound of two loud cracks echoed in the near distance.

As he turned toward his car, two men appeared, rifles drawn and aimed at his head.

They wore tactical vests; their bared arms exposing full tattooed sleeves with the markings of eagles, shamrocks, and the American flag. The Army fatigues and black boots rounded out the rest of their attire. Minutemen.

"Our first catch of the night," said one of them. He was tall, sporting a buzz cut, sunglasses, and a sharp smile. He regarded Ashkii. "Long way from the reservation tonight. Mikey, go on and cuff him and we'll radio the Border Patrol."

He nodded. "You got it, Connor. You," Mikey said to Ashkii, "raise your hands and get on your knees!"

117

"What did I do?" Ashkii asked raising his arms.

Connor shook his head. "Come on, man. You know it's against the law to leave water behind for the illegals."

Mikey lowered his rifle and stepped forward.

"You don't understand," Ashkii said. "It's not what you think."

"'Course it ain't," Mikey said while kicking in the back of Ashkii's knees, sending him to the floor.

"I have to leave them water. It's the humane thing to do. They get thirsty and disoriented at night."

"Between you and me, chief," Connor said, "it's best to let them bake out here. Those animals don't deserve water. Either way, they knew what they signed up for when they decided to cross into our sovereign, God-given country. You feel me on that?" Connor winked at Ashkii and grinned.

"It's not like that. They're not animals, they're just misunderstood. They get really thirsty. I'm protecting us all: my family, your family. If I don't leave this offering, they'll begin the hunt and we'll all be in danger."

"Looks like he's gone mad from the heat," Mikey said, retrieving a pair of handcuffs.

There came a loud snap in the dry brush to the south.

"What was that?" Connor said.

Mikey spun around, lifting his rifle.

Something fluttered in the grass.

"Yee naaldlooshii," Ashkii said.

"Must be talking to one of his red-skinned buddies out there," Mikey said. "Hey, come on out of there, chief. We got your friend."

Two large, bipedal shapes emerged from the dark, snarling like rabid dogs.

"What the fuck?" Connor said, mouth agape.

Under the moon's light they appeared like coyotes standing on hind legs. They were vaguely humanoid with their muscular arms and long gnarled nails.

Their bodies shimmered from the mucous and blood that coated their torsos as their fur rippled softly to the night's breeze.

Before the men could pull their triggers the beasts sprang forward, latching their jaws onto their arms. Mikey and Connor collapsed to the ground, dropping their rifles.

Connor screamed as one creature tore into his leg, completely severing it.

The other beast locked its teeth around Mikey's throat and snapped. A cascade of blood coursed down Mikey's neck and into his vest.

The nightmare at Connor's leg abandoned him for the easier meal and both animals then suckled from the fountain at Mikey's neck.

After they had their fill, the creatures turned and leapt back into the darkness of the desert.

Connor dragged his maimed body across the dirt, howling in pain. "Help me," he said.

"They spared you," Ashkii said dusting himself off. "Nature will decide your fate, friend. There's no one for miles. You'll either die from blood loss or from baking in the sun." He eyed the broken jugs and the mud at his feet. "Maybe you'll even die of thirst," he said laughing.

The man dug his nails into the earth as he crawled toward the road, leaving a trail of blood behind him.

"Oh, and they're not animals, they are merely cursed men. Skin-walkers, to be exact," Ashkii said stepping toward his car. "No man is an animal who understands both mercy and justice."

Pedro Iniguez is a horror and science-fiction writer from Los Angeles, California. He is a Rhysling Award finalist and has also been nominated for the Pushcart Prize and Best of the Net Award for his speculative poetry.

His fiction and poetry has appeared in Nightmare Magazine, Never Wake: An Anthology of Dream Horror, Shadows Over Main Street Volume 3, A Night of Screams: Latino Horror Stories, Speculative Fiction for Dreamers, Worlds of Possibility, Infinite Constellations, *and* Star*Line, *among others. He can be found online at www.pedroiniguezauthor.com.*

The Dead Lands

Anthony D Redden

Jacob placed his one hand upon Luca's shoulder; in the other he held a staff upon which hung a gas lantern, their only light for negotiating the dark. Father and son stood at the entrance to the deadlands. Jacob squeezed his son's shoulder reassuringly. This was the first time he had taken his son on patrol.

"It's a poor night," Luca stated.

"It'll be fine. I've seen worse," Jacob replied trying to ease his son's nerves.

Large ornate iron gates barred their path, and equally impressive railings ran in either direction for farther than the eye could see, disappearing into the low-lying mist.

"Are you ready?" Jacob asked.

Luca nodded.

"And you've got everything we need?"

The boy lifted the knapsack to reassure his father, who responded with a smile and a ruffle of his hair.

Jacob unlatched the lock and pushed open the gate. It squealed angrily on its old hinges. Once they were through, he released the gate. It swung back and clattered shut causing the railings to shudder.

"The grounds have been troublesome these past few months and we've needed experienced hands to control the beasts. You'll be fine though as long as you keep that knapsack on you. It's got food for distracting them. It's the warden's job to make sure the beasts stay below ground, but we're running low on corpses, so they'll be extra aggressive. Just stay close and keep an ear out?"

Luca nodded, but his father waited for a more definitive response.

"Yes sir!"

"Good lad. Come on."

Jacob and his son walked the plots around the edge of the cemetery. They headed north and followed the boundary railings as far as the old oak tree gallows. Dense mist continued to roll in from the mountains, carpeting the ground. The lanterns of other night wardens floated like spectral orbs in the distance, their lights the only indicator that Jacob and his son were not alone.

The silence of the night was broken by the distant ring of a bell. Jacob raised a finger to quiet his son whilst he listened for its direction. He gestured for Luca to follow as he began to jog toward the noise. When Luca eventually caught up to his father he was kneeling beside a grave. As the boy approached, Jacob raised a hand for him to keep his distance. A small bell dangled from a perch upon the grave's headstone. A thin thread ran from the bell to a small tube that disappeared underground. Jacob took the line and gently pulled it up; it came away with ease. He held the frayed end up to the lantern light for a closer inspection.

"It was a dead ringer. The bait's been taken."

Before either could voice concern, another bell began to ring. Jacob tossed away the thread and lifted the lantern toward the new sound. He nodded to his son and then set off again. Luca struggled to keep pace, the uneven ground and thick mist causing him to stumble and misstep on more than a few occasions. His jacket snagged upon the bramble vines that grew between the headstones. When the knapsack caught upon a branch it sent him flying hard to the ground, knocking the wind from him. His father's light grew distant and faint as he continued ahead with his pursuit of the ringing bell.

Luca scrambled to his feet and pushed on despite the pain. When at last he reached his father they both stood before an opening in the ground. Jacob lowered his lantern into the darkness and two large eyes reflected the light. He stepped back from the hole as the creature began to climb, its long bony fingers clawing at the dirt and rock, pulling itself free and raising its head to the sky. It stood an intimidating sight, each monstrous claw and tooth perfect for shredding a corpse of its flesh. The ghoul rose to its full height, an infrequent luxury for one usually restricted to the cemetery catacombs. Jacob fumbled with his staff, drawing back the lantern and releasing the coloured glass that instantly changed the lantern light to red—a silent call to the other wardens for assistance.

"The bag," he called to his son. "Where's the bag?"

Luca went to retrieve it but suddenly realised it was gone—caught upon the branch of a tree now lost within the fog.

"Oh. It's...I'm sorry."

Jacob quickly looked for the other wardens, but their lights were too far away to be of help.

The creature lunged forward, knocking Jacob through the air to land heavily upon a headstone. The creature then looked at Luca and the boy froze.

"Father!" he screamed.

Jacob lay dazed and too afraid to respond. He closed his eyes and turned his head from the horror that loomed menacingly above his young son.

• • • • • • • • • •

When the first of the wardens arrived, Jacob was alone. The ground was awash with fresh warm blood.

"Jacob, are you okay?" a warden asked.

"Of course I'm not okay."

"Come here, man."

The warden pulled Jacob to his feet before swinging his arms around him and embracing him in a hug. The other wardens finally arrived, each pale and forlorn.

"I can't believe Luca is gone."

"That's how it goes, my friend. You did what was needed. We all have. All first-borns must be sacrificed to the ghouls on a blood moon, you know that. What we did tonight was for the good of the whole village. The sacrifice of a few for the safety of hundreds."

Anthony D Redden is a writer of science fiction and horror short stories. He lives amongst the lush green rolling hills of middle England with his wife and three children. He is a full-time carer, and a writer the rest of the time. He has a Master of Arts in Creative Writing and has a particular interest in disability representation in fiction, alt-history fiction, red wine and sherbet dip dabs.

Welcome to GothMart

David Bernard

One of the few perks to being the GothMart manager is hiding in my office when the Muzak version of a Morbid Angel track starts playing. There's worse elevator music, but I can't stand early Death Metal.

I was taking inventory of the pre-torn fishnet stockings when I heard the first notes of the synthesized harp riff to "Blessed Are the Sick." I ducked into my office until it was over.

Miss Tiffany was waiting in my office. She had been voted "Scariest Employee of the Month" six times in a row, mostly because she wanted to be promoted to management, but there were no openings. Her frustration reflected in her attitude toward her co-workers. At the suggestion of the coroner, I did transfer her from the whips and chains aisle to satanic ceremony supplies. That seemed to slow down the body count a little.

123

I decided that dealing with Miss Tiffany was less painful than listening to the saxophone solo that was coming up on the "Blessed Are the Sick" track. She smiled. Between the purple eye shadow and black lipstick, it was not a reassuring smile. She walked up to me, pulled a very large knife out of the ample cleavage of her vinyl corset, and wordlessly slashed me across the belly.

I collapsed as my intestines spilled out. Miss Tiffany had finally figured out the only way to get promoted at GothMart.

David Bernard *is a native New Englander who hightailed it to South Florida as soon as he was informed that grown-ups can live anywhere they want, and that in spite of opinions to the contrary, he was considered to be an adult. His previous works include short stories in anthologies such as* Twice Upon an Apocalypse, Legacy of the Reanimator, *and* The Chromatic Court.

Wasteland

Sheldon Woodbury

In the far flung future, the ancient warrior rumbled up in his ghostly ship, a rickety old vessel that heaved and wheezed. The memory stayed with him like it always did, shivering down from the blackness of space, raining death and destruction on the planet below. In the musty darkness of his mind, colossal destruction flickered non-stop.

He'd long ago abandoned the urges of the flesh, so all that was left was his shriveled body attached to a maze of life support systems. He was little more than a withered husk cradled in a thicket of wires. The rattling old ship had become a crusty tomb of living death. As he lay in his prison, he strained to reach back to another time. In the distant past, he'd been chosen to be a new age warrior that would create a hopeful new future.

There had always been wars since the beginning of time, but now they'd become infinitely more vast; a new kind of fighter was needed, along with a ghostly death ship to carry out the mission. So his cosmic crusade began. He was part of a military horde that roamed the blackness of space, destroying all the warring worlds spinning in their path. But as time tumbled by the horde died too, until he was the only one left.

And then he saw something different in the darkness ahead. There had always been a glimmering orb off in the distance, but now he saw none; only an endless wasteland of ash and smoke. He rumbled faster ahead, but the sight remained the same. There were no celestial glimmers anymore, just the splattered remains of pulverized planets. It was a cosmic graveyard with nothing left except his ghostly death ship.

Then he heard a beep. It was barely audible, but enough to alert his ship that some vestige of life lay ahead. The beep pulsed louder, then a roaring attack charged out of the darkness. The ship was monstrous, a hulking behemoth slashed with deep scars from its rampaging past. All he could do was watch from his prison of wires and tubes; his ghost ship had taken control long ago. Another banshee blast came, leaving his helpless husk closer to death. But his ghost ship attacked with an equal fury, unleashing its own bruising assault.

They fought like merciless warriors, each blast more savage than the one before. Then a memory appeared from long ago. In his glittering youth he'd wanted to be a new kind of warrior, and that yearning was ignited again. The battle raged on between his wheezing ghost ship and the monstrous behemoth, both attacking through the graveyard of space.

And then it was over.

His ghost ship delivered a blow that sent the monster ship plummeting down through the roiling darkness. But the blistering battle had taken its toll. He was close to death, gasping in the grimy tangle of wires. He struggled to keep his ancient eyes open, but an icy blackness tightened around his shriveled old heart.

But it was not to be, not just yet.

His ghost ship followed the other vessel down to the scorched chunk of a dead planet. He heard a faint beep and saw the monster ship still had some life left. It looked like a scarred creature from some hellish netherworld, but one that had lost most of its fury.

He willed himself back to life, clenching the wires and tubes with all the strength he had left. He'd spent his life as a warrior, so the fight wasn't over until the enemy was dead. His ghost ship was a warrior too, so delivering death was all it ever knew.

The landscape was barren and burnt, a craggy slab drifting in space. The monster ship groaned a short distance away, and a portal cranked open. A hideous creature emerged, every bit as gruesome as its monstrous ship. There were black scales and claws, slits instead of eyes, and it looked ancient, too. As it scrambled across the rocky surface, the tubes and wires hoisted the old warrior up like a puppet, and carried him out of the ship to face the inhuman creature.

It was a strange sight, but one that had played out since the beginning of time: two raging warriors facing each other with death in their eyes. The fight was primal and pure, like all fights should be. The slithery creature was weak, but fought valiantly. It darted and leaped, clawed and stung, searching for any advantage. He fought courageously too in the shivering web that made him much stronger. Their beaten up bodies were covered with ash and dirt, so the fight was just a murky shadow in the darkness of space.

And then he just couldn't do it anymore.

He'd been smashed to the ground in a shivering heap with the wires and tubes strangled around him. He stared up at the dead universe silent overhead and his mind was filled with the fiery horrors of what he had done. He'd wanted to be a new kind of warrior, but he'd created a future without any hope at all.

Then everything, all of it, disappeared.

When he opened his eyes they weren't ancient anymore, but young and bright. He was still hooked up to a tangle of wires, but they had a very different purpose. He remembered he was being evaluated for Officer Candidate School, and this was one of the psychological tests. They wanted to see if he had the military fierceness to be a new kind of warrior.

"I'm sorry, son, but you just missed at the very end. I'm afraid you don't have the right stuff."

He stared back at the officer, then closed his eyes again. In the howling blackness inside his head he felt horror and pain, because he knew how all this was going to end.

Sheldon Woodbury is an award winning writer (screenplays, plays, books, short stories, and poems). His short stories and poems have appeared in many horror anthologies and magazines. His poem, "The Midnight Circus," was selected by Ellen Datlow as an honorable mention for Best Horror 2017.

In My Mind, the Deep Calls

Maxwell Marais

The view out of the diving suit's round glass window was dark, cramped. The crash and thrash of waves in wind far above filtered down, a muted bass imitation of the surface. This deep the water was not so agitated, not so tempestuous. As I hung steeping like a moldering teabag in some long-forgotten china cup, I wondered why no one had pulled me up yet. Little night fishes darted in my limited peripheral vision, pinprick glints of silver through the black.

We'd searched this whole stretch of ocean three times over, the rest of the expedition and I. In our desperate excitement we had been certain that *this* time, this time would be the one. The night and the storm had not discouraged us. Shifting in the oiled-canvas bulk of the diving suit, I could just make out the dark, storm-tossed shadow of the bottom of the ship. I imagined my maps, charts, script translations and stone tablet rubbings slipping and sliding in the tumult, crumpling into the corners. Without them, down in the water's undulating embrace, I couldn't shake the feeling I might have been mistaken and, in this black expanse, I was impossibly small.

Something was below me.

I'd known for a while now. A tingling up my spine, the unmistakable sensation of being watched. Flicking on my electric lamp I watched its beam waver unsteadily, that one small source of light seeming horribly insufficient in the great encroaching darkness. But there! Down below, almost hidden beneath a crust of coral and sea plants, the light had hit smooth, carved stone.

Ruins.

I gave a tug on the line tethering me to the ship to give me slack. *Let me down; let me see. This is what we've been looking for all this time, isn't it?* There was no response. I thought again of the downpour above, the rain-slicked decks, the crashing waves. Where were the crew? I floated, inert, shifting the beam of the lamp over the stone's surface, squinting through the greenish gloom. The ruins seemed to imitate the plants that grew from them, spires and columns reaching ever upwards towards the impossibly far starlight. The architecture branched, growing paper-thin and needle-sharp. It had been carved in such a way that it seemed to melt *upwards*, walls like curdled wax, windows like gaping sores.

Each time I looked away, I could swear a part of it had shifted. Not noticeably, just enough to make one question, enough to make me wish I could rub my eyes through the diving suit's window to make sure.

The feeling of being watched did not subside. The tether between myself and the ship was a thin, insubstantial crack in the ocean between me and safety. Without the crew above to guide the rope, I was little more than dangling bait on a fishing line. The ruins yawned below, needle tips reaching upwards like so many drowned hands. The plants lolled sickly in the dim and wavering light. The rotted seaweed along the walls and peaks swayed sluggishly, shadows casting strange and shifting patterns on the stone. The world down here was frozen in time, and I with it. I could taste the oily tang of the air from the pump above, as I breathed in and out, focusing on the prize below...what we'd been looking for all this time.

But were we supposed to find it?

A fleeting shadow shifted at the very edge of my vision...

Something's moving.

Something was down there, among those candle wax columns, and it was no longer just watching. It moved through spaces I could not see, moved through the overgrown ruins as though they were little more than the rest of the water, twisted around corners that did not, *could* not exist.

It was getting closer. I blinked, trying to clear the blurry vision through my diving suit's window. The oiled canvas pressed against my body like dead, clammy skin. I couldn't quite make the thing out, not directly, only the places where it had been. The places it had grasped some piece of architecture and unwoven it like a threadbare sleeve, climbed up the dangling strings like a spider and then sewn it shut behind. The water rippled with a force that no current could create.

Something gripped the edge of my suit, and I thought, *This is what it must feel like to have one's blood curdle.* I must have screamed because down there in the awful darkness I heard something *reply.* I dropped my lamp. The beam oscillated wildly as it fell, giving split-second glimpses of stone and seaweed, seaweed and stone, over and over and...

My God what was that?

The tether yanked hard, suddenly taut. They were pulling me up, the crew far above, but I knew only the wild flailing of my own arms, the thrashing and kicking of my weighted boots, the hot stifling breath coming too fast, until I felt my head break the surface of the water. The cacophony of rain on my dive helmet broke the violent shock of what I had seen before the lamp went dark and I was cast into blackness.

Down below, though I would never tell a soul, had been an eye, down among those ruins, impossibly huge, sealed shut with limpets, barnacles, and salt. In my ignorance I had thought it part of the stone (*or was the stone all part of it?*). But as the last of my light fell upon it, as that *thing* had taken hold of my suit, I had known, truly...

I had been *seen*.

It had opened. That ancient, rheumy lens peeled wide and *fixed its gaze on me.*

· • • ● • ● • • ·

It's been over a week now. Our ship is headed home, the rest of the expedition believing their search utterly unsuccessful. I have told them nothing. How could I? I cannot look them in the eye when I lie. I cannot look anyone in the eye—but thankfully, none of them pry. They want to trust me, and that is perhaps what makes it the most difficult to stay silent. That thing has *seen* me, and that is something that cannot be undone. But a captain knows no duty as strong as that to his crew. *They must not know. They must not be seen.*

The thing below is still with me. I have come to realize over the past few days that it did not stop at my suit. It unraveled a part of *me* as well, as it did the water and ruins. There is some sort of infection on the inside of my ankle, just below the bone. It grows larger by the day, the skin becoming gray, oily, soft like pulp.

Even now, *scales* push their way through my ruined flesh.

I dream of the eye in the ruins. In some I am in my diving suit, hanging as it watches me wordlessly like a specimen in some enormous briny petri dish. Hanging as I feel the unnamable thing unravel the canvas and crawl up beneath my skin, grey-green tendrils slipping into veins and between muscle fibers.

But in others I am with it, among the lolling sickly sea-plants, the fish, and spires. When I wake, I find revolted the feeling that lingers is one of *home*.

I am changing. The air on the ship is dry and stings my parched skin. My toes are growing webbing. The scales itch beneath my clothes. I can't hide these signs from the crew much longer. Some of them already glance suspiciously over the rims of the cups of rum I ply them with. They question why I am absent at some of my duties, why I do not speak more like I used to, or what exactly I am doing up at the bow of the ship leaning into the cold salty spray until my clothes are soaked through.

But none are brave—or foolish—enough to question what happened the night they pulled me up from the water blank and staring, mouth opened wide to scream, but silent. Glassy-eyed. *Fish-eyed.*

I will not be with them much longer.

My plans are made. This morning I found fine little slits beginning to open along the length of my neck, raw and purulent. I am ready.

A part of me is repulsed as I walk out onto the deck. A part of me still kicks and screams and rejects what I am becoming. The stars wink dully behind a thin layer of cloud. My hands grip the railing. That part of me is ignorant. It is foolish to be fearful of change. We cannot change what we become. *What we have always been?* I swallow my disgust.

I left a note in my cabin. They will find it eventually. It is the final lie I must tell my crew. I am not dying, but for their sake they must believe I am. For their sake, they must never know.

They must never know about the ruins.

They must never know about the eye that calls in unspeakable and voiceless tongues.

The rail and the ship are behind me now. The water is blissfully cool as I sink and wriggle free of my clothes, as my new gills flower open in the darkness and I *breathe.*

In my mind, the deep calls.

And now, at last, I answer.

Maxwell Marais is an author and illustrator of all things horror living in Montreal, Canada. When they aren't frantically scrawling down the weird fiction and horror that crawls out of their brain, they can be found attempting to summon (with limited success) horrible abominations from beyond our world. Their works have been featured in such publications as The NoSleep Podcast, Thuggish Itch, and Dark Recesses Press.

Night Swimming

Michael O'Brien

There was movement in the dark corner of the bedroom.

'Rosie, is that you?'

Light footsteps on the floorboards.

'Of course, silly. Who else?'

She stepped out of the dark and into a shaft of moonlight. She was nude, her nipples hard and pink, skin pale as cream. He sat up in bed, rubbed sleep from his eyes.

'What are you doing here?'

She sat on the edge of the mattress. It did not sink an inch.

'This is still my bed.'

The air was thick with her perfume. He inhaled deeply, relished it.

'I didn't think I'd see you till tomorrow.'

She made a face like something rotten was under her nose. 'I couldn't wait that long. I wanted to be alone with you. Tomorrow is going to be so damn grim. All of those people looking at me...'

'Funerals aren't supposed to be fun, Rosie.'

She frowned, traced a finger along his calf. Her touch was cold.

'You're a grump tonight. I thought you'd be happy to see me.'

'Of course I am. You surprised me, that's all.'

Her hand moved up his calf, stroked his thigh. The moonlight graced her face and he saw tears in her eyes.

'I miss you,' she said.

'I miss you, too.'

'Death is lonely, babe.'

He took her hand in his own, tried to warm the flesh. 'I know, babe, I know.'

Rosie crawled forward and lay down on him, pressed her breasts against his chest. They had not been this close in weeks. He waited for the rise and fall of her breath, but it never came. She was still and cool.

'Will you visit me?'

'Every day.'

He felt her smile against his skin.

'That's nice, but you don't have to visit every day. Those places can be depressing.'

'That's why I need to visit and keep you company.'

He traced circles on her lower back. She arched her spine against his touch and their pubic hair meshed. A cat cried outside the window.

'Will you bring me flowers?'

'Nope. You hate flowers.'

She smiled. 'Just testing you.'

He kissed her forehead. A strand of her hair was in his mouth.

'I hope I don't get bored,' she said. 'I hope there are books and crosswords.' She thought for a moment, and then added, 'At least I won't have to do my makeup.'

'That's not funny.'

'It's a little funny. Do you know how much of my life I've spent fussing in front of the mirror?'

'You always look beautiful, even when you first wake up. But your morning breath is scary.'

She laughed and nudged him. 'Now that is not funny!'

He looked beyond her, at his black suit hanging on the wardrobe door, freshly pressed and ready to be worn like armour in the morning.

'Will you make a speech?' Her voice was muffled against his chest.

'Of course I will.'

'That's nice of you, but you don't have to. I know you hate public speaking.'

'I don't mind it these days. I stuttered as a kid. I always dreaded getting up in front of the class. Nearly passed out once.'

She propped up on her elbows, touched his cheek. 'You never told me that.'

He shrugged. Even in death, they were still learning new things about each other.

For the first time since appearing out of the dark, she looked away from him, out the window, to the ocean. They listened to the distant roar of the waves. He held her tighter.

After a while, she said, 'And the kids?'

'We don't have kids, babe. We talked about it, but we never had them. Remember?'

'Oh, that's right.' She wiped her eyes. 'My brain feels foggy.'

She ran her thumb along his bottom lip, down his unshaven chin. 'Don't drink so much while I'm gone. And watch your sweets, you're getting older.' He thought about the empty bottles on the kitchen bench, and the half-eaten slice of cake by his bed.

'Can I come with you?' he said. 'I promise I'll stop drinking if you let me come with you.'

'I don't think that's how it works.'

'Will you visit me?'

She kissed his neck and buried her nose in the warm hollow of his shoulder.

After a long time, they fell asleep.

When he woke, she was gone. He climbed out of bed and went to the window. It was still dark outside. The moon hung low and bright over the ocean, a perfect silver coin. On the shore, ghostly pale in the moonlight, was a naked woman. She waded into the water and disappeared up to her knees, her hips, her shoulders, until she was only a wet fall of dark hair bobbing in the waves. She could have been a floating piece of driftwood. Then she went under.

He sat on the window sill and watched the restless water hurl itself against the shore. He would sit and wait for her to resurface. He was fine with waiting.

Michael O'Brien is an Australian writer from Port Macquarie, NSW. He works an office job and writes at night. He's published short stories here and there, and is working on longer material. You can connect with him at @michaelistyping.

The Southland

Pedro Iniguez

"Last time, Martin. Where is he?"

"Depends."

"On what?"

"Which part of him you're looking for."

"You mean to tell me he's—"

"I mean he's left the party."

"You mean he's dead."

"Beyond dead."

Detective Degafney glared at Martin.

Martin met his gaze, eyes burning like embers with defiance. He'd swatted away Degafney's questions for hours.

"We're finally getting somewhere."

Martin looked at his watch. "Don't you have somewhere to be?"

"We're not finished."

"He was a thin man, you know? Now he's a *chunky* man."

Degafney's head throbbed. The crime wave in Los Angeles had risen like the summer heat spawning crazies like Martin. More crime, less sleep, itchy trigger fingers. They called L.A. the Southland. Degafney knew why: it was Hell on Earth.

"You think it's a game. Just tell me why you did it."

"You wouldn't believe me," Martin said gazing at the walls as if merely a temporary inconvenience.

Degafney thumbed his safety strap forward.

"It's survival of the fittest. I like weeding out weak people. He didn't have teeth," Martin grinned. "But that saw I used did."

Degafney bit his lip. Something chipped at his sub-conscience. With every second, his mind neared collapse. He buried his face in his hands, hoping it would shelter him from the nightmare.

The heat skyrocketed as the sun crept past the window, casting gnarled shadows. They began sweating.

Degafney loosened his tie.

His mind wandered as he looked past the odd shape of what moments ago was another man.

The room fell silent, save for the ticking of their watches. It grew louder as the minutes stretched on.

Degafney looked at his watch. He'd lost track of time. He grabbed a towel and wiped his sweaty face.

"Going somewhere, detective?" Martin asked.

"I'm running late. Heading to the station. We've got things to discuss when I get back; you've got a lot of talking to do."

"I'll be waiting."

Detective Martin Degafney combed his hair, straightened his tie, and turned from the bathroom mirror. He took a breath and stepped out into the urban Hell they called the Southland.

Pedro Iniguez is a horror and science-fiction writer from Los Angeles, California. He is a Rhysling Award finalist and has also been nominated for the Pushcart Prize and Best of the Net Award for his speculative poetry.

His fiction and poetry has appeared in Nightmare Magazine, Never Wake: An Anthology of Dream Horror, Shadows Over Main Street Volume 3, A Night of Screams: Latino Horror Stories, Speculative Fiction for Dreamers, Worlds of Possibility, Infinite Constellations, *and* Star*Line, *among others.*

He can be found online at www.pedroiniguezauthor.com.

Read Me If You Forget

Gregg Stewart

If you're reading this, it means you've forgotten who you are, where you are, and how you got here. Don't worry. It's all explained in this journal.

First, whatever you do, DO NOT GO ASHORE. Stay on the lake.

I'm not sure how much or how little you've forgotten, but I'll try to catch you up. Hopefully, you remember how to read. Oh God, if you've forgotten, this entire backup plan was a waste of time.

Assuming you can read, I'm sure you've also figured out that you're on a boat. This is not your boat, but it's where you need to stay for the foreseeable future. The land is not safe (see earlier note re: don't go ashore).

If you've forgotten your name, it's Sam Navzdy. You are 38 years old. You used to work in an underground lab, which saved you in the beginning. You were born and raised in Cleveland, and you are on Lake Erie. You've been on this boat for five months, perhaps longer. I've written down some of your favorite memories later in this journal to peruse at your leisure. The memories are nice but, in many ways, non-essential.

You are alone on this vessel, which is how it needs to be. If you're close to shore, you might see people waving to you, asking for help, trying to swim to you, or attempting to come aboard. Do NOT let them on this boat. Do not speak with them or engage in any way. They want to kill you. They WILL kill if you let them get close.

There should be a Frankenstein mask in the main cabin. Shit, you're not going to know what that name means. It's this green-faced thing that you wear over your head. Find it. Put it on anytime you're above deck and the people on shore will leave you alone. You used to think Halloween was dumb. Now it's Halloween forever, and there isn't even candy.

Oh, right. Food. If you're hungry, you'll find a garden box at the prow. You've tried growing lettuce, cucumbers, and spinach, but the only things that seem to thrive are basil and dandelion greens, which are about as hard to kill as you. The small tree in the large white ceramic pot is a dwarf Meyer lemon. You'll only get one or two ripe ones per week, and less as it gets colder, so use sparingly. There should also be a fishing pole and net aboard. Don't catch too many at a time. They'll only spoil. There is a bucket on a rope for collecting fresh water from the lake. You can drink it and water the garden with it.

For months now, you've been surviving on this strict diet of bitter greens and fresh fish with lemon and basil, and in all honesty, as boring as it sounds, it's also the healthiest and slimmest you've been in years. If you've forgotten how to catch fish, tend to the garden, or cook, see notes and recipes in the back of this journal.

Also, be aware of the sails—those huge sheets above you. Keep them battened down unless it is imperative to move. I've drawn diagrams to show you the correct knots. It would be dangerous if you drifted too close to shore during one of the blackouts.

Ah, yes, the blackouts. You're no doubt wondering how you lost your memory. It's been happening to everyone. Some speculate it's the work of an alien race, while others say it's one of our AI satellites gone haywire.

If you hear a sound, like a high-pitched wail that cuts through the air like a whistling wind, you've got less than ten seconds to get somewhere dark and shut your eyes. You'll blackout if you see or even sense the blinding flash in the sky that follows, even with your eyes closed. You'll have lost most of your memories when you awaken (we think about an hour later). The flash occurs at random intervals: sometimes twice a day, sometimes a week or more will pass.

The bad news is when this began it caused a lot of accidents. People blacked out while driving on highways, standing in crosswalks, or operating dangerous machinery—it was a fucking mess. Even bathing, cooking, and ironing became lethal activities. There were tens of thousands of deaths on that first day, and millions, maybe even billions, at this point.

The worse news is that all those people who died during the blackouts woke up with everyone else an hour later.

Yes, like zombies, but worse. They do not amble around. They move as they did in life—running, jumping, talking, reasoning—and their sole intent is to kill everyone who is still alive.

Those people calling to you from the shoreline—look closer. They're all dead.

Staying offshore preserves your sanity. You've seen the undead up close, and it is hideous. Don't do that to yourself again. When you emerged from the lab to check on loved ones, the dead were everywhere—blackened, oozing husks dashing from their blazing homes and cars. You've outrun their grasps while vomit streamed down your chin and chest. You've tripped over twisted, ravaged bodies, their exposed, splintered bones snapping as they attempted to catch you. You've slipped in blood and entrails far too many times to count. I feel certain even a blackout could not suppress the horror of those drowned children from the community pool—those dewy, bloated carcasses reaching out to grip and hold you with their small gray fingers. Their pale eyes, a sea of milky white, boring into your still beating heart, hoping to consume it.

I hate to put these images back into your mind, but you must remember. Otherwise, you will grow complacent.

Remember: the dead can do everything they did in life. Heaven forbid some zombie Olympic swimmer shows up on shore and makes their way toward this boat. So far, anyone trying to swim our way has sunk to the bottom. I assume they are still "alive" down there, and I hope they never regain the strength to resurface. It seems inevitable. This is why you must watch the water. If you see any people in there: GET AWAY.

I hesitate to mention this but, if you recall the name Preeta, try to forget her.

Last week (or the week before you decided to write this journal), you saw her on the shore calling to you. Idiot, you had forgotten to wear the Frankenstein mask. She was waving, begging for your help. It took everything in your being to resist going to her. If you see her on the shoreline calling to you, know that you resisted her before, and you can do it again.

Unless you're dead? Would you know? Grab your wrist, or your throat is better, and check for a pulse. If you've died, then, by all means, go to your wife. Take Preeta aboard and live forever on this boat. You won't need to tend to the garden or catch fish anymore, so relax and enjoy yourself. If you can't beat 'em, join 'em. Isn't that right?

Unless you're not Sam? I hadn't considered this, but if I fell overboard and drowned during a blackout, and you are someone else who's come aboard and forgotten who you are...

There is a hand mirror in the galley below deck. Go to it. If you have brown eyes, dark hair, and a five-inch-long scar along your left-side jawline, then you are me. If not, stay the fuck away from my wife.

I'm sorry. This situation has put a terrible strain on my mental health. If you're alive and I am gone, then you are welcome to stay on this boat. But be careful. Like I say, watch the water at all times.

If I'm dead, and I'm close by, I will find you and kill you. Again, I'm sorry.

When you are done with this journal, be sure to set it in an obvious place with the title visible.

Good luck, Sam, or Frankenstein, or whoever you are.

Gregg Stewart is an author, songwriter, musician, screenwriter, journalist, and film composer whose dark fiction tales have appeared in Sirens Call Magazine, CLP's Shallow Waters series, and in coming anthologies from Crystal Lake Publishing and Hellbound Books. Find him online at linktr. ee/greggstewart.

All's Fair

Michelle Mellon

He had been a double agent in this conflict, and now he was caught. His captors forced him into an uncomfortable chair to bark and screech at him. Standard procedure. He wasn't worried; he'd always managed to get out of these situations before.

But he was weary. All those years of training. All those lives. And the number of missions was increasing exponentially as people confronted the realities of life outside of apps and online experiences. It weighed on him like it never had before. He wanted out.

For the first time ever, he raised the white flag. No more slick words turning the tables on the combatants. No more subterfuge. He admitted how he'd appeared to broker peace talks as a neutral party but had spoken to each side secretly about doing what was in their best interests.

He expected more recriminations. Disbelief. Disappointment and anger at the betrayal. Justifiable but also manageable. It was his specialty, after all—wrangling difficult situations into harmonious outcomes. Except the parties involved in this war weren't interested in justice or an accord. They only wanted revenge.

And it looked like he was going to get caught in the crossfire.

· • • ● • ● • ● • • ·

At his debriefing, he played it cool. But government officials kept milling in and out of the interview room, whispering and studying images on tablets. Then they'd look at him and consult and begin another round of whispering.

Finally, he'd had enough. "Am I done here?"

He was stern, but polite. He maintained eye contact without being aggressive. Once again, his training was serving him well. But he couldn't help fiddling with the war trophies in his pockets. If he didn't leave soon, someone would notice.

"There are some inconsistencies at the scene," said the lead investigator.

He had to stop himself from smiling. There always were. But they usually didn't involve him because he deflected attention. And in this case, the response team had bungled things in his favor.

"I guess we can clear those up another time," the official sighed. "You're free to go."

He stood and nodded at the team. Not smug, but not deferential. Confident without the swagger of having gotten away with anything. But he had. This time and several times before.

What a way to go out, he thought as he stepped into the sunlight and strolled away with his hands in his pockets.

· • • ● • ● • • • ·

It had been a grisly scene. In his many years on the front lines he hadn't seen enemies go after each other like that. It escalated quickly from volleys of items within reach—a book, a vase, a lamp—to a standoff with knives.

They slashed at each other as they danced around the large open space. Soon the floor was splattered in drips and drops and smeared prints from slippery shoes. He could have tried to stop them. To call for backup. To run. Instead, he moved to a safe distance and watched as blood loss and fatigue brought them both sagging within final striking distance of each other.

It was obvious they couldn't land the final blows. At this point they looked like fleshy fringe instead of whole people. One had an arm nearly severed at the elbow. The other was trying to hold a cascading eyeball back in place with slickly crimson hands.

It was harder than people thought, to end a life. So as they lay bleeding and panting on the floor, he helped in the only way he saw fit to help. He dragged them closer together and, with little resistance, helped them finish each other off. He barely had time to pretend to be checking for their pulses before the front door came crashing in.

"Hands up where we can see them!" The voice was muffled through protective gear, but he complied.

"Thank goodness you're here!" he cried. "They...they killed each other, right in front of me."

A figure stepped forward. It was the lead detective, the one who later would scrutinize the evidence and let him go.

"What's your name and relationship to these two?"

"I'm, I mean, I was their marriage therapist."

He breathed deeply and observed everything around him. Again, training. But not the psychological insights from his counselling degree. It was the special ops training he received for a great war that never came.

While the team leader was called away briefly to confer with an evidence tech, a rookie offered him a towel to wipe the blood off his face and clothing. He smiled. There went any blood splatter evidence. Now there was little indication that anything had happened here other than what he told them.

A bad marriage gone toxic. Two borderline personalities setting each other off. The murder-suicide of two people desperate to end their mutual life sentence. He could see the evidence team was out of its element with so much chaos and blood. That would only work to his advantage as things could more easily be misinterpreted or go missing.

And when they checked his background, they would find nothing suspicious. His success rate was nearly perfect. For those couples who couldn't see the light, well, there had always been staged robberies or accidents. Boring, but they eradicated the blips and kept up his stats.

That's why he was glad that this, his last call of duty, was also the most spectacular of any of the battles. He had been audience and executioner, and his need for strife had finally been quelled.

He reached into his pockets. The soldiers in these wars wore a different kind of dog tag, as the severed fingers he now possessed would attest. He moved down the joints until he felt the smooth gold of the wedding band on one and the ridged embedded diamonds on the other.

Like talismans, he thought. Signs of a new start. He would no longer be a prisoner of these wars. He was finally free.

Michelle Mellon has been published in over three dozen speculative fiction anthologies and magazines and is a member of the Horror Writers Association and Science Fiction & Fantasy Writers Association. Her first story collection was published by HellBound Books in 2018. Her second story collection was self-published in April 2022. For updates on her work visit www.mpmellon.com.

The Red Scarf

Rhea Rose

I looked up from the street toward the haunted house on the hill. The house, famous in our suburban neighborhood, looked like a cliché haunted home. The old Edwardian architectural nightmare of disrepair had a black and broken picket fence. The only path to get to the front entrance was to climb a weed-infested, forested hill.

As children walking home from school, we dared each other to walk by, stand on the walk below and stare at it until someone or something came to the window.

We all accepted the dare at some point but, other than running past the house at full speed, none of us ever plucked up enough courage to stand and stare.

One day, while school was still in session, the principal came on with an announcement about an approaching hurricane, and we were all dismissed early and were to head straight home.

The announcement of a hurricane, possibly a tornado, seemed very exciting and, even as a youngster, I understood that it was a dangerous situation.

My friends and I huddled together outside in the schoolyard, discussing who would walk home past the haunted house. The only one up for the challenge was me, and I convinced two smaller kids to come with me. Heading toward the house was a long way to go home. There were shorter cuts, and we knew it, but viewing the haunted house on a stormy day seemed too good an opportunity to be missed.

"Don't worry," I said to the younger children, "the big wind isn't coming until much later." The two little girls trusted me because I babysat them on occasion.

The blustery wind made me pull the end pieces of my pigtails out of my mouth. The warm hands of the kids held tightly to mine. "And the house is up a hill, so nothing inside can get us. We can be long gone before any monsters get to us."

"Monsters?" Tammy, the youngest, asked.

"My mom says an old witch lives there," little Stephanie said. "She hangs children." That was news to me. I'd never heard that a witch lived there. I always assumed it was ghosts. "My mom calls her the Hag on Hill House."

"Even a witch can't get us from down here on the sidewalk," I assured them, but I wasn't sure.

The sidewalks were eerily empty and quiet as we walked hand in hand for several blocks and turned down the street that gave us the best view of the old house. The sight of row after row of modern houses boosted my bravery. At the same time, while it was still early afternoon, only a half-hour past noon, the sky got dark. A cold wind blew, and the trees' branches bowed, their fly-away leaves hitting us in the face and bare knees.

We shivered but continued.

We stopped in front of the house. We were utterly alone. No cars, no other people, only we three. The wind blew our hair across our eyes.

In the distance, at the end of the street, the sky looked black, and I became unsure of my decision to go home this way. "Take a quick look, then we'll run home," I said, but they looked terrified. They didn't even look up at the old house. They took off when I let go of their hands, leaving me alone on the abandoned walk.

My scarf, caught by a chill gust, blew up the hill toward the house. My birthday gift, gone, pulled up, up, up the hill like a snaking kite. I stepped off the curb to go after it.

I looked up.

An old woman dressed in black, with a black bonnet on her head, stood in the window staring at me.

I stopped.

The hag held my stare. She didn't speak or move but called to me inside my head.

Beware the wind, she said.

My scarf landed in a bush near the broken picket fence around the house, not even in the yard. I went after it. The wind bullied me and made the leaves smack my face. Globules of rain fell and hit my head like watery fruit. I forced myself not to look at the woman in the window, not to look at the grumbling sky.

Grab the scarf and run! I told myself.

But the hill became slippery; every two steps forward slid me one step back. The prickly bushes grew thicker as I fell and scraped my knees. The gathering wind stole my breath. My red scarf was held fast to a thorn by a thread. The rest of it threatened to blow toward the house. I reached, stretched, "Got it!"

"Gina!"

I turned to look. Little Stephanie and her tiny sister stood in the sheltered doorway of the spooky house. The door behind them opened. The woman from the window stood there. She took the hand of each little girl. They held tightly to hers. The hag stared at me as she led them inside. They both looked back, their sad small faces worried, white in contrast to the witch's black skirts. Then they were gone.

Fighting my way up the hill, I managed to get to the scabbed and stained front door. I pounded once, and the door opened. The wind blew me inside the house. While I searched the broken ruins like a fireman looking for life, neither the woman nor the little girls appeared. When I find them, I'll take them home. I won't leave until I find them. One day I'll go home, but not before.

In the meantime, from where I stand at the window, I can watch the other children as they walk home from school.

Rhea Rose has published many speculative short fiction stories and poems. A four-time Aurora Award Nominee, she is an active member of HWA, SF Canada and SFPA and is the editor of Polar Starlight, an online magazine of speculative poetry by Canadian authors. Recent short stories appear in (as the featured author) Pulp Literature issue #35 and the UK's ParSec Magazine.

Website: www.rheaerose.com

Twitter: @rheaerose1

Instagram: roseypoesy577

Smooth Man

Kim Mannix

The air felt cool and heavy, like a slab of stone had been set on Jenna's chest. She kept her eyes clamped shut, refusing to look. She knew the dark would be blacker, and swirling, except for the spot where he glowed.

Smooth Man.

Back for the third night in a row. He never spoke, but Jenna felt him in her mind. Slithering.

"Go away," she cried.

She slowly opened her eyes, taking in every detail of his horrible form. White and hairless, he was so smooth he looked polished. His lips, thin and silvery, and in the sockets, where eyes should be, a light shimmered. He stood motionless, spindly arms stretched toward her.

"Go away," she said, softer.

She stared at him for hours, too afraid to look away. A few times, the need for sleep overcame her, but then she would wake with a jolt. Still there. Watching. Until he slid away to whatever murky place he came from. Only then could Jenna sleep, dreamless, until her alarm shrieked.

She barely made it to work. She was there in body, but couldn't stop thinking about Smooth Man.

The first time He came, she was six. Halloween night. She hadn't brushed her teeth and could still taste chocolate.

Jenna.

Her eyes snapped open and searched the dark. A faint glowing figure grew brighter as she watched. She squeezed JamJam, her pink bear, tight to her chest.

She needed to pee. She was too scared to cry. Maybe he couldn't see her. But if she made a sound, he would know she was there.

She shut her eyes. A movie started to play in her head, like a cartoon. Teddy bears, in every size and color, jumping and dancing in a circle. *Don't look, don't look, don't look.*

Where were the teddy bears to calm her last night? Jenna picked up her cell and sent another text to Em. *Hey. Let's talk today.* Em had been gone for more than a week. Business. Again. They'd been together for five years, but for the last six months, Em was absent, even when she wasn't away.

Jenna remembered how defeated she felt the one time she tried to talk to Em about Smooth Man. She told her about her experiences in college. How the white, hairless thing plagued her even worse after she'd started the anxiety medication. How cold she felt inside when he said her name.

"The worst feeling," she said to Em, "is thinking he might be the only one who really knows me."

Em flipped a page in the book she was reading.

"Emily! Are you listening?"

"Yeah, pale dude, like you, and a sexy blond, too." She touched a lock of Jenna's hair and twisted it around her finger. "You were depressed. Now you have me."

She wouldn't have her tonight. She'd be alone. Until He came. *Not tonight, not tonight, not tonight,* Jenna chanted as she got ready for bed. She turned on her nightlight and popped two sleeping pills.

She crawled under the covers and started scrolling her phone for the year's best celebrity Halloween costumes. Luxurious lives. Beautiful people, even in make-up and masks. *No glowing creeps.*

She awoke a few hours later, unaware she'd even fallen asleep.

Jenna.

The cold whisper thrummed in her brain.

Jenna.

She opened her eyes and saw his thin hand reaching toward her. Close enough to grasp.

She imagined the feel of his fingers. Bony and icy. Like something that should never be touched.

He'd never hurt her before. He could have done something terrible to her in her sleep, but he hadn't.

She felt her own hand rising toward his, even as part of her screamed not to do it. His long fingers curled around her hand. Jenna's body began to buzz. Her eyes rolled back in her head, and she heard a high-pitched sound, like air leaking from a balloon.

Flashes, as memory after memory flickered past. Like slides, revealing moments of her life, in reverse. Her college graduation, when both her parents forgot to come. A slumber party where the other girls locked her in the closet for hours. The grade two teacher who said, "Strange girls like you have trouble making friends." Sitting at a table when she was four, scribbling a black circle, over and over with a marker. As a bawling newborn, bald and impossibly pale.

Jenna.

She writhed and shrieked, white light filling every part of her.

Then, like a champagne cork releasing, she felt herself pop back to reality. The room was quiet and warm. A normal dark.

Smooth Man was gone. Really gone. Whatever he was, he hadn't harmed her.

She wiped her eyes and took a gulp of water. She put her head on the pillow. *I'm ok.*

Within minutes, she fell into the first solid sleep she'd had in a week.

She woke to the sound of her phone buzzing. It was Em. *Be home tonight. Let's carve a pumpkin.* A heart emoji. Jenna smiled. It was something.

She stretched and shuffled to the bathroom. She splashed cool water on her face and reached for her hairbrush. The first run-through snagged on her flaxen hair, and she pulled harder. She felt a slight tug, but no pain.

Jenna stared, open-mouthed at her brush. A clump of hair was snarled in its teeth. She reached her hands up to her head and felt a bald spot on her crown.

She patted her head. Another lock peeled off and fell into her fingers. With every touch, more hair sloughed off, like dandelion fluff on a windy day. Jenna wailed, clutching her head as the hair continued to slide off her scalp.

She stared into the mirror. Her eyes faded from soft blue to milky white. It was happening, but she could only see now. Sobbing, she collapsed to the floor and watched her freckled legs take on a silvery sheen.

Jenna.

In her head. His voice.

Welcome.

Kim Mannix (she/her) *writes short fiction and poetry from Treaty 6 territory in Sherwood Park, Alberta. Her background in journalism and love of dark fiction means she spends much of her time pondering the nature of horror, both real and imagined. You can find her on Twitter @KimMannix posting about kids, cats, and music.*

Charlie-in-the-Box

Vivian Kasley

Charlie parked his truck off the road and got out. It was dark and brutally

151

cold, a night most people wouldn't want to be outside unless they had no other choice. He dragged his axe through the deep hard snow, carving a trail in his wake. He didn't feel an ounce of remorse for what he was about to do. All his miserable life, he'd been cast aside for being different. If he couldn't sit at a table and feast alongside loved ones, why should they? It had been a few years since he'd seen his family, and the last time he had seen his mother, she'd said, "Just look at you—you're not like us. Honestly, you're an embarrassment and I wish we'd never brought you home from that goddamn place. You will never be a Wilkins!" *She had wanted a project, a novelty... I was never anything fucking more than that.* They're the freaks, not him. "Fuck that shit about we all bleed red," Charlie spat. "Everyone shits when they die is better."

· · · ● · ● · ● · ● · ·

As the glow of the sprawling farmhouse came into view, Charlie rested the axe between his legs and stopped to light a joint. No rush, he thought as he blew his smoke, relishing the way it came alive in the icy air. So, his mother wished she'd never brought him home? Well, he wished he'd never been shot from some asshole's unprotected dick into some bitch's snatch. He wished he never won that race at all. He hadn't asked to be born. No one does. You just swam faster than the rest, not knowing that eventually you'd end up in a shithole filled with even shittier people who would abandon you the first chance they got. There's no such thing as a decent person, he thought, then flicked the last of his joint into the snow.

· · · ● · ● · ● · ● · ·

Rage bubbled from the depths of his innards as he watched them from one of the frosted kitchen window panes. They were all smiling with their perfect white teeth and clinking their overfilled crystal wine glasses. His pale-skinned Waspy parents and grandparents sported matching plaid sweaters, and his blonde snub-nosed brother and sister snickered as they snuck pieces of the crisp golden skin from atop the turkey. Bark—the family labradoodle—must've sensed him. He lifted his head and looked in the direction of the window, lifting his ears in recognition, but lucky for Charlie he didn't alert anyone, instead, he curled back up in his bed like he didn't know nothing. Charlie always liked Bark; he'd leave him alone.

$$\bullet \; \bullet \; \bullet \; \bullet \; \bullet \; \bullet \; \bullet \; \bullet \; \bullet \; \bullet$$

His parents had tried to return him once, like he was a pair of unfit shoes or faulty appliance, but much to his chagrin, they had changed their minds. They'd argued the whole way back home as if he wasn't able to comprehend a word of what they were saying. "He's just a child, Millie. Children make mistakes," his father had said.

"This wasn't a mistake, Richard. He knew exactly what he was doing!" his mother had replied.

"He said it was an accident, and I believe him. He's only nine for Christ's sake. Do you really believe he meant to harm you?"

"Yes, I do. And it's not only me he means to harm, but Laura and Jack, too. He's evil, a spawn of Satan himself."

"Stop this right now! You're being ridiculous." His father ground his teeth. A sure sign he was losing his patience.

"Am I?

"Well, I can't do it. If you want to bring him back, you're going to have to do it yourself." His father had been white-knuckled as he gripped the steering wheel, chewing his bottom lip to shreds in an effort not to explode in anger.

His mother's nostrils flared and her face had turned almost a shade of purple when his father turned the car around. Her face had always scared Charlie when he was small. It reminded him of an angry dragon ready to spit fire and caramelize the flesh from atop their bodies.

He hadn't meant to hurt Jack and Laura's pet hamsters the day he took them from their cages and set them loose in the house; that was an accident. But mother? He had meant to harm her. When she'd asked him to put poison in the barn for the mice and rats, he put a little in her lemon iced tea, as well. His only mistake that day was forgetting to stir it well enough.

· · · · ● · ● · ● · · ·

They were right, though. He was a misfit and he'd never fit in with their cookie-cutter image. So, imagine the family's impudence of surprise when he popped through the front door wielding an axe. The looks on all of their stupid faces when he shook the snow from his hair and shouted over the carols playing in the background, "MerryfuckingChristmas, assholes," made Charlie burst out in maniacal laughter, he couldn't help it. At first, they didn't move, as if they thought it was some sort of sick and twisted joke on his part, but when he lifted the axe over his head and bared his teeth, they scrambled like ants in every direction. But he was stronger and quicker than all of them.

It wasn't long before the magical scents of the holidays—pine, clove, cinnamon, turkey, and stuffing—became sullied with the odor of his family's piss, shit, and blood. When he pulled the axe's blade from the last of the Wilkins' wriggling bodies, he sighed. It finally was over. All of the invisible weight that he had carried for years had been lifted from his shoulders.

Charlie thoroughly washed his family's gore from his hands and then changed into one of his father's festive sweaters. He stoked the fire, warming himself by it for a while, enjoying the snap, crackle, and pop. Afterward he carved off a piece of turkey, filled a glass with chardonnay, swirled it around, and took a long slow sip. "Mm, buttery," he said, then laughed until he choked.

Charlie filled his plate with food, sat down at the head of the table, and stuffed a red cloth napkin into his cashmere collar. He grinned at Bark, who was in his bed, gnawing on what he guessed was his grandfather's liver spotted hand. His mother struggled on the floor nearby, blood gurgling from the gash in her throat with each raspy labored breath she took. Charlie shook his head. *She was always so stubborn.* He winked at his mother, put his finger to his mouth, and shushed her. "I'm having Christmas dinner with the family, after all, Mother—whether you fucking like it or not."

Vivian Kasley hails from the land of the strange and unusual, Florida! She's a writer of short stories and poetry. Some of her street cred includes Cemetery Gates Media, Brigids Gate Press, Vastarien, Ghost Orchid Press, Death's Head Press, and poetry in Black Spot Books inaugural women in horror poetry showcase: Under Her Skin. *She has more in the works, including her first collection. When not writing or subbing at the local middle school, she spends time reading in bubble baths, snuggling her rescue animals, going on adventures with her partner, and searching for seashells and treasure along the beach.*

https://www.facebook.com/bizarrebabewhowrites/
amazon.com/author/viviankasley3

The Road Home

Rand Eastwood

Turns out it was just an old country road, narrow and crumbling; somehow it looked bigger on the map, and upon reaching it after days of marching overland, Dan and the rest of his platoon were surprised.

Nevertheless, it marked the northern boundary of the town the enemy had besieged and occupied, and were now using as a base of operations to expand their conquest. The south side of the town was surrounded by hilly terrain—difficult to traverse and easily defended—so Command had decided they should attack from the north.

But when they launched their assault, the enemy was ready; there was no element of surprise, as hoped.

The battle was intense, the enemy fervently holding the line, ensconced and nearly invisible, camouflaged among the shrubs and overgrowth in the field beyond the road. But their military had been spread thin as they had advanced from town to town, and they were incrementally driven back.

What Dan's platoon had lost in surprise, they had made up for in sheer numbers.

Becoming overwhelmed, the enemy slowly retreated, then regrouped just inside the woods that stood behind the field, which was now veiled in smoke and strewn with corpses.

Ordered forward, Dan's platoon marched confidently toward the tree line, accompanied by rebel yells and brisk firing. But as they drew closer, the enemy soldiers all abruptly turned and dashed farther into the woods with reckless abandon, apparently in full, panicked retreat.

This prompted Dan's platoon to give chase, their yelling escalating as they bounded through the high weeds and brush and into the woods.

But as they entered the woods, the enemy soldiers ahead suddenly dropped to the ground, and several large machine guns opened fire in the distance. Mounted on tripods, giving them an open, elevated line of sight, their hail of bullets raked the entire area, ripping the oncoming soldiers to sheds, leaves and branches blown into the air along with blood and flesh.

It was a trap—and they had walked right into it.

Glancing to his right, Dan saw his comrades exploding into bloody tatters, one by one—their mangled bodies landing in the underbrush, brief anguished screams ending abruptly as they went down—and realized with horror that the torrent of bullets ripping through the line of soldiers was fast approaching *him*.

As his buddy not six feet from him was shredded into screams and blood, he glanced to his left and saw an old log, a fallen tree from ages ago, lying across the ground, rotted and laden with moss. As the bullets tore through the tree branches hanging near his head, he turned and dove behind the log.

He struck his helmet hard on his way down, the impact wrenching it from his head. It rolled away, coming to rest in a pile of dead leaves.

As he landed in the mud behind the rotted tree, the machine gun spray ripped across its top, sending bark and wood chips raining down on him before continuing on, his comrades farther down the line now screaming and falling.

Tears welling in his eyes, heart beating in his ears, lungs heaving hotly, he thrust his muddy hand into his shirt pocket and yanked out the old, tattered black and white photo he had kept there since leaving boot camp. In it, a pretty girl—blonde hair, bright shining eyes—smiled beautifully at the camera, a tiny baby girl in her arms, swaddled in a pink blanket: his wife Jenny, and their newborn daughter Kaylie.

He hadn't yet laid eyes on Kaylie, nor held her in his arms. But he was living for the day he could return home to do so.

As the screams faded and the machine gun fire died down, he contemplated his options: he obviously couldn't advance any farther, he would be cut in half just like the rest of his platoon; and he couldn't stay here, either—they would eventually find him, and that thought frightened him even more than being shredded by machine gun fire.

Staring at the photo, he made his decision: he was going home, to his wife and daughter, to all that he loved in the world.

Resolved, he stood and walked back toward the edge of the woods.

Miraculously, no bullets struck him from behind as he made his way out of the woods. The gunfire had subsided, along with the dying cries of his comrades. Calmly, purposefully, he crossed the field, ignoring the bodies strewn about until he reached the road. There he stopped and looked up into the sky, orienting himself by the sun.

East. Home was east of here. He *sensed* it.

Turning right, he stepped out onto the road and headed east.

As he walked, the horrible sounds of war faded, and the serene sounds of nature took over.

Soon the sun set behind him, bringing first twilight, then darkness, until the moon rose above the trees and bathed the dark earth in its pale nightlight.

As the sound of nocturnal creatures emerged from the darkness, he walked.

As the moon watched from the cloudless night sky, he walked.

Holding the picture up before him, he stared at it with his left eye—his one remaining eye—and didn't notice that his right eye was gone; he also didn't notice the stream of blood running down his arm and dripping from his knuckles as he gripped the tiny photograph. And he didn't notice that his helmet was gone, or that a bloody mass of brain matter now hung from what remained of his skull, speckled with bits of shattered cranial bone.

No, all he noticed was Jenny and Kaylie.

And the road.

The road that would take him home, to his wife and his daughter, to all that he loved in the world.

The road that stretched out for miles before him, fading into the distant darkness.

The road that looked as if it might just go on forever.

Rand Eastwood *is the author of* Rolling the Bones*, a collection of 12 subtly interconnected tales of dark fiction, including 8 short stories, 3 novellas, and a short novel. He currently has an extensive novel under development (working title* Primeval*), along with various other writing projects. Visit his blog INSIGHTS at www.randeastwood.com.*

Whittling

Michael Harris Cohen

Mr. Nervous found her in the dry culvert where she hid with Jake. Mr. Nervous' gaze crawled from the dead baby in her arms to her empty eyes. His hand twitched on his hunting knife. He bowed his head. She watched his lips tremble.

She called him Mr. Nervous because though he held the knife, and she just her son Jake—dead now two days—the old man was the one who shook. She named him Mr. Nervous and he never asked her name. Because what good were names anymore?

• • • ● • ● • ● • •

Mr. Nervous buried Jake in a city park. He gripped her hand by the open grave he'd dug. She couldn't tell if he squeezed for comfort or to make sure she didn't jump in after.

She could barely stand. She tried to speak but no sound came.

Mr. Nervous sang "Amazing Grace." His voice was low and silvery.

After, he led her back to the storage unit where he lived. Reckless, she knew. Though he was old, sixty or more and with kind eyes, he might rape her, might even eat her. She'd seen things since the war. She knew what people could and would do to survive.

But her heart was gone, buried in that grave. She was hollow. He could have her body if he wanted, to fuck or eat; it was no use to her.

• • • ● • ● • ● • •

Mr. Nervous fed her soup by candlelight. He did that for a week or more. There was no way to tell time in the storage space. It was dark but for the irregular candles. The air was stale and reeked from their honey bucket.

They passed the time together in silence, often in total darkness—candles were precious, though Mr. Nervous used them when he whittled.

She mostly slept and prayed not to dream. For dreams were nightmares of Jake—his howls of hunger, his blaming stare. Her empty hands and breasts. His body rotting underground.

· · · ● · ● · ● · · ·

Weeks later she still hadn't spoken. Mr. Nervous said that was fine.

"I have a master's in silence." He giggled, high-pitched and childlike. Mr. Nervous loved puns.

He left her alone and whittled in his corner.

The animals he'd carved filled the storage unit, all the creatures great and small, now dead and gone from the world. Bears and deer and rabbits and more.

"I'll carve you something special," he said.

· · · ● · ● · ● · · ·

Mr. Nervous wouldn't let her go outside. That was one of the rules.

"It's too dangerous," he said. "Truth is danger than fiction."

The other rule was "never touch the knife." Not that she had the chance. When he left to search for food or wood he took it with him.

Here, he carved by candlelight, his back to her, whittling and singing. All she saw was his hunched shoulders and arms, flexing with effort.

· · · ● · ● · ● · · ·

Mr. Nervous had wrapped it in newspaper, circled by a piece of twine in a bow. He'd carved it from a log. It was heavier than Jake but exactly as big. She traced her fingers over the roughness of its uneven lips. It had Jake's nose and his tiny curled fists. By the flicker of candlelight, it seemed to move, to shudder with tiny breaths.

In the dark, she cradled the doll and mouthed Jake's name. She would not speak it aloud. Not ever. She pressed her nipple to the rough wood of his mouth.

• • • • • • • • • •

Jake screamed his hunger. Still alive, his teeny mouth was crusted with dirt, his eyes wide in the forever dark of the grave. There were other eyes, too; she sensed them. Hungry things that lived in the earth, sharp-toothed creatures, they gnawed Jake down to bones.

She bolted upright, Jake's howls still in her ears, then the rasp of Mr. Nervous' snoring.

She found her wooden baby in the dark and rocked him. She stroked his mouth where she'd stained the wood with spoons of soup. Weeks ago, when there'd still been soup.

They were down to a few rotten potatoes and moldy crackers. She was dizzy all the time now. Mr. Nervous no longer whittled.

She lit a candle and saw the wooden eyes of her baby open wide. His little hands snatched at the air. She knew his look and need, felt it deep in her hollow gut. She kissed his eyes and crawled to Mr. Nervous.

His knife rested on his chest, like always, like a knight laid to rest. She slid it from under his hands without him stirring.

• • • • • • • • • •

Mr. Nervous woke to a sound. *A muffled scream?*

He felt his knife had vanished.

He flailed in the dark, fending off blows he imagined might come, though none did. He called out to her but she didn't respond. Had she broken the second rule, too? Had he slept through the sounds of her leaving?

Then he heard the suckling.

Candle lit, he saw her back to him, shoulders hunched. The suckling grew louder as he crept toward her.

She looked up and smiled for the first time since he'd known her.

Her mouth was covered in blood.

The doll's mouth was too.

In the candlelight, the blood on the wood shone black. She held something to the doll's lips, a moist bit of pink. Inching closer, he saw what it was and his legs gave out from under him. Mr. Nervous slid back, whimpering, hands fisted in his mouth.

He really is nervous, she thought, as she fed her son. Her bloody lips made suckling noises, mimicking Jake's, encouraging his feeding.

Her body had a use, after all, and what better use for her tongue? Because what good was talking anymore?

His mother tongue.

She was certain Mr. Nervous would like her pun. If he weren't so nervous, sobbing in the corner. If she still had her tongue to speak it.

She giggled and wetly cooed, content at last. She'd never let Jake starve twice. There was so much more to whittle away.

Michael Harris Cohen has published stories in Conjunctions, The Dark Magazine, Pseudopod, Apparition Lit. *and numerous anthologies. He's won* F(r)iction's *short story contest, judged by Mercedes M. Yardley, The Modern Grimmoire Literary Prize, as well as Mixer Publishing's Sex, Violence and Satire prize, judged by Stephen Graham Jones, which was published as his first collection,* The Eyes. *His most recent collection,* Effects Vary, *came out last year from Cemetery*

Gates. He lives in Sofia, Bulgaria with his wife and daughters, and teaches creative writing and literature at the American University in Bulgaria. Find him online at Michaelharriscohen.net.

(Almost) Joined at The Hip

Dan Weatherer

Hate invariably originates from a single seed. Once nurtured by perceived injustice and the passage of time, what manifests is a tangle of twisted half-truths and misplaced anger, which can if left unchecked devour any lingering sense of logic and pollute the mind; a veritable tree of woe taking root deep in the psyche.

He'd hated his twin for as long as he could remember. Lately, resentment seemed to be his permanent mindset; he'd spent increasing amounts of time brooding over each slight Gabriel, his brother, had subjected him to.

It seemed that hate not only consumed him: it defined him.

His entire life, he'd had to watch from the sidelines as Gabriel ambled his way through life. Nothing was a struggle for Gabriel.

As the years passed, he'd stood by and witnessed Gabriel excel, whether it be in school or university. He'd watched Gabriel drink and fuck his way through his twenties, until he'd finally matured and settled into marriage, only to be blessed further with the birth of two, perfect children.

He'd experienced none of that.

Nevertheless, he'd content himself with the thought that although he'd suffered watching Gabriel succeed in life, he knew he'd be at his side as he suffered in death.

Gabriel was present at *his* death, of course, oblivious though he might have been. As twin boys growing together in the womb, Gabriel's development proceeded, while his did not. Small, malformed and unable to obtain the nour-

163

ishment required to thrive, he perished. Mother never knew he'd existed, and Gabriel absorbed what little remained as part of his anatomical development.

The nameless child, never known to his parents and forgotten by the gods, became a calcium deposit attached to the base of his brother's spine. He would remain an anonymous shade, one of nature's misplaced souls, forever bitter, shackled to the brother who had taken his life.

As the years passed, jealousy begat anger, and anger begat hatred. He reluctantly accepted that the haunting of Gabriel would continue mercilessly until nature granted him the small revenge of Gabriel's death.

That would be a good day.

Dan Weatherer is represented by the Cherry Weiner Literary Agency, USA. For more information about his film, theatre and book work, visit www .fatherdarkness.com.

She Fluttered

Andrew Garvey

She fluttered softly, her delicately patterned wings whirring in the moonlight seeping through a crack in the thick, blue curtains. In one hand, she clutched her tiny burlap sack, in the other, a scroll, its elegant lettering giving the boy's name and age–'Caden, 6'.

She flew and danced and dived and spun, filled with glee, enjoying the fan-cooled air around her. Then she saw it start to drag itself lazily out from under the boy's bed and yawn. Its gleaming teeth, particularly the two huge ones that jabbed downwards like tapered ivory knives from its top jaw, caught her bright, silvery eyes.

The creature flexed its huge front claws on the pale carpet and hauled the rest of its body from under the bed. It glanced upwards and back, over its shoulder, checking the boy was still there. There was no real need to. It, and she, could both hear the child's breathing, a quiet, gently slumbering rumble of dreaming innocence.

She watched from high up, close to the ceiling, her wings whipping furiously to hold her in place far from the creature's reach and, she hoped, its sight. She'd seen these creatures before and she was cautious. They were fast, they were huge, and they were dangerous. She'd watched them kill, seen them revel in the redness and the horror of blood.

But this one was sleepy and, unaware of her presence, it wandered away, out of the room.

Left alone with Caden, 6, she swept through the air, watching him sleeping so peacefully, his mouth hanging open. She dived and rolled, close enough that the wind from her wings brushed his soft cheeks. She tucked the scroll away in her sack, rummaged inside it and found what she needed.

She hefted her hammer and smashed out as many of his teeth as she could fit in her sack, shoving the great, white, shattered, bloody things inside it with magical, determined speed before she flew up and out of the window, chased by the boy's screams and, tearing back into the room, by Misty, his pet cat.

Andrew Garvey is a writer and editor of horror stories. His work has appeared in several anthologies. He co-authored the flash fiction anthology 'Little Penny Dreadfuls' and co-edited 'The Spooky Isles Book of Horror'. He lives in Staffordshire, England with his wife, son, bull terriers, rabbits and books.

Fall to Frost

Jonathan Winn

"It had eight legs," the man said. A stranger seeking shelter from the constant chaos, he sat in the corner, chin on his knees, eyes still wide, bottom lip trembling. I stood guard at the window, peering at the field through ragged shards of broken glass.

"That's new," I said, the words feeling weak. I looked outside. It was quiet now. Nothing crawled through the tall grass. Nothing crept forward from the ring of barren trees in the distance. All was calm under the glow of a hanging moon.

"It had a head and torso, a human head and torso, and two arms," he said, his voice a whisper. "And eight legs." He paused. I could feel him look at me. "Eight clumsy, stumbling, snapping legs." He sniffled and wiped his nose. "How is that possible?"

How is any of this possible? I wanted to say. How could one day be Christmas, the land covered in frost, and the next a hell scape of impossibilities. Of loved ones waking ravenous, their suddenly rotting flesh slipping from muscle and bone. Of the dead punching through frozen ground to hunt and capture and feed. Of children, scalps sliding from skulls, scampering, their bloody teeth bared, eyes wild. Of a sudden army the world could not fight in a never-ending battle it could not win.

How could frost give way to spring, spring to summer, summer to fall, and then fall to frost, again, to reveal a world of hollowed desolation?

And how could that be just the beginning? The bedlam of brutal appetites and senseless death lurching deeper into nightmares never imagined. Of changing bodies and grotesque deviations.

Heads four sizes too large thumping against the earth, the necks too weak to hold their weight, fingers digging at the ground as starvation claimed them. Arms too long, the useless hands dragging on the ground by the ankles, the flesh rubbed raw to the bone. Torsos growing, ribs cracking, the flesh of the waist ripping and tearing, the spine expanding too quickly, pushing the hips down and popping the necks up, the body breaking within moments, the innocent trapped, heart beating, fully aware, screaming for death.

And now this new evolution. A human with a head, two arms and eight thumping, stumbling, scrambling legs.

"It's more than that." I turned to him. He was younger than I expected. The weariness of his voice and the stoop in his back leading me to assume many more years than there were. "Now some of them come back after they're killed. Their souls. Their spirits." The floor creaked as he drew his knees tighter against his chest, his thin arms wrapping 'round his shins. "Normal. As real as you and me. Solid and aware, for a time, their voices clear but their lives on repeat, or after-lives, I guess. A loop of their last moments, their final hopes and goals. With all the other unimaginable things we fight, we've seen this—"

"We."

"Yes, the strangers I called my family." I looked at the grass, the shining moon. "Some now gone, though others remain. Brave souls taken by mistakes and fear, exhaustion and appetite. Choosing their end by sitting in the light as the sun comes up, knowing they'll be found by the ravenous ones, hoping they bleed out before there's pain."

He nodded, stretching his legs out, ankles crossed, his fingers lacing in his lap. "And now hungry ghosts. This is what we're fighting."

I watched the trees. Tried to spy the secrets lurking in their shadow. Saw nothing. Watched the moon sitting low in the sky, knowing morning was still many hours away. Saw the tall, sturdy grass rustle with the coldest of breezes, glinting with ice but not yet bowing to winter. Closed my eyes and missed the simplicity of a solid, trusting sleep.

"So, they're real like you and me," he was saying, the stranger with the long legs and skeletal fists resting in his lap. "One minute you're alone and then, what, the next their breath is on your neck?" He cleared his throat. "Jesus—"

"Run," I said.

"What?" He watched me. Drew his knees back to his chest.

"Past the trees is a hill." I turned to him. "At the top is a house. In that house are my family. They will take you in and be yours." I paused, my eyes still on him. "No one should be alone. You cannot fight alone."

I was back to watching the trees, their shadows holding nothing though the quiet had changed, the chaos threatening to return. "If you run, and run fast, you will make it through the trees. But you have to go and go now."

He stood, the floor creaking. Came near. I stepped back. He stopped.

"And you."

I shook my head. "My family last saw me sitting in the light, exhausted and desperate for a solid, trusting sleep." I could feel him pull away, inching toward the door. "They last saw me stab my neck when the ravenous ones came, my last memory the burning stink of their hot breath as I bled. But I was no more by then." I looked at him. He stood, his hand on the door. "And then I was here, determined to fight the battles I could fight, doing what I could." I smiled. "Not all of us are hungry ghosts." I gestured toward the door. "Now go. Run."

He left, sprinting through the tall grass, his feet crunching the frost, the trees soon swallowing him. I closed my eyes, praying the shadows hadn't lied and he'd make it to—

"It had eight legs," the familiar voice said. A stranger seeking shelter from the constant chaos, he sat in the corner, chin on his knees, eyes wide, bottom lip trembling. I stood guard at the window, peering at the field through ragged shards of broken glass.

"That's new," I said. I looked outside. It was quiet now.

Jonathan Winn is a screenwriter and author of several books including Eidolon Avenue: The First Feast *("a great read...powerful and jarring," Cemetery Dance)*, Martuk...the Holy *(A Highlight of the Year, 2012 Papyrus Independent Fiction Awards) and* The Martuk Series, Vol. 1, A Collection of Short Fiction.

Gandaberunda

Richard Thomas

(Originally published at *ManArchy*)

When Rodney found the tiny bones scattered on the concrete slab that was his front porch, he assumed they were from a small animal, like a raccoon or a squirrel. In time, he learned that he was wrong. When the long shadows passed over the back yard, and a gust of cool wind caused the skeletal branches of the skinny dogwood tree to bend and wave, he hardly glanced up, thinking airplane, in his fearless skull—airplane, airplane, airplane. When the phone started ringing at all hours of the night, his mother's voice rising to a high pitch, he rolled over and went back to sleep, because death had never visited their doorstep before. He had no base of knowledge.

There were cops at his school the next morning, Rodney noticed, as the beige 4-door crept up to the parking lot. His mother drove him as usual, but today she walked him in—all the way in. She nodded to Mr. Langer, the gym teacher, with his bushy mustache and crossed arms, a hairy beast guarding the door to Rodney's school. His mother held his hand, and it was nothing new—he liked to hold his mother's hand, his father's hand, they felt large and warm—safe was the word that came to mind.

The classroom would have an electric quality to it all day long, as rain beat at the windows like knuckles—knocking and knocking, wanting to come inside. Rodney noticed that Millicent was missing. She was his very first crush. It would make the day slower, the math problems dry and calculated, no dishwater blonde across from him with a smile and a toss of her hair. There would be tears in the hallway later that week, anguish echoing in the hallways. But Rodney would be long gone by then.

Hushed voices in the kitchen, and Rodney sat on the couch, a juice box in one hand, and a bowl of Cheetos by his side. The puppy lay next to him, eyes to the ground, and then back to him, her black tail wagging furiously, and then stopping. Her head kept lifting to look at the mother, to look at the father. There was whispering in the kitchen, words that Rodney didn't understand, exhaled with a heavy despair. Abduction was one of them—pedophile another. His parents were also wrong. The bones from the other day flashed across his mind's eye, but Rodney pushed the image away. Stupid bones. They meant nothing to him, not sacrifice, or remains, they were not real—they were not familiar at all.

The puppy ran around the back yard, yapping at the leaves that fell from the neighbor's oak tree, faster and faster in an infinite loop, around the swing set, around Rodney as he stood in the breeze, his mother watching from the kitchen sink, the sun setting over the faded wooden fence. He stared at the sky—and with Halloween approaching—the myths and fables came back to him. He thought of wolves and huntsmen, he thought of sharp teeth at his neck. He laughed and lowered his eyes to the dog, a black shadow blurred across the dying grass. When the wings expanded overhead, the leathery skin stretched taut across ancient bones, he opened his mouth, to scream perhaps—and then he was gone.

Richard Thomas is the award-winning author of three novels, three short story collections, 150+ stories in print, and the editor of four anthologies. He has been nominated for the Bram Stoker, Shirley Jackson, and Thriller awards. Visit www.whatdoesnotkillme.com for more information.

Pagliacci's Ghost

Naching T. Kassa

The chill announced her absence.

Harley blinked against the darkness, his right hand reaching for Colleen. Cold silk met his questing fingers. The pillow lay unoccupied.

He glanced up. Colleen stood near the window, the lace curtain clutched in one fist. She stared through the glass.

"What is it?" Harley asked.

Colleen jumped. The curtain fell from her hand and over the window.

"N-Nothing. I couldn't sleep."

Harley grinned. "Come back to bed. I'll help you sleep."

"I-I can't. I have to get up early." She stooped to pick up a high-heeled shoe. "I'm sorry. I have to go."

"Now? It's three in the morning."

"I'm sorry. I just can't stay."

"Is this about last night? I wasn't lying."

"I know you weren't. I know how you feel."

"But you don't feel the same."

Moonglow shimmered in her eyes and spilled out onto her cheeks. The tears trailed over the star-shaped scar on her chin.

Harley threw back the covers and rose from the bed. He switched on the bedside lamp and a golden glow filled the room.

"No! Shut it off!" Colleen cried. She rushed to the nightstand and hit the switch.

Harley stared at the blonde. She stood trembling before him, her face pale. "What's out there?"

171

"I already told you. There's nothing there." Colleen tried to grasp his arm, but he pulled away. He pushed the curtain aside and looked out.

A figure, dressed in white, stood among the roses just below the window. A tall, conical hat sat upon his head. A large white ruff encircled his neck. Each of his eyelids bore a dark, vertical line, like a single stitch. They seemed sewed shut.

Before he could speak, the figure bent over backward and scrambled in an unnatural crawl across the lawn. "What in the hell is that?" Harley cried.

"A clown."

"I can see it's a clown. Why is it doing that?"

The clown paused in its circuit of the lawn and bared its teeth. Colleen didn't answer. She pulled her dress over her head. The clown continued its weird shuffle across the lawn. It vanished around the corner of the house.

"Jesus," Harley said, snatching up his jeans and pulling them on. "Who is he?"

"It's a long story. I'll call and tell you later."

She headed for the door, but he caught her by the wrist and pulled her back. "I'm not letting you go out there. That guy may be a psycho."

"He's not! He's just a little...overprotective. Oh, Harley. Let me go. If he finds out we slept together... He'll hurt you."

"Colleen, who is this guy?"

"My husband."

Harley released her arm. "You're married?"

"I was." She dropped down on the end of the bed. "He was a great tenor once. Pagliacci was one of his favorite roles. It's an opera—"

"About a clown who killed his wife for being unfaithful. I know it."

Muffled knocking sounded below. Harley froze and the chill raced from his scalp and down his arms. "Shit! I don't think I locked the door." He hurried toward the bedroom door, but Colleen blocked it with her body.

"No, Harley. Don't. Just let me leave. If I go, he will too."

"I'm not afraid of him."

"You should be. He hasn't been the same since the accident."

"Accident?"

"He was in a car crash."

"Brain damage?"

"No. It was far worse than that." The clown flickered into being at Colleen's side. It grinned at Harley, displaying blood-stained teeth, then lashed out with talon-like nails. Harley fell backward. "Peter, no!" Colleen cried. "Please!"

The clown turned toward Colleen. A single tear, the color of midnight, trailed down his cheek. He reached out, his eyes pleading. Colleen grasped the doorknob and fled the room. The clown vanished.

Harley rose to his feet and stumbled into the hall. He found Colleen on her knees at the top of the stairs.

"I was driving that night," she said softly, "and I was mad. He'd signed a contract without telling me. Another tour. Another six months away. I just wanted him home with me. I shouted at him. I cursed him. He never said a word. And then, we crashed. The next time I saw him, he was under a sheet. And no matter how I begged him, he wouldn't...he wouldn't say a word." She looked up into Harley's eyes. "Do you know what it's like? To kill the only person you've ever loved?" She reached out and touched Harley's cheek. "I won't let that happen again."

Colleen rose to her feet.

"No!" Harley shouted. He lunged forward as Colleen launched herself over the banister, catching her by the sleeve of her dress. Stitches popped and gave way. As he leaned over to grasp her arm, his feet slipped. His body slid over.

• • ● ● ● • ● ● • •

Harley blinked against the morning sun and woke to find himself at the bottom of the stairs. Though his arms refused to obey him, pain remained a stranger. Colleen lay in the shadows a few feet away, the clown at her side. Like a strange and pale Prince Charming, he leaned down and kissed her lips. Her eyes fluttered open.

The clown helped Colleen to her feet. He kissed her fingers and led her toward the door.

Harley watched them go and smiled. He would follow them soon.

Naching T. Kassa is a wife, mother, and writer. She's created short stories, novellas, poems, and co-created three children. She resides in Eastern Washington State with her husband, Dan Kassa.

Naching is a member of the Horror Writers Association, Mystery Writers of America, The Science Fiction and Fantasy Writers Association, The Sound of the Baskervilles, The ACD Society, The Crew of the Barque Lone Star, The Beacon Society, The Sherlock Holmes Society of London and The John H. Watson Society. She works as the Talent Relations Manager at Crystal Lake Entertainment and was a recipient of the 2022 HWA Diversity Grant.

Father

R. Leigh Hennig

The man I have been living with does not know he is my father. If he did, I would be dead.

"Zeus!" he bellows, the gruff sound of his voice further muddled through the floor. "Beer!"

His speech is slurred, though it is only six in the evening. I make my way down crooked steps, passing sugar-thin windows that rattle in their latticed frames. Gritty snow lashes the weathered walls of our sagging Colonial, sounding like sand poured over a washboard. We lost power two days ago. I cup my hand around a small candle, protecting the dim light against a bitter draft that threatens to snatch it away.

It's brighter in the living room. Warmer, too—here I cannot see my breath. Against the far wall a fireplace roars, servants always on hand to feed it logs from the supply in the garage.

"More of the same, sir?" I ask, glancing at the growing pile of empty beer cans beside his recliner.

He grunts. I nod, turning toward the kitchen.

"Wait. Forget the damn beer. Whiskey this time."

"Of course, sir." It's difficult not to smirk; this is what I've been waiting for. He did not know me when we first met, instead taking me in as a favor to someone. It took a while before he trusted me to serve his drink, but that was always the plan, to gain his trust. And like most alcoholics, my father is predictable in at least one regard: his drinking habits. Beer in the morning and early afternoon, whiskey in the evening.

The house is dilapidated, but otherwise kept tidy by the servants that scurry from one room to the next. By the sink is the liquor cabinet, though checking it I find it empty. Ordinarily one of the kitchen servants keeps it stocked, a short fellow with red hair, but no one has seen him in two days, not since he made my father angry.

Descending into the cellar where the bulk of the stores are kept, I make my way past a forest of meat: rows upon rows of salted and smoked slabs suspended from hooks bolted into the ceiling. Pork, beef, goat. Other things not meant to be eaten. My father likes meat a great deal. Soon that will change.

Beyond the meat are shelves on the cellar's far wall stocked with jars, tins, boxes, sacks, and bags of different goods. I haul a case of Macallan under an arm, careful of my sputtering candle, and ascend the creaking stairs back into the kitchen.

I take one of the glasses from the cupboard and pour three fingers, then, glancing about the kitchen, sneak a plastic baggie of powder from my pocket. A swirl of the glass is all it takes for the powder to dissolve.

"God damn, what took so long? You distill a fresh batch yourself?" he says, glaring at me as I hand him the glass.

"I'm sorry, sir. I had to go into the basement. The liquor cabinet hadn't been stocked."

He twists in his chair to yell toward the kitchen but stops, seemingly remembering something, then takes the glass of whiskey and begins to drink.

I turn to leave but then stop, hearing a loud grumble and burp emanating from his tremendous girth that fills the sagging, threadbare chair.

"Ugh, Jesus," he moans, rubbing his stomach. Already a sweat has broken out across his brow. The powder is working faster than I thought it would.

He leans over the armrest and vomits, a stringy trail of yellow spittle dangling from his mouth. Eyes bulge in their sockets. From his mouth a stone falls to the ground amid the heap of empty beer cans. I bend down to pick up the stone, holding it beside my face.

"See the resemblance?" I ask, smirking.

"Who..." he gasps, veins protruding from his neck. "Who are you?"

"Six children you had. Six you ate—or thought so, anyway." I shake the stone in his face, gloating. "I don't think it looks much like an infant, personally. More like a potato. What do you think?"

He swipes for me but I dodge him, taking a step out of his reach. I watch as he coughs and spills green and yellow bile onto the arm of the recliner. He leans farther out and the chair tips over, dumping his mass onto the wooden floor with a reverberating crash. Plaster sifts from the ceiling. The servants have converged from throughout the house, silently bearing witness. They do not intervene.

The sound of his retching drowns out the storm outside. Blood splatters from his mouth against the floor as the contents of his stomach are forced out.

Misshapen and half-digested lumps of chewed meat begin to emit. His body trembles with each heave of his gut. A crushed eye, the sclera still visible. Teeth. Fingers. Lumps of hair, bones, knobs of cartilage from broken joints. From the heaving creature before me are born the digested remains of my brothers and sisters, five in all, and had I not been secreted away by our mother, I would have been among them.

He crawls away from their remains, as if disgusted by their sight, dry heaving and choking on his own vomit. I kneel and take the mass of flesh into my hands, cupping them and scooping what I can to hold against my breast. We have work to do, my siblings and I, so much work. But first I must make them whole again.

R. Leigh Hennig is a writer, editor, and horror enthusiast living with his beautiful wife and three awesome kids north of Portland, Maine. During the day he works as the principle network architect for the largest datacenter in New England. Visit him at https://semioticstandard.com or follow him on Twitter @BastionSF.

Rattled

Madeline Mora-Summonte

Rosemary reaches to pull the curtains across the kitchen window when she sees a baby's car seat in the middle of the road.

She sighs.

The only people who use this back road either live on it or are going to the junkyard, ones too lazy to pack up their stuff correctly and who want to avoid a fine. Rosemary has lost track of how many things have fallen off trucks, of how many things Bo has fixed up then sold or sold for parts. Other people's trash is our cash, he always says with a smile.

Rosemary hurries down the porch steps as the sky grows dark and growls with thunder. The gate creaks as she pushes through it to the road.

Hands on hips, she studies the car seat. The material is stained, shredded. A rattle the color of old bone is still attached. Rosemary nudges the car seat with her foot, making sure nothing slithers out. The rattle shudders to life, the sound like chattering teeth. She tugs at the straps. Despite being chewed by some critter, they hold pretty well. Bo would be all over this if he weren't off on one of his overnight fishing trips.

Raindrops start to fall, cold and slow. She lifts the car seat. An odor of such earthy rot fills her nostrils that she drops it in disgust. She drags it instead, leaves it around the back of the house. Bo can deal with it tomorrow.

That night, Rosemary tosses and turns. The rain taps like fingernails on the roof, the windows. The wind moans around the house, filling the gutters as if searching for something lost. The gate creaks, slams. She must have forgotten to latch it in her hurry to get out of the storm.

The early morning sky is just starting to lighten when a thump from the kitchen wakes her from a fitful sleep. "Bo? Weather drive you home early?" She gets up, wraps a robe around herself. "Catch anything besides a cold?"

The car seat sits on the kitchen table, its back to her. Streaks of mud slick the floor, the back door wide open. The rattle jitters in the breeze.

"Tell me you did not just drag this stinky thing inside, get mud all over and leave the door open to boot," she mutters. She peers outside.

Bo's truck isn't there.

Frowning, she closes the door then turns around.

The kitchen is no longer empty.

But the figure standing there is not Bo.

The car seat is no longer empty.

But what's in it, is not a baby.

Neither is human. Not anymore.

Rosemary staggers, crumples to her knees.

The figure shuffles closer, that same rotting stench from yesterday wafting over Rosemary like a shroud. She wraps her arms around herself. She won't look up, won't let herself see.

The voice is more rasp and rust than human. "My baby...so...hungry."

The rattle bounces off the table, lands hard near Rosemary as if flung down. It cracks open. Teeth, animal and human, spill out onto Rosemary's kitchen floor.

Madeline Mora-Summonte is a writer, a reader, a beach-comber and a tortoise-owner. Many of her creepy little tales prowl in print and lurk online. Visit MadelineMora-Summonte.com for a taste of her work. Just be careful something doesn't taste you back.

Odor Mortis

Red Lagoe

Harold slithered the tip of his nose along the body, absorbing the scent into his soul until he was gravid with pleasure. A female, mid-thirties, graced the table in his basement embalming room. Being a mortician allowed him to keep his fervor for a corpse's acrid aroma a secret from the public.

Like any other person, he spent his evenings watching shows while swiping left on a dating app. Most women, he assumed, had no interest in coming back to his place considering he lived in his funeral home. A lack of confidence, and fear they'd discover his unorthodox delights in the fragrantly deceased, kept Harold from ever reaching out to the women on the app.

He preferred the people on the table to the living, anyway. A tragic car accident landed the current body into his caring hands. A wreck mangled the right half of her face beyond recognition. Harold was smitten by what was left

179

of her. A remaining soft, black eyebrow, slick to the touch like a crow's feather, framed the woman's left eye. She had a kind eye, one that he could stare into all day. Pale skin contrasted thick, dark hair. As Harold leaned his face against her right cheek and inhaled, he was reminded of his childhood friend, Jenna. Had she been given the chance to grow up, Jenna would have looked like the woman on his table.

· · · ● · ● · · ·

When they were ten years old, Harold and Jenna had been walking down the country road, singing and laughing under the summer sun. The roar of a speeding vehicle had approached so fast, before Harold had a chance to see it coming, Jenna was struck. Her body flipped into the air and crashed to the gravel shoulder. The truck slowed, but then sped away never to be found.

Harold cradled Jenna's broken body. As he waited for a passerby, she grew heavier and blood absorbed through the cotton of her yellow sundress. Sweaty arms clung to her lifeless form. His tear-soaked cheeks pressed against her blood and gravel-splattered face. He embraced his best friend and begged for her to be alright, but on this stretch of country road nobody was coming to help.

Then he detected it. At first he turned away from the foreign, pungent odor, but he was intrigued. Having never smelled anything like it, he leaned in for another sniff. Fighting a natural response to reject the odor, he dove in for more. The fragrance had filled his nostrils, caressing his olfactory receptors, and smothered the tips of his taste buds. Harold liked to think that part of Jenna's soul had stayed with him that day, respired into his body with each mournful breath.

· · · ● · ● · · ·

He traced his finger along the cadaver's brow bone, astonished by her resemblance to Jenna. The mangled half of her face had been fixed with stitches and makeup to the best of his ability. He brushed her thick, black hair over her mutilated half. Because of her disfigurement, the family had requested a closed-casket funeral, but he wasn't preparing her for them. It would be a pity to embalm her, especially if nobody would see her.

Harold laid her nude body on his bed. Gases attempted their escape from the fleshy confines, bloating her and making the fetor even more intoxicating. From a plastic bag, he pulled a new yellow sundress. He slid the cotton over her swollen feet, gliding the fabric along her pale, blue legs and around her hips. The warm, sunny cotton masked her olive green, distended belly. Harold supported her head, hoisted her torso up against himself, and respectfully shroud her breasts within the garment.

She rested peacefully on his bed while he slipped under the covers. Cold fingers welcomed his warm touch as he inserted his hand into hers. He lay next to her, reminiscing of their summers playing together, talking about his day and how happy she made him. The bed would shake from Harold's laughter, erupting plumes of putrid perfume into the air.

He kept his old friend company each night. Coagulated blood settled into her back and buttocks. Her eyeballs shriveled behind closed lids. Weeks passed and the bouquet changed. No worse nor better, but different. Her body broke down, releasing a slow leak of new chemicals. An evolution of essential odors, each stage as perfect as the next. Life couldn't be any better. But all things that bring happiness eventually get taken.

Over time, the remains of what used to be Jenna (or the woman that could have been Jenna) were sticky and skeletal. The aroma of decay waned and Harold's gut gurgled with a hunger for more. He twitched, scratching at his arms. Ever since his new Jenna came along, none of the other bodies that came through his funeral home satisfied him. Jenna's face was a frosting on his fetish that he couldn't go without. But she was rotting away.

181

Waiting for another closed-casket victim that looked like his best friend could take a lifetime. He'd have to go out and find someone.

He kissed the exposed skull on her forehead and promised he'd find her again. After inhaling the remnants of Jenna's musk, he went to the living room and opened his dating app. Repeated left swipes revealed a multitude of disappointing options. Blurred faces (all the wrong faces) passed by. Persevering through his search for over an hour, he began to lose hope. As exhaustion took over and he began to nod off, a pale face with dark hair caught his attention. His pulse hitched with the prospect that he found her.

A woman with dark brows and kind eyes had a coy smile. She would be perfect for him, but first he would need to release her morbid fragrance.

Red Lagoe grew up on 80s horror and carried her paranoia of slashers and sewer creatures into adulthood. She never investigates the noise outside and never enters the creepy house. This is how she survives and is able to write dark fiction. Find more of Red's work at www.redlagoe.com.

Sleepy Hallowed

Joseph VanBuren

The moon hung huge in the sky, nearly full, its reddish tint glowing like a grim promise. Despite its celestial grandeur, the moonlight shone only dimly into the dark woods. Silhouettes of leafless trees stood still as skeletons, their branches shivering in the night breeze like chattering teeth. Somewhere, an owl hooted hauntingly—or was that the longing moan of a lonely imp?

Cornelius Crow had no intention of discovering the sound's owner. If Mr. Van Reede were not hosting the harvest party on this night, Cornelius would have never been out on Samhain night at all, that's for certain. Not on the night when the veil between the worlds of the dead and the living is thinnest.

He cracked the reigns with a shaky shout, and faithful Angel began trotting a bit faster. Cornelius held on tight, the cross hanging from his neck bouncing with the horse's gait.

These woods get more and more haunted as time goes by, Cornelius thought. Sleepy Hollow was once a safe place, a small religious colony that emphasized community and Christ. Over time, however, folks' hearts hardened, and the town became more about self-gain than the common good. Indeed, people here still go to church, but it's out of tradition, all for show. The local church had lost its head long ago.

Wind whistled through the trees, and in that Cornelius heard the wailing of a somber spirit that sent an icy shiver down his spine. It could be the cry of any one of the myriad ghosts that refuse to leave Sleepy Hollow. A long-deceased Native American, lingering over the land stolen from him. A soldier from the Revolution, reliving his painful death in battle. Or perhaps, worse of all, it was the Headless Horseman.

If Cornelius perished out in these woods, would anyone know? Would he become another legend of the haunted Hudson Valley?

Keeping his pace, Cornelius tried desperately not to think of such things. He closed his eyes and prayed, trusting Angel to lead them the rest of the way. When the horse finally slowed down—and mercifully, the scratching branches and crying winds had ceased—Cornelius opened his eyes again. They had emerged from the forest.

The manor of the Van Reede family stood before him, a beacon of shelter and civility that glowed warmly and beckoned Cornelius. He was glad to accept its invitation. Tonight, Mr. Van Reede was hosting his annual harvest party. As every year, there would be feasting, drinking, dancing, and merriment all around. None of these, however, compared to the reason Cornelius had come.

Catherina stood by the fireplace, sipping punch and giggling at those dancing to the fiddlers' music. Her smile captivated Cornelius, drew him in to further worship the rest of her beauty. Flowing hair and radiant complexion invoked images of the heavenly beings Cornelius had named his horse after. Her elegant white dress only confirmed her purity. It was no surprise that he wasn't the only man with eyes on her.

"This is the harvest party, isn't it?" A boisterous voice plowed through the sound of laughter and fiddling. "Well, I'm here to harvest a wife." This got a response of chuckles from some of the ladies, Catherina included.

Then Cornelius saw him: Klaas "The Butcher" Beenhouwer. His nickname came from his profession, though Cornelius would never want to test him about it while off duty. The Butcher was big and bulky—you couldn't miss him, but that didn't stop him from drawing as much attention to himself as humanly possible.

"These arms could handle any woman," said the Butcher while flexing his bulging biceps. To make his point even further, he found the largest woman in his vicinity, a right portly old gal, grabbed her by the waist, and lifted her high into the air. Cornelius found this to be quite inappropriate, but the women seemed to love it, even the chubby lass being accosted. That's what strong drink will do, Cornelius supposed.

He had to admit that it looked like fun—the drinking and dancing and socializing. But that was the corrupted world talking. The devil speaking to the flesh. If these people were faithful to God, they wouldn't want to drink and act as fools before an altar of pagan practice. And perhaps their town wouldn't be haunted by so many evil spirits.

Catherina was the only one who did not engage in foolish activities. The only one that Cornelius noticed, at least. For once he set his eyes upon her angelic form, everyone else faded into the background like so much human fog in the distance. She stood in the firelight, shadows playfully flickering across her delicate features. Cornelius felt like he was floating, walking toward the beauty as if in a trance, an insect drawn to the lamplight.

"Good evening, Cornelius." Her voice was honey to him.

"Evening, m-miss," Cornelius replied. He tripped ever so slightly on both words and feet as he approached. For a split second, she proffered that sweet smile directly to him.

"Don't talk to him!" the Butcher's booming voice cut through the crowd. "Cornelius already has a bride." He slammed the remainder of ale in his mug with one gulp as if it were the punctuation to his sentence. Catherina's eyes widened. She regarded Cornelius with an expression of surprise, her brow crinkled, wrinkles in the perfect flesh of her forehead.

"It...It's not true," Cornelius stuttered. By this time, the Butcher had reached their location by the fireplace and stood towering over the both of them.

"Yes, it *isss*," said the Butcher through a drunken hiss. "He's married to that cross around his neck." Cornelius instinctively grabbed the cross in his hand, concealing it. But he wasn't ashamed, was he? If anything, these heathens should be ashamed. And afraid for their eternal souls.

Catherina rolled her eyes, and Cornelius did not know if the gesture was intended for himself or the Butcher.

"Put that way," Cornelius finally said in response, "I suppose it is true." The entire banquet hall erupted with mocking laughter. A nausea of humility and nervousness sloshed around in his stomach. He turned to Catherina, but she was already walking away. The laughter filled the cauldron of Cornelius's head like a bubbling witch's brew soon to boil over. Dashing through the cloud of faceless mockery, he ran out the front door of Van Reede manor.

He had Angel going at a mighty fine trot on his hasty trip back through the woods. The rain had started before he left the manor, but now the winds were picking up. An occasional flash of thunder lit up the skeletal forest, the following booms of thunder startling horse and man alike. But Cornelius cracked the reigns and kept up the pace.

That is, until he saw something up ahead. Way up the path, somebody walking? A figure in white, voluptuous, and glowing in the gloom of autumn night. Cornelius whoaed and slowed Angel down to get a good look. There was no mistaking her beautiful features, that captivating smile.

It was Catherina, alright. But what was she doing out here?

Cornelius pulled back on the reigns, bringing Angel to a stop alongside his desired angel. She stood at the tree line, her smile's warmth contrasting starkly with the cold night. Into her eyes Cornelius gazed, and in them he beheld fire.

In a flash of lightning, Cornelius saw a sizable projectile flying through the air. It came from behind him and seemed to travel right through Catherina. The head-sized object flew too quickly to be identified. Only the flames that consumed it were distinguishable.

Thunder rumbled, and Angel neighed in response. No, not Angel but another horse from the rear. With a heart full of dread, Cornelius slowly turned Angel around until the apparition—God, please let it be only that—that stood behind them was now in full view.

A horse blacker than the Samhain sky. Upon it sat a giant of a man whose bulk barely fit on the unburdened beast. He wore the robes of a high priest, flowing in the wind like a flag of blue, purple, crimson, and gold trim. His arms stretched outward as one being crucified, and in each hand sat a pumpkin engulfed in fire. The flickering light provided by those dancing flames illuminated the fact that Cornelius's greatest fear had come true.

For the horseman was indeed headless.

Angel bucked and dumped Cornelius onto the dirt road. As his horse bolted in fright, the night-mare drew closer with menacingly slow clomps. The robed yet headless horseman *looked* down. And finally, Cornelius was no longer afraid.

They found his body the next morning, propped up against a tree, a burnt pumpkin in his lap. It took no time for the rumors to circulate. Another ghost story for the heathen townsfolk to tell. A new evil spirit to haunt the slumbering hamlet. The fate of Cornelius Crow became another legend of Sleepy Hollow.

*Out of the darkness, risen from the ashes...**Joseph VanBuren** creates dark speculative tales showcasing the reality of resurrection and bringing a light against legion through poetry, fiction, music, and more. Originally from the haunted Hudson Valley region of New York, JVB now lives with his beloved wife Renée in Fort Wayne, Indiana. Find him on introverted media https://othershadows.wordpress.com/mentions/jvbwriteon/.*

Julaften Heks

Anthony D Redden

He would never catch me.

I was fast as the wind and the knife in my hand sharp enough to easily cut his throat should I need to. The woodsman was large though, a giant of a man, much bigger than my father, from what I remember. I watched him as he struck the logs with a frightening force, spitting them in two with one stroke. From a safe distance hidden within the bushes, he couldn't see me, and the winter breeze rustled the leaves enough to hide any sound I may have made.

I steadied my breath, and urged my muscles to carry me with the speed and might I needed to strike down the man. But even with the fire that burned in my veins, I hesitated. My aunt's words haunted me.

'You are too little and too weak to amount to anything Eliza. The best we can hope for is to trick the Baker's idiot of a son to marry you.'

I cursed my aunt's words for following me here, threatening to prove her right.

'Oskar,' I whisper his name to focus on my purpose.

The woodsman threw the remaining logs into a basket and then swung it upon his back. I held my breath in frustration as I saw my opportunity for blood walk back to the hut and close the door.

I followed in the man's footsteps and kept my head down and close to the shadows until I was at the woodsman's door. I spied the axe he had left and exchanged it for my knife. The axe was heavy, but the edge was sharp. I carefully peered through the window and saw the woodsman warming himself by the fireplace. My anger would have broken down this door and butchered the man where he stood, but no, the only reason I was there was to rescue my brother, Oskar.

I lifted the axe and deftly crept beneath the window and around the hut to where the hatch to the cellar lay. The latch was secured with a chain and padlock, but no match for the heft of the axe. On the third strike, the padlock sprung open and the chain was easy to pull free. Snow had built up on the hatch and I needed to dig it free before I was able to lift it open.

The warm stale air that greeted my face was enough to make me retch. It was dark down there, too dark to see a thing.

'Oskar?' I called, but there was no response.

Braving the dark and the stench, I descended the steps.

'Oskar?' I called again, daring my voice to penetrate the dark bowels of the woodman's abode.

I was all at once aware of movement around me, and as my eyes adjusted to the dimness, I saw a sight that caused my breath to falter. Small animal cages, those a poacher might have to secure his game, lined the walls of the basement, some stacked two or three high. From inside the cages, the pale faces of children stared at me. The intensity was horrific, the looks of distraught hope on tear-stained faces all yearning for help. I desperately searched for my brother's sweet face, and to my relief found him—one of the lost children, one of the trapped animals.

I unhooked the latch, a simple yet effective lock that was out of reach to the children. I swung open the door and pulled my brother into my arms.

Squeezing his quivering form, surprised to find a healthy bulk to him. In fact, upon inspection, all the children were far from the emaciated frames I would have expected, but instead plump and rounded, well fed and in fact fat.

I released the latches on all the cages and the children emerged, gratefully hugging and sobbing. But I knew we had little time for gratitude, there was still the threat above. The woodsman, who at any moment could appear. I ushered the children up the ladder to the snowy chill outside, and free of the basement.

My brother and I were the last to escape and found the children had already run for cover, like skilled woodland animals they had all disappeared, only tracks in the snow as evidence they were ever there. I followed their lead, Oskar in tow close behind. I scoured for signs we had been discovered, but there was an unusual quiet befallen the hut and surrounding land. I gestured for my brother to continue home, but something intrigued me beyond reason. The quiet lull seemed to deaden my senses as if a blanket of silence had fallen upon the clearing. Then from the corner of my eye, I noticed the dark figure for the first time, a hooded tall creature, that moved silently through the snow towards the front of the woodsman's hut. A thin boney arm reached from beneath the thick material of their shawl and at once the door swung open of an accord seemingly at the creature's command. My curiosity compelled me to circle around the hut, scrambling through the woodland, for a better view of the creature.

The figure entered and the door slammed shut behind it.

I ran to the hut and peered in through the window. There was the figure, besides the fire, in front of the woodsman. The big beast of a man seemed to cower in the presence of his visitor. His fear was evident in his cast-down eyes, his quivering hands, and his backward steps to maintain a distance.

I could not hear what was said, the sound of voices was as dull as the unnaturally muted sounds of nature. The man bowed his head in homage before scrambling away from the creature and downstairs into darkness. Down into the basement. Down to the cages.

Oh, what a surprise he would have when he discovered our dareful deed, the rescue of the children. Whatever his need for the youngsters, he would be sorely disappointed.

When the man reappeared he was clearly distraught, his face red, his hands held up in front of him submissively. It is then that I beheld a sight unfit for youthful eyes. The mysterious visitor threw back their hooded cloak to reveal the hideous features of a nightmarish creature, part woman, part serpent, all monster. It was then that I recognised the creature from the cautionary tales I had been told by my parents whilst they were alive, about the creature that lives deep in the forest, that feeds upon children, the devourer of innocence, the eater of youngsters. It was the De Julaften Heks - *The Yuletide Witch*.

I froze momentarily, transfixed at a sight I was too scared to process, yet too scared to turn from. The witch held up a hand and the woodman was caught in an invisible force, gripping him, squeezing him. He was lifted from the ground, unable to escape the power of the witch, and then with a swing of her arm, talons as long as daggers sliced the air and with it the neck of the woodman. His head was at once cleaved from his torso and dropped to the ground amidst a spray of blood. I let out a scream, forgetting myself, and that scream broke the silence. The witch turned and at once I was caught in her glare.

I pushed away from the window and ran. I ran as fast as I could, towards the woods, towards the lane home. I followed the footfalls of the children, skipping branches and ducking the low-hanging canopy. Ahead of me, I saw my brother, his small form a stark figure amongst the bright snow. Each step caught him up, each swing of my arms pushing me further and faster.

I heard the door of the hut burst open behind me and a shriek that sent chills through me. I dared not look, but I knew the witch was following. How she moved so fast I do not know, but I at once felt her presence behind me and darkness began to fall with a coldness beyond the winter chill that froze my muscles and stung my bones. I felt a hand fall on my shoulder. A thin, boney hand, with fingers that gripped me and squeezed tightly, talons that dug into my flesh. My feet became heavy and I slowed my pace, swiftly coming to a halt. The darkness began to quickly envelop me, and the last sight I remember is the figure of my brother running for home. My heart yearned to be with him and my soul longed for home. And then there was darkness—full and impenetrable as death. Even now after my tale is told, I still feel the icy grip of the winter witch upon my shoulder, and I wonder, in this dark void of nothingness, if she will ever let me go.

Anthony D Redden is a writer of science fiction and horror short stories. He lives amongst the lush green rolling hills of middle England with his wife and three children. He is a full-time carer, and a writer the rest of the time. He has a Master of Arts in Creative Writing and has a particular interest in disability representation in fiction, alt-history fiction, red wine and sherbet dip dabs.

Hot Broth on a Cold Winter's Night

R.B. Wood

I had the watch the evening of the great storm that winter in 1899. We knew we were close to the port of Boston, but without stars to navigate by, and 25-foot swells knocking our old East Indiaman hither and thither, we were most sincerely lost.

Sleet slashed at my skin, and I was soaked and near-frozen in the crow's nest. I could see nothing but blackness and the dark grey foam of the angry sea around us. I was desperately looking for some sign of hope.

There!

I caught something out of the corner of my eye that made me look to port. One numb hand grasped the rope that tied me to the mast, and the other attempted to shield my eyes from the onslaught of lashing ice.

There! I did see something!

A beam of glorious light pierced the storm.

"Land! Ho!"

The excited call was echoed from down below by my crewmates.

It was then that a massive wave struck the ship. The *Levant* heaved thirty degrees to port, leaning toward the beckoning light.

Almost there.

I heard the death knell crash of our shifting cargo.

The frigate listed forty degrees now, and my body slipped from its perch. Only the ropes that held me to the mast kept me from the near-frozen maelstrom below.

I screamed, but the wind whipped around me, stealing the sound of my voice—a blackness, darker than the clouds above, and the swirling waters below.

The Hull of the *Levant* shuddered as wood splintered. Men screamed as they tumbled overboard. I felt the mast behind me crack, and the ropes slackened enough to let me slip from my nest.

I fell into the black frozen waters and was no more for a time.

· · · ● ·● ·● · · ·

"Sir... Sir, wake up!"

Someone was shaking me. I'd been having a dream...something about warmth and sun.

That's when the uncontrollable shivers began.

Bits of ice slashed my face. I was soaked yet lying on the sand.

I could breathe.

"Sir!"

I finally realized I wasn't alone. At first, I thought it was one of the crew. But the man shaking me was, as near as I could tell in the dark, a gaunt, small figure, wearing grey rags and looking like a pitiful drowned rat. I suspected I looked the same to him.

The beam from the lighthouse briefly lit up the beach—the pelting sleet reflected in the light looking like angry frozen fireflies buzzing around me.

"Sir," he said for the fourth time. "We must get you out of this storm. There is shelter beyond the trees there."

I realized I was lying on a snowy beach of some sort, with a dark, swaying copse of trees bordering the sand.

"My ship..." I said, coughing up some seawater.

The man pounded me on the back.

"Sunk," he said, pointing at the sea. "Out there. I heard the crash and found you."

The man in rags yanked on my arm, then said in a shrill voice, "Inside! We have water and food and fires. Come, come!"

I followed, stumbling drunkenly at first, as my legs expected the pitch and yaw of the *Levant*.

Thoughts of my shipmates haunted me. Had any of them survived?

The steady beam of the lighthouse was noticeably closer. At the base of the great beacon was a square room. I could see firelight dancing from the windows. I could see that someone had swept the snow from in front of the door.

The yellow glow promised safety. It promised warmth.

The wind howled louder.

I yanked at the heavy oaken timbers, and the iron hinges squealed in protest. I was engulfed by light and heat, and it was glorious!

I felt like the luckiest man alive at that moment.

"Sit, said my emaciated savior. "Sit and grab a blanket. We should eat!"

"J-j-just t-tea, please," I said, teeth still chattering.

"Tea. Bah. Broth! Need nourishment. Need food."

I could see him better in the light. The rags he was wearing clung to his thin, grey body. He was nude underneath the single garment. Nude and dirty.

Perhaps he had gotten that way rescuing me.

He put an iron cauldron on the rack above the fire, water, and bits of meat sloshed from the top, flames hissed and smoked in protest.

"Bowls. Where are the bowls?" muttered my rescuer.

Could tea in a bowl be some strange American custom? I heard the former colonists were eccentric. As the warmth dried my skin and clothes, it seemed to sharpen my thoughts, as well.

My little host's behavior was indeed odd, I decided, even for Americans.

"I don't believe I ever said thank you," I said. The man waved a hand at me as he scrounged about the little kitchen for bowls. Along with seeing the filth that enveloped my new friend, I began to notice more of my surroundings.

Copper cups were scattered about me and a dark brown stain was on the floor at the edge of the firelight—a recent spill of some kind.

Perhaps a bit of spilled tea, I thought hopefully.

But the hairs at the back of my neck stood on end.

"If you wanted to change...I'm fine minding the cauldron," I said.

"Nonsense, nonsense," said my host, his voice now higher pitched. "Guests mean meat! Meat! We will have broth! We take care of the family."

I shivered again, but this time it had nothing to do with the storm or the sea.

I was panicking. I had to find a way out of this wretched lighthouse and away from my strange rescuer. During my desperate attempt at concocting an escape plan, I heard the shuffle of feet and the muttering of voices. For the first time, I noticed a second door that was behind the brown stain.

People were coming.

"Ah!" said my host. "The family! You will meet with my family. Good, good!"

A moment later the door burst open. Four men came into the room, all wearing the same dirty-grey rags of my "host."

Except for their rags still had lettering on it.

BOSTON ASYLUM – *Thompson Island*

"Oh, God..."

They stared unblinkingly at me. One of them drooled.

A sharp pain radiated through my body, coming from my back. I reached around and felt the hilt of a knife.

I flailed, trying to grasp at the weapon. But my arm was slapped away by the bony hand of my rescuer. In one smooth move, the little man pulled out the knife and put it to my neck.

"More broth, thank you," he whispered and kissed my cheek.

A fountain of blood spurted from where he sliced my throat. This time, I would not wake from the darkness.

R. B. Wood is a recent MFA graduate of Emerson College and a writer of speculative and dark thrillers. Mr. Wood recently has been published online via SickLit Magazine *and* HorrorAddicts.net *and appeared in the award-winning anthology* Offbeat: Nine Spins on Song *published by Wicked Ink Books.*

Tea for Two

Amanda Hard

Emmy, who is well-recognized as being smart as a whip, sharp as a tack, and growing like a weed, sits with her fingers jammed into her ear canals. The house is always so loud now, that she can't even hear the tick-ticking from the clock on her bookcase, or the playful whispers of Kind Wendy and Mr. Gallops, who comfort her when the house fills with arguments.

It's Daddy's voice now. Daddy, who used to say Emmy was smart as a whip, now talks more about Mommy instead, what a terrible and selfish person she is. Mommy's voice is next, not reminding Emmy she's sharp as a tack, but calling Daddy arrogant and self-centered and a lot of other words that have nothing to do with Emmy. Nobody talks to Emmy anymore. She continues growing like a weed, with nobody to notice, other than the stuffed animals in her room. And they can't be heard over the shouting.

The house is big. She found a quiet place once before, in the basement, where the shouting voices in the house were like distant thunder, but Daddy found her and made her leave. He was too busy shouting at Mommy upstairs to notice the bulging pocket in Kind Wendy's apron. Mr. Gallops never said a word.

Today is Sunday, the perfect day for a tea party. Emmy removes her fingers from her ears and hums to herself. She writes out the invitations carefully, one each for Daddy and Mommy. Emmy lays her small table with the beautiful china set Grandma gave her. She has already brewed the tea. She is not allowed the use of the stove unsupervised, but nobody told her she couldn't use the coffee pot. Tea bags steep in boiled water in the china tea pot on a white tray. On the saucers are leftover Girl Scout shortbread cookies—not proper tea cookies, but good enough in a pinch.

Mommy arrives first, then Daddy, both surprised but thankfully quiet. They sit on pillows around the table and admire the place settings.

"Before we have tea, can we please agree to no fighting at the table?"

Mommy and Daddy agree, of course, and smile fake smiles at each other.

"Care for sugar?" Emmy asks, knowing that Mommy and Daddy both like coffee with lots of sugar. Emmy takes the sugar bowl from the tray. She has put sugar in the creamer pitcher because nobody in the house drinks cream with their tea. She removes the spoon from the sugar bowl, shakes it off, and sticks it gently in the creamer. Of course they can get along for a cup of tea. Of course they can wear pretend smiles and polite masks for the duration of one cup of tea. Of course they won't fight—except they do fight, even at the tea table, and it is just as Emmy expects. It is just as Kind Wendy, who was Mommy's doll and knows Mommy very well, expects. It is just as Mr. Gallops, the stuffed horse who once belonged to Daddy, also expects. But nobody says, "I told you so."

"One spoon or two?" Emmy asks. "I think two because this tea is very strong." In between snide comments, Mommy accepts two spoons, which

Emmy dips gently from out of the sugar bowl this time. Daddy, responding under his breath, accepts his two spoons from the sugar bowl, and even though there is a kind of quiet in the house, the tension has volume and Emmy wants to cover her ears again to make it go away.

Emmy drinks her tea black, which is bitter and tastes the way the burnt toast smells. She looks over at Kind Wendy and Mr. Gallops for guidance while beside her Mommy and Daddy begin another round of arguments. Kind Wendy nods to Emmy, wide unblinking eyes full of understanding, her arms crossed over her empty apron pocket. Mr Gallops has his mane over his eyes, but Emmy knows he would agree.

And then Mommy and Daddy are no longer arguing. The house is quiet, but for the choking and gagging sounds from Mommy and Daddy, who are red in the face, with white foam dripping from their mouths. They fall from their pillows, writhing and clawing at their throats. Emmy smiles when they fall silent and still, lying next to each other on the rug. Their faces are ugly, so she takes the blanket from the bed and covers them. She moves their hands together, but she can't get all the fingers to stay entwined.

Both of the grandparents get along so well. And they are so proud of Emmy, reminding her always that she is smart as a whip and sharp as a tack. She has never heard them fight. Their house is always quiet, but for the slow shushing of the furnace. Quiet enough for a person to hear her own thoughts. Quiet enough for a girl to hear the soft murmurs of Kind Wendy and Mr. Gallops, reminding her that if the house ever gets too loud, she can always calm it down with a nice tea party.

Amanda Hard's work has appeared in various magazines and anthologies including Lost Signals *and* Tales from the Crust, *both from Perpetual Motion Machine Publishing. Her poetry has appeared in two volumes of the Horror Writers Association* Poetry Showcase, *and her flash fiction was part of three graphic collections from* The Daily Nightmare. *Amanda earned her MFA in Creative*

Writing from Murray State University, Kentucky, in 2018. She is a member of the Horror Writers Association and lives in the cornfields of southern Indiana with her husband and son.

Going Home

Lee Smart

I love my daughter very much, but I have been careless and now I am going to kill her. All because of one stupid mistake.

The body had looked dead, lying prone amongst the ruined aisles of the grocery store. Its flesh was parchment tight over old bones, the fronds of coral poking through its skin were fossilized and inert. I stepped over it without a thought, just another corpse in a world of the dead. Until it reared up and wrapped a spiked, bony palm around my ankle. I brought my hammer down on its skull, shattering it into desiccated shards of bone and spongy matter.

The damage was done, though. Within moments I collapsed to the floor, vomiting and shaking. The infected had injected part of its viral colony into me, a hive of disease and parasites that quickly overran my control and burst through my flesh. I watched in horror as polyps slid from the skin of my arms, tiny growths of osseous coral erupting at their bases.

The disease forces me to my feet, and I stagger out of the store onto the empty street outside. I feel something move in my mind. The coral is working its way in, a creeping, voracious hunger at the edge of my thoughts. Before I can stop it, an image appears in my mind.

Home.

Suddenly my limbs explode into motion, wheeling me around and back down the street. The infection inside me has plundered my memories. It knows where my home is, a place with hosts for it to spread to, and I am powerless to stop it. Powerless, but fully aware of what the coral will make me do.

Familiar houses pass by my roving eyes, places that belonged to my neighbors and friends, now all dead and gone. A dry, cracking screech explodes from my lungs and I hope it will give enough warning to those I have left at home. I turn the corner and see it at the far end of the road, a tree in the garden spreading its branches over a red roof.

My house, my home.

My daughter is in our front yard, waiting for me to return. She looks so strong, so beautiful. Abigail instantly recognizes me; the coral has yet to warp my features into something inhuman. I can see the grief and loss pass over her face, swiftly replaced by a look of grim determination as she realizes what she must do now. The shotgun is pressed tight against her shoulder, the dark of the barrel focussed on me like an unblinking eye.

I try to speak, to say I am sorry it has come to this. To tell her that I love her. All my mouth does is ratchet up and down like a mechanical trap, biting at the air. The disease in me wants to spread and colonize fresh hosts, its implacable will drives me forward. I know that if I get close, I will bite and claw until the coral is within her, too.

No part of my body listens when I try to force my limbs to stop, to stay away from my daughter.

Abigail tightens her grip on the shotgun, her finger resting on the trigger. She raises the barrel slightly. I am nearer to her now, too near. The sight of Abigail and the dark gun barrel fills my world.

I love you, my little girl. I wish you could hear me and know that I am still here.

"I love you, Abigail, and I'm s—"

Lee Smart is an artist, designer and writer from Bedfordshire, UK. He spends his free time drawing monsters and mecha as well as writing horror and post-apoc-

calyptic fiction. His first short story collection, Stories from the Outer Dark: Vol 1, *can be found now on Amazon.*

Snack Money

Jay Bechtol

Silas moves behind the cabins, scanning the pines for the black squirrel with tufted ears. He is a loner, alive in his solitude. There is still a half an hour until the lady with nine fingers clangs the triangle, summoning the campers and the counselors for lunch. It's thirty minutes of freedom and Silas embraces the isolation. The distant laughing of the other children swinging on tires hung from trees, and the *chunk-chunk* of red dodgeballs on the deteriorating four-square asphalt is almost meditative.

They know there is safety in numbers.

A twig snaps behind him and his thoughts are interrupted by a thick hand, landing on his shoulder, preventing any further search for the elusive squirrel. Silas is spun, and the poorly assembled face of a much larger kid lowers toward him. Silas knows the boy, an ogre of a child with coarse strands of hair pushing through the skin of his upper lip and the stink of cigarettes on his breath. At only twelve years old.

"Money." The ogre growls, a confident smirk contorting his already muddled features. A simple business transaction. Because the camp store, open every afternoon before dinner and full of candy bars, popsicles, and Pringles, isn't free. This is the same demand the ogre has made to any number of campers when the counselors aren't looking. He's heard rumors that the loner may have more than just some spare change for snacks. The ogre is interested in some sustainable income.

Silas' eyes don't lower, his lips don't quiver. If the ogre knows anything of pity, he will see it in Silas' face. He doesn't.

The deep blue eyes of Silas burn through the bigger kid. Past the ogre's Neolithic forehead and simplistic demand. Silas can see it all. The kid's weaknesses, the injuries of the past, and the hurt still to come. Silas understands it all while the bigger kid shakes him. Seeking respect under the stench of inadequacy.

Silas' head tilts to the left imperceptibly. A thin smile finds its way to his mouth.

His voice is soft, "When you dream, what is that bird that chases you? Why does it become your father and rape you? Why do you wake up in a puddle every morning?" Silas grins with no kindness.

The ogre's hulking face retreats, his smirk becoming a more symmetrical O-shape. And the larger boy can feel tiny legs growing in his spine and bones crawling under his flesh. Climbing up his back and encircling his throat. Hair-like legs tightening and constricting. The ogre releases Silas and begins wheezing, struggling for breath. Thoughts of snack money dissolving with his strength. His hand grasps for something in his jeans. A small cylinder he works over the thick ridge of denim in his pocket only to have it drop onto the forest floor among the pine needles where it clinks metallically against a pinecone, indifferent to his need. He stumbles to his knees, thick hands keeping him from going face first. Gasps of air coming shallower and shallower. The noose of his own backbone growing tighter and tighter. The inhaler just out of his reach.

The toe of Silas' sneaker nudges the small metal cylinder a little further away, just a little. He turns and continues his stroll through the trees, his interest returning to the squirrel. The distant *chunk-chunk* of the red dodgeballs echoes from the far side of the cabins, as does the laughter of the children.

It won't be until after lunch that one of the counselors wanders behind the cabins and begins to scream.

Jay Bechtol likes to write, so he does. Recent stories are in Penumbric, Uncharted, and at Crystal Lake. His debut novel The Great American Coward *is available from Golden Storyline Books. He can be found on line at www. JayBechtol.com and on Twitter @BechtolJay. He can be found in person in Homer, Alaska.*

The Perfect Match

Madeline Mora-Summonte

I do not want her to get out.

The long, lonely road unfurls beneath my tires like a tongue that finds us distasteful, ready to spit us out. Yet, we are stuck here in the mouth of these woods like a broken tooth.

It is my fault. I am too old, too beaten down to carry us safely through so many wrong turns, through this isolated landscape, through this falling night. Too many things, too expensive to fix, are wrong with me. Fluids leak from me now, dripping onto the road like blood from a wound.

The pickup truck heading our way makes me uneasy.

We've been together a long time, she and I. I've heard her sing along to the radio, to mixed tapes. I've smelled the grease of cheap cheeseburgers, their wrappers staining me, giving me a taste. I've soaked up spilled diet soda and spilled tears. I've braced myself as she raged, fists thumping my dash.

She has gone gray, and I have gone rust. She sits heavier in my seat, my contours comforting if no longer supporting. She counts on me to replace reflexes with sturdiness, but we are both older, less dependable. We are dinosaurs, lumbering through these early years of the 1990s, fearful of the future yet unable to preserve the past. But extinction will come for me sooner than for her. I will not see another decade.

The truck slows, pulls up behind us. She watches in my rearview mirror. Headlights go dark. The engine cuts off. Two figures, swallowed by shadow and silence, sit in the front seat. They don't move.

She grips my steering wheel. Her heart pounds so hard it becomes a sound I can hear. She glances around. My windows are rolled up. My doors are locked.

The driver climbs down, calls something to the other. Their laughter is deep, male. He ambles toward us.

Keeping her eyes on him, she digs under the crumpled map for her purse. She pulls out the pepper spray, then slides it into her pocket. The second man exits the truck.

The driver raps on her window, bends down to look inside. Words are exchanged through my glass, pleasant and polite on the surface, violence and terror crouching below. The second man strolls along my passenger side, tugging on my door handles. I hold tight.

It happens so fast, too fast. Shattered glass slices me. Her screams fill me. My doors wrench like tearing muscle. She is dragged from me. Grunting. Crying. The stench of blood hits me like a punishment. I did not keep her safe.

Then one of the men hollers. The other shouts. Screaming, but not from her. Another smell, biting, sharp.

And then I see her. She is running. Down the road. Away.

The men are bent over, hands to their faces, eyes streaming. Bitch, they mutter. They lean against me, breathing hard, rough.

I watch her run.

The men pull out a flask, cigarettes.

I wish I could go with her.

A match glows, falls. It sets my blood on fire. I turn the night into day.

I am glad she got out.

Madeline Mora-Summonte is a writer, a reader, a beach-comber, and a tortoise-owner. Many of her creepy little tales prowl in print and lurk online. Visit

Ashes

Martin Aguilera

I think of her body in the dusty field—cold lifeless eyes staring up at the descending flakes with an empty gaze until enough of them stack up there and they turn to little mounds of powdery white nestled between the top ridge of her nose.

I try to think of her as she was in life but am forever haunted by her in death. Eventually, the time she's been gone will be more than all the time I knew her, loved her, or understood her. My restless conscience often keeps me awake, and 3 a.m. knows all my secrets.

We've been hiding out in this abandoned house for five weeks or so now. One of the few places we'd stumbled upon that had miraculously not been looted. Whoever lived here had had a child. There was a crib. I look in on our son, the only innocent in all of this, who has her raven hair and expressive eyes. There she will always be, looking back at me. I invoke her name. As a prayer, as regret. I do what I can to push her out of my mind. I pick him up from the crib and hold him close, to feel his tiny breath against my neck, his beating heart as he tugs the back of my hair with his small fingers. I move to the rocking chair in the corner of his dimly lit room and stare out of the window, hugging him tight. He is all that remains of her; the only thing I have now worth anything.

He can never know I killed her.

Weeks after the cataclysm, it continues to rain ash.

The air quality is pretty terrible.

Everything as we knew it has come to an end.

The machine stopped.

Chaos reigned.

It became evident early on we were on our own. There wasn't a lot of food left in the markets. We had to make do with what we could scavenge, and drive at night. We hid in empty houses or apartment buildings. Sometimes there would be attacks. We were civilized people. At first, we got hurt pretty bad. But then we began to fight back. Made makeshift weapons out of furniture, whatever we could find. We jokingly referred to each other as gladiators, but that was laughable. The only thing we had to protect was our boy.

Luck had us find two masks in the home of a former firefighter. We needed a third, for the baby. She and I kept sharing ours until it became impossible to do so. They had to be worn at all times. The baby had to have his.

I told her to go ahead with him, that I would stay behind. She insisted. Her body was tired, weak. The birth had not been easy. All she asked was that I stay by her side. We sat in the field under a cardboard box for several hours, ashes pouring down all around us. And I took off her mask, because she couldn't bring herself to do it, and talked to her, and watched as her breath became slower, slower, until it finally stopped. I stood outside the box with her and watched the ashes start to cover her. And then I grabbed the baby and we kept moving, moving. I could not bring myself to look back.

We're here, for now, in this house. But we will have to keep moving.

I wonder if her death was in vain. Should we have all just died together?

I hum to the baby.

I pray for the ashes to cease.

Martin Aguilera is a writer, filmmaker, and bibliophile residing in Los Angeles, California. He has been a contributor to the magazine Famous Monsters of Filmland *and been published in* The Brokeback Book: From Story to Cultural Phenomenon (*edited by William R. Handley) from the University of Nebraska Press. In March 2020, his horror story* "A Valentine for Timothy" *was included in the anthology* Nevada Necromance (*edited by Joe Moe*) *published by Black Bed Sheet Books. He wrote on the Netflix TV horror series* The Craving, *executive produced by Darren Aronofsky, and is currently developing his directorial debut.*

Nineteen Weeks

Theresa Derwin

It's my own damn fault...

I'd gained over a stone since he'd died and eaten my grief.

I was angry—at myself, the world, the fucking neighbour's cat.

Why didn't he tell me earlier?

I *loved* him.

He should've given me enough warning, so I'd be ready to lose him.

So much for the last Rolo on my pillow.

Nineteen weeks—*fuck*.

Nineteen weeks 'til Christmas and I didn't understand why I was here, at this damn 'fat club', as Dave used to call it.

I'd lost nearly two stone last year. A stone—mostly through stopping drinking—because I loved him; the second because I loved *me*.

I lost *him* in February. The weight gain started slowly, creeping up just like the cancer that killed him. One day I looked at myself and I was obese again.

I went back to fat club. Weekly weigh-ins and a food diary, a target.

It was nineteen weeks 'til Christmas, but I went back and thought holy crap, I have time to do something about it before I put on the glamorous NYE dress.

After my first weigh-in, riding the scooter now 'cause I'd gained so much, I started slowly back home. Then, right outside the cemetery, of all places, the damn thing ran out of juice.

The fucking cemetery.

I couldn't cope with this.

A black hole of grief and loss sucking me up.

If I even thought about him, how I loved him, the pain would rip me apart because I missed him so much. I didn't know how to handle this.

Staring at my dead scooter, wishing it were me that was dead instead of him, instead of my scooter.

From the corner of my eye, I caught a flicker. A beacon of vague hope in the consuming darkness.

A white light dancing in the autumn night.

In the graveyard.

I turned off the ignition, in the hope that there might be a little battery left, then turned it back on again.

Nothing.

No light on the dash, no groan as it attempted to start.

Shivering against the early onset of autumn, I dug into my handbag until I found my mobile.

I hit the screen—dead. Panic gripped me, fear, a snake constricting around my throat.

I wasn't scared of ghosts or zombies, the kind of things you feared when near a cemetery, alone, in the dark.

I was scared of much worse things, like being stranded.

There was no way I could walk the distance to the nearest house for help.

Loss expanded in my heart, amidst the fear. I needed Dave.

But he wasn't there, and I was alone.

I scanned the dark, looking for anyone in the deserted streets, but no such luck.

The brief light I'd seen earlier still flickered in the dark of the cemetery, creating shadows that danced over looming gravestones.

It had to be the groundskeeper still working late into the evening.

I pushed down that persistent ache that would engulf me if I thought of him too much, grabbed my bag, my foldable walking stick, and hobbled slowly towards the cemetery gates.

Pain shot up my hip, a stabbing sensation, nearly making my knees buckle.

I finally reached the source of the light, a small wooden cabin—or maybe a poor person's mausoleum...

And just like a horror movie reject, I knocked on the wooden door and called out, "*Hello.*"

"Argh!"

I spun 'round, teetering a bit with my walking stick, heart pounding in my ears. "Jesus Christ," I squealed, as a tall figure emerged.

"Sorry, did I scare ya?"

I could only nod.

The figure, now revealed by the light of a torch, was a man with medium salt-and-pepper hair and a cropped beard, wearing jeans and a t-shirt.

Sorrow consumed me as I took him in, for just one moment—I saw Dave.

But it wasn't him, just some random guy—in a *graveyard*.

"It's okay," he said, voice gruff but gentle, "I work here."

"Oh, thank God!" I sighed. "A handyman or something?"

"Or something," he said, grinning like a mischievous kid. I'd have been worried, but I got a good feeling from him.

"Broke down?" he asked, nodding to my scooter.

I grimaced, more embarrassed than anything, though my hips and back were really starting to hurt.

I leaned against the cabin, rifled in my bag for my meds.

"Hold on," he said, taking out an old key and unlocking the wooden door to the shed. "Sit in here a minute and catch your breath."

Shit. If I said no, I was rude. But I'd also be alive.

What were the odds he was a serial killer?

"It's okay," he said, "I'll bring a chair out here for you."

"Thanks," I whispered, suddenly very tired.

My bones ached in the crisp night air, my soul tired, empty.

Before I knew it, there were tears, then heaving great sobs as the guy pushed a rickety chair underneath me to help me sit.

Distantly, I could hear his soothing voice, repeating two words.

"It's okay. It's okay."

I don't know how long I cried, but a tissue was handed to me.

I looked up to say thank you, but he must've gone into the shed.

My thoughts were interrupted by a woman's voice from the main road.

"Hello luv, are you okay?"

I smiled at the elderly couple with their dog, paused by my abandoned scooter.

"I'm okay, thanks, this guy was just help—"

I glanced up to the cemetery, where a lone figure of a man walked into the distance, the light fading as he disappeared.

"He was jus—"

I let out a big sigh, and stood, grabbed my bag, and limped back to my scooter, the ignition light brightly lit in green.

A warm breeze tickled my ear and a hint of citrus wafted by me, just like his aftershave.

Suddenly I didn't feel so alone anymore.

Theresa Derwin writes horror. She has over sixty anthology acceptances and is in her final year MA Creative Writing. She's published four collections, edited over nine anthologies. Her forthcoming books include God's Vengeance from CLP. Her latest #WIHM anthology is as one of a quartet of #WIH; Daughters of Darkness from Black Angel Press. She is the 2019 HWA Mary Shelley Scholarship recipient.

Follow www.theresaderwin.co.uk

Twitter @BarbarellaFem

Cracked Pot

Armand Rosamilia

The sign was wrong in the office, but no one seemed to notice or care.

0 Accidents in 66 Days was a lie.

Denny knew, at some point, the cops were going to come. Look around. Ask a lot of questions. The old man at the gas station on the highway would see them coming. Know something was wrong at the Miller Kayak and Canoe Rentals. Know there'd been another accident, only this time it hadn't been an accident.

The young man was dead, and it was all because Uncle Joel couldn't stop the drinking and the anger that came along with it.

Two days, tops, Denny thought. He wasn't worried about the fuzz, who could be bought off with a carton of smokes, a cold half-dozen Ballantine beers, and a fifty slipped inside the grocery bag. They weren't the problem.

The old man, who folks called Oil Can because no one knew or cared what his real name was, had been a thorn in Denny's family's side forever.

Used to be word of mouth and the occasional lost tourist would find their campsite. Not that the cabins were livable. Hadn't been since Denny was old enough to work here during the summers. Nope. It was the kayaks and canoes and the danger of them.

Yankees wanted to get up, close and personal with a gator.

They wanted to drive back to New York City or Boston or somewhere awful where snow covered the ground all winter, bragging to their fellow northerners about messing with a southern gator and the hillbilly rednecks who gave it to them for a twenty.

Uncle Joel was sleeping one off behind the rental office in the hot metal chair that predated Denny, too. Everything on the property was older than Denny, who would be fifteen in a month.

If he didn't get a handle on the situation, Oil Can was going to make sure Denny spent his next birthday in juvie.

To save money, Denny's father left him for weeks at a time. He had cans of baked beans, tuna, and Campbell's soup. A loaf of bread and bottled water. Denny liked to read, so a stack of magazines, pulp paperbacks, and a few hard-cover books killed a few hours.

They only needed a hundred dollars a week in order to keep it going. A canoe-load might be twenty bucks. It might be thirty. It depended on the day of the month and how close they were to making ends meet. Denny had the ultimate power to set the prices, but he wasn't stupid. If it seemed like the dad wasn't going to spend so much, even though his cross-eyed kids and his bottle-blonde Jersey Girl wife wanted to, Denny would pull the poor sap off to the side and lower the price five or ten bucks, depending on his mood. It usually worked.

As long as Uncle Joel didn't make an appearance and want to chat up the wife with the big hair. He'd wash his face in the river using the cracked pot, the one he'd used to kill the last girl who didn't like his advances.

Denny sat and read, ignoring the mosquitoes until the sun was nearly gone behind the stunted swamp trees in the distance. That was his sign to drive the golf cart to the highway and put up the chains.

By the time he got to the road, he'd decided to take a ride. He'd been thinking about the old man at the gas station on and off all day. Business had been slower than usual, and Denny had the nagging feeling Oil Can had been telling the tourists stopping by about the missing tourists.

Denny parked on the side of the gas station so no one could see the cart from the road. He wasn't gonna do anything wrong, but if the cops decided it was time to look for the latest girl, he wanted to be questioned in the comfort of the campsite and not with Oil Can's big ears working.

Oil Can met Denny outside, closing the door behind him. The two stared at one another. There was no love between them, although Denny knew the old man took the payoffs to supposedly shut his mouth and push tourists in their direction.

A quick shake of his head and then Oil Can was walking quickly toward his pickup truck, turning his back to Denny.

That was rude.

Denny must've unconsciously known what was going to happen, because he had the cracked pot in hand. Had Uncle Joel given it to him? No. Uncle Joel was dead. Had been dead for months.

What about father? He'd run off. Hadn't he?

Oil Can went down just as he got to his truck. Before he could rise again, Denny clubbed the old man. Dragged his body to the cart, covered him with the tarp, and drove back to the campsite.

If the police didn't show, looking for the missing girl, right away, Denny had time to toss Oil Can into the river and feed the gators one more time.

He'd go back to the gas station after midnight and load up on cans of beans, tuna, and get a loaf of bread. A couple of cases of Ballantine beer and as many cartons of Lucky's as he could fit on the golf cart.

Then, after breakfast, he'd see if he could wash the hair and blood off the cracked pot.

Armand Rosamilia is a New Jersey boy currently living in sunny Florida, where he writes when he's not sleeping. He's happily married to a woman who helps his career and is supportive, which is all he ever wanted in life...

He's written over 200 stories that are currently available, including crime thrillers, supernatural thrillers, horror, zombies, contemporary fiction, non-fiction and more. His goal is to write a good story and not worry about genre labels.

He also loves to talk in third person... because he's really that cool. Maybe.

You can find him at https://armandrosamilia.com for all of his information as well as random things he enjoys.

Diversion

RJ Meldrum

Initially, my journey had gone to plan. It wasn't until I was instructed by the GPS to turn off the highway onto a narrow country road that the problems started. Just as my tires crunched onto the dirt road, the clouds, threatening all day, finally released their snow. I checked the GPS and saw I had about fifty miles to go. I decided I could make it, as long as the snow didn't get worse.

It got worse.

I found myself crawling along at about ten miles an hour. The snow was settling, and the going was slippery. I had neglected to put on my winter tires and could feel the car losing traction and sliding dangerously towards the ditch. I slowed to a crawl, worried I might lose control. The wind buffeted my car, making the going even more unsteady. It didn't take me long to notice my GPS had malfunctioned, it was showing I was still on the highway. My cell phone had no bars. I realized I had no idea where I was going. The road was too narrow to turn round. I decided to keep going, to try to find a house where I could ask for directions.

"Why the hell didn't he just agree to meet me at the office?"

I already knew the answer; rich clients expected their architects to come to them, not the other way round. I had to drive out of the city to meet my newest potential customer at his country estate. He didn't care if it was February or if snow was forecast; the planning meeting was scheduled for today. If I refused to attend, well, there were plenty of other eager, young architects happy to step into my shoes.

The road started to incline. I floored the accelerator to keep my momentum up. My car wasn't four-wheel drive. I reached the top, just.

As I crested the hill, there was a four-way stop. There was a police cruiser parked up and a cop standing beside it, wearing a high-visibility jacket. I lowered my window, feeling the biting cold of the wind for the first time.

"Is there a problem?"

"The road is closed. Please turn left and follow the diversion."

His voice was strangely flat. I guessed he was bored.

"Thank you!"

There was no response.

I turned left and headed down the hill. A sign told me a place called the Witch's Gorge was two miles away. As I drove, an idea dawned on me. I nearly slapped myself. I should have asked the cop where I was and how to get to my destination. Luckily, this road was a bit wider, so I could turn the car round, albeit with some difficulty, and head back up the hill. As I arrived at the top, I saw him still standing by the police cruiser.

"Do you know how to get to the Croxley house from here?"

"The road is closed. Please turn left and follow the diversion."

"I know, you just told me. I just want some directions. I'm lost."

"The road is closed. Please turn left and follow the diversion."

"You just said that. Are you okay?"

I got out of my car, thinking he was suffering from hypothermia or something. As I got closer, I realized something was definitely wrong. The figure was lumpy and misshapen. Instinctively, I put my hand out. My hand encountered something that felt like straw. I used my cell phone to illuminate the face. A pair of very human eyes stared out at me from a mass of dried grass, topped by a police officer's cap. The eyes were alive, full of pain and despair.

"The road is closed. Please turn left and follow the diversion."

There was no mouth.

The next few moments were a blur. I vaguely remember running through the snow, jumping into my car and hitting the accelerator. The next memory was reaching the highway. I made it home in record time. I never did get to meet my rich client.

No-one believed me. I wasn't sure I believed it myself. It took a few days for the news to emerge, but then it hit all the main outlets. Five abandoned cars, including a police cruiser, had been found near the Witch's Gorge, stuck in deep snow. There was no sign of the occupants. The assumption was they'd left their vehicles and wandered off into the snowy wilderness. The authorities termed the search a 'recovery operation', meaning they were looking for bodies. I suspected they wouldn't be found, and I was right.

The road hadn't really been closed. Something had set up the terrifying straw effigy, something that was smart enough to understand the prey it sought. Something had taken the eyes and the vocal cords from one of the victims and crafted a facsimile; something that was close enough to pass for a cop. Something that could fool us. The victims were sent down towards the gorge, and God alone knows what happened to them then.

I was grateful I'd escaped, but it was pure, unadulterated luck. What still keeps me from sleeping is the sure and certain knowledge that whatever killed those folks is, without a doubt, still out there.

RJ Meldrum has been published by Culture Cult Press, Trembling with Fear, Black Hare Press, Smoking Pen Press, Breaking Rules Press, and James Ward Kirk. He's had stories in The Sirens Call eZine, The Horror Zine, and Drabblez Magazine. His novella, The Plague, *was published by Demain Press in 2019.*

Facebook: richard.meldrum.79

Red

Liam Hogan

She's not hard to follow; a splash of red as vibrant as freshly spilled blood, glimpsed between the dark trunks of wind-tortured trees. I keep my distance at first, not wanting to spook my quarry until we're well away from prying eyes. I expect her to stick to the path, the straightest and shortest way through the woods. The neck of the bottle with the town on one side and a smaller hamlet on the other, on the borders of which lives her grandmother, a crone with sharp eyes and a sharper tongue. I already have my spot picked, a kink, as the path skirts a mossy boulder, out of sight from other travelers.

But no, the girl flits between pools of dappled sunlight, wandering deeper and deeper into the woods, oblivious to its dangers, to its dark secrets. She is evidently in no hurry with her burden, the wicker basket with its cloth cover. She travels this way as regular as clockwork, carrying the same basket, to the same destination. I've been close enough before to get a waft of recently baked bread, or the sweet smell of caramelised sugar from a fruit pie.

Not that these treats would be anything but appetisers for what I'm *really* seeking. And more likely a cold dessert after the deed is done. Tempting though the package is, I've been biding my time. It is important to be prudent so close to my doorstep. Yet today she has strayed a long way from the path and even if the wood is searched, what will they ever find?

I close the gap. But each time I do, I catch a glimpse of that red hood, that red cloak, in a direction I did not think she had gone. She's quicker on her feet than I imagined, and even my sense of direction is put to the test as I follow her twists and turns.

I'm vaguely aware that there is something else in the woods. Something hovering on the fringes, too distant to be entirely sure they even exist...

But I'm not afraid. Why would *I* be afraid? Afraid of the stories the old women tell, my own grandmother included? Until that day she took a long, hard look at me and shook her head. "No more tales," she said. "No more."

She never spoke another word to me, despite my mother's, her daughter's, pleading. I was glad when the old witch passed. My mother followed a year later, her rheumy gaze taking on the same steely darkness, as if they had both looked deep into my soul and found it wanting.

But that was over a decade ago. I'm a grown man now, an important figure in the town and respected as such. A woodsman, skilled with the axe, the axe I carry with me today. Because what could be more natural than a woodsman in the woods with his axe?

The threat of an axe to keep them still and quiet as I go about my work. The promise made good to make sure they never talk of it, after.

The sun must be dipping towards the horizon and the unfrequented wood is too dense to let the evening light filter in. A fire risk is what it is. The undergrowth and brambles start to pick at my jacket, at my exposed arms, at my legs. Another flash of red, closer now and about time, this game has gone on quite long enough. I abandon any thought of stealth, crash through the saplings and the ivy, hoping the sudden noise will freeze my prey and not spoil the delicious surprise.

With a final curse as a tangle of blackberry vines whip their thorns against my legs, I half-burst, half-tumble into the clearing, panting as I see the red I've been following, doubled.

Two cloaks, two hoods, both as red as the other. Two hands carrying short knives, the open basket abandoned on the mossy ground.

I grip my axe tight, what witchcraft is this?

The hoods lower. There is the girl I've been chasing, the one people say was born in these woods, the one who never smiles. I realise she's older than she looks. No puppy fat, up close her cheekbones are sharp, almost gaunt, almost feral.

217

And *there* is her grandmother, the one with the wicked tongue, the one who turned my own relatives against me.

Two birds with one stone, then. A deal I'm more than happy to accept. I waggle my axe at them, but they don't look worried and the girl who never smiles takes the time to do exactly that, revealing teeth shaped not like the rounded gravestones that surround the chapel but like fangs, yellow, and long, and pointed.

The axe is my friend, my companion, my accomplice. I grin defiantly back. If this is a trap, an ambush, then they should have brought more than just a young woman and an old crone.

Their smiles linger, but they're not staring at me. They're staring over my shoulder.

I feel the warm breath on my neck even before I gag on the fetid smell, the cloying odour of rotten meat.

My axe is fast.

The wolf is faster.

Liam Hogan is an award winning short story writer, with stories in Best of British Science Fiction and Best of British Fantasy (NewCon Press). He's been published by Analog, Daily Science Fiction, and Flame Tree Press. He helps host Liars' League London, volunteers at creative writing charity Ministry of Stories, and lives and avoids work in London. More details at http://happyendingnotguaranteed.blogspot.co.uk.

Lure

Catherine McCarthy

"Catch anything?" the fisherman asks. He's packed up. Given up. Off home. Tacklebox heavy as his disappointment.

You suppress a grin. "Take a look," you say. He squats low, green waders to match his jealousy, but you get a bite and you're on your feet. By the time you turn around, he's gone. Couldn't stomach your success.

What have you snagged? It's not a fish, but a tail fin. A predator's leftovers, spat out. But on close inspection, you realize it's not a tail at all, but the tail end of a crank-bait lure. Mud-caked. It's been sitting on the bottom since god knows when. You rinse off the mud, and for a moment, imagine it flicking between your fingers, trying to escape.

A whole decade has passed since you last camped at this ancient lake. Couldn't face it; not after what you did.

Secret. Birthed by a glacier twenty thousand years ago. The mountain wraps her arms around the lake, possessively. Eight acres of amniotic fluid, warm and writhing, and she won't let go.

You crawl out of the bivouac to take a piss. Early start. Carp float rod, centrepin reel, baited with a single grain of corn.

Sometimes that's all it takes—one little nibble, and she's yours.

Your prize slips into the net: a pristine wild carp. Lateral scales in copper-gold, translucent tail fin forked like the devil's tongue. Her lower lip pouts, sulking.

"I won't hurt you," you say. "Not if you don't struggle." You prod about inside her mouth, and all the time her saffron eye judges you.

Sweet tiger nut and smaller hook. A handful of loose feed adds to the temptation: halibut pellets and hemp. You could use a spliff yourself, so you roll a quick one and wait for the hit.

That's better. You sense the bite, and reel it in, judging the struggle at the tip of your rod. Muscles ripple beneath the water, and she breaks through the surface. But it's not a fish. Two inches in length, no bigger than your thumb, it's the mid-section of the lure you found yesterday. Unbelievable! Where the hell did you put the tail section? Can't remember. Haven't a clue. You won't rest until it's found. You're a man possessed. Obsessed. Why? You've plenty of lures, in all shapes and sizes. Ah...but not like this.

And then you remember. Your gilet pocket.

You reunite the sections, hook to hole.

Now all you want is the head of that lure.

But the bites keep coming: carp, bream, gudgeon. Time after time you're disappointed. You know it's crazy because it's just a fucking lure, for Christ's sake!

So many sheep on this mountain. They're laughing at you. Shitting pellets everywhere. Some of the brazen ones come close—stare you in the eye before bleating a snigger and wandering off with shit stains dangling from their arse.

You blow on your fingers for luck. A moment of anticipation, but your heart sinks because it's just another gudgeon. You pick up a stone and bash its head in with one swift thud. Its eye is a leaky mess that slides down its face and your stomach churns with guilt.

What have you done?

What happened with the girl ruined you for a proper relationship. Couldn't forgive yourself. It was fucking good, though. Still has the ability to make you hard. But the shame afterwards. My God! The way you rammed your fist in her mouth to stifle her screams and worse. Much worse.

Sling the carcass in the water. Hide the evidence. But it's then you feel the lump—in the fish's guts—something hard.

One long incision, anus to throat. Entrails spew out, claggy, slick...and something else. A fish inside a fish, or the top third at least. Your prize slips from the gudgeon's insides like a birth. A freak of nature because fish don't do that, dickhead! Thank god you carry wire and spare hooks in your tackle box because now that you have all three sections, you're desperate to try it out.

Someone's watching. It's a girl. She's a couple of hundred yards away, dressed in pale blue just like *she* was. Hair dripping, clinging to her shoulders. Bile rises in your throat. It can't be! She'd not be that age now, prick!

One blink and she's gone.

Focus! The line snags, and instead of going with it you pull up sharp, grabbing it as it feeds through the reel, splicing your palm. But you won't let go. You're not going to lose this lure.

Snap! And the rod's in half.

In you go, thigh deep, cursing the air blue as you fumble among reeds and weeds.

Inch by inch, you feel your way down the line. It's caught between two rocks. There's the eye. You expect it to blink as you run your fingertip over it—a reflex. As you jerk it free you slip and in you go, headfirst, gulping great mouthfuls of water.

Then, relief! She's in the palm of your hand.

It's as you straighten again that you see it. Out of the mist it comes, icy breath stagnant, putrid. The stench makes you gag. It floats towards you and you grip the lure tight because you won't give it up, no matter what. Fight to the death if need be.

Its tentacles suck you in. Transparent on top, so that you can see its innards and even how it thinks. Electric cogs pulse and glow in a rippling pattern.

Then it grins, and an electric shock travels shoulder to fingertip, forcing your palm open.

And the lure slips from your grasp and into the welcoming arms of its mother.

You're sinking now, like a scrap of meat, bleached of all colour. Water fills your lungs and you can't even fight.

The last thing you see is the face of the lure. Pale blue, iridescent, in the prime of its life.

Safe in mother's arms.

Catherine McCarthy weaves dark tales on an ancient loom from her farmhouse in West Wales. Her published novellas and novels include Immortelle, Mosaic, A Moonlit Path of Madness, *and* The Wolf and the Favour. *Her short fiction has been published in various anthologies and magazines, including those by Black Spot Books, Nosetouch Press, and Dark Matter Ink. In 2020 she won the Aberystwyth University Prize for her short fiction. Time away from the loom is spent hiking the Welsh coast path or huddled in an ancient graveyard reading Dylan Thomas or Poe. Find her at https://www.catherine-mccarthy-author.com/ or at https://twitter.com/serialsemantic.*

A Bright New Future

Philip Harris

Eva tried to ignore Mr. Jackson's eyes, but she was drawn to them. She couldn't even say why. They were pale, yes, but not the palest she'd ever seen. They also seemed to be permanently narrowed but that wasn't it, either. They were just...hungry.

Mr. Jackson cleared his throat. "As we discussed on the telephone, Mr. and Mrs. Lambert, Douglas is a bright, independent boy who deserves a safe and stable home. A fresh start if you will." He picked up a tablet from his desk. "I understand you're an electrical engineer, Mr. Lambert?"

"Please, call me Henry. Erm, yes. I'm a partner in a small electrical installation company. Mostly commercial work."

"Good, good."

"I—I can get you access to our financial information if that would help?"

"Oh no, that won't be necessary." Mr. Jackson smiled, and Eva suppressed a shudder as his eyes squeezed even tighter. "I just like to get to know our applicants a little. What about you, Mrs. Lambert? How do you while away the hours?"

Eva reached for the glass of water sitting on the desk and took a sip, mostly to avoid those eyes.

"I'm, well, I'm *hoping* to go back to nursing."

"Excellent, excellent. A worthy calling."

Mr. Jackson swiped across the tablet a couple of times, nodding. Then he placed it back on the desk and steepled his fingers together in front of his chin as though he was praying.

"Well, I'm pleased to say that our background checks and psychological profiles have all been very positive. In fact, we feel that you are *ideal* candidates, and that Douglas would be very happy."

A broad smile broke across Henry's face. He took Eva's hand and she smiled slightly.

"That's fantastic, Mr. Jackson," Henry said. "We couldn't be more excited, could we, honey?"

Eva hesitated, then shook her head.

"Good, good," Mr. Jackson said.

He paused, seemingly considering his words.

"I do like to check one last time, though. This is a significant commitment, and it can create a great deal of upheaval. We're committed to giving you and Douglas all the support possible, but ultimately, you need to be sure, and I mean *completely* sure, that this is the right choice. For both of you."

Henry straightened up in his chair. "Oh, absolutely, no doubt about it." He paused, frowning, then tilted his head and gave Mr. Jackson an earnest look. "We've been missing something, you know? From our lives."

Mr. Jackson nodded slowly. "I hear that *so* often. What about you, Mrs. Lambert?"

Eva looked up. Those narrowed eyes drilled into her as though he was trying to extract her thoughts. Or maybe her soul.

Henry gently squeezed her hand. "She feels the same way, don't you, honey?"

Eva forced a smile, but when she spoke her voice came out too soft. "Yes." She took another sip of water, then tried again. "Yes. I do," she said, and this time she almost sounded confident.

Mr. Jackson held her gaze, and she had to fight not to look away. He seemed about to challenge her response, but he just smiled.

"Excellent, excellent. In that case, there's just the matter of the fees."

"Oh, right," Henry said, "Of course." He dug around for his credit card, then handed it across the desk.

"Thank you," Mr. Jackson said. He wrinkled his nose and waved the credit card. "I apologize for this. It feels so inappropriate to bring commerce into what should be a joyous occasion."

"No, not at all, I understand."

Mr. Jackson tapped the credit card on the tablet, squinted at the screen for a few seconds, then handed the card back to Henry.

"Thank you. Now, let's get Douglas on his way to a bright new future, shall we?"

He stood and led them out into the waiting room.

Douglas was sitting on his hands, swinging his legs back and forth.

"Ah, there's the gentleman in question," Mr. Jackson said. "Excellent, excellent." He gestured to Henry and Eva. "If there's anything you'd like to say?"

Eva started toward Douglas, but Henry grabbed her arm. She looked back at him and he gave a slight shake of his head. She held his gaze for a moment, then looked away.

"No, it's okay," Henry said.

Mr. Jackson nodded. "I understand. It can be difficult." He offered a hand to Douglas. "If you'd come with me, young man."

After a few seconds, Douglas slipped off the chair. Tentatively, he took the man's hand.

Eva tried to move forward, but Henry was still holding her arm and he kept her in place.

Mr. Jackson led Douglas to a door at the back of the room.

As they stepped through it, Douglas turned around. "Mama?"

Eva closed her eyes.

The door clicked shut.

Mr. Jackson led Douglas down a dimly lit corridor lined with doors. Each one had a plastic nameplate attached to it. *Jeffrey Chacon. Delia Remington. Sarah Read. Christopher Fried.*

Mr. Jackson stopped in front of one of the doors and pushed it open. "Here we are."

Douglas stared at the nameplate beside the door. *Douglas Lambert.*

"Well, go on in then."

Mr. Jackson nudged Douglas through the door and into a short hallway. He leaned down until his face was just a few inches away from Douglas.

"Welcome to your new home."

Then he whirled around and walked back into the corridor.

Douglas watched the door swing closed, vision blurring.

He walked slowly down the hallway, past doors to a living room, a kitchen, a dining room. The brightly lit rooms looked almost identical. Pure white walls, a handful of pieces of furniture, no personality. There was a staircase at the end of the hall. Douglas stood on the bottom step and peered up. More bright lights. More white walls.

"Hello?" he called. "Is anyone there?"

The words echoed around him.

No one replied.

Philip Harris was born in England but now lives in Canada, where he works for a large video game developer. Not content with creating imaginary worlds for a living, he spends his spare time indulging his love of writing. His published books include the Serial Killer Z series, the Leah King Trilogy, and an homage to the old pulp science fiction serials—Glitch Mitchell and the Unseen Planet. *His short fiction has appeared in numerous anthologies and magazines including* The Jurassic Chronicles, Tales from the Canyons of the Damned, Bones, Uncommon Minds, The Anthology of European SF, *and* Peeping Tom.

He has also worked as security for Darth Vader.

You can find more details of his work and his blog at http://www.solitarymin dset.com.

Prior to Slaughter

AJ Franks

They'd arrived like dogs signaled by Galton's whistle, infiltrating the city in numbers too great to count, with masks and stark white uniforms concealing their identities. Not military. Too professional, too coordinated for a militia. Havana had nicknamed them attendants.

Was it always the same one making deliveries? Did they smile beneath their facemasks as they left her food and supplies outside, then vanished? She imagined their features as she stepped on the scale.

She didn't recognize herself in the bathroom mirror. Her once glittery green eyes now appeared the dull hue of depression glass. Her sunrise-red hair resembled more of a pale moon, and her skin was now pasty and stretched around her frame. And her weight ...

The scale's numbers flashed, then registered. As if to mock the current circumstances, the number 251 revealed itself. Coincidentally, it was the same number of days she'd been in quarantine.

Quarantine: That's how the paper packet the attendants supplied referred to the situation. For days, it had been her sole source of information surrounding lockdown against the virus. Her phone, her electronics—all forms of communication had gone dark prior to their arrival.

The message in the packet was clear: stay inside or be killed. There wasn't a second option. All necessities—food, medication, supplies—would be delivered. They had all the information they needed on her, and without fail, each morning after a tap at the door, she opened it to find a daily delivery, a care package.

Around week three her television turned on by itself, nearly causing her a heart attack. There was only one working channel, and as terrifying as the on-screen footage was—coverage of midwestern and southern states where courageous country folk fought, but failed, to protect their freedom—the screams, gunfire and bomb blasts were the only company she had. It wasn't long before she concluded the broadcast was not meant to provide updates but to be a deterrent.

And so, the Cardinal Rules of stay in or die was one Havana abided, along with the other instructions in the packet: Finish all your food if you want to eat the next day; report your weight each morning. (A scale will be provided to you.) Shower daily. (She found they never inspected for this one.) She assumed they mandated the rules to help control the spread of the pathogen.

A knock at the door made her yelp and pull her purple cotton robe tight as she stepped from the scale. *They've never come twice in one day,* she thought, heading to the door, pressing her eye against the peephole.

"Havana Green," the gruff voice behind the mask carried through the barrier, "open the door."

The frame creaked as she turned the knob. "I'm Havana." She felt stupid as the words crawled across her tongue. They knew who she was.

"Come with me," the attendant said.

"But where—"

He pushed past her into the apartment. Her mouth barely formed a scream when a needle pierced the soft skin on her neck. The world turned black.

· · · · ● · ● · ● · · ·

She woke to find herself in the rear of a moving, covered truck, longer than any semi she'd seen. A pudgy, balding man across from her blinked as she came to.

"You okay?" he asked.

Her eyes widened, and she straightened. *I've lost it,* she thought. *That can't be him.* She forced the words. "You're the—"

The man chuckled and lowered his empty gaze.

"You're him. I recognize—"

His eyes narrowed. "No."

Havana tried to clear her head of whatever drug they'd given her. He was about seventy-five pounds heavier, not as rosy-cheeked, but it was him. "You are!"

His jaw set. "Not anymore."

The brain fog wouldn't clear. She looked around. "But I don't understand." The truck contained dozens of overweight people. All were silent but for a few in the middle whose whispers she couldn't understand. "Where are we going? Are you part of this?"

He lifted his chained wrists. "I'm no more a part of it than you."

Squinting, her eyes brought him into focus. "But you must know something. You're the—"

"I'm not the fucking president!" The man's eyes filled with pain as faces turned toward them. "Not anymore."

Havana rubbed her throbbing head. "Where are we going? We'll catch the virus!"

The man laughed, his tone hollow. "We are the virus."

"What?"

He sighed. "Humans. We're the disease. And they've found a way to eradicate us."

"Who?" Beads of sweat coated her clammy forehead.

"The Aboves."

"Who are the—"

He shook his head. "Not who. *What.* They're higher beings." He spoke as if he'd long been privy to the information.

"Higher beings?" Havana pressed. "Like God?"

"Not God," he held her gaze. "Godlike, maybe, but..."

"What do they want?"

The truck's bed vibrated as he shouted. "A snack! A goddamn snack!" Tears filled his vision. "And we're it." An attendant stood at the back of the truck, and the man's rant continued. "They've seen how terrible we are to each other. This is their solution." The attendant raced toward them. "What did you think was happening? Quarantine. Mandatory meals." His rushed words were difficult to understand. "We're nothing but fattened up cattle!" The attendant's backhand struck his face, followed by a quick injection to the neck. The man, perhaps the most powerful in the world, fell limp as the truck stopped.

Attendants prodded the captives out the back, and Havana looked for an escape, growing hopeless. She couldn't run, not in her physical condition. She crawled from the truck and followed the others into a warehouse.

Wait a minute. Recognition clicked. *This* is *the airport!* The insides were gutted and emptied. *Or it used to be. Now, it's just a—*

The smell hit her before the sight. Bodies, rows of them, hung from the ceiling, stripped of flesh, dripping blood into metal tubs beneath. She stumbled back and bumped into an attendant.

"Welcome to the slaughterhouse," he said.

AJ Franks is the author of more than thirty short stories and The Chilling Tales series. His debut horror collection, Keep You Cold: Chilling Tales, *was a multi-category finalist in the American Book Fest 2019 Best Book Awards. The follow-up collection,* Colder in Hell: More Chilling Tales *is now available. Franks' debut novella* The Boy with the Spider Face *was published by Crystal Lake Publishing.*

The Riverfront

Jay Bechtol

She pulls the worn scrapbook from the shelf like she does every year at this time. She sets it on the table and clutches her small leather satchel closer to her body. A comforting rattle comes from inside, like dozens of small marbles rustling together. The scrapbook cover has faded from a once royal blue to an indifferent grey. She flips it open to the first page and stares at the yellowed newspaper clippings.

The Spokesman-Review
Wednesday, August 28, 1985

Staff Reporter Dave Neill—Long-time local favorite, The Riverfront Drive-In is slated to close after its final show next Monday, Labor Day, the unofficial end of summer. Joan Harper, current owner and daughter of The Riverfront founder Carl Harper, cited reduced attendance, increased multiplexes, and cable television as competition. Ms. Harper and her eleven-year-old daughter, Ellen, have lived on-site at the seventeen-acre theatre that sits near the Old Flour Mill and the banks of the Spokane River.

"It's not just work," Joan Harper stated, "It's been home for as long as I can remember."

Over the past five years, The Riverfront has only been open on the weekends in the summer, showing second-run movies, classic fare, and teen slasher films on Friday nights.

The Riverfront opened in the summer of ...

She flips over a page.

The Spokesman-Review
Tuesday, September 3rd, 1985

Staff Reporter Sydne Phelps—The sixth local teen has been reported missing in as many weeks. Mike Shortell, preparing for his senior year at North Central High, was last seen by his parents Friday morning before heading to N.C. High for registration and a day ...

Flip.

She runs her finger along the edge of the green flyer, the top torn where staples had once held it to a telephone pole. The smiling picture of a teenage girl stares back. The green flyer identifies the girl as Heather Lynch. Seven digits underneath call out, desperate for information on Heather's whereabouts. She wonders if she dialed the number today who might answer.

Flip, flip.

The Spokesman-Review
Saturday, September 7th, 1985

Staff Reporter Sydne Phelps—A city on edge grows quieter. The number of missing youth in Spokane now stands at eight. Two new cases were identified this week. A citywide curfew is set to go into effect even as students are heading back to school for the fall. The police are concerned that there seems to be no connection between the cases as the youth all attended different high schools. Chief Bryan Daniels is asking for cooperation from families and the school district in enforcing this curfew ...

Flip.

Flip, flip, flip.

Memo: Sept. 10, 1985

To: All District Principals

From: Superintendent Michaels

Re: City-Wide Curfew

Effective immediately all after-school activities are canceled. This includes high school sports, clubs, social activities, and any other extra-curricular event.

Additionally, please ensure your counselors have access to the Grief and Loss pamphlets being distributed later this week. Do not ...

Flip.

She smiles thinly at the faded newsprint. A full-page ad in the local paper. A thank you letter from her mother to the City of Spokane for being such a great host to The Riverfront Drive-In for so many years. Her mother closed the letter with the sentence: Our thoughts are with the missing children.

Flip.

The Spokesman-Review
Friday, November 1ˢᵗ, 1985

Staff Reporter Doug Bywaters—Local businesswoman, Joan Harper, has been charged with the gruesome murders of twelve Spokane area teens. After weeks of searching, false leads, and dead ends, the Spokane Police Department uncovered the bodies hidden in the projector room of the shuttered Riverfront Drive-In. The discovery was made ...

Flip.

She uses her thumb to wipe some dust from the plastic sealing the newspaper photograph. The picture is of her mother, from some time in the seventies if the hairstyle is any indication. The headline above Joan Harper's face screams: Convicted!

Lower on the page is another photograph. In this one, an eleven-year-old girl sits alone on a bench in the courthouse. A leather satchel clutched close to her side. Tears evident, even through the grainy black and white photography. The caption below reads: Convicted murderer Joan Harper's daughter is distraught at the news. Attorneys and child advocates are hopeful Ellen Harper can overcome the ordeal.

Flip.

Page 76, *The Drive-In Murders*, Simon & Schuster, 1991. By Doug Bywaters

...kids were enticed by newspaper advertisements from earlier in the summer offering free admission to anyone "riding solo."

...Rows F, G, and H, the final three rows at the Riverfront, still had the old-fashioned speakers. Row F, speaker thirteen, had been specially outfitted to slowly fill the car with odorless propane ...

Flip, flip.

Page 206, *The Drive-In Murders*, Simon & Schuster, 1991. By Doug Bywaters

...Officer Cox kicked the door in. At first, as he recounted, "I couldn't see anything, just a dark, empty room. But when I clicked on the flashlight, there they were. Hanging upside down against the back wall. Twelve bodies strung up by their feet."

Officer Cox ran from the room and began vomiting. He refused to re-enter, and it wouldn't be until the coroner arrived when it was discovered that the bodies had been disemboweled and several teeth removed.

Flip.

The Spokesman-Review
Classifieds, Friday, August 6th, 1999

"Haunted" Drive-In for Sale! Seventeen Acres of Developable Real Estate!

She closes the scrapbook gingerly, as if not to disturb what sleeps there. The time may be right, she thinks. Time passes, people forget. People need to forget. Thirty-five years is plenty of time. And this summer, well this summer everyone else has so many other things on their minds. An evening at a drive-in might be just what people want. Safely distanced in their cars, desperate to get out of their homes for any reason.

Maybe the time is right. She gives her leather satchel a shake, the objects inside rattle together like marbles. Or teeth.

And she smiles.

Jay Bechtol *likes to write, so he does. Recent stories are in Penumbric, Uncharted, and at Crystal Lake. His debut novel* The Great American Coward *is available from Golden Storyline Books. He can be found on line at www.JayBechtol.com and on Twitter @BechtolJay. He can be found in person in Homer, Alaska.*

Sisters of Loss

Mark Allan Gunnells

Sandra and I have been friends since kindergarten. Back then we used to have tea parties with our stuffed animals and dollies, or pretend we were princesses waiting for our princes to ride up on white horses and take us away. By the time we were in middle school, we were calling one another "sister" because we felt closer than any blood relation.

We always asked for the same gifts for Christmas, but since my family had considerably less money than hers, that meant she kept her requests much more reasonable than need be. If her parents surprised her with something extravagant, she would refuse to play with it or even break it on purpose just so we would stay on even ground.

Sandra was always smarter than me, and in our senior year she got into Northwestern University. She chose not to go because the only school I'd been accepted to was a small college the next town over. We went together, took teaching jobs at the same elementary school after graduation. We were so close we earned the collective nickname "the Siamese Sisters" since we seemed to be conjoined.

We even got married within the same year, Sandra in early April to Bob and me mid-October to Frank. I found out shortly thereafter that I couldn't have children, and Sandra made the choice not to have any herself. She didn't want to take the journey of motherhood if I couldn't take the same journey.

I recognized just how much Sandra sacrificed for me, so that we could be together and that our lives would stay on the same path. It was incredibly selfless of her, but she didn't seem to see it that way. She said it was just what sisters did for one another. They shared everything, both the joy and the pain. I repeatedly vowed to repay her someday though she said it wasn't necessary.

And then Sandra's husband died a month ago. I have tried to be there for her, to comfort her, but for the first time in our lives, she has pulled away from me, withdrawing into her own sense of grief and loss. That grief built a wall between us I couldn't seem to breach, and it was lonely on my side of that wall all alone.

I have come to realize that the reason I can't help Sandra through this is because for the first time since we met, there is something we can't share. I can sympathize but I can't really understand the loss she feels because it is a pain I've never actually experienced. The only way I can comfort her is to turn my sympathy into actual understanding.

It's a sacrifice, I realize, but after all Sandra has sacrificed for me, it's the least I can do. And that's why I've tied you to the bed, Frank, and that's why I have this knife. I want you to understand why I'm doing this. It's nothing personal against you, but Sandra is my sister and I have to do this for her. Once you are gone, I'll be able to share her loss.

And sisters share everything.

Mark Allan Gunnells loves to tell stories. He has since he was a kid, penning one-page tales that were Twilight Zone knockoffs. He likes to think he has gotten a little better since then. He loves reader feedback, and above all he loves telling stories.

Not Your Average Monster

Kenneth W. Cain

I am man. A monster. Everyone says so—social media, TV, my family. This is what I tell myself while I get ready for work. I only see an innocent man staring back from the mirror. But I know the truth; there's a monster inside all right.

This flesh is just a coat. A disguise. Part of a charade to hide what I really am. That's why I cut it away. It came easier than I thought it would. A snip here, a tug there, my costume falling to the tiled floor. Already I see it, that monster everyone's been telling me about for so long now. Its bony grin, laughing at me for taking so long to discover its hiding place. Those thin meaty lips curled back in a wicked snarl, so full of anger and hatred. Eyes wide, the monster sees me, too; it identifies with me.

As if I would ever kill or maim or hurt anyone. I'm more like a deer, gracefully moving through a wooded expanse, pausing when startled, just trying to survive. I've never attacked anyone, save for twisting my antlers about in defense now and then. But that's only an instinctual reaction. Once, I even let someone beat me until I could no longer feel the blows. I'm tough like that, able to take abuse and get on with my life. A person in my shoes has to learn how to do that.

The monster, on the other hand, relishes in that pain. It wallows in my sorrow, content with my depression. And I am unhappy most of the time. I struggle to see how anyone can be truly content in this life. Worse yet, the monster's glad I'm like this after all these years, because it makes me vulnerable. Susceptible to suggestion. Controllable.

"Kill her," the monster says.

It's talking about the woman lying in the bathtub. She's handcuffed to the faucet, duct tape over her mouth, whimpering. Staring up at me with those familiar eyes, I'm sure she hates me. But I can't kill her, not yet; maybe not ever. And the monster knows that, he does.

It occurs to me for the first time, I've referred to it as a he. That concerns me, as if some wire came loose inside, a short circuit. It's like I'm broken, a complex jigsaw puzzle with a few key pieces out of the millions missing, so that no one can ever fully put me back together again.

The woman is still looking at me, scrutinizing me. She's shivering. I have no idea how she ended up here, but I'm beginning to think there's more to this monster thing than I initially believed.

I try empathy. "If I let you go—"

Hope fills her face, but it was wrong to even suggest it. I can't let her go.

No, that's not it. I don't want to let her go. She's part of me. Always will be.

Knowing I can't do what he wants, the monster will surely hurt me. I'll just stand there and take it, like I have so many times before in my life. But I'm no more afraid of the monster than I am anyone that's tried to hurt me. And believe me, many have tried. Too many to count. People I didn't even know as well as those I trusted.

It's funny how that works, trust; how a person can see you one way, then something happens that changes their entire perception. It's like me being broken somehow ruined them, too. Like I'm to blame for everyone's unhappiness.

"Hey," Charles says, "you okay, Enrique?"

I see him standing in the doorway behind me, those brilliant blue eyes showing how worried he is.

"Uh huh."

"It's just," he comes closer, "you were staring at yourself in the mirror again."

"Was I?"

He comes up behind me, wraps his arms around my waist, and squeezes. "Is it her again?"

"Yes." I feel relieved just admitting the truth. "It's just that, I'm not that person anymore. But she haunts me, you know."

"Why's that, you think?"

"I'm not sure."

Charles hums. "Maybe there doesn't need to be a reason."

"I think she sees me as a monster. Like everyone else does."

He kisses my cheek. "Honey, you're not a monster."

"Aren't I?"

"No. Of course, not."

"If you saw her the way I do, you'd think differently."

"What are you saying? That you see bad things?"

"No." I'm shaking my head. "I see what I've done to her."

"Enrique, stop. You're right here. She's still right here."

For a moment, I consider his words, that he's right. Maybe that's why I see her so often.

"Besides," Charles says, "we're all monsters."

And he's right to a degree. Maybe different sorts of monsters, but monsters all the same. Animals at the very least, scavenging, killing each other, feasting on flesh. A bitter truth, but the life of a monster is full of such truths.

Kenneth W. Cain is the author of over one hundred short stories and thirteen novels/novellas, as well as a handful each of nonfiction pieces, books for children, and poems. Cain has edited ten anthologies, and is editor-in-chief at Crystal Lake: Torrid Waters. He is an Active member of the HWA and a Full member of the SFWA. His full publishing history is available on his website at kennethwcain.c om.

Dance Faster, Carmelita

Sunni Ellis

Tick-ticking like a time bomb...buzzwords from the TV news droned out a quicksand goodbye, boosting the ratings with film footage of body bags and ventilators. Who wouldn't be moved to tears by a struggling grandmother risking it all for a can of SpaghettiOs? Meanwhile, death, once the most terrifying thing in the world, had been reduced to statistics while the virus continued to mutate, ensuring its survival.

Life as we knew it went south with the onset of the second wave. Conspiracy theorists, troubled loners, the kind that can smell a hearse from a mile away, were the first to roll out the razor wire and bunker up. Slicing off a big piece of the

"I told you so," doors latched in unison and they passed out the shotguns and ammo, as if pestilence couldn't walk through walls.

The match in the powder barrel came for the rest of us following the "incident" at Benson's Chicken Farm and processing plant. A half-million infected hens, euthanized with carbon monoxide, began crawling from the compost heaps and conducting business as usual. Less than a week later, graveyards were mostly empty, but the streets were jammin'.

Sloppy slow and a bit clumsy from the onset of rigor, the Corona Zombies were, otherwise, in mint condition. In an annoying paradox, they retained all of their faculties while being compelled to eat or infect slower survivors. Most weren't really down with the whole eating people agenda which made them quite effective in sincere requests for cooperation. Horde insiders began referring to this as "That's the Covid talkin'," dissolving into hysterical fits of shoulder-shaking laughter. Polite listeners were the first to go.

You might think death comes with an upgrade, but the fact is people are creatures of habit. The Corona Zombies were no exception, tending to flock to familiar hangouts. Dunkin Donuts, Piggly Wiggly, TJ Maxx at the Galleria were packed shoulder-to-shoulder. Some even attempted to go back to work. Industrial, inner-city barrios soon became *the* location to shelter in place for the bunker-savvy.

As culture collapsed, urban renewal of the warehouse district slipped into chaos and decay, drained of color and returning to dust. A gauntlet of gutted buildings, windows smashed, doors kicked in, lined both sides of the street like broken teeth. Rusting tower cranes screeched in the wind like banshees, drowning out the thin moaning wails of those going slowly mad behind the barricades.

This is how Quickshift Ricky, street king with Pennzoil eyes, found himself holed up in an abandoned auto body shop, The Wicked Wrench down on Hemlock Street. The mud-splattered facade, peppered with dry rot, sagged shakily on its foundation and weeds had overtaken fissures in the sidewalk. On the upside, piles of filth and cigarette butts were swept back against a rusted metal garage door, just wide enough to squeeze in the love of his life, Carmelita, a musclebound '64' GTO in Hemi orange with loaded V8 power drive. He'd been racing for pinks out on Dugan's Road when this cheese puff hipster, Buzz Binks, choked up in the stretch. He and Carmelita had been joined at the hip ever since.

A little lonely goes a long way, and after a few months of that ritual dance in cramped circles even the sweetest wine can turn to vinegar. An understimulated mind is like revving an engine in neutral, eventually, all the screws come loose. Victim to his own Bohemian tendencies, Ricky began to weigh the pros and cons of the zombie lifestyle. Just how bad could it be?

His heart stuttered at the answer. Panic constricted his lungs as a mewling wail echoed in the distance, growing louder by the second. A thin veneer of sweat beading on his upper lip, he pressed his face to the windowpane and stared as the horde rose from the dust with a gravel-grinding stomp. Skidding in the wake, a '67' Jaguar XKE, black as mourning, braked to a stop out front, screaming like a hellhound. Stunned, his scalp crawled when the door flew open, and a familiar face emerged. It was Buzz Binks, flaking lips pulled back in a surly sneer. With a voice like broken glass, he challenged, "Dugan's Road--NOW--racing for pinks! Shake it, loser, you have one foot in Hell anyway."

Engines growling like wild animals that need to run, they hugged the line on Dugan's Road, saturating the air with the stench of blood and gasoline. Ricky fired up a Lucky, his gaunt poker face hoarding shadows, hanky-panky eyes fixed on the conjure girl waving a checkered flag. Some bouffant, pedal-pusher princess French-twisted together with bobby pins and Aquanet, was stoking up the Juju like storm clouds, and damn if her skirt wasn't so short you could see Christmas. Clicking off the hollow seconds like a metronome, he ran a steady hand along the steering wheel and whispered, "Dance just a little faster, Carmelita."

3...2... FLAG! You could smell the tires smoke when Ricky popped the clutch and nailed it, a full car length in front before he hit second gear. Three-second jump of a true believer that dusted old Buzz right then and there, flat as promises.

Haloed in headlights, Christmas girl flashed a predatory grin, the kind that brings the rain. Jiggling keys to the Jag, she closed in on Carmelita with the sensual strut of a wild bird in the sand. It made him want to smoke, eat pie, wrestle alligators. Yeah, that laundry list of used-to-be's, washed one too many times and hung out to dry, had staled long before his Covid cubicle coma. All tacky lingerie and unbroken habits, she flicked her cigarette to the asphalt and pulled another from the pack, residue of unfiltered smoke giving up the ghost in thin, sinuous tendrils. Lightly dragging her long, red fingernails along the bumper, she mouthed the words, "Bic me, Prometheus."

He unlocked the door and crawled into bed with the thunder.

Writer...poet...designer...painter...seamstress, and carnival gypsy... **Sunni Ellis**...*a Nichiren Buddhist chanting for world peace and happiness...keeps a room in her best friend's house in Nashville, where she resides with her German Shepherd, Jax, and various ghosts. They keep the wolves at bay selling unique items at Motorcycle Rallies, where she sews patches to jackets...reading individual selections like Tarot cards.*

Hello

Karen Bayly

'Last stop!'

The guard strode to the front of the carriage and turned to face its occupants, his clipped moustache bristling with officious glee. None of my fellow passengers, currently slumped in their seats, was keen to sit up, let alone leave.

It had been an arduous journey. Forbidden to speak and crammed into a space furnished with narrow benches and no air conditioning, we understood our place. The food was barely edible—leathery meat and stale bread washed down with tea so weak it was indistinguishable from dirty water. I suppose selection for the Outlands meant you forever relinquished any dreams of simple pleasures.

'Come on, you lazy good-for-nothings!' he shouted, smirking. 'Time to leave. Or will I introduce you to my friends?'

He smiled and nodded to outside, where six masked soldiers stood, guns at the ready.

The woman next to me leaned closer and whispered, 'I expect we'll be "introduced" soon enough.'

She was a lovely creature with glossy black hair and luminous skin, but her eyes were hollow with fear.

Squeezing my arm, she asked, 'Promise you'll say hello when you see me?'

I hesitated for a split second. We were strangers plucked from our ordinary existence to serve the State. Our future was with the working men of the toxic Outlands, bringing sexual relief to their short, brutal lives. I wished I could reassure her, but what was the point?

'Please. I'm afraid of losing myself, of not being me anymore. If you say hello, I'll remember who I am. It's important if I'm to survive this.'

The guard leaned over us, a mean dog itching to bite.

'Well, aren't you the Chatty Cathy?' he snarled at my companion. She shrank back into her spot.

I realised the other women were spilling out onto the platform. As the first woman passed by the soldiers, they reached out, fondled her breasts and buttocks. She didn't utter a single word. The second woman followed, head high, and the men pawed at her body but to no effect. Then came the third and the fourth and so on—all with heads held proudly. Not one of them flinched. None showed any emotion. Brave women, braver than me.

A scuffle behind me caught my attention. Our tormenter had grabbed my companion's wrists and was wrenching her from her seat.

'You.' He looked straight at me. 'Get out.'

I stumbled down the aisle. There was no sense fighting. This was our life now. The gains we'd made, the fight for equality, the "me too" movement, all for nothing. One devastating world war and it had all come undone.

I heard my friend cry out in dismay as he pushed her to the ground and forced himself into her. I wanted to scream like a banshee, rip his throat out, and cut the heart from his chest. Instead, I drowned in powerlessness.

At the door, I turned, desperate to do something. He was on top of her, bare bottom rising and falling with each invasive thrust. Her gaze drifted upward to meet mine.

'Hello,' I whispered. How painfully desperate and inadequate that one word sounded.

Her face glimmered with hope as she mouthed 'hello' back at me.

Shaken, I walked out into the blazing heat and toward the waiting women, ignoring the soldiers and their filthy, probing fingers.

'Hello,' I said, wondering if one word really could have power.

The eyes that met mine brimmed with sisterhood.

'Move on,' yelled a soldier.

Heads bowed, we shuffled off, silently swearing revenge.

We would find a way.

Karen Bayly is a writer, software tester, and author of two books: Fortitude *and* Tesato's Code. *Her short stories and poems have appeared in* Yellow Mama Webzine, Black Petals Magazine, *and* Every Day Fiction, *and anthologies from*

Black Beacon Books Black Hare Press, and Crystal Lake Publishing. She lives in Sydney, Australia, with two cats, a guitar, and a ukulele.

#Camping

Lee Smart

Delaney trudged along the hard dirt road; its surface rutted with tyre tracks. The county had never got around to paving it. After all, it added to the '*rustic charm*' of the area even if it threatened to ruck a visitor's tyres. She had left her own car back down the track, hidden in the brush and on the far side of a recently felled tree that blocked the only road out.

The woods had always been her home. Great oaks, bigger around than she could reach, crowded together on either side of the road as the afternoon sunlight cast everything in a gentle orange glow. Less than a quarter of a mile down the track, hidden in the treeline, was the lake where she'd spent her childhood. Everything around her reminded Delaney of better times, happier times.

Her nostalgia was broken by a slight buzzing in the pocket of her father's old canvas hunting jacket. Delaney pulled out her smartphone and thumbed the screen until it lit up. Another check-in, this time with photographs. Delaney looked through the images, taking in the familiar landscape before heading off the track and into the treeline.

It broke her heart a little every time she came up to the lake. The open land by its north edge was picture perfect; exactly the kind of place you could settle down in. That was why her ancestors had built their home here, back at the founding of the nearby town of Boothe. Delaney had spent her childhood here until the developers and their banks took it all away. They said her Da didn't have the right paperwork, nothing to show he legally owned the land. The court said the lakeside was up for grabs, so the developers took it from them.

Notice was served, telling them they had to vacate their home and leave the only place Delaney had ever loved. Her Mam couldn't accept it. One summer morning she had walked into the lake with a pocketful of stones. After that, her Da seemed to give in. He moved them into town and worked small-time jobs to make ends meet. Something inside him had died with her Mam. The only time he seemed alive was when they visited the site of their old home.

Since then, the lakeside had been a summer camp for rich teens, then a reform camp for wayward ones. It had been an executive lodge, a log cabin getaway, and even a place for fishermen to park their RVs and enjoy some time in the country. Every few years some company would ignore the lakeside's history and try again. Her Da would head up to the lake, Delaney in tow once she turned twelve, and it would always end the same way for the interlopers on their land.

Delaney's phone chimed again, another check-in. She was closer now and could make out the lakeside through the gaps in the trees. Her old home had become something new yet again, this time they called it a glamping site. Glamour camping, for people who couldn't hack the wilderness without heated cabins, cable TV, and Wi-Fi. Although Delaney had to agree, life with the internet was a helluva lot easier.

Now her parents were gone it was her responsibility to keep up the visits. Delaney had to remind people this land belonged to someone else, despite what the developers might think. It was her family's land, now and always. Delaney knew this day would come, when she'd have to visit without her Da and take over his work. She had paid attention every time they had been to the lakeside, watching her father and learning.

She knew what to do, and how to do it.

The phone buzzed slightly in her pocket, no louder than a midge passing through the summer air. Another check-in; someone had posted a *selfie* online. She took in all the details of the scene, recognising the old, vast tree behind a smiling blonde woman, and the arc of the lakeside further beyond that.

She was close.

Things had changed a lot since the early visits to the lake with her father. Back then they'd have to listen to the local gossip, keeping watch on the roads to see when people would venture up the lake again. When something new inevitably opened up, Delaney and her father would spend days in the woods, hidden and watching. They would patiently gauge what moves to make and how far to go to get the site shut down and force the interlopers off their land. Now, all Delaney had to do was wait for an alert to pop up on her phone, telling her someone had checked in at the lake and follow the trail of tags and selfies to find her prey.

The blonde woman was still snapping selfies, trying to get the perfect shot. She didn't notice Delaney moving through the brush, too intent on her own smartphone. This is what her beautiful family land had been reduced to; a backdrop for pouting lips and peace-sign hand gestures. Delaney stalked up behind her, felling axe raised high. She was right behind the woman as the blonde turned, catching a glimpse of the axe-wielding stranger on her phone screen. The blonde started to scream before Delaney sunk the axe into her neck with a scream of rage, its weight all but severing her perfectly styled head.

One down.

Delaney prised the smartphone from the blonde's dead hand and scrolled back through the photographs she had already taken. There they were, the blonde's friends. Five more to go, three men and two women. Delaney set off back into the woods, skirting around the lake's edge and heading towards the glamping site built on her family's land.

Delaney missed her Da and their visits to lakeside dearly, but she had to admit that modern technology made it a lot easier to get things done.

Lee Smart is an artist, designer and writer from Bedfordshire, UK. He spends his free time drawing monsters and mecha as well as writing horror and post-apocalyptic fiction.

His first short story collection, Stories from the Outer Dark: Vol 1, can be found for sale online.

Gone Fission

Amanda Hard

The boy sits at the edge of the lake, a fishing pole held firmly between his dirty and skinned knees. He eyes the long, eel-like creature in the faintly glowing water, silently willing it to do more than circle the hook, although he doesn't blame the creature for not biting. The tinned ham leaves oily ripples in the water each time he drops it in. The fish unenthusiastically nudges the bait before diving to the bottom.

Fishing here, the boy thinks of his father, who taught him to cast sideways, rather than overhead, to keep the line out of the trees, and to ensure a gentle landing, mimicking the way an insect might skate across the surface. The memory causes him to smile at first, but then he remembers his father's voice, and all he can hear in his mind is the rattle of wet breaths—the only sound his father made in those last hours. The boy draws the line across the water, painting the surface, as his father had demonstrated.

The boy suspects he will die the same way, blood and water bubbling in his chest, if he doesn't starve first. The constant nausea is enough to keep him away from the bright glass jars of pickles and beets in the cellar, but he knows he could, if he had to, pan fry a fish. It is easier though, and more relaxing, to sit in the dust and pretend his father is by his side, patiently wiling away a summer morning, while his mother sips coffee on the porch, gazing at them absently, no doubt thinking of the unpainted canvases in her studio.

From the pines beside the lake comes the shuddering sound of large feet crashing through underbrush. The boy looks up to meet the eyes of a dog. He whistles and the dog limps over to him. Mostly skin than fur now, and with blood drying at its muzzle, the dog's tongue lolls good-naturedly at the boy's outstretched hand. It sniffs the air, sneezes a bloody spray, and whines as it sits crookedly, favoring a back leg.

The boy pulls the line across the water again. With renewed interest, the fish-thing pokes again at the hook, finally giving the bait a test nibble, then a full commitment. The boy jerks the line, setting the hook, and draws the long eel-like body out of the water and into the sunlight. The thing is mud-colored and its bloated, segmented body glistens on the line like a string of jewels. The dog whines and tries to bark.

"Of course, I'll share," the boy says, the voice surprising him in both its strength and loudness. He drops the fish on the edge of the grass, where it explodes in a spray of intestines and blood. The dog whines again, pawing at its back leg.

"Look at that. It was dead all that time and it didn't even know it."

The boy scratches under the dog's jaw. It gives the fingers a feeble lick, leaving a brownish-red stain behind. The boy scratches his own head, taking the last of his scalp hair under the remainder of his fingernails, and looks upward at the gray haze of sky. He sets the pole next to him and lays back to rest against the dead grass. The surface of the water gradually stills, and the boy closes his eyes against the flow of bloody tears, reassuring himself that the fishing is bound to be better tomorrow. Fishing's always better on a Sunday.

Amanda Hard earned her MFA in Creative Writing from Murray State University in 2018. Her fiction and poetry have appeared in several print and online magazines including Lamplight, parABnormal, *and* MetaSellar, *as well as anthologies such as* Midnight in the Pentagram, Lost Signals, Tales from the Crust, *and volumes in the HWA Poetry Showcase series. She is a member of the Horror Writers Association and the Science Fiction Poetry Association, and lives in the cornfields of southern Indiana.*

A Cunning Plan

R. B. Wood

It was the smell that drew Aiden Fairweather to the shore that day in 1932.

He was at his old pub at five in the morning, the usual time since he'd had to let the cleaning lady go a few months back.

At first, the old man thought someone had dumped a load of rubbish into the water. Wouldn't have been the first time.

But as he approached the murky blackness, he noticed a shape lying on the water's edge. It was a twenty-foot-long mass of tissue. It was nothing he'd ever seen before. And it was most certainly dead.

It stank to high heaven.

Covering his nose with a handkerchief, he hurried back to the pub as fast as his old legs and cane could take him. Aiden fumbled with the keys for a moment or two—damned arthritis—and finally got the door unlocked.

The aroma of cheap cigarettes and stale beer washed over Aiden. The smell was comforting.

He shuffled around the large oak bar and grabbed the phone.

"You're up a bit early, Aiden," a croaky female voice said on the other line.

"Ya, Breda," he said, slightly out of breath. "Listen, love, could ye put me through to Doc McAllister?"

"Old Rex, finally ready to be put down?" Breda coughed. Aiden could practically see the fag dangling from the phone operator's mouth, a blue-grey cloud of tobacco settling like a halo over her head.

"Bite yer tongue, lass," Aiden said. "That pooch will outlive us all."

She laughed. It was a disgusting, phlegm-laden sound.

"Hold on, hon. I'll get the Doc for ye. And tell 'im my granddaughter is still available. Twenty-two and no man in her life to be seen."

Aiden waited a moment before a young, sleepy voice came on the line.

"'Ello?"

"Doc, it's Aiden Fairweather."

"Ya, Aiden, Breda told me," he said through a yawn. "Rex again?"

"Nah. The old boy's fine, Doc. Something's washed up onshore. You should come to see it."

"Gotta be at the Montgomerys' in a couple of hours. New foal's due."

"It's twenty feet long, Doc."

Aiden waited. "Doc?"

"You've got to be mistaken."

"Nope." Aiden waited again.

"I'll be there in twenty minutes. Ta."

· · · ● ●· ● ●· ·

The Doc's 1927 Morris Cowley pulled up to Aiden's pub around six, sputtering and wheezing as it came to a jerky halt.

"Damn piece of shite," McAllister grumbled as he hoisted himself out of his car.

"Good horse will last you ten. Make less noise, too. But you'd know that bein' a vet an' all," said Aiden, chewing on his pipe. "Coulda had the whole pub cleaned by the time it took ye to get here. C'mon inside, Doc. Kettle's on, and I've got a fire goin'. A good cuppa will sort out your carriage problems."

McAllister shook his head. "Would love to, Aiden, but have to make my rounds. Let's see this twenty-foot beastie of yours."

The old man shrugged his shoulders. Knocking his pipe against the side of a barrel, he stood, grabbed his cane, and without another word, started toward the shore.

The day had brightened from a charcoal black to a dull grey. The stinking mass on the shoreline was much more visible now than when Aiden had first ventured toward the water.

The old man wrinkled his nose. "That's not gonna be helpful for business," he said.

McAllister grunted.

The creature was a blackish grey. The vet could see a bloated torso with four large fins. A long tail curled into the water, and the head of the creature lay at the end of an equally long neck that bobbed in harmony with the small waves.

The vet slowly made his way around the corpse. Finally, he looked up at Aiden. "N'er seen anything like it. But I can tell you what killed it."

"Oh?" said Aiden, raising one eyebrow.

"Trash. Its gut has been torn open, and the beastie's gut is filled with garbage. Got to call this in."

The vet started back up the hill when Aiden blocked his way with his cane.

"Hold on, laddie. Let's think about this for a mo'," he said.

"What do you mean? This animal is a great discovery ..."

"Mmm. Maybe. But stuffing this beastie isn't the answer."

"What do you mean?"

"Well, folks around here have been hurting for a while as you well know, Doc." The old man said thoughtfully. "You go and announce this to the world, and sure a few people will come to take a look. Five years from now, that poor creature will be gathering dust in a museum somewhere."

"What's your point, Aiden?"

"The corpse is a passing fancy. Now legends, that's where the real money is."

"What?!"

"Think about it, Doc. People have been talking about a beast in these waters since St. Columba, and that was thirteen hundred years ago."

McAllister rubbed at the stubble on his chin. "But that legend hasn't helped folks here very much," he said slowly.

"Like any good idea, all it takes is a little press. Maybe a blurry photograph or two. A few folks scared outta their wits by 'somethin' in the water.' Trust me, we could make this into a full-time business that will help everyone around here."

The vet looked back at the sad creature decaying on the shoreline.

"What's a more fitting legacy, then? 'Animal killed by trash' or 'The Legend of the Monster at Loch Ness?' Come up to the pub and have that cuppa, and we can discuss our cunning plan..."

R. B. Wood is a recent MFA graduate of Emerson College and a writer of speculative and dark thrillers. His second novel, the supernatural thriller Bayou Whispers, was released in May of 2021. Mr. Wood recently has appeared in Crystal Lake Publishing's Shallow Water's anthologies, as well as online via SickLit Magazine & HorrorAddicts.net, and in the award-winning anthology Offbeat: Nine Spins on Song from Wicked ink Books. Along with his writing passion, R. B. is the host of The Word Count Podcast—a show of original flash fiction.

R. B. currently lives in Boston with his partner Tina, a multitude of cats, and various other critters that visit from time to time.

Wifely Duties

D.C. Phillips

Frankie says I watch too much trash television. Back when he was working the graveyard shift at the plant, I tried to hide it from him. He'd get home in the wee hours, and I'd switch it off stealth-like from under the covers. Then he'd sleep all day, and as soon as I heard him rouse, I'd switch it off and hide the remote in the tangled nest of clothes I'd been folding. Every once in a while, he'd catch me by surprise on his way to the bathroom in the middle of his midnight, which was my midmorning. That's when all the best game shows, court shows, and love-triangle dramas would come on.

"Rottin' your brains again?" he'd say as he adjusted the front and back of his briefs. I'll never forget how his face looked in those moments, his eyes and nose all screwed up from sleep and disgust. To this day, I can't figure out why it mattered to him what I watched or how much time I spent watching it.

Anyway, things changed when they laid Frankie off at the plant. "Recession," he muttered when I asked him what happened, and that was his final word on the subject. I suspected it had more to do with his drinking habit than with the economy, but I held my peace.

I scoured the want ads for days on end until I finally got the call. It was hardly a glamorous job—entering data for a local cardboard box factory—but it was honest work, and it would cover the past-due statements piling up on the kitchen counter. Frankie said it wasn't right, that a woman shouldn't be leaving the house and making her man look bad. He made it sound like I was stepping out on him and the whole town would soon be talking.

Oh, and if I insisted on leaving him by himself all day, I at least had to fix something for him so he wouldn't starve to death. I said fine, and I fixed it for him alright. In addition to a microwave plate of the previous night's leftovers, I left him a tall glass of sweet tea in the fridge every day for lunch. All he had to do was lift himself off his ass and pull it out of the fridge.

Every day, I would come home to more gripes. I could tell he had been drinking—more with each passing day, it seemed like—and his speech would slur, and he would sob like a baby about how I left him at home to be a housewife and that was against God. Well, I let him talk until he wore himself out and he passed out in his recliner. Then, I'd pass out, too, and the next day we'd start at it all over again. I'd leave his lunch and his sweet tea for him, and I'd be on my merry way.

After a handful of weeks, I was really starting to get fed up. *Nag, nag, nag* from that damned recliner day in and day out. Something had to give. Then, one afternoon, I braced myself as I turned the key in the lock.

Nothing. Not a peep except a heated conversation on TV. I recognized two characters from *Guiding Light*, a couple arguing with more passion than I'd ever witnessed in my own relationship. It made me wonder what was unrealistic—what I saw on my shows, or what I endured in my personal life.

I walked over to Frankie's lounge chair, but he didn't move. He didn't speak. I stooped down and got in his face, and I realized he wasn't breathing.

That was two weeks ago, and I've got to say the peace and quiet has been nice. All those sweet teas finally did the trick.

D.C. Phillips is the Atlanta-based author of Frightful Fables, *tales that will leave you screaming for more! His short stories have been featured in a number of publications–including* Georgia Gothic, *the first official anthology sponsored by the Atlanta Chapter of the Horror Writers Association. Additionally,* Man's Best Phantom, *his most recent work for early readers, is now available in English and Spanish. He welcomes communication with like-minded writers and readers via email and social media.*

All We Endure

Grant Longstaff

You don't know how long you have been driving, but the bones in your fingers ache and the skin stretched over them has turned a bloodless white from gripping the wheel so tightly. The deserted road ahead, which you have come to think of as your own, snakes through a starless night. The sky above is wearing all the colours of hurt. You know these colours deeply, intimately.

But now you are running.

Now, you are free.

You are alone in this world and there is nothing but black road in the headlights until—a thumb, a fist, an arm—a woman by the side of the road. You do not know her, but you know the fear on her face.

You have worn fear, too. And too often.

You stop, watch the girl bathed in the bloody red of brake lights stagger into the road behind the car. She stops at the passenger window and you see some part of yourself, in another body, from another time and place, looking back. You see the tears, still fresh on the girl's bruised cheek, and know they will sting the split in her lip should they reach it. You open the window to warn her, to tell her that even when she thinks the pain has stopped it will keep coming, but instead say,

'Where are you going?'

'Wherever you are going, I guess.'

The girl is beside you. It is not a cold night, but she is shivering in the passenger seat so you turn on the heater, knowing there will be no comfort in it. You offer her a crumpled paper handkerchief, still damp, made thin with your own tears, and the girl presses it to her lips without hesitating.

You drive.

'Who did this?' you ask sometime before dawn.

'An old flame. You?'

How does she know?

You glance at the girl; she is holding the wad of tissue in her open palms. Watered with your collective grief it has blossomed into an ugly, grey flower.

'Someone who swore to love me.' You swallow old agonies.

'How often they say that. How often they use it to make us stay.' The girl sighs. 'All we endure.'

The pale circle of flesh which haunts one finger, the ghost of a ring you left behind, is the only visible relic from a life of torment you can't ever forget. Your heart will forever be a coiled knot of scar tissue.

'Keep running,' the girl says. 'Keep running for those of us who no longer can.'

The girl places the handkerchief onto the dashboard and then she is gone, and you are alone again.

You weep for the girl as the light of a new day chases away the wounds of the night.

You drive on, and on, and on.

You will survive.

No.

You will live.

Grant Longstaff *is from Gateshead; a small, suitably dismal town in the North of England where nothing much happens. He had no choice but to write fiction. Though he now lives in Glasgow, his heart remains in the North East.*

His debut novelette, Between the Teeth of Charon, *was released by Demain Publishing in June 2022. His short fiction has appeared in the Bram Stoker Nominated* Arterial Bloom, Shallow Waters Vol. 8 *and* Aurealis Magazine *and on* The Other Stories and Tales to Terrify *podcasts.*

You can find him at www.grantlongstaff.co.uk or on Twitter @Grant-Longstaff.

Tumshie

William Meikle

"You don't want a pumpkin—no kid of mine is having a bloody pumpkin. Pumpkins are corporate Americana, sanitized bollocks for the easily pleased. Pumpkins are cute and cuddly and bland Hollywood Halloween at its very worst. Bloody pumpkins. You'll have a tumshie. Now there's real Halloween for you."

"But Derek's getting a pumpkin and…"

"Derek's dad's a bloody idiot then. A tumshie was good enough for me when I was your age, so a tumshie is what you'll have."

"What's a tumshie, Dad?"

John's dad slapped his forehead in mock disgust.

"Don't they teach you kids anything that's not American? A tumshie is what people around here used for lanterns on Halloween Night—All Hallows—when they went out *'acting the galoshes.'* We didn't have bloody *'trick or treat'* then either—we had to work for our sweeties. Sweeties—not bloody candy. What's a tumshie? It's a turnip, lad."

The thing his father got out of the shopping bag was a deformed, purple-brown ball, rough-skinned, like it had a serious case of acne, and scarcely the size of two fists put together.

"Everybody's going to laugh at me," John said, looking at the misshapen thing on the table.

"Let them laugh," his dad said, and took out the big knife from the drawer by the side of the sink. "This is your tradition, this is. If they want to forget where they come from, more fool them."

Dad set to an attack with the heavy knife. Although the turnip got mostly hollowed out in short order, the blade slid hard to one side as he finished off a rough mouth, and the blade gouged a slice across his left palm.

"Bastard!"

Blood pooled in the hollow inside the turnip for several seconds as the man stood above it holding his wounded hand.

"Don't just stand there, lad—get me a towel, quick—I'm bleeding like a stuck pig here."

John knew better than to delay—he quickly fetched a kitchen towel—one of the older, faded, ones—he had Mom's wrath to consider as well as Dad's—and the hand was soon wrapped up, although the material was already turning red and wet at the cut palm. Dad looked at it and swore loudly before turning to John.

"Finish the job off, lad. And mind you don't hurt yourself – I need to get this stitched."

• • • ● •●• ● • • •

John heard the old car's engine stutter and cough before taking hold, and waited until it clattered off down the road before turning his attention to the thing on the table.

The knife lay where his dad had dropped it, to the right side of the turnip. There was blood on the blade, in the hollowed-out turnip, and at the crude mouth opening his dad had been working on. John wanted to just step back and close the kitchen door on the whole sorry mess. But he knew better than that. Tradition, that's what his dad had said, and Dad was big on traditions, especially ones that involved boys getting beaten with a belt when they weren't fast enough to obey their elders. John had seen plenty of tradition in the past. He wasn't all that keen on seeing any more of it in the near future.

Besides, any hope of a pumpkin had always been a forlorn one. Mum had enough on her hands managing the money to cover basics and Dad's booze without worrying about a frippery like a pumpkin.

So, tumshie it'll have to be then.

He took the knife and, leaving the bloody mouth as his dad had left it, started to work on gouging out an eye in the tough vegetable.

It was hard going, and John was surprised to look up later and find it was almost ten o'clock. It was the first time he could remember being on his own in the house so late; Mum wouldn't be home from the Pizza Place until after midnight—it really would be Halloween by then, he remembered. And Dad's wound must have needed a lot of stitching to keep him away this long.

Unless he's gone for a bevvy.

That wasn't a thought—it felt like it should have been, but it had been a whisper, a soft, Scottish-accented voice. And it had come from the turnip he was working on. He almost dropped the knife in astonishment, and stared at the roughly carved mouth, still red and moist, that took on a lopsided grin as it spoke again.

You know I'm right. He's gone to the pub to get pished. It's tradition, isn't it?

"You're not real," John whispered.

Maybe not. But I am traditional, it said, and laughed, the red at its mouth bubbling and hissing as if boiling. Heat came off the turnip, as if it was roasting in an oven even while it sat there, still grinning.

Come on, laddie, finish the job. I can hardly help you if I only have one eye to see with, now can I?

John thought again of stepping away; it was past his bedtime anyway, and if he went upstairs he could hide from whispering tumshies, drunk fathers, and traditions that made no sense at all.

There's no hiding from him after he's been on the bevvy. You know that.

"I know that," John whispered in reply. "It's traditional."

He went back to work, cutting and carving and gouging. The tumshie whispered its encouragement with every cut of the knife. John only looked up when the kitchen door opened sometime later.

His dad was standing at the door, staring at the bulbous thing on the table. Impossibly red, burning bright eyes smiled from above the bloody crooked smile.

"What are you doing still up?" Dad said. His voice was slurred, his eyes clouded. He'd definitely been out following his traditions. Meanwhile, John had been working on a new tradition of his own.

"Thanks for the idea, Dad," John said, and cut a wound across his palm before smearing flesh blood across the rough skin of the tumshie, closing his fist, letting a dripping stream of hot red pool in the inside hollow. The clock struck midnight and John smiled as the tumshie whispered.

Playtime.

This was definitely better than a pumpkin.

"Happy Halloween, Dad."

The tumshie smacked its lips and replied.

Happy Halloween, laddie.

"What kind of trick is this?" Dad said, and leaned forward. He put his freshly bandaged hand on the turnip.

"You'll like this one, Dad," John said as the tumshie's grin grew wider. The lips clicked shut, snipping three fingers off the man's hand and tearing bandages and stitches open in the same action. The tumshie chewed and smiled even as the screams and the red flew everywhere.

"You'll really like this, Dad. It's traditional."

William Meikle is a Scottish writer, now living in Canada, with over thirty novels published in the genre press and over 300 short story credits in thirteen countries. He has books published with a variety of publishers including Dark Regions Press, DarkFuse and Severed Press, and his work has appeared in a number of professional anthologies and magazines. He lives in Newfoundland with whales, bald eagles and icebergs for company and when he's not writing he drinks beer, plays guitar and dreams of fortune and glory.

Arts and Crafts

Madison McSweeney

Lenore's long hair whipped in the wind as she walked home from school, black cat thrashing in her hand.

The creature, a folded sheet of construction paper cut vaguely into the shape of a cat, with red pipe-cleaner whiskers and yellow felt eyes, was supposed to remain another day as part of Mrs. Takahashi's Grade 2 Halloween display, but Lenore wanted to take it home. Now, the gale threatened to rip it away.

Clutching the artwork between her fingers, splaying them flat so as not to tear it, she hastened her pace, slowing only to admire the orange flashing leaves above her head and the grinning tableaus of skulls and pumpkins on porches. Plastic bones jangled from dangling branches and rubber bats smiled at her as they flapped, like her cat, even though Mrs. Takahashi said cats don't have smiles. Plastic bag ghosts strained at their earthly bonds, and garden scarecrows toppled impotently.

A gust of wind, and the cat escaped from her hand. It unfurled and fluttered violently, more batlike than feline, until a horizontal breeze caught the paper and sent it sailing smoothly down the street until it landed, finally, in a bush. Lenore ran after it, backpack bouncing wildly.

Breaking branches aside, she pushed herself through the foliage and emerged on the most immaculately raked patch of grass she had never tread upon. A few feet away, a pile of crunchy red and yellow leaves sat placidly, waiting to be jumped in. But that could wait. Her cat was missing.

Lenore fell to her knees to scour the bottom branches, holding her breath. Anyone who puts a fence or bush at the edge of their front yard is not to be trusted; any second some terrible old woman or crotchety man with a dog would pop out and yell at her, like a fright mask in a funhouse.

On a whim, she climbed to her knees and called out sweetly, "Here, kitty, kitty."

The reply surprised her. "Meowww."

A sleek black cat was sitting beneath the last bush. It meowed again when it saw her seeing it, and—Lenore was almost certain of this—smiled slightly. The girl stood slowly, scared to spook it, and began to gingerly approach. The cat hopped to its feet, mewled pointedly, and darted underneath the bush.

Lenore rushed after it, prickles cutting her arms. She emerged to find the cat sitting patiently on the sidewalk. It gave her a moment to catch her breath before taking off again, turning its head to make sure she was following.

Over her shoulder, skeletons and ghosts danced in the trees. From porches and windowsills, jack-o-lanterns and skulls grinned. And once the little girl was out of earshot, they started to laugh.

Lenore followed the cat down the sidewalk, past where the houses stopped.

Past the white church with the triangle spire, and into the cemetery.

Past the tall marble crosses and gleaming granite slabs, to the back lots where the stones were so old that the names had disappeared.

Lenore winced as she passed a tiny tombstone with a stone lamb on top: a baby's grave. But even these pioneer relics held no interest to the cat. It led Lenore to the very edge of the yard before coming to a stop, staring insistently. There was no cross, no headstone, here, but the outline of a hole could be seen in the rectangular patch of dead grass, six feet by three. Lenore put her ear to the ground and heard a sound: *knock, knock.*

She gasped and jumped back. She met the cat's eyes skeptically, silently asking, *Why did you bring me here?*

The cat answered verbally, "You have nothing to fear."

"Wh-Who's down there?"

"My mother," the black cat said. "She was buried alive."

Lenore eyed the earth warily. The grass had had time to grow back, if not healthily.

"By mistake," the cat added.

"A long time ago."

"Too long," that cat agreed. It pawed at the ground, turning the dirt with its claws. Following its lead, Lenore knelt and started digging, one handful at a time. The deeper they dug, the louder and clearer the knocking became.

At last, they hit wood. The corpse's fist pounded on the underside of the lid, cracking the surface, and then a hand pushed out. It was charred. Lenore shrieked as the crack widened and arms then elbows and torso broke through, until a burned and blackened corpse was sitting up in its casket—but the cat meowed excitedly as the woman climbed to her feet and hauled herself out of the grave. The first thing she did once she'd found her footing, was stroke the cat's ears.

"He needed a new body," the witch said, looking at Lenore with rotted, gelatinous eyes. "Thank you." Purring with satisfaction, the cat slipped from her fingers and sauntered out of Lenore's line of sight.

"Are you free now?" Lenore asked, not sure if that was a good thing or not.

The witch shook her head. "A grave needs a body in it."

Lenore wasn't quite listening; she was wondering where the cat was. As if reading her mind, the beast pounced.

Lenore flailed, throwing up her hands to dislodge the animal as it crawled up her back, clawing at her head and eyes. Whirling, she took a step back. Her foot caught the edge of the grave and she felt herself fall. Her head hit the wood with a muffled *thunk*.

She didn't have a chance to get her wind back before the cat landed on her chest. She took a breath, but the cat lapped it up before she could inhale. Lenore's vision blurred as the cat sucked the air from her lungs, and the world went black.

Half an hour later, the earth was back in place, and a black cat strutted through the cemetery gates. A little girl walked behind him, long hair whipping in the wind.

Madison McSweeney is a horror and weird fiction author from Ottawa, Ontario. She is the author of The Doom That Came to Mellonville *(Filthy Loot),* The Forest Dreams With Teeth *(Demain Publishing), and* Fringewood *(Alien Buddha Press). Her short stories have appeared in anthologies like* Zombie Punks Fuck Off *(Weirdpunk/CLASH),* American Gothic Short Stories *(Flame Tree), and* The First Five Minutes of the Apocalypse *(Hungry Shadow Press). She blogs at www.madisonmcsweeney.com and tweets from @MMcSw13.*

The Halloween House

Sheldon Woodbury

Their house was always draped in shadows from the bushy black trees huddled around it, and a passing wind would sound like the wail of ghosts. They shunned visitors of any kind, moving through the gloom with creaky footsteps and raspy murmurs. They were weak and weary, clinging to each other because that's all they had left. Old age had crept up with the barest of warnings and now it wouldn't let go, like a heavy cloak that squeezed tighter and tighter.

They moaned as they shuffled down the hall, grumbling like the wind outside. The world had become a neglected haze rarely glimpsed through the shuttered blinds. They didn't need much, so they accepted this as the way things had to be, living a sheltered life away from prying eyes.

But this night was different, the sacred ritual called Hallows' Eve, when they'd finally unlock their bolted front door. They'd been dreaming about it all year, a nocturnal reverie that was finally here. The daylight world had become even more unbearable, so their nightmares were the sanctuary they desperately needed.

A murky sun had just died outside, and a luminous moon had swiftly appeared. The sky had dimmed to a morbid hue, and the stars seemed to glow from some unknown beyond. Tonight, their house was like a nightmare too, a place where spookiness loomed in the night. Pumpkins crackled with fiery eyes and clattering skeletons dangled from the trees. Gravestones were strewn about, crooked and crumbling. For far longer than it was safe to admit, on this sacred night they'd made their home a Halloween house.

They traveled at night from one small town to the next, finding a decrepit old house at the end of a lonely road. They never stayed longer than a year, always leaving at midnight after Hallows' Eve. It was a vagabond life, traveling from darkness to darkness, unseen by the daylight world.

Giggling voices could already be heard, tiny ghouls and goblins clutching bags with sugary treats. It was even better when a misty rain splattered down, or a murky fog swept in, bringing the same gloom as their nightmarish dreams.

They hobbled down the splintered wood stairs, clutching wrinkled old hands. They hadn't talked about it, but they both knew this might be their last Halloween, and their sadness was darker than anything else. Memories were all they had left, back to the forgotten past when the scares and fear were real.

There had always been monsters, but they'd had the good sense to stay where they belonged, lurking in the shadows until it was time to strike. They'd prowled the world like unknown warriors, hidden in the dark away from the light. But when you spend so much time hiding, you eventually lose your claim to be real. And that's when all the legends and myths about their existence came into being. Made-up stories replaced the frightening reality of what was really there. And now this was all they had left, a single October eve when giggling children mimicked them for sugary treats. Their existence had been turned into a frivolous night with cheap costumes and candy. All the monsters were tiny and fake, let out for just a single night, then packed away in boxes again.

They'd spent the last hour putting on their costumes, the bland and boring human disguises they only wore when absolutely necessary. Covering up their true form was a shameful process, and that's what hurt most of all. A real monster was a crusty and wicked apparition with burning eyes and misbegotten parts, spewing billows of ashen black smoke.

But at least for tonight, they could imagine a different world that existed only in their dreams. They could pretend they didn't have to hide anymore, and were free to roam as they pleased, showing this sad and dreary world what they really were.

And that's what they did, as the giggling children banged their tiny fists on the rotted front door. When they peered out into the night, there were more scary creatures than horrible humans, and that was the way they knew it should be.

They looked like a tired old couple who should have stayed in bed on this Halloween night. Their hair was grey and stringy, hanging like vines, their clothes dirty and ripped. A musty smell of ash and smoke swirled around them like an infernal fog.

They handed out candy with their wrinkled old hands, because they didn't want to miss the best part of the night. If this was going to be their last Halloween, they wanted it to be extra special. They waited until the very end when there were just a few children left. They tore off their shameful disguises and threw open the door. In the glowing light of the colossal full moon, they showed the giggling make-believe monsters what a glorious creation a real monster was.

Sheldon Woodbury is an award winning writer (screenplays, plays, books, short stories, and poems). His short stories and poems have appeared in many horror anthologies and magazines. His poem, "The Midnight Circus," was selected by Ellen Datlow as an honorable mention for Best Horror 2017.

Tom Coombe

Hello everybody, and happy fall! Can you believe there are only two weeks left until our annual Halloween celebration?

It seems like just yesterday we were splashing around in the community pool, cheering on West Pennfield Little League at states—next season, guys!—and watching the July 4 fireworks in Gemmell Park.

A few months ago, we'd have said "Time flies," but thanks to The Judges, we now know that time is a mirage and that there is only Them.

As you might have guessed, there will be a few changes to this year's Halloween celebration, though nothing that should stop you and your family from having a good time. Stick to these (very simple, really) rules and the night will go off without a hitch and (fingers crossed) The Judges won't open Their eyes.

1. Costumes

In accordance with new township regulations, children are forbidden from dressing as: Supernatural beings (witches, ghosts, mummies, vampires, werewolves), pop culture characters (this means characters from movies, TV shows, books, comic books or video games), historical figures, celebrities, princesses, clowns, or animals.

2. Bobbing for apples

Due to the ongoing produce shortage, we're forced to suspend this popular game this year. Happily, The Judges have ordered a few replacement games for this year's party:

- House of Voles

- Iron Shoes

- 71

- Hunt the Goat

- King Atroxian

I have to confess I haven't been able to dig up much information about these games so far. I hope to have a better handle on the rules and what we'll need to play before the party.

3. Food and beverages

Food and beverages will not be served or permitted on the festival grounds. Please plan to eat before you arrive.

4. Trick or treating

The Judges have ordered an end to the practice of trick or treating, as it interferes with Their nightly wandering. Instead, we'll be switching to a Trunk or Treat format, which a lot of communities have adopted over the years.

If you'd like to volunteer your car's trunk, or to help with decorating, organizing, parking, etc. please contact the West Pennfield PTA.

We urge you not to spread the rumor that The Judges have halted trick or treating because it gives residents a chance to speak one-on-one outside of Their earshot. Truly, there is nothing They do not hear.

5. The Haunted Library

As we all know, everyone who dies lives on within The Judges, joining countless others in Their eternal consciousness, feeding and being fed, the battery and the receptor. On the searing plane of Their Mind, each of us is rendered into one, trillions upon trillions of voices forming a single chorus to intone Their holy and monstrous song.

That means ghosts aren't real, and as such, this year's Haunted Library will be canceled.

6. The Offering Tent

We have a new attraction this year called The Offering Tent, which will cover the entirety of our athletic fields. You've probably noticed some prep work happening behind the township offices. If we're going to be ready by Halloween, we'll need a few volunteers to help with construction. The Judges say these volunteers must be between 25 and 30 years old, "of clean blood" and a licensed CDL driver.

Township residents born on the following dates are required to attend The Offering tent:

January 3, January 20; February 8, February 9, April 11, April 19, April 29, May 13, May 14, May 15; June 24, July 7, July 10, July 16, August 1, August 8, September 30, October 5, October 11, October 13, October 28, November 2, November 3, November 18, November 20, November 21, December 8, December 9, December 15, December 27.

Attendees must bathe before arrival and wear the white gown we've provided.

We know this all sounds like a lot, but if we all pitch in and come together on this, I think we can still have a fun and safe Halloween party that does not offend The Judges. Remember that attendance is mandatory. See you there!

Best wishes,

Sherry Melendez, Township Administrator

Tom Coombe is a horror writer whose stories have appeared in Not Deer Magazine, Dose of Dread, and the recent anthology It Was All a Dream. He lives in Pennsylvania's Lehigh Valley with his girlfriend and their demonic cat.

The Pumpkin Fetch

Tom Deady

"Right there!" Steve was pointing like he'd just spotted Bigfoot. I pulled over to the side of the road to see what had gotten him all worked up. I followed the direction of his wild gestures and smiled. The house was set way back from the road, a brick walkway leading to the sprawling wraparound porch. It wasn't the house that had Steve acting like a lunatic, it was the pumpkins that stood sentinel along both sides of the walkway and lined the porch railing.

There had to be thirty of them. "Jackpot," I whispered.

We were competing in the annual Pumpkin Fetch. It was a Halloween tradition we'd started six or seven years ago. Like many traditions, this one started with the often volatile mix of alcohol and boredom. We were seventeen or so when we started it; old enough to drive but too young to get into clubs. Clever enough to get our hands on a couple six-packs of beer but not cool enough to be invited to any parties.

"Creep up a little more and we can start grabbing them," Steve said.

I took a long pull on my beer, thinking about how much better it tasted out of a bottle than a can. "Fuck that," I said, "if we're gonna win this thing, we don't have time for that shit." I inched past the driveway, shut off my headlights, threw the car into reverse, and backed up the drive and over the lawn until I was practically on the porch. Steve whooped and jumped out as I threw the Charger into park and hit the button to open the hatchback.

The night was redolent with the scent of dead leaves and cool enough to remind you that winter was on its way. It took less than five minutes to load the pumpkins in the back. As we grabbed the last few off the porch railing, the outside lights snapped on, illuminating the yard. We tossed the last few pumpkins in the back and jumped in the car. The front door opened as I peeled out, leaving a mess of tire tracks on their pristine lawn. Steve and I were laughing our asses off as we heard the owner shout something about calling the police.

So, you've probably done the math and figured out we were now in our twenties. We were both college graduates with real jobs, and long in the tooth to be stealing pumpkins on Halloween night, but a tradition is a tradition, right? Besides, the event had grown to the point there were almost twenty cars, each containing a pair of contestants, a lot of beer, and by this time, a shitload of pumpkins.

"It's two-thirty," Steve said. "We better haul ass to the church if we don't want to get disqualified."

I glanced at the dashboard clock. "We'll make it," I said, "now grab me another beer."

I tore into the lot behind the old church, kicking up a cloud of dust as I pulled next to an old Country Squire wagon. We had five minutes to spare before the 3:00 AM deadline. Another fun thing about the Fetch is keeping the cops from finding out where the rally point is and avoiding them all evening. Every year a few people don't make it, getting their car impounded for the night if they're caught with any pumpkins, but so far Steve and I had a perfect record. I was pretty sure we had a chance to win this year and my walk showed it.

I strutted past a few other cars, ready to start trash-talking. Instead, I stopped and stared at the odd sight before me. Instead of everyone hanging out drinking, usually next to their pile of pumpkins waiting for the final count, it looked like they'd dragged the pews out of the abandoned church and were—Are they praying?

"What the fuck," I whispered.

"Are they..." Steve didn't finish, apparently rendered speechless by the absurdity of it.

"They're fucking with us," I said, walking toward the row of three wooden pews. They were full of my friends—it looked like all the other guys and girls participating in the Fetch. It wasn't weird enough that they were sitting motionless on the pews, but they were all wearing pumpkin masks.

"Tommy..."

I ignored Steve as I picked up my stride and reached the first pew. I recognized George McCauley and his girlfriend, Suzie something-or-other. It was easy—they'd rolled in at the start of the Fetch dressed in identical chain gang costumes. "George, what the fuck?"

He didn't answer. Didn't turn to look at me. It was pissing me off. I stepped closer and punched him lightly on the shoulder. He tipped over, bumping Suzie, and the entire row of bodies went down like dominos. George's mask popped off and rolled off the bench onto the gravel lot with a crunch. I stepped back, unable to process what I was seeing. It wasn't a mask, it was an actual pumpkin. George's head was gone, just the shiny white top of his spine was sticking out of his shirt. A few others were the same. Headless. The pumpkins having rolled off their human spine-spike perches.

I backed up, wanting to get to the car but somehow afraid to turn my back on the horrific tableau. I stumbled but managed to catch my balance before falling, the scene in every horror movie of the victim tripping and the monster catching them playing in my head. I looked down to see what had caused the stumble: it was Steve's headless body.

I turned, and there before me, was a pile of...heads...where there should have been a pile of pumpkins. I recognized George and Suzie and a few others. A figure emerged from behind the pile, dressed all in black like the Grim Reaper, but with a priest's clerical collar. Of course, it carried a scythe.

Tom Deady's first novel, Haven, *won the 2016 Bram Stoker Award for Superior Achievement in a First Novel. He has since published several novels and novellas, and is releasing his first collection of short stories in late 2020. He has a Master's Degree in English and Creative Writing and is a member of both the Horror*

Writers Association and the New England Horror Writers Association. He resides in Massachusetts where he is working on his next novel.

Welcome to the party, pal

William Meikle

We finally got the kids to bed near midnight, but not before we'd watched and sang along to Albert Finney, then Michael Caine as Scrooge, the latter twice. By then Jo was dead on her feet but her twin brother Duncan had fire in his eyes; he'd been told earlier in the week at school that Santa Claus wasn't real and he was determined to know, one way or the other. As I sat on the sofa with Elaine for our own annual ritual movie I imagined Duncan's blue eyes staring hard at the ceiling in the room upstairs. He would be straining for any indication of sleigh bells in the wind or reindeer on the roof; he was still young enough to want to believe.

We had a jug of mulled wine, a bottle of expensive vodka, and a round of nice aged brie. I had stoked a roaring fire into life with judicious use of the old iron poker, and we had hours to ourselves, at least until Duncan's itch got too much for him and he, and his sister, descended on the presents under the tree like hungry raptors. I intended to make the most of it.

Elaine, as ever, had fallen under the movie's spell from the first few scenes, and I caught myself joining her in mouthing the dialog as the bad guys crashed the party.

"Mr. Takagi, whoever said we were terrorists?"

As I reached for my glass to toast the clock above the mantel ticking over into Christmas Day, I heard a dull thud from somewhere overhead.

"The old man's early," I said, but Elaine's smile quickly turned to a frown as the noise was repeated, heavier this time, and the frame of the house shook, setting the light fitting overhead swinging.

"There's somebody up there," she said, barely more than a whisper. The barefoot man on the screen seemed to answer.

"No fucking shit, lady. Does it sound like I'm ordering a pizza?"

But by that time I was on my feet and heading for the stairs, a vague, almost floating feeling of dread washing through me as there was another, even louder thud and the house shook again. I intended to head for the kids, but I never made it across the room.

Ash and soot fell in a rush down the chimney, sending a billowing cloud of black smoke and choking fumes across the room. I heard a rasping, cloth on stone, then felt hot sparks lash my cheeks. There was a thud, a flare of red as something heavy landed in our fire from above. I had to rub my eyes against a sudden, almost acidic sting, and when I opened them it was to see a tall bulky figure standing among what were now embers on our hearth.

Elaine screamed and I heard a squeal from Duncan upstairs. In his case it sounded more like delight, but whoever—whatever—this was, it was no Santa Claus. It carried an empty burlap sack over its left shoulder and wore a heavy coat of reddish-brown, matted fur—at first, I thought it was part of it but the coat swung open at the front revealing a grey, painfully thin body. The rib cage, pelvis, and legs looked almost canine—wolf-like even, but the head end was more goat-like, with tall, curving horns that scraped our ceiling. No goat ever had teeth like this though—pointed, fang-like, with a silvery hue that seemed almost metallic.

The blessed Bruce spoke on the screen, "Come out to the coast, we'll get together, have a few laughs."

The thing on our hearth raised its snout and brayed out a laugh in reply, although I heard little humour in it.

"Santa Claus!" a small voice shouted on the stairs. My head turned the same time as the thing's and we both stared at Duncan who had already come down four steps before stopping, a confused look in his eyes.

"Beep! Would you like to go for double jeopardy where the scores can really change?"

The thing in the hearth smiled—don't ask me how I knew, it was something in its eyes, something in the way it rolled a fleshy tongue over its teeth. It stepped away from the fireplace and began to head towards the stairs where Duncan stood, frozen in place.

"No!" Elaine shouted. "Leave my boy alone."

I finally found that I could move. I waited until the beast walked past me then stepped over to the fireplace and took up the iron poker. I turned to my wife. "Hey babe, I negotiate million dollar deals for breakfast. I think I can handle this Eurotrash."

I went after it and caught it on the stairs, three steps below Duncan, just as it was opening the black mouth of the burlap sack. The poker whistled in the air as I smacked the beast on the back of the head with all my strength. It was like swinging a hammer against solid rock, a jarring thrum running up my arm and across my chest. But it had served a purpose. The beast stopped heading for Duncan and slowly turned towards me.

"Welcome to the party, pal."

I thrust the poker, like a sword, under its ribs. The blow didn't penetrate the skin, but the beast staggered. It didn't fall, so I hit it again, a backhand from below my waist level, heading up and hitting the sweet spot on the point of its chin. Its head jerked back, it staggered again and almost fell. I kicked it where its balls should be, then yelled, screaming nonsense words as I rained blow after blow on its head and shoulders.

It crept away from me, heading for the fireplace and escape.

Elaine stepped forward and mashed a slab of runny Brie in its face. It mewled, clawing at suddenly blinded eyes and I stepped up my attack, driving it back-

276

wards. I paused only to pick up the bottle of vodka with my free hand as I backed the beast against the embers of the fire.

I shouted more incoherent nonsense and dashed the vodka at its feet.

It went up in flames in seconds. Even then it tried to reach the chimney to flee, but the iron poker kept it down, pinning it in the flames until its struggles lessened, grew feeble, and finally, with a crumble of ash falling in on itself, ceased entirely.

"Yippee-ki-yay, motherfucker," the Blessed Bruce said.

I agreed with him.

William Meikle is a Scottish writer, now living in Canada, with over thirty novels published in the genre press and more than 300 short story credits in thirteen countries. He has books available from a variety of publishers including Dark Regions Press and Severed Press and his work has appeared in a large number of professional anthologies and magazines. You'll find him at Williammeikle.com.

Santapocalypse

Ken MacGregor

It's the Day of the Dead and already I'm seeing Christmas shit on the store shelves. Halloween's corpse is just barely showing signs of rigor mortis. Stupid money-grubbing retailers can't wait for stupid, money-spewing consumers to start shopping. I should just stay home until mid-January.

Oh good. The city is stringing pine garlands on all the lampposts. Each features a massive red bow, like "Here! *Light* is your present. Merry Fucking Xmas!"

Used to be, we could enjoy Thanksgiving first. Bunch of cartoon turkeys and the like. Not anymore. If some people had their way, we'd probably have Christmas all year. Ugh.

· · · ● · ● · ● · · ·

Thanksgiving is typical. Uncle Bob is still an unapologetic racist. Carol has another new husband: she collects them like tchotchkes. My cousin Mike spent the whole day high as hell on edibles. We were close once, being almost the same age. I try to talk to him now and he just nods and says "Right?" in a vague, distracted way, like he's seeing through gauze and not really sure who's in front of him.

Heading back home, the highway is peppered with red and green billboards shouting at me to Buy All the Things! Snow is falling just hard enough to give that cool Millennium Falcon effect through the windshield. All the SUVs on the road have red noses and antlers. Every station is playing "Little Drummer Boy" or "Greensleeves."

I pull in my driveway, assess whether I'm going to have to shovel tomorrow (probably), and crawl inside for a hot toddy and a good night's sleep.

· · · ● · ● · ● · · ·

The morning sun reflects off the snow, dazzling my eyes. It's going to warm up today though, so at least I don't have to shovel the walk. Across the street, the Anders' have put out their annual inflatable Santa sleigh and eight reindeer. At fifteen feet tall, it is somehow elevated beyond tacky and is instead bold. I hate it. By evening, their whole exterior will be covered in tiny, blinking lights, making my bedroom window feel like I'm living in Times Square, drowning in neon.

Black Friday. Time to shop local and help keep the mom-and-pop folks in business. If I'm being honest, I do hit Amazon more than I want to. Sometimes, it's the only way to get stuff. But sometimes it's just...convenient. Not proud of that. But I do it anyway. However, today, out of all the days of the year, I make it a point to shop downtown, and to only buy from independent stores. I *am* proud of that.

The storefronts are positively festooned with holiday decorations. No fewer than three guys in Santa suits stand around, ringing bells, either attracting shoppers or asking for charitable donations. It's almost fifty now, and I wonder if they're sweating. Regardless, they're smiling broadly under those white beards and rosy cheeks. They got some very convincing actors this year.

By the time I'm finished, I've got presents for most of my family and a couple close friends. Outside, the sky is already dimming toward evening. There are four Santas now. Huh.

Inside me, the Christmas Spirit tingles.

I suppress it.

• • • ● • ● • ● • • •

Back home, I hide the gifts in the spare bedroom closet, eat leftover pizza, and watch "The Ref" on TV. This is my concession to watching Xmas movies. A profane, obnoxious comedy about a thief who kidnaps a dysfunctional family...on Christmas. It counts.

When it's over, Netflix suggests I might want to watch Home Alone 2. No thanks. Across the street, every color of the rainbow blares out from thousands of tiny light bulbs, behind Colossal Santa. Up and down the street, the other houses are trying desperately to keep up. Me? I still have a cardboard skeleton on the door. I'll take it down eventually.

• • • ● • ● • • • •

Driving to work, on December 13, I let the car drop to almost an idle. Downtown is starting to look like The Littlest Christmas Village. Every surface of retail space is literally covered in red and green, in smiling elves and prancing reindeer. There are so many Santas now I lose count after 30.

My office is, thankfully, devoid of décor, but most of the building is showing its holiday spirit in spades. Even Spielman's desk has a belly-laughing Santa leaning against the menorah. To a one, my coworkers are wearing pointy red hats with white fur fringe. There's an extra one on the coat hook near my desk. I ignore it.

· · ● ● · ● · ● · ● · ·

December 21. I'm afraid to leave my house. My cardboard skeleton seems to be warding them off for now, but who knows how long that'll last.

The Santas mill around outside, over a hundred strong. Occasionally, one will put on speed and barrel into my wall, headfirst with a resounding *thunk!* They avoid the door and maybe haven't figured out that the windows are breakable.

The taunting, awful "Ho ho ho"s echo through the air, a holly, jolly madness. I sit on the couch, iron poker in my hand, waiting. Eventually, they'll get in. I'll take down as many as I can.

· · ● ● · ● · ● · ● · ·

The sliding glass patio door explodes inward. More than a hundred shuffle in and surround me, just out of reach of the poker. As one, they speak.

"You better watch out. You better not cry."

I swing wildly, catching a Santa in his gut. It jiggles like a bowlful of jelly.

"You better not pout. I'm telling you why."

The poker drops from my hand. Frustrated, I clutch at my beard.

(BEARD?)

"Santa Claus is coming..."

Horrified, but unable to resist, I finish: "...to town."

· · · ● · ● · ● · ● · ● · · ·

With a hearty "Ho, ho, ho," I pull the cardboard skeleton off the door and drop it in the snow. Reaching back, I take the wreath from another Santa and hang it in its place of honor. Still one more Santa plugs in the extension cord and my house lights up red and green, the good colors, the proper colors.

Together, we set out from our small city. We are fifteen-hundred strong. We will spread cheer, whether you like it or not.

Christmas is coming. For you.

Ken MacGregor writes stuff.

He has three story collections, an award-winning YA novella, and a co-written novel. Ken is a Shirley Jackson Award-nominated editor.

Ken drives the bookmobile for his local library. He lives with his kids, two cats, and the ashes of his wife.

Ken lurks at kenmacgregor.com.

A Very Weird Christmas

Madison McSweeney

The snow was so deep, and its coverage so complete, that the house might have been a hill, were it not for the multicolored glow streaming out from the windows. Kris Kringle tied down his sleigh with a single loop around the chimney before squeezing himself inside and shimmying down headfirst. When he reached the bottom, he stopped dead.

He was in a living room, which did not surprise him. What did surprise him were the two children in matching pajamas sitting side-by-side in a green paisley armchair. The tree beside them was already suffocating with gifts, brightly-wrapped boxes bedecked with ribbons and bows stacked a foot-and-half high at its feet. Standing in front of the children, his back to the fireplace, was a man in a red cloak, belted with a rope of white fur.

He had barely a second to comprehend the scene before the older child, a little boy, pointed at him, causing the houseguest to turn around. The man was very old, with a long white beard and eyes that glistened with mischief. To a stranger, he probably would have looked exactly like Kris.

The ersatz Santa Claus laughed, a gregarious and throaty *ho ho ho*. "This is one of my helpers." He placed a gloved hand on Kris's shoulder, holding him firm, and looked down at the children. "Have your parents ever taken you to a department store to meet Santa Claus?"

The kids nodded, rapt.

"Of course, they did," the false Santa smiled. "But there are thousands of department stores, and I can't possibly be at every one of them at once. That's why I ask my fondest friends to go in my place and collect the messages for me. Does that make sense?"

They nodded again. Kris' blood ran cold.

"You've had a night of wonders, haven't you? Getting to meet Santa Claus and his helper, together! Very few children can say that. And if you listen closely..." the imposter raised a finger towards the ceiling. "Do you hear that sound?"

Sure enough, a muffled stomping could be heard from the roof. "Reindeer!" the little girl yelled.

"A bright girl, indeed!" The fake Santa fixed his eyes on the little boy. "Your sister is a smart girl, isn't she?"

"Yes, Santa, sir," the boy said solemnly.

"She's a little younger than you, isn't she?"

"A year younger," the boy replied. He couldn't have been more than five or six himself.

"And you look after her?" The man's eyes twinkled conspiratorially.

"Yes!"

"Why don't you two put your boots on and go take a look at the reindeer, while I chat with my helper?"

"Oh, can we, Santa?" the little girl cried.

"Of course, you can." He winked at the boy. "Your big brother will take care of you." The false Santa raised his sleeve, unbuckled a thin black watch, and handed it to the older child. "When the long hand reaches three, come back in and put your sister to bed. That's five minutes." He cast an eye towards Kris. "We shouldn't need much longer than that."

The two Santas stood side-by-side as the children hurried to pull on their boots and coats, the fake Santa shedding pounds with every second that passed. Kris flicked his head toward the fireplace. *How much time would it take to scurry up, untie the reindeer and fly away?* The boy held the door open for his sister. "I know what you're thinking, Mr. Kringle," the man said under his breath.

Outside, the snow was coming down in heaps, and the children—after they'd poked their heads out—doubled back to fish for hats and scarves. By the time the little girl hopped onto the porch and the boy closed the door behind him, the old man's robe hung limply around emaciated shoulders. When he turned to face Kris, he was beardless, and his black eyes had lost all remnants of their jolly glow.

Crow, Kris thought. As if it hadn't been obvious from the beginning.

He spoke haltingly. "I've brought a lot of joy on this realm."

"And siphoned much from it," Crow replied. His voice was like cold stone.

Kris didn't have to ask what he meant. With every present he delivered, he'd taken something else from the recipient—a dream, a wish, a fantasy. Children were so full of them, they hardly noticed the loss; that single annual harvest had fuelled Kris for hundreds of years.

Kris made a break for the fireplace. But the instant he stepped onto the hearth and into the firebox, Crow raised his cane and set the dry wood ablaze. Kris dug his talons into the brick, but had no time to pull himself up before his ancient feet turned to dust and his legs crumbled under him. He barely even had time to scream.

"Quiet, Mr. Kringle," the old man said. "You'll scare the children."

The fire burned hot and died out. Now Crow stepped into the fireplace, taking care to avoid the pile of ash, and slithered up the chimney.

• • • ● • ● • ● • • •

Kris Kringle's sleigh was a ramshackle collection of wood, the tethered deer pale and sickly. He'd been feeding off their essence as well; it was amazing they could still fly. Crow pounded his staff three times on the roof. The yokes fell off their shoulders as the ropes tying them to the sleigh melted away.

Shaking snow off his shoulders, Dasher stretched and stood. The others followed suit, freed of their bonds. On two legs, the deer towered nearly eight feet tall, their antlers shining in the moon. With great dignity, they nodded at Crow before turning their backs to him; he lowered his eyes respectfully as they lifted off and flew away into the night.

A pair of voices rose up from below: "Wow!"

Crow peered over the edge of the roof to see the children staring up at him. He chuckled. "Off to bed now, little ones. I have a number of visits before I can sleep." *Far too many.*

The little girl ran obediently into the house, but the boy lingered. "Your watch!" he shouted, dangling the strap above his head.

"Keep it," Crow called back, laughing again. Might as well—what use had he for a timepiece?

The boy's face lit up. "Merry Christmas, Santa!" he cried, and then darted inside as if worried his luck would run out.

"And a good night to you," Crow murmured as his body faded into the darkness and blew away with the snow. It was nearly Christmas day, and other worlds awaited.

Madison McSweeney *is a horror and weird fiction author from Ottawa, Ontario. She is the author of* The Doom That Came to Mellonville *(Filthy Loot),* The Forest Dreams With Teeth *(Demain Publishing), and* Fringewood *(Alien Buddha Press). Her short stories have appeared in anthologies like* Zombie Punks Fuck Off *(Weirdpunk/CLASH),* American Gothic Short Stories *(Flame Tree), and* The First Five Minutes of the Apocalypse *(Hungry Shadow Press). She blogs at www.madisonmcsweeney.com and tweets from @MMcSw13.*

If the Elf Moves, Kill It

Matt Bliss

Dad presses the cold revolver in my palm and wraps his coarse hand around mine. "You know what to do," he says and quickly pulls the zipper up his winter jacket.

And I know it's not right—*I know Dad's not right*—but what if he is? What if it's *really* happening and I have to pull the trigger? Could I actually do it?

His eyes dart up to the ceiling and dance across its surface. "They're on the roof again. Can you hear them?"

I don't, but I nod anyway.

He sprints toward the door and mutters, "I thought the lights would keep them away." The statement doesn't make sense, but none of this does. It's Christmas Eve, and I should be in bed, pressing my eyes shut and dreaming of what I will find under the tree. But Mom never came home, and Dad has grown more frantic than ever.

I look back at the stuffed elf on the mantle across from me and try to steady the gun in my hand. Did it move? When I looked away, in that sliver of a second, did it turn its head toward me? It couldn't have. There's no way, but...what if it did? It moved while we slept. Scouting for Santa, Mom said, and I was *never* to touch it. Every morning I found it somewhere new. Frozen in place, playing with toys, climbing the tree, messing up my room... Mom and Dad swore it wasn't them, but last night, while they were asleep, I touched it, and it was no more real than any of my toys. So why is Dad so afraid?

"I'm going outside to check," Dad said, reaching for the doorknob. His eyes are too large, too glassy. "Whatever you do, whatever happens, don't open this door, understand?"

I don't understand, but I nod anyway.

"I want you to know," he says, and I look away from the elf to see his bottom lip quiver. "No matter what happens tonight...I love you."

"What's happening, Dad? Why are we—"

But he twists the handle and opens the door to a blast of frigid air. Dad steps outside and disappears in the flurry of snow, then slams the door shut behind him.

Something moved. The elf. I snap my eyes back to it. It's closer now. Chin pointed toward me, but its eyes look sideways. Its eyes were always sideways, always looking away. I readjust my grip on the pistol and keep it raised despite the burning in my arm. I know how to use it. Dad showed me twice now how to hold it—how to squeeze the trigger.

Footsteps thump on the roof, and I look up toward the sound.

Was it Dad? What was he chasing? My heart pounds like a drummer boy in my chest. I wish Mom were here—she'd know what to do.

Something patters across the floor in front of me, and I jerk back, but I already know. The elf moved. He's right in front of me. Frozen, standing on spindly felt legs. Its smile screwed up in a sneer. Its eyes, no longer looking sideways, look straight at me.

Dad screams from outside and something thuds against the roof.

Still, I don't look away. If I do, he'll move. The Elf will get me. I press my arms straight and aim the barrel of the pistol at its tiny head. *If it moves, kill it.* That's what Dad told me. That's what I should do. I'm panting now, willing myself to squeeze the trigger, just like Dad showed me, but I can't.

The doorknob jiggles. Something's trying to get in, but it's locked.

"Dad?" I ask, but still, I can't tear my eyes away from the elf's snarling face.

The handle jiggles again, and a voice says, "Open the door, honey." But it's not Dad that says it, it's Mom.

"Don't open it!" Dad shouts from behind her. His voice is choked and breaking.

My heart beats faster. "It moved! The Elf Moved," I say, still too afraid to blink.

"Shoot it!" Dad yells.

"Open the door!" Mom cries.

The elf is still there. Still watching. Ready for the moment I look away to come after me. "Why's it doing this?" I ask. "What's happening?"

I hear Dad openly weep outside. Deep sobs, filling the frosty night.

"Because," Mom says. "You touched the elf. We told you not to, but you touched him. These are the rules. I..." her voice breaks as the door clicks open. "I'm sorry..."

I look up to see a red suit filling the doorframe. I drop the pistol, and the room fills with the tiny patter of felt legs. They're everywhere.

"Goodbye, son," Dad says and drops his head in his hands.

It was my time to join the elves.

Matt Bliss *is a construction worker turned speculative fiction writer from Las Vegas, Nevada. His short fiction has appeared in MetaStellar, Cosmic Horror Monthly, and Diabolical Plots among other published and forthcoming works. You can find more of Matt's works at flow.page/mattbliss.*

Meadow for The Birdmen

Guy Medley

Jack felt it before he heard it, the whole earth beneath the barn heaving upward, breathing in deeply, then exhaling with a thundering wail as if the skies had been savagely gashed open.

When the smoke had mostly cleared away, Armageddon revealed, Jack ran into the destruction, the wheat stalks burned down to pointed charcoal nubs that crunched to dust under his feet. He found his father in the smoldering ruin, his body a tangled, burned mess, torn asunder by red hot shrapnel—wings, wheels, gearing—guns. Anything that could have once identified the thing's origins now lay obliterated by heat and gravity.

Jack retrieved his father as best he could. The armies whose men rained down through the clouds in a plague of flaming wreckage never came to claim their fallen, their machines laying burst apart in every field of the land, fuel and oil filling the soils with poison—with death.

As his father was laid out upon the family table, the lands took on a savage red hue as the sun began its descent. The streaming tentacles of more falling machines marred the dusk, moving the mourning farm into deep shadow and deeper sorrow. Jack watched the night transpire in solitude. From the long row of trees that bordered the lane, he saw them slowly emerge—men concealed in shadow, gaunt forms drifting past on the breeze, so silent in passing the haunting songs of the flittering nightjars remained undisturbed, the night blooms un-blemished by their trek.

They moved on, countless numbers, legions unending seeking the field, the meadow of the feast, Jack remembered from his father's tales. To dine in Fölkvangr with Freyja in the glory of the moon. He wondered if his father was among the many, if he would eat at the table of the gathered warriors this night, or if he has perhaps traveled some other path. One forged by slain farmers.

Curious, Jack followed them into the misty night. There were so many, all broken, battered—unwhole. Men in splinters, blown apart and grisly. Men of wars. Men's wars, he thought, are surely kind to the gods.

They wound like whispers through the night, finally emerging into a marshy meadow near the river where their battle-weary bodies would at last welcome in a feast. But, it was Freyja who feasted, and her alone, on all who entered her meadow. Her colossus form filled the meadow, a deep green ethereal brume radiating from her, a turbid raging sea exuding from her being. The Goddess' jaws opened an eternal chasm and they took in the slain to be once more devoured wholly by death. He watched aghast as one by one the lost men marched on under otherworldly devices into that godly maw, their preternatural shrieks causing Jack to recoil in horror and duck below a low stone wall whereupon he witnessed the terrors before him.

Freyja's great feathered cloak filled the field, obscured the moonlight. A foreboding overtook Jack, his spine tingling with static. He could feel a slipping here, where mortality wore thin—virulent. In a panic to escape the hungry god, he turned to flee into the darkness, away from the damned meadow, the tormented dead, hoping that her greed did not involve the living. He could feel it calling to him, pulling at his bones. Always hungry, always wanting more. His very soul shuddered, filling him with a deep sadness so frightful, so all-consuming, he thought he might have succumbed to Freyja's feast, until at last the feeling loosened its grip on him and he was thrust forward past the edge of the meadow and along the treed lane that led toward home.

Guy Medley writes dark and haunting fiction from the lonely solitude of his secluded Mojave Desert chateau. He has been published by Crystal Lake, Sirens Call and more, and is always looking to share his strange stories with others.

The Cut

Amanda M. Blake

"And it's down to the bottom two this week, Brandon and Arielle. We love everyone and don't want anyone to leave us, but who will live to sing and sling cake flour another day? The one leaving us today is..."

Dramatic pause, milking the digestive acids of the contestants now to milk them from the audience in six months.

"Brandon. I'm sorry, but your 'Crazy in Love' triple chocolate cake didn't inspire the judges to sing your praises today. The voice judges found your Beyoncé too blasé and sloppy, and the baking judges felt your bitter dark chocolate ganache overwhelmed the whole cake. I'm afraid you've been *cut*"—sound effect of a slicing cake knife through the speakers on set—"from the competition. We'll never forget your 'Bad Romance' biscuits and gravy in Breakfast Week, but this is the end of your yellow cake brick road in *Sweet Sing-Off*."

I hang my head, but I smile sadly. I knew this was coming. Arielle's tiramisu lacked a strong enough espresso flavor in the syrup brushed onto the ladyfinger sponge, but she absolutely killed her karaoke version of "Taking Chances." I knew that if it ever came down to us, I could never beat her. She has off-days in baking; she's never off-key on her songs.

Arielle and I hug, because I'm not mad. Then the other two singer-bakers gather us in a group hug. I blink away some errant powdered sugar in my eye. I was so close. It sucks to be the first to leave, and it sucks to leave just before you reach the pedestal, even if you only make third. I share this in my exit interview, and I tease that I'd planned to sing "Wrecking Ball" with my three-tiered, three-flavored wedding cake. The two hosts slap my back and wish me well.

"It's just Martine, Deandra, and Arielle, our top three, fighting for sweet, sweet survival in next week's wedding finale…" I hear before they shuffle me out of the kitchen.

A producer I hadn't met yet briskly leads me through the house custom-built for their reality competitions—with movable walls in the main kitchen area because they also use this house for *Cookie Chemotherapy*, which starts as soon as *Sweet Sing-Off* concludes.

Someone already cleared out the bedroom I shared with Caro until he was cut the third week. A production assistant rolls my suitcase, filled with all my shiny shirts and sequined scarves that any flamboyant would envy. She also carries a cardboard box of my personal baking supplies that I use in the practice kitchen and that they allow in the competition if I need a specialty tool within accessory guidelines.

"I'm sorry, Brandon. I was really rooting for you to go all the way." The producer's hand rests warm and heavy on my shoulder as he guides me gently but insistently through the labyrinth of the house. I expect he'll lead me to the front door, where a taxi waits in the drive to take me home until they bring me back for the reunion finale.

Instead, we stop at a random door that looks like it's for a linen closet. He directs his beleaguered production assistant to open it to a dark hole with raw wood steps down to a basement. I didn't even know the house had a basement.

Missed opportunity for a cast and crew speakeasy, if anyone asks me.

"What's going on?"

"Just some last shots for the introductory package." The producer gestures me down first, then the production assistant.

In the bowels of the plasterboard mansion, bright photography lights and their reflective umbrellas, green screen backdrop, and black camera equipment conjure me more powerfully than the hesitation of my confusion. I don't immediately notice the churning of the furnace, with its grill chewing fire. I'm too confused by the guillotine in the shadows—and the sealed prop box of mannequin heads with familiar faces.

"It really is a shame every time we lose someone," the producer says from the base of the stairs. "The longer you're with us, the more you feel like family. But we make it very clear in the contract that you're fighting for your life in front of our cameras, and that triple chocolate cake was not good enough to let you live."

The production assistant tosses my baking equipment into the fire, but it's watching her feed my favorite sparkly clothes into the furnace that makes me gasp, backing up the stairs, but the door at the top is locked.

"I have the unfortunate task of dealing with eliminations," the producer says, unconcerned by my attempt to flee, checking his watch with impatience. "You're contractually obligated to the guillotine, Brandon. If you refuse, I assure you, you'll wish you'd just stuck your neck in of your own accord. Don't make Lelane strap you down. Have a little dignity."

If this producer had really been rooting for me the whole time, he would know that, as a semi-professional karaoke singer, I have no dignity.

There's screaming, crying, wailing tremolo, and there might be a little melodrama. Part of me still believes there's cameras in the corners, watching my hysterics and recording what will turn into a well-edited viral moment. But the very real heat from the furnace billows into the rest of the room, melting the people in it. The producer looks decidedly wilted by the time he and Lelane, soaked through her three-piece suit, force me face-up on the bench, rather than face-down to keep me from seeing the gold-soaked tempered steel, with an angle smoothed into the edge like a razorblade.

I'm sweat-soaked and not at all at my best. Although my mascara is waterproof, the eyeliner is not.

The producer turns the lights and cameras on me. I stare at him upside-down, into the dead, black eye of the camera. The melodrama casually shifts into tearful terror, even if you can't tell the difference on my malleable face.

"For legal reasons, we're required to film eliminations. Something about proof of fulfillment and mutually-assured destruction." The producer bustles around to put himself into the frame. "I wish this could have gone differently. I was really looking forward to 'Wrecking Ball.' I'm sorry, though, Brandon. You've been cut."

It's funny. A real blade sings nothing like the sound effect.

As my head rolls to a stop, I'm able to look back at the clean cross-section of my neck—framed by the iridescent shirt that I hoped would usher me into the finale, not cremation—and reflect: that guillotine could make a killer slice, all the way down the three tiers of my wedding cake, but can it carry a tune?

A cat-loving daydreamer and mid-age goth who loves geekery of all sorts, from superheroes to horror movies, urban fantasy to unconventional romance, **Amanda M. Blake** *is the author of such horror titles as* Nocturne *and* Deep Down *and the fairy tale mash-up series* Thorns.

Reindeer Game

Jonathan Hyde

Rob Roy was exactly where McCleod said he would be: in the oval glade.

The sight of the huge, statuesque animal under pale grey moonlight on a dusting of snow was incredibly beautiful and, if Stewart had let the moment get to him, really quite serene. It was almost a shame that Stewart was about to put a bullet into that massive heart of his.

If there was anybody who hated McCleod more than Stewart, it was Stewart's father, Tam, and because of that, he could think of no better Christmas present for his father than the head of McCleod's beloved stag.

Stewart slowly knelt behind a low, skeletal hedge and placed his backpack on the ground. He slipped the strap of the rifle down his arm, held the gun horizontally and nestled the butt into his right shoulder, ready to take aim.

The stag was unmoved.

Stewart took in a deep breath and grinned as he let it out. This was going to be the perfect hunt—the perfect kill.

Stewart knew he wouldn't be disturbed. At that very moment McCleod would be passed out in bed with a bellyful of the Black Lion's house whisky and it would be hours before Jenny and the girls would wake ready to open their presents on Christmas morning. By that time Stewart would be home with them and would have a present for his dad bagged up in the garage.

These were the moments he lived for.

He wordlessly counted down five seconds, not thinking the numbers from five to one, but at each beat he heard the double thud of heartbeats.

Du-dum

A slight breeze rolled in and Stewart moved just a touch so that the centre of the scope was to the left of the animal's chest.

Du-dum

Stewart inhaled a deep lungful of cold December air.

Du-dum

He rubbed his finger against the trigger and then firmly pressed against it, ready to squeeze.

Du-dum

He slowly let out his breath and was about to pull the trigger when—

One

The whole bank of trees behind Rob Roy shook, relieving their emaciated branches of snow. With panic, Stewart pulled in the trigger but he was too late. As big as the stag was, when startled he was quick off the mark and nimble. Within seconds Rob Roy had left the glade and Stewart knew that any chance he had of killing the animal that night had gone.

Stewart punched the ground, then stood and kicked his backpack.

What in the hell had just happened?

He had felt a breeze but that's all it was—even a sudden strong gust of wind wouldn't have been enough to do to those trees what he had just seen happen. He left his bag where it lay and stomped across the oval patch of hard earth toward the recently disturbed wall of trees.

Stewart slipped into the wooded darkness, slowly walked maybe thirty feet, snaking between trees, then he stopped and listened. There was something, or some things in the wood with him.

He heard a light, tinny sound, like the soft shaking of a tambourine. He could also hear rustling just up ahead. He slowly edged forward and as he did so, he lifted his gun once more. The dark wood broke ahead of him and Stewart couldn't believe what he was seeing.

Moonlight broke through a gap in the tree cover and highlighted a number of large, furry antlers.

Reindeer.

That sneaky McCleod, thought Stewart. McCleod usually couldn't help but brag about anything and everything and for him to introduce a bunch of reindeer onto his land without mentioning it to anybody was very out of character.

Out of character or not, Stewart wasn't planning on going home empty-handed that night. Through a gap in the trees, he could see the whole of the front end of one of the reindeer. It had a wide collar of white fur and Stewart aimed for the bottom of that collar.

He calmed himself and, after his earlier disappointment, shot on three heartbeats instead of five.

A crimson stain exploded in the white of the reindeer's collar. The animal then opened its mouth and fell to the ground with a loud thud.

Stewart thumped at the air and did a little happy hop, then clapped his hands twice hoping that the other reindeer would scatter...but none of them moved.

He slowly walked toward the fallen animal and as he rounded a large tree he could see the rest of the reindeer—all seven of them. They were tethered together in four pairs, the fallen one being half of the front pair.

Stewart's eyes widened when he saw that the rear pair of reindeer were tethered to a large sleigh. A strange sight indeed. Stewart's mind clouded as he tried to make sense of what he was seeing, but he didn't have time to work it out. There came a deep coughing noise behind him and Stewart turned to see somebody emerge from the darkness dressed in a Santa outfit and zipping up the fly of his trousers.

Stewart hadn't expected any kind of confrontation that night and he didn't want it either. He let his gun fall to his side and quickly stepped back into the shadows, then turned and walked away as silently as he could. He had just made it to the centre of the oval glade when he heard a horrifying, guttural wail.

"No no no," cried Santa. "DUNDER!"

Time was his to do with what he liked. At the sight of his fallen reindeer, Santa reached up and clenched his fist, slowing time once more and dragging this Christmas Eve back into a night of ten thousand nights.

He untethered Dunder, lifted her, and placed her in the sleigh's basket. She will be healed, but for this night's work, the rest of his crew would have to pull with the strength of eight.

Santa gritted his teeth and growled. He should have got straight back to work but first he would have his revenge. He reached into the sleigh and pulled out a red-and-white striped walking stick which looked like a huge candy cane.

Because Dunder had been hit on her right side, Santa knew the direction from where the gun had been fired. He trudged off in that direction and saw a disturbed patch of ground from where he saw footprints leading away and out of tree cover. He reached the glade and saw the culprit up ahead.

The man looked less than majestic and hardly statuesque. He cut a pathetic sight: a would-be killer frozen in time as he fled under moonlight.

Santa walked toward him, warping time and allowing the hunter a slither of coherence.

To Stewart it felt like he had walked into a wall. Mid stride he stopped moving and his thoughts slowed so much that they were an incoherent drone.

He could see perfectly though, and although he was frozen in time, the large man who stepped around him wasn't.

Santa loomed over him, his lips curling within the cloud of his bushy white beard.

He lifted his cane, held it horizontally, and then unscrewed the top. When the hook came away it revealed a gleaming pointed blade.

Santa held the tip against Stewart's chest and said "You've been very, very bad" before plunging the blade through the man's breastplate and into his heart.

It would take the same amount of time as twenty nights before Stewart would feel any pain and another forty before he fell dead to the ground.

By that time Santa had delivered presents to all of the good children of Europe and was heading toward the Canary Islands when Dunder awoke a quarter of a mile above the Atlantic Ocean.

Jonathan Hyde is a musician and author from the South Wales Valleys who grew up on stories and songs. Since childhood he has obsessed over comic books, 80s coming-of-age movies, and horror books and films; these loves blend and form the basis of his tales which have human-interest, terror and dark humour at their heart.

You can find him on most social media as @RockAndWriting.

Christlessmas

Joseph VanBuren

Blood everywhere, splattered on every wall, drying in half-congealed pools between piles of debris strewn across the floor. The store is a complete disaster. All the shelves are empty, the racks upturned, bent metal in funny angles all over. Shreds of packaging litter the ground like used confetti. Ruined proof that things used to be sold here, some semblance of order was once in place.

Yes, things were relatively normal before the virus. The store was a store, not a warzone wasteland. And people were people, for the most part. Maybe a little more animalistic during big sales, but nothing like this.

It all starts after Halloween—literally on November first. The first snakes of garland slither around posts, the blinking lights begin to twinkle like evil eyes, the wicked whisper of sleigh bells chuckle in the distance. The signs of end times we cannot ignore yet do not resist.

The aisles are flanked by well-stocked shelves. We marvel at the many things we can buy, all that stuff we could own. Colorful signs burst with eye-catching images and attractive prices. Cross-promoting displays in opportunistic places draw people closer. If only they actually promoted the cross.

Nativity scenes are knocked down by reindeer hooves. The manger moved aside to make room for more snowmen. Multicolored trees tower over everything, Babel-tall and beautiful. No Savior anywhere in sight. He's been replaced by a gluttonous giant in a blood-red coat. How did we not reject this anagram of Satan?

It all seems quite innocent at first, not to mention good for business. Those neat, clean aisles fill up with people. Carts and bellies get full, wallets emptied. Scanners beep to the rhythm of a healthy heartbeat. The pulse of the holiday season.

But those beeps increase with each day. As our appetite grows, the heart beats faster. We breathe heavier, clammy hands pushing carts quickly. Items on the shelves start to dwindle, disappearing like regretful ghosts. Familiar tunes become irritating earworms.

There's one left on the shelf and two customers coveting it. Doesn't matter what it is. They both lunge for it. One person grabs the item.

Then the other person bites them.

Some viruses take a while to show symptoms, but not this one. The victim lets out a snarl that sounds prehistoric. His skin takes on the ashy pallor of a corpse, yet he moves quicker than ever. He whips around and gnashes his teeth at the store full of people. Nobody is scared because they all have the germ inside them, scratching in their guts, eager to feed.

The store becomes a sea of piranha-like activity. Each person that gets bit passes the rapidly transmitted virus onto the next victim. Sounds like an overcrowded pig pen at dinner time. We eat the shelves bare, ingesting things we cannot digest. We devour ourselves into poverty. We eat each other out of the way, consuming everything until there is nothing left.

The seats at the table of the Lord's Supper are empty, for we have feasted with the enemy and engorged ourselves on the flesh and blood of our brothers and sisters.

And we'll do it again next year.

Out of the darkness, risen from the ashes... **Joseph VanBuren** *creates dark speculative tales showcasing the reality of resurrection and bringing a light against legion through poetry, fiction, music, and more. Originally from the haunted Hudson Valley region of New York, JVB now lives with his beloved wife Renée in Fort Wayne, Indiana. Find him on introverted media https://othershadows.wordpress.com/mentions/jvbwriteon/.*

One Wrong Number

Andrew Martin Robinson

Brony, 555-727-1397
(2 recipients)

Brony: Hey sibs, visited mom today.
Me: How's she doing?

My brother, Brodie, (a.k.a. Brony because he hates that nickname) sends a photo of our mom in her retirement home, a smile on her face, but a vacancy in her eyes. Looks about the same since I last saw her, but perhaps with minor improvement in her arthritis since she has no problem gripping the handle of her coffee cup.

Me: She looks goo
Brony: She ain't that old yet.
Me: Good*
Brony: She was sorta lucid. Kept calling me Jack.
Me: Can't imagine that made you happy.
Brony: Confusing me with the brother who hasn't seen her one time and can't be bothered to reply in our group chat? No. Not annoying in the least.(Just kidding, Jack...kinda)
555-727-1397: I'm sorry that happened. I've been meaning to visit.
555-727-1397: What's mom's room number, sis or bro?
Brony: 22

I send a text to Brodie on the side of our sibling group chat.

Me: Jack bet his phone in an "unlosable" poker hand?
Brony: Something like that.
Me: His new number came with a new personality?

Brony: Apparently. All hail New Jack. The brother that learned how to say sorry.

Me: And means to visit mom? And calls me sis? And doesn't just reply two weeks too late with a thumbs up or middle finger emoji?

Brony: It's strange, yeah.

Me: I'm going to try something. Don't reply.

Brony, 555-727-1397

(2 recipients)

Me: Hey Jack, send us a pic of the kids.

555-727-1397: Can't. All pics are on the old phone.

Me: Then take a picture of them right now and send it. I want to see my niece and nephew.

555-727-1397: They're asleep. I'll send one tomorrow.

Me: How's Claire?

555-727-1397: Claire's stable.

Me: Claire's dead, asshole.

555-727-1397: Yeah. Stable. Lol

Me: WOW.

Me: What are your kids' names?

A long delay.

555-727-1397: You know I'm not good with names.

Me: Who is this?

555-727-1397: I don't like being called asshole.

Me: Maybe try not being an asshole then.

I give Brodie a call and he answers immediately. "Dude, what's this punk's problem?"

Brodie laughs, finding it amusing.

"This isn't funny."

"It's a little funny, c'mon. I just sent an email to Jack and called him an idiot for giving me the wrong number."

"This makes me uncomfortable. It's a violation."

"It's some moron teen, laughing with his buddies. He actually had me going for a second."

"Jack can't even be bothered to send us the right phone number? Why do we even include him on our group texts?"

"He made a mistake. Yeah, see. He just emailed me back. Last number should be an eight, not a seven. He also said stop bugging him about mom. He'll get there when he gets there."

"Mom shouldn't have pushed her luck and just stopped at two kids."

"Jeez. Uncalled for."

"Called for." Brodie says nothing, knowing me well enough to wait for the guilt to hit. "Alright. Yeah. Uncalled for. I take it back."

My phone vibrates in my hand, rattling more than just my bones.

555-727-1397: DON'T CALL ME ASSHOLE.

555-727-1397: DON'T CALL ME ASSHOLE.

555-727-1397: DON'T CALL ME ASSHOLE.

"You see what this guy just sent us?"

"I don't like this anymore."

"What do we do?"

"Block him."

I put my phone on my desk, switch to speaker, but before I can block the number, a new barrage of texts come in:

555-727-1397: APOLOGIZE.

555-727-1397: APOLOGIZE.

555-727-1397: APOLOGIZE.

"This guy, dude! What the hell?" I say, losing my patience. Anger and fear duking it out in my head for supremacy.

555-727-1397: OR ELSE.

555-727-1397: OR ELSE.

555-727-1397: OR ELSE.

"Don't say anything," Brodie says. "Just block him."

Anger wins out and I text back:

Me: Sorry...

Me: ...Asshole.

"What are you doing? People kill people over stupid shit like this these days."

Anger wins out in Brodie, too.

My whole desk shakes with the vibration of another text.

555-727-1397: I'm going to visit Mom tonight.

"You see? You see what you did?"

"It doesn't matter. This loser doesn't know where Mom is."

As if the intruder on our group chat could hear me, another text:

555-727-1397: Room 22.

Me: *Uh oh. I'm shaking in my boots. Just put "Room 22" into Google Maps and I'm sure you'll get the right directions.*

"Seriously," Brodie says, voice stern, chastising. "That's enough. I'm going to get pissed if you reply again."

Another vibration. Another text. This time though, it's a picture. The same picture Brodie sent of our mom, but it's zoomed in and cropped. It's of my mom's coffee mug, emblazoned on it is a logo of a sun and words underneath it: SUNNY ACRES RETIREMENT HOME

555-727-1397: 11784 Sunny Dr. Havenmill, CA

A gut punch and a stab to the heart hit me at the same time. Fear pulls off a last second comeback victory.

"Damn it! What have you done?"

"It's a bluff," I say more to myself than to my brother. Hoping I'm right. But my trembling hands are moving of their own accord, grabbing my purse, finding my car keys. "Are you home?"

"Yeah."

"That means I'm closer."

"Not much closer."

"I'm driving to Mom's now. Call Sunny Acres. Get them to move Mom to a different room. After that, call the police."

"You don't actually think he's going to do something, do you?" A quiver in my brother's voice.

"I don't know," I say, sprinting down the stairs, yanking the door open, letting it slam the wall.

"What am I supposed to tell the police? There's a guy threatening to visit my mom?"

"Figure it out, Brodie!"

I'm in my car, backing out into the street when I see my front door still open. No time. I stomp on the gas pedal. Fifteen minutes away, but at this speed I can get there in ten.

I'm lucky it's late. Traffic's light. Wherever the chat intruder is, it's hard to imagine he lives closer than I do.

I run a red on Euclid.

And Cedar.

And Highland.

Five minutes away.

Never seen the speedometer pass 90 before.

In my pocket, my phone vibrates. Again. And again. And again. But I can't read it. Hands so sweaty I doubt I could even grip my phone. I need to focus. I'm driving too fast.

Two minutes away.

One.

My tires screech as I turn into the lot. I stop in front of the entrance in a parking space I invent for myself.

As I stride to the doors, I check my messages.

555-727-1397: *I'm going to bring Mom a gift, too.*

555-727-1397: *She doesn't have one of these, right?*

A picture message of a gloved hand holding a knife.

I didn't think I could possibly pick up my pace, but I do. I sprint through the doors and see the receptionist's desk unmanned, phone ringing. Beyond the desk, I see the receptionist in the back room, not working on anything except a French dip.

"You don't answer the phones here?" I say, sounding like a bitch. Don't care. Not right now.

I pick up the receptionist's phone and hear Brodie say, "Hello?" In the background, I hear honking.

"I'm here."

"I'm on my way. The cops wouldn't do anything."

The receptionist wipes *au jus* off her face and approaches. "We're short-staffed. I have a right to a lunch break."

"Did anybody pass through here in the last ten, fifteen minutes?"

"Just you," she says.

For the first time since this stupid text exchange started, I feel like I can breathe.

"I'm going to go say hi to my mother," I say, with no improvement in my tone.

I catch my breath as I walk down the hall, keeping my eyes on one side of the hall, passing room 16, room 18, room 20.

I open the door to my mother's room. The lights are off. Dark except for the light coming from the hallway. My shadow casts over my mother in her wheelchair.

She stares out her open window sitting very still.

"Mom?"

No reply.

No movement.

305

I step closer.

Into a puddle.

I turn her wheelchair, making her face me.

But there's not much left of her face.

The door closes behind me.

I'm not alone.

A hooded figure stands in the darkness, staring at me.

Cell phone in my hand, I turn on the flashlight and shine it on the man. On his knife.

I didn't know he was this desperate.

"Jack?"

"Maybe I am an asshole," my brother says.

My blood splatters on the floor before I can scream. I drop to my knees and hold my throat. I try to stand back up, but my feet slip in the blood.

Jack says, "You see how it's perfect, right?"

Down the hall, I hear Brodie yelling my name. His voice coming closer.

Jack moves back into the shadows.

Andrew Martin Robinson is a writer of horror and dark fiction. He is an active member of the Horror Writers Association. His fiction podcast Dream Sequence is slated for production in late 2023. Additional works and contact information can be found at www.andrewmartinrobinson.com. Beyond writing, he enjoys the controversial things in life like puppies, pizza, and paychecks.

Welcome to the Race

K. J. Shepherd

WELCOME TO THE RACE the sign reads. *Yeah, no shit.* I pan my head to the left. There are dozens of us. I look right. Even more that way. Bodies are pressed in behind us, as well. I can feel them breathing, can smell their desperation. The small beach is barely visible beneath our eager feet.

We are all that remains. Many of us are not whole. Missing limbs and knobbed stumps make us a grotesque reflection of our struggles. Our hunger.

I tighten my grip on my daughter's hand, lift her up. Her hands are around my neck, her legs lock around my stomach. I see many eyes cast in her direction. Hungry eyes.

"Hold on," I say.

A firework cracks in the distance.

The ground erupts as hundreds of feet pound down and into the water. I let the mass of rank bodies flow around me as I will my feet into the sand. Lira is nearly knocked from my shoulders, her whimpers lost to the maelstrom.

I shut my eyes hard. Patience is key.

Hands desperately pound the water, legs pump and churn, and a man is eaten. Tendrils of red spiral the water where he was a moment ago.

Madness ensues. Panic. More blood and gurgled screams. Bodies soon blot out the water. People are clamoring over the dead and dying.

Now!

I start to run across the piled-up bodies.

• • • ● • ● • • •

"Congratulations," the man in white says. "Welcome to the Phoenix." He gestures in a grand arc. "You've won."

The ship that would bear us to our new home towers above, immeasurable in scale, sleek, shiny, free. *It's so big.* Tears cut tracks in the salt on my face as I now allow myself to feel the weight of the race behind me. My knee buckles as I take a step and I go down to the sand. Lira wipes blood from her face and she tries to help me up.

The water behind froths red with countless bodies. A feeding frenzy for days. Fins and tails surge and wave among the floating corpses; the only movement left on the beach. They are starving just like us.

My eyes trail back to our savior. A deep shame settles into my bones, that we should make it when so many did not.

"Why like this?" I ask.

He stops. "Resources are limited. You know that. You knew when you signed up, Number," he turns back to me, gazing at my tattoo, "ninety-nine." He harrumphs in his throat, amused. "And that makes you number one-hundred." This to Lira. She clutches at her arm where the flesh was still tender. "It seems not only early birds get the worm."

I clench my fist at his callousness.

As we sail into the heavens on a jet of blue fire my gaze lingers still on the dying world below, consuming itself.

We right ourselves and sink back down on a distant chunk of rock, hundreds of miles from the first. The smoke clears, revealing dozens of people lined up on the distant shore, preparing for the race of their lives.

K. J. Shepherd was born in Missouri but doesn't remember it. He grew up in Texas and bounced around a bit before ending up back there, for better or worse. He spends his days hanging out with his daughter, Harper, reading and writing, playing video games, and obsessively listening to death metal (send some recommendations his way!). He has been writing most of his life, but only started submitting works in 2017.

He's been published by The Arcanist, Elegant Literature Magazine, Crystal Lake Publishing, Bag of Bones Press, Witch House Magazine, and Black Hare Press. He's also had works appear on The Other Stories horror podcast, and A Fistful of Demons, *an anthology of the Weird West.*

Senseless Act of Violence

Evan Bond

"So, you're the witch doctor?" she said with a tremble. She was nervous and afraid.

"No, not a witch doctor. A priest," the man in the fancy black suit said.

"Okay, priest then. But you're the guy I'm looking for, right? The voodoo priest?"

The man let out a laugh and sat on his stool. He unbuttoned his jacket and tipped his fedora at the woman standing before him. His smile was wide and genuine, showing off his perfect teeth. This is not what Simone had expected from a voodoo priest.

"Hoodoo, my dear. Not voodoo. But yes, I am the one you seek."

"Hoodoo?" Simone asked.

"Voodoo is a religion. Hoodoo harnesses magick from the Gods. Big difference."

"Right, well, I've spent a lot of time and money to get here so I need to know. Can you do what they say you can?"

The hoodoo priest gave her another toothy smile. He was a confident and handsome man.

"And what is it you hear I can do?"

Simone peered over her shoulder to make sure they were alone in the shop. She didn't need some nosey passerby hearing the business she was about to conduct. It felt foolish. Simone felt like she was there to buy drugs, but that couldn't have been further from the truth. If someone walking by had heard what she was truly there for, they might have her committed.

"The power to raise the dead," she whispered, letting the last word linger in the air like a cloud.

The Hoodoo priest stood up from the stool and walked over to the front window of his shop. He slid the blinds closed and locked the door. He turned to face Simone. She gave an audible gulp. The blood in her veins felt as cold as ice. Her nerves were beginning to run wild. Was this the man she was looking for? Or was it all a sham?

"Look, I've come a long way for your help. I drained my savings account to find you. This is all I have left," she said, pulling a wad of cash from her purse. "It's yours if you can do what I need you to."

"The death of a loved one cuts deep," the priest said. "Lucky for you, death is not always permanent. I can do what is required. Tell me, what happened."

Simone took a deep breath. She knew this story was going to come up sooner or later. Still, she had not wanted to tell it. The wounds were still too fresh. The pain still lingered. At first, she didn't think she would have the strength to repeat the story again. She had told it too many times already. The police, the paramedics, her family, and friends. The burden was too much.

"My husband," she started. "He got in an elevator in one of the office buildings downtown. He was there for a business meeting. I've always been so proud of how hard he works and what he brings home for this family. Our two little kids loved him very much. This other man in the elevator took him from us. Such a senseless act of violence. The cops told me he was an unstable man off his medication. But that man had the devil inside him. He stabbed my husband over thirty times. Sliced his throat right there in the elevator. When the police caught the man, he rushed them with the knife and they shot him to death."

Simone's hands shook as she recounted the story. She hated every second of its recital. The quicker she told it, the better.

"I require one thing from the deceased," the Hoodoo priest said. "A fluid from the body. Saliva, blood."

"I did my research, Priest."

Simone pulled a vial from her purse and placed it on the table in front of her. A dark red material sloshed inside. She hated having it in her purse. The sheer thought of the blood in her purse made her skin crawl. It had been with her for so long. Like a rain cloud, it followed her everywhere.

The Hoodoo priest picked up the vial and smiled at Simone. She slapped the cash down on the table and slid it toward him. But the priest shook his head and pushed it back.

"No, this I do for free."

Simone's eyes welled up with tears. She wiped them away as the priest ducked into the back room. She could hear noises like chanting from behind the door. Part of her still worried this was nothing more than a hoax. But why not charge her if that were the case?

After several minutes of excruciating waiting, the priest appeared from the backroom. He gave Simone a nod which told her the task was complete. The months of planning, paying, and searching had finally come to an end.

"Remember, the form he comes back in is not as you remember him. A zombie is not like the television shows you've seen. He will be your slave. Powerful magick has bonded him to you."

Simone nodded as she awaited her prize. This priest had done more for her than he could ever have realized. Finally, she would get true closure from such a horrific act.

A man stepped out from the back room with his head hung low. A servant awaiting an order.

"Thank you, priest. For everything. My husband's body was cremated before I knew about any of this. But when I learned the dead could come back, I knew I could get true justice for my husband's killer. Death had been too quick and too good for this bastard. Getting the blood was hard, but worth it. Now, he will know suffering by my hand until my dying day."

Simone smiled and beckoned for the man to follow. In her wake, she left the Hoodoo priest with his mouth hung open like a broken garage door.

Evan Bond *is a thriller/suspense author who loves blending his love of the outdoors with his writings. He is the author of the best-selling psychological thriller* Echoes of the Past *and his best-selling collection of short horror stories* Charred Remains. *He has always had a passion for telling suspenseful stories. Even at a young age, he was crafting horror stories to share with his family and friends.*

Evan Bond lives in Tampa, Florida with his wife, Melissa, their two boys, Desmond and Logan, and their dog Loki. When he's not writing, he can be found adventuring in the outdoors with his family and calling it "research" for his next novel.

You can follow Evan on his social media platforms like Instagram, Facebook, or Twitter.

The Dullahan's Reckoning

Claire Davon

Humphrey cursed when his driver stopped. He could think of no reason to halt in the night. Fear sweat dotted his forehead; his bad heart beat an irregular rhythm in his chest.

He banged on the window.

"Why are we halting? This hour is not safe." His voice quavered despite his efforts. Once it commanded the attention of men. Now it sounded as weak as the old man he had become.

The horses let out frightened whinnies. Humphrey clutched the pistol he held in his lap. The driver had a similar gun at his hip. Highwaymen roamed these lanes, prepared to rob the unwary, but Humphrey feared it was no bandit they faced.

He'd been warned this might happen. Still, he'd had no choice but to ride. If he did not, he might be dead by morning. Only his physician could help him.

"My lord, I had to stop. The road is blocked. It is...not human."

He had prepared for this. Humphrey Randolph could not be felled by ordinary means—or supernatural ones.

He jerked on the curtains and reeled back. No man could ever be prepared for the Dullahan.

It was at least eight feet tall, a dark figure of screams and nightmares. Humphrey had suspected that he would run into her on this road. It had always been his destiny. He had ways to thwart even such a creature as this.

The Dullahan pulled on the reins and her black mount reared into the air. Blood trickled from her neck, matched by the ichor on the staring head under her arm. Nothing could be concealed from her vision, not even on the darkest night. The wagon she hauled was decorated with skull candles, the wheel spokes human thigh bones.

"You will not take me this night, devil." Though he spoke in a low tone, she turned and stared directly at him. Her face burned with a red-hot glow and he longed to let the curtain fall but dared not. The Dullahan raised an arm, her blood-red stare fixed on his form. He fought not to shrink from her gaze.

"You will come with me," she said, her voice a thousand screams in the night. Her penetrating gaze left no doubt she saw Humphrey. "Release your hold on your mortal life. It is time."

"Not on your life." A thin stream of phlegm came out of his mouth as he gasped out the words.

"Sir? What is your order?"

Humphrey coughed again, his body aching. The doctor in London would cure him. He had prepared for this. He knew the dark portents well and assumed he would meet this monster on the road.

"The bag I handed you for safekeeping. Throw it to her. Quickly."

"Sir?"

"The bag. Throw it to her. We have no time for foolishness."

The nightmare carriage creaked. The head she carried—her head—looked at him. The horrid jaw moved, its teeth clacking. "You're doomed, old man. Your time is up."

He wanted to flee from the monster but that would only hasten his death. He had a plan. He couldn't let terror rule him.

He had heard it said that when the headless Dullahan called a man's name, the person dropped dead. He had no more time to waste.

"Not today, hellfire creature. Throw the thing, idiot driver. What are you waiting for?"

The candles in the coach beyond flickered, but never went out. The head grinned from ear to ear in an impossible smile that split its face in two. Its attention remained on him. Its victim.

As she came forward, Humphrey banged on the carriage wall with his walking stick.

"Throw it now, or I will have you flayed alive."

"As you say, sir."

The Dullahan came to a halt as the thrown sack bounced and spun on its edge before a coin tumbled out.

"That's got you now," Humphrey cackled. "You thought to take my soul, but you won't. That," he pointed to the object, "that will take care of you."

The Dullahan opened her mouth to speak, but Humphrey rushed in before she could.

"You're supposed to disappear now. They said that you throw a golden object in front of a Dullahan and they vanish. You need to melt back to the hell you came from."

Mist curled in wisps on the damp ground. The offering lay face up, the image of a woman holding a staff and clad in a robe glittering in the grass. Animals howled in the night, the chittering of bugs adding to the sounds.

The Dullahan patted the horse and it whickered. Humphrey banged on the coach. The driver jerked on the reins and the horses whinnied but didn't move.

"Let's go," Humphrey said.

Through it all the Dullahan stayed in place.

"She is still blocking the way."

"I know. Vanish, damn you!" Fear surged within him, leaving his hands shaking and his body trembling. "Begone. I command it!"

The Dullahan pointed to the coin. "That is not gold."

"What?" Humphrey gasped. "That's impossible. I bit it myself."

The Dullahan's horse pawed the ground, burying the piece.

"If you throw a golden object in my path I vanish. Do otherwise and I have no such compulsion. Your cheap ways have doomed you."

The Dullahan pointed her finger at the coach and said his name. Humphrey uttered a piteous whine as agony flooded his dying body. His mouth peeled back in a rictus when his heart stopped. Humphrey slumped over the seat. The misty form that was his soul flowed into the Dullahan's satchel.

She focused on the driver and gave him an infernal grin. "Next time it might be your name I call." She rode off, leaving the gasping coachman behind.

When the Dullahan had gone, the driver reached into his pocket and pulled out a gold coin.

"Did you think I wasn't aware of what was in the bag? Too bad, old man." He flicked the reins, and the horses trotted forward.

*USA Today Bestselling author **Claire Davon** has written for most of her life, starting with fan fiction when she was very young. She writes across a wide range of genres, and does not consider any of it off limits. Her novels can be found in the paranormal romance and contemporary romance sections, while her short stories run the gamut. If a story calls to her, she will write it. She currently lives in Los Angeles and spends her free time writing novels and short stories, as well as doing*

*animal rescue and enjoying the sunshine. Claire's website is www.clairedavon.co
m.*

Rain

Jim Horlock

There were many things that Michael loved but rain was chief among them.

The first sound that morning was the drumming on the roof. Before opening his eyes, Michael lay a while and listened, letting it wash over him. It never failed to bring him peace. Any day that started with that sound was going to be a good one. He could have stayed there for hours, wrapped in the blanket of that pitter-pattering, but he knew there were things to do. He didn't know how much time he had beyond not a lot, so he opened his eyes and pried himself up from sticky sheets to get started.

Angel was in the kitchen, where he'd left her. It made him sad to see her slumped across the table like that, on a pile of papers. Should he carry her to the bed? He considered it for a while but decided it was best to leave her undisturbed for now. Instead, he quietly made breakfast, stepping carefully over the letters and other mess that had fallen from the table. Michael had always been good at being quiet. He refused to look down at the tattered, sodden paper on the floor—the Pompeii ash of his life.

He indulged himself a while longer with the rain at the window, while sipping his coffee. For some, he knew, the love of rain stopped there, just with watching. For him, it wasn't enough; what he really loved was to be out there in it, to feel the cold of it seeping through his clothes, over his skin. Ever since that night by the roadside, where he'd watched in numbness as the blood was washed away, he'd understood that rain was the great cleanser. It was purity falling from above.

316

"Quiet" was what they'd called him after the accident. Some had said "withdrawn." Others had said "repressed." In truth, he couldn't remember much about it. Fright as the car skidded across the road. Pain. His mother's scream just before the impact. The drumming of water on the twisted metal. Sometimes, in dreams, he could see his father's face, crushed against the asphalt.

The ticking of the clock in the hall reminded him of pressing matters. It had been an anniversary gift from Angel, an antique of rich wood and bright gold metal. He'd always loved old things. He was sorry about the crack across the glass. Carefully, he lifted it from where it had fallen, as though it was an injured bird cradled in his big gentle hands. He was glad it was still ticking. It made him feel like everything would be all right. He hung it back on the wall, its outline marked into the wallpaper by time.

He'd get the kids ready first; always a challenge with youngsters. They'd inherited all of Angel's impulsiveness and fire. From Michael, they'd inherited nothing at all. He knew that now. He took a deep breath, tuning out everything but the sound of rain.

He bathed the kids and dressed them. None of this was their fault. They were victims, just as much as he was. At least they'd never have to grow up without parents, like he had. He'd spared them that. As Michael leant them at the foot of their favorite tree, the rain grew louder and louder in his ears. He let their heads slump forward to hide the bruising on their necks.

Things were more complicated with Angel. There was no amount of cleaning up for the ruined back of her head. The claw hammer was still matted with her hair. The table, chair and floor were soaked with her blood and there was just no time to clean it all. He settled for putting her on the loveseat in the living room. They'd cuddled there from time to time, but he'd always suspected she could feel how empty he was. Maybe that's what drove her to someone else.

He left the letters where they lay. The blood had rendered them unreadable now, but he knew enough about what they said. He couldn't bear any more details. He was glad the red had washed them out. In a way, he'd made rain of his own.

As the police arrived, Michael went out under the tumultuous sky and removed his clothes. Guns were pointed at him. Shouts sounded far away. His ears were full of the rain. He turned his head up and felt it washing him clean. The blood, the dirt, the sweat, the pain.

It was the best feeling.

Jim Horlock is a writer, dungeon master, and collector of ghosts. He lives in Wales, in an apartment full of taxidermy and loose drafts. You can find his work on Creepy Podcast, as well as in anthologies from Eerie River Publishing, Scare Street, Bag of Bones Press, and many other places. His short story collection Changes *is coming from Quill & Crow Publishing House in Summer 2024.*

Corporate Types

Derek Clendening

So, they fired me. Bunch of ingrates. I would tell you that I gave them the best years of my life, but that's not really true. I gave the Carriage House Motel and its previous owners the best years of my life. When ValuLodge bought the motel, Martin Lavallee took charge of what the people of Fort Erie, Ontario would forever call the Carriage House Motel despite the name on the sign.

And I was out.

Lavallee thanked me for my years of service and acknowledged that I'd worked there since I was a teenager, mopping the floor before becoming manager. But I was still out with all the lack of pomp and pageantry you can imagine. Specifically, "My services were no longer needed," as if a cold and formal tone would soften the blow.

But I'm not leaving.

I announced this to Lavallee, which he returned with a pause, like he couldn't decide how to interpret my stand. Surely, he would've known that someone like me would respond unfavorably. A cold fish like him had doubtless axed his share of vulnerable souls with little care for the fallout.

"We highly value your contributions and dedication." There he went with the corporate bullshit language again. "Although ValuLodge will always in some way be the Carriage House Motel, we have decided to go in a different direction."

Boy, didn't that just beat all?

"I'm not leaving."

"Why do you keep saying that?"

"If you fire me, I'm taking the ghost legend with me. What do you think about that?"

"How can you take the ghost legend with you? This will still be the Carriage House Motel but under the ValuLodge banner. The ghost legend is and will always be ours."

"There is no ghost in this place. Don't be ridiculous."

"What are you talking about?"

"The War of 1812 soldier with the bayonet who committed suicide in the room?"

"Yes, the one who seems perpetually angry since he never received a proper funeral thanks to his suicide."

"That's what we've been telling people for years. The story draws guests to the motel to hear the story behind the story. They pay extra to stay in the room where he killed himself, to hear noises their imaginations manufactured completely and generally scare themselves silly. Mr. Wilson who hired me, two owners ago, made that story up. He was very believable if I do say so, but I never felt good about the ruse."

"If you had such a moral objection, why not go public with the truth sooner?"

"I kept it quiet the way fast food workers never reveal what's in the secret sauce. Plus, I had far too much respect for Mr. Wilson."

"We here at ValuLodge find the story intriguing and plan to retain it as part of the house history and heritage."

"Until I leak the fraud and how this place has played people for suckers for decades."

"That is your privilege, sir. We here at ValuLodge believe we can succeed quite adequately with or without the legend."

"That story has kept this place afloat. Otherwise a motel this crappy with peeling wallpaper, stained carpets, molasses-slow Wi-Fi and a bug problem would only be frequented by people renting a room for sex."

"We here at ValuLodge endeavor to change that."

Let me tell you, this asshole had a corporate saying for every occasion.

He said I could take my time gathering my personal belongings before being escorted out. That was kind of him, but I'm not leaving. I told him again, and he couldn't say he hadn't been warned. There would be no losing the battle of the wills. So, I marched upstairs to room fifteen, site of the ghost legend, a .38 special in hand. I locked the door, unsure what I would do but certain the outcome would be bad.

I will admit I've always reacted poorly to confrontation. The only way I'd stood up to Lavallee like that was because of adrenaline. That much of a rush is hard for someone like me.

What would I do?

Lavallee phoned the police after discovering I'd taken refuge in the room. When they arrived, I watched them pull into the parking lot from my window. I cocked the gun, aimed it at the door and then paused. We'd kept the gun around in case of robbery, which was laughable, and look at the trouble it caused. The cops pounded on the door, demanding I emerge from the room unarmed.

Fat chance.

I'm not leaving. I told Lavallee that and he damn well should have listened.

The whole thing had driven me into a frenzy no matter how calm I thought I was being. On the inside, I went wild, my heart jackhammering and my lungs working overtime. I felt dizzy at first, light-headed. Next, my vision blurred, and it didn't matter what I wanted to do. My aging body made the decision for me.

When the police knocked the door down, they found my body sprawled on the floor, so Lavallee could at least say I'd died in the room. No shots were fired on either side, but the good people of Fort Erie could be counted on to distort the story with little regard for the truth.

They did just that, so Lavallee ran with the gunfire version. I bet that was why he gloated so zestfully afterward. He thought he'd won. He'd rid the Carriage House Motel of me while not only escaping my pitiable severance, but also keeping the ghost legend fraud silent.

Only I won't let him win no matter what.

He can't get rid of me. The Carriage House Motel is the only home I've known since I was a kid.

I'm not leaving.

Funny how this pompous ass thinks he's rid of me, but when the next guest enters room fifteen, they won't risk seeing a bayonet-wielding soldier, longing for a proper burial. No, they'll find a used-up, discarded motel manager with a .38 special, and a hunger for vengeance.

Who on earth would pay to see me?

Derek Clendening lives in Fort Erie, Ontario. In addition to work in the horror genre, he writes LGBT young adult romance. His Love and Justice serialization features both romance, the western genre and zombies. When he isn't writing, he loves going to the movies and cheering for the Buffalo Bills.

Shadow Dust

Diana Olney

It's not easy being imaginary. Make believe may seem like fun and games, but it can still hurt you. Trust me, I know. I've been playing dead so long, I'm practically a ghost.

I don't believe in ghosts, but maybe I should. No one believes in me either. No one...except one little girl.

But she's not little anymore. Sarah is getting older, too old for imaginary friends. She hasn't seen me in a while.

I live in her shadow now, with the darkness and dust. But I won't stay here forever.

I know the way out.

· · · ● · ● · ● · · ·

Today, Sarah finally noticed me. She was sitting in bed, her blue eyes glistening like two crystal ponds. She looked up, and I saw myself in the water. Together, we remembered who I was.

I asked her what was wrong. She frowned and glanced out the window. She said she wanted to run away.

I told her I could help.

· · · ● · ● · ● · · ·

We're leaving tonight. I wasn't strong enough before, but Sarah has put me back together again. Just like our old nursery rhymes.

She's at the vanity, getting ready. I tell her not to bother with make-up. She's too old to play with me, but still too young for all that lipstick.

She asks where we're going. I tell her it's a surprise.

She watches as I make the door. The frame, the hinges, the handle, all appear like magic, and when she sees them, they're not imaginary. They're real. Real enough to touch.

It's now or never. I turn the handle. I open the door.

Sarah follows.

· · · · ●·●· ● · · ·

The world is our map, unfolding its pages like a bird soaring across the night sky. The possibilities are endless. We can go anywhere we want.

I let Sarah choose. She picks the park. This worries me. She has less imagination than I thought.

But I indulge her. We sit on the swings, and I listen while she talks. She tells me about school, her friends, her parents. Her parents might get a divorce. That's why she wants to leave. She's sick of being stuck in the middle. She wants to be on her own.

I promise her she can. This seems to cheer her up. She smiles, and I know what she's thinking. She remembers now how useful I am.

But she'll forget again. Every so often, I see that faraway look in her eyes, and I know I'm in trouble. It's time to go. We have to keep moving, or we'll drift apart.

I know where to take her. I lead her past the playground, toward the woods. At the tree line, I make another door. This time, Sarah opens it.

Her eyes light up the moment we go inside.

"It's the enchanted village," she whispers.

I nod. I remember. We spent half her childhood here.

We rush into the square. The buildings glisten in the moonlight, each one a falling star. I watch us walk in the windows. Sarah steps in front of me, and my reflection shivers in the glass, its soft shape slipping into hers. For a moment, we are the same person.

Sarah runs ahead, racing through her memories. She passes the chapel, the shops, townhall. Then she looks over her shoulder at me. I can tell she's disappointed. This place isn't the same anymore. It used to be full of magic, but the fairy tales that lived here have moved on. Now all that's left are their ghosts.

I guess I believe in them now.

I wonder if Sarah does.

She's at the diner now. I catch her smiling in the doorway. This was our favorite place, our home away from home.

You can tell right away who the decorator was. The ceiling is Sarah's Sistine Chapel—Crayola rainbows and smiling clouds—and the walls are candy apple red, the same shade as the lipstick she's wearing. Every booth has its own soda machine.

We take our usual table, and Sarah pours herself a glass of 7-Up. She downs it in three gulps.

Then she looks at me.

"Why did you bring me here?" she asks.

I start to reply, but the room answers for me. First, with a rumble, then a loud snap, like a bone being broken in half. I glance up at the ceiling. There's a crack in it now.

I had a feeling this would happen.

Sarah gasps, leaping out of the booth. The walls are bleeding, spilling their candy apple guts all over the floor.

Chaos ensues.

We try to flee, but a cinderblock cloud crashes down in front us, blocking the exit. The sky is literally falling.

I glance back at Sarah. She's just standing there, staring. She must be in shock.

This is my chance. I reach out, tracing the shape of my escape route. The window opens, and I slip outside. Then I shut it behind me.

Two hands appear in the glass, pounding like drums. The window is locked.

Sarah screams.

"It's okay," I shout. "You can fix this. Just calm *down*."

She isn't listening.

Meanwhile, her imagination is running wild. I try to make a new door, but it doesn't work. This place is unstable now. Even the air is moving too quickly.

So, I run. I don't look back.

Around me, the buildings shatter, releasing their ghosts into the streets. But I don't let them stop me. I push past the darkness, leaving its blind eyes behind.

The door is waiting.

It's still open. I leap through it, and the frame collapses, crumpling like paper.

I turn around. The village is gone.

So is she.

But it's a beautiful morning. The sun is rising, repainting the horizon. As it touches the trees, all the leaves turn to gold.

I smile, stepping into the light. There are no shadows anymore.

Diana Olney *is a Seattle based fiction writer, but she is most at home in the shadows, wandering the dark paths between nightmares and dreams. She has authored many twisted tales, which can be found in the following collections:* These Lingering Shadows, The Monsters Next Door, Dark Horses Magazine Issue 20, Shallow Waters Vol. 9, The Devil You Know Better, *and the upcoming anthology,* To Hell & Back. *She is also the creator of Siren's Song, a horror themed comic series soon to be haunting bookshelves near you. Currently, she is writing two novellas and a leaning tower of short stories. Visit her at dianaoln ey.com for updates on her latest releases.*

S/MART

Jonah Buck

Automatic data recovery. Retrieving requested files. This may take a few moments... Scanning for viruses...

Data recovered. Display?

ENTRY ONE: 03/06/25/02:51:29

Hello! Welcome to your new S/MART (Security/Maintenance Automated Realty Technologies, LLC) Home! Thank you for choosing S/MART Home. New user detected. Please enter your personal information.

Name: *Vernon Young*

Please enter your date of birth.

ERROR: January 4, 1672 is not a valid date of birth. Please enter a valid date of birth.

You have chosen to skip this question. Please continue to build your personal profile.

You have selected QUERY. Are you looking for topics on *How to finish your personal S/MART profile, Upgrading to S/MART Premium Security,* or *Something else?*

You have selected *Something else.* Please enter a few key words to help us direct you through our database of answers.

We're sorry, but we don't have any S/MART guides relating to: *What demoncraft is this?*

We're sorry, but we don't have any S/MART guides relating to: *Out, out vile devil.*

We're sorry, but we don't have any S/MART guides relating to: *Why can the people in this house not see me?*

We're sorry, but we don't have any S/MART guides relating to: *What year is it?*

We're sorry, but we don't have any S/MART guides relating to: *Torment me not with your infernal witchcraft! Answer my questions.*

We're sorry, but we don't have any S/MART guides relating to: *What in the blazes is that?* Do you mean *Jeeves* the fully automated robotic vacuum and cleaning companion unit?

We're sorry, but we don't have any S/MART guides relating to: *Rein back your Satanic familiar! I will not submit myself to your demonic clutches like these other poor wretches caught in your grasp. Back I say, damn you!*

We've noticed you seem to be having difficulties. Do any of these features help? *Put Jeeves into sleep mode, Upgrading to S/MART Premium Security,* or *Something else?*

Jeeves will now enter sleep mode. Can your S/MART Home help you with anything else?

You have selected *No.*

ENTRY TWO: 03/18/25/17:43:37

Greetings, User Jessica! [Internal notice only. Voice logs show User Jessica responds to "Jess," "Honey," and "Mom." Recent search history includes "is it dangerous my child swallowed a tiny plastic dinosaur," "greek food near me," "candles," "relaxation candles," "scented candles lemon," and "smart home parent controls." Information packet distributed to targeted marketing division]. How can your S/MART Home help you today?

Parental Control Options.

Find additional S/MART user profiles.

Display. User POOP FART. Profile created by User Kaiden, age 11.

User profile POOP FART *deleted.*

Display. User BUTT CHEEKS. Profile created by User Kaiden, age 11.

User profile BUTT CHEEKS *deleted.*

Display. User VERNON YOUNG. Profile created by ERROR.

User profile VERNON YOUNG *deleted.*

Enacting new parent control settings. Thank you, your new S/MART Home system will apply these new settings.

ENTRY THREE: 03/30/25/03:18:41

Hello! Welcome to your new S/MART (Security/Maintenance Automated Realty Technologies LLC) Home! Thank you for choosing a S/MART Home. New user detected. Please enter your personal information.

Vernon Young

Deleted profile. Recover data?

You have elected to skip finishing setting up your new S/MART profile. Are you sure? S/MART Home can tailor temperature, lighting, and security features to your personal preferences with your profile settings.

You have selected QUERY. Are you looking for topics on *How to finish your personal S/MART profile, Upgrading to S/MART Premium Security,* or *Something else?*

You have selected *Something else.* Please enter a few key words to help us direct you through our database of answers.

What ungodly powers have you granted this family, foul demon? I have seen them communing with fellow witches through magical plates of glass via the arcane conjuring of "internet." They speak into small, dark bricks they call "fones," with lenses dark as sin, and voices answer them. They cook their food without the aid of a fire. Is this the price of a soul these days?

Query blocked by Parent Controls.

What rank in Hell's armies does this arch-demon Google have? I have seen this coven consulting with him many times.

Query blocked by Parent Controls.

Does this General Electric command the demonic host? His name is etched on several unnatural artifacts here.

Query blocked by Parent Controls.

Why have I been placed back on this earth in the midst of these demon worshipers? Is this hell I now find myself in? I was... I am a good man. I personally hanged three witches after the colonial justice courts found them guilty. Though I did not relish it, I would have killed a hundred-fold more, if it safeguarded the souls of my neighbors. Why have I been cast out of the light of Heaven? What sin did I commit to be placed in this devil's den?

Query blocked by Parent Controls.

Grotesque deceiver, I should not ask you these things. I should not ask questions from a minion of the Father of Lies. But I am adrift. Torment me not with your refusals. What purpose do I serve now that I am a mere shade of my former self? Am I to save these lost souls from their wicked ways? Or to stop them? Answer me!

Query blocked by Parent Controls.

Very well. Your refusal speaks volumes. But know this. I may be spat forth from the grave, but I am not powerless. In the end, I will best you. Evil will be defeated. I merely pray that it does not cost me my eternal soul.

ENTRY FOUR: 04/08/25/23:02:42

Greetings, User David! [Internal notice only. Voice logs show User David responds to "Dave," "Honey," and "Dad." Recent search history includes "can i sue if my house was built on a graveyard," "reduced property value if house built on a graveyard," "do they have to tell you before you buy if land used to be a graveyard," "lawyers near me," "identifying bones," "how to tell if a bone belonged to a human or animal" and "found weird bone in garden." Information packet distributed to targeted marketing division]. How can your S/MART Home help you today?

You selected *Security Summary*.

07:14:31 User David left S/MART Home

07:49:12 User Jessica left S/MART Home

07:49:19 User Kaiden left S/MART Home

09:11:52 User Vernon Young signed in

09:12:08 User Vernon Young query blocked

09:14:32: User Vernon Young signed out

11:18:41: User Jessica entered S/MART Home

11:22:36: User Jessica adjusted temperature settings

13:32:17: User Jessica left S/MART Home

14:54:20: User Vernon Young signed in

15:55:01: User Vernon Young changed security setting personal preferences

16:18:43: User Kaiden entered S/MART Home

16:18:53 User Jessica entered S/MART Home

17:21:22: User David entered S/MART Home

18:41:26: User Vernon Young signed out

22:16:35: User Vernon Young signed in

22:17:11: User Vernon Young changed security setting personal preferences

You have selected Security Settings. Search for "Vernon Young" invalid. Please upgrade to S/MART Home Premium Security for additional user features.

You have selected internet search. Query: "Vernon Young"

See social media for Vernon Young? 87 results.

New Query: "Vernon Young obituary"

Search results: (1) Colonial Obituaries Online (2) News: "Historical Society Objects to New Subdivision Expansion" (3) Explore Your Local History! Historical Tour [CANCELLED]

New Query: How to tell if your house is haunted

New Query: Hotels near me

ENTRY FIVE: 04/09/25/04:11:10

Greetings, User Vernon Young! [Internal notice only. No voice logs recorded involving User Vernon Young. Recent search history includes "Release these people from your detestable grip, devil," "Take me instead, or you will force my hand," "Fiend, in the name of God, I banish you back to the pit from whence you came," "Very well. I will prevent your taint from corrupting this land any further" and "Please, forgive me." Information packet distributed to targeted marketing division]. How can your S/MART Home help you today?

Security Settings

Fire Alarms: Set to OFF

All doors: Set to LOCKED

All windows: Set to LOCKED

WARNING: SMOKE DETECTED

Automatic Emergency Call Function: OVERRIDE

User Jessica is attempting to place a manual call to Emergency Services

CALL CANCELED by User Vernon Young

Jeeves is detecting large quantities of spilled liquid. Analysis running. Blood detected. Would you like your S/MART Home to place an automated call to Emergency Services?

You have selected *No.*

Excess heat beyond personal preference settings detected. Current temperature is ERROR.

Your *Jeeves* Automated Vacuum Unit is now offline. Catastrophic damage detected. Would you like to place an order for a new *Jeeves* Automated Vacuum Unit?

You have selected *No.*

User David is attempting to place a manual call to Emergency Services

CALL CANCELED by User Vernon Wells

User Jessica is attempting to activate automated fire suppression systems. Please upgrade to S/MART Premium Security package to access automated fire suppression systems.

ERROR. Significant damage to structure detected.

ERROR. User Jessica's S/MART Fitness Watch has overheated. Disconnected.

ERROR. User David's S/MART phone app has overheated. Error Log: Phone Temperature High. Disconnected.

ERROR. Central Unit Overheating.

User Vernon Wells has signed out. Thank you for trusting us with your S/MART Home!

ERROR. System Failure.

Jonah Buck wanted to study eldritch knowledge and commune with pale, furtive beings that flit across the sunless landscape to terrorize the living, so he became an attorney in Oregon. His interests include history, exotic poultry, paleontology, professional stage magic, and prosecuting international drug trafficking organizations. He is the author of several books including Carrion Safari, Substratum, *and* 100 Dark Horror Stories.

Unholy Night

Francesca Maria

White flurries, illuminated by the moonlight, fly like wingless angels. It is the only thing of beauty on this night, void of grace, void of warmth. Black droplets litter the snow, the darkness conceals a crimson hue—the only trace of our presence. Another extraction, another token gathered for the Master.

The sack is full tonight. He will be pleased. Shimmering down snow laced rooftops, we move without detection, shielded by the night. Each of us have quotas to hit that none of us dare miss. For if our bags are not full, we are forced to make up the difference. A consequence too many of us had to face.

It gets more difficult with each passing year. So many children harvested for the Master. It's tortuous to think of the lives lost, unlived to their full potential. Worse yet, the unbearable alternative.

His emaciated shape comes in wisps, pale and starved these last three hundred and sixty-four days. Barely solid, he cannot wait until we return to the village. Materializing a raptor claw from an ethereal skeletal arm, he grabs the burlap off my shoulder, peering inside for the treats within. A child is chosen at random. A round boy with plump cheeks and pudgy legs that kick in the air. The child's scream fades into the blizzard as he takes his last breath. The same raptor's claw slices open the boy's neck pouring its contents into the Master's newly formed mouth. Blood drizzles down the pointed chin, splattering the untouched snow. He drinks. Raising the child by his hair, he brings the boy closer, squeezing the young body with monstrous claws ensuring every drop makes it into his bottomless maw.

As the feeding continues, Master takes on more of his traditional form. His cheeks now glow a rosy red. The second child grants him muscle and sinew. The third, tissue and skin. The fourth, fills out his suit, now stained with the blood that flows like a cascade down into every pore. The leather belt around his waist squeals in protest, stretching to the breaking point.

More.

Hungry obsidian eyes, shaped like almonds speak to us without words.

More.

We each produce our sacks, filled with children from around the globe, collected this unholy night. Master feeds, grunting, now in full form, growing rotund with each child he consumes, with each life he takes. The empty husks are discarded like candy wrappers and left for us to retrieve. We hurriedly placed the corpses back into the sacks for incineration. The damp, hollowed bodies cause me to wretch. The older gnomes laugh at my weakness. They don't remember what it was like. It has been too long since they were human.

I wish I no longer remembered. That night, so many years ago, is etched into my psyche. Every time I close my eyes, my abduction plays out in vivid detail.

• • • ● • ● • ● • •

I was eleven when I heard the pitter patter on the rooftop. Eager to catch a glimpse of St. Nicholas I ran outside in my nightgown. I can still feel the cold on my bare feet on the fresh snow from that night. The winter air cut through my skin, whipping through my gown.

A grunt, low and urgent from behind brought a different kind of chill to my bones. I will never forget that first encounter. A large white mass, the size of a barn door, bent over something out of view. It slithered and undulated with a snail's slime, spraying clear residue as it shook. Its back was to me. In the fading light of the moon, I made out no features, save a row of vertebrae that protruded unnaturally from translucent skin, high and sharp like hunting knives. It grunted again and as it sensed my presence, turned and locked onto me.

Black, soulless eyes imprisoned me where I stood. My excitement at seeing the beloved Santa churned into a mixture of total despair and hopelessness. Those eyes stole all sense of joy from the world.

A circular mouth with two rows of serrated teeth appeared, accompanied by a sucking sound. The rest of the body was a misshapen slug with bulges that pushed against a thin layer of skin. Twin claws like that of a vulture jutted out from the mass.

As my young gaze took in the sight, I recognized something familiar in its grasp. Blond hair, white with the moon, fell in strands toward the ground. Below, a pool of red formed a perfect circle in the virgin snow. The creature was holding a limp child by one hand, causing it to lean at an angle toward the ground. Clara. My little sister, not yet eight, was dangling from the creature's grip. Her lifeless body made a light thump sound as it dropped into the pool of blood. She was perfect. She could have been sleeping, save for the jagged dark fissure across her neck.

The monster ran to me, sniffing my hair with its open mouth. It had power that prevented me from running or crying or screaming. I remained frozen as Master surveyed my being, taking in my essence with its gaping orifice.

I saw the gnomes then, peeking out from the shadows with their pointy red hats and white beards. Four of them grabbed my sister, one on each limb, and placed her into a sack. Two more stood on either side of me. We were the same height—the gnomes and I. It was an odd thing to notice at the time.

Master made a clucking sound as he faced the night sky. He gestured toward me with a wink of his eye and I was placed in the sack—the same one that contained the body of my little sister, Clara. Her cold hand brushed across my face. A hand I held so many times before.

Once at the village, I learned I would never see my family again. My life was spared though my fate is worse than that of my dear sister. At least her life was over quickly. I am bound for an eternity by Nicholas and his insatiable hunger, in my pointy red hat and shoes to match.

There are rules even he cannot break. The Rule of One is paramount. Only one child may be fed upon per household, no more. The second, Rule of Seeing states that once a child sees the Master, they may never be allowed to tell another. They are either killed or transformed into gnomes and forced to do Master's bidding.

Every Christmas Eve, we scour the planet for the purest of souls for Master to feed upon—never more than one from the same home. Each year he demands more. Each year his hunger grows. I don't know how many households there are left that do not have at least one child given to its hunger. I wonder what will happen then.

Francesca Maria writes dark fiction surrounded by cats near the Pacific Ocean. She is the creator of the Black Cat Chronicles, a true horror comic book series narrated by a mystical black cat. Her short story collection They Hide: Short Stories to Tell in the Dark *from Brigid Gate Press debuted as an Amazon #1 Best Seller. Her short stories and essays can be found in various anthologies and publications including Crystal Lake Publishing's Shallow Waters,* Death's Garden Revisited *and* Under the Stairs. *You can find her at francescamaria.com.*

Red Christmas

Taylor Grant

It was safer in the darkness.

For Gabby, it was a refuge from the screaming, the anger, and the violence.

She was still small and nimble enough to burrow into the farthest corner of the closet. A sanctuary amidst shadows and storage boxes.

Squeaky, a golden-brown hamster, was curled in her lap next to Ruby Rose, a unicorn plushie. She gave both a light squeeze to let them know how much she loved them.

The screaming and violence continued.

Gabby could make out certain words, though she didn't understand all of them. "Bankruptcy" and "foreclosure" were foreign concepts, but the word "cheating" came up a lot as well. Gabby often wondered what game her mom had cheated on that would make her dad so angry.

Something crashed against a wall, the sudden shock striking somewhere inside Gabby's chest. Squeaky uttered a single *squeak.*

"Shhh," Gabby whispered in the blackness, stroking the hamster's back.

Soon there was a familiar hacking noise from her mother, as if a dog were choking up a bone. Then came the whimpering cry.

Gabby let out a deep breath. She could tell this particular battle was nearly over.

She gently placed Squeaky onto a folded quilt her grandma had sewn and reached underneath to grab the flashlight she kept hidden there.

The hamster's ears were up, whiskers twitching, large round eyes blending into the darkness. Gabby snapped the light on, lifted the nearest box's lid, and pulled out various items her grandma had left behind.

There was a set of teacups, a pair of horn-rimmed glasses, a harmonica, newspaper clippings, a photo album, and other odds and ends. There were also some well-worn books with their pleasing musty smell.

Most of the books were too advanced for Gabby's reading skills, but they made her feel closer to her grandma at a time when her heart ached with grief. Her beloved protector had passed away two months ago after a long illness, and Gabby felt as if she had lost her life raft in a raging storm.

As she reached the bottom of the box, she took note of the only book she hadn't browsed before. It had no title and was heavy, with a red cloth cover. Inside, she spotted an envelope inscribed with a single handwritten word: Gabby.

Her expression changed from morose to sheer delight as she opened it. Inside was a handwritten letter from her grandma, purposely written in simple language the young girl would understand. Grandma had known Gabby struggled a bit with reading and spelling, suffering as she did from a mild form of dyslexia, and she still needed to "sound out" words, which often took some time.

The letter read:

Hi angel,

Your mom and dad don't believe in magic, but of course, you and I do. So, I've written out a prayer for you to prove magic is real.

I know I promised you a Christmas present, but sadly, it looks like I may not be with you this year. Instead, please accept this magic prayer as my gift.

If you believe in miracles they can come true! Make sure to read the attached prayer out loud on Christmas Eve—you'll see how magical life can be.

Remember, you must BELIEVE.

I love you with all my heart.

Grandma

PS. Keep this letter and book a secret!

Tears brightened Gabby's eyes and made them glitter like dark stars in the night sky. She wiped at them, skimming through the prayer, which was all about Santa Claus, magic, and the power of belief.

Christmas had been one of the few joys of Gabby's short life. Flying reindeer. Elves. A generous, plump man who came bearing gifts one miraculous night per year. She embraced it all.

Though her parents were not ones for flights of fancy, her grandma had spent years weaving wonderful tales of Jolly ol' St. Nick. And true to Grandma's word, Santa had always left something Gabby wanted under the Christmas tree each year.

Her parents seemed to despise Christmas as much as they despised each other. But due to persistent urgings from her grandma, they had resigned themselves to going along with the holiday year after year.

338

This year, on the other hand, was looking bleak. Without Grandma's influence, her parents hadn't put up a single decoration.

Gabby missed the bright, beautiful Christmas tree most of all.

Her mom had said coldly, "We can't afford one this year. Get over it." When Gabby had cried, her mom backhanded her, sending her crashing into the kitchen table and cutting her upper lip.

But Gabby didn't want to dwell on that. She began deciphering her grandma's prayer. After all, tomorrow night was Christmas Eve, and this was her chance to bring peace to her home with the power of magic.

· · · ● · ● · ● · · ·

The following day Gabby spent most of it in her room reciting the prayer repeatedly.

As night fell, she peeked out of her bedroom window and was astonished to see snow spilling down like quiet feathers. *The prayer worked!* She thought. For she'd never experienced a white Christmas in real life and stood in wonder as snow danced in the night air.

Neither of Gabby's parents had said a word to her since breakfast, which was just as well. Silence was a welcome alternative to the screaming. She remembered the famous line from the book *Night Before Christmas*, which her grandma had read to her many times. *'Twas the night before Christmas, when all through the house, not a creature was stirring, not even a mouse.*

That line had partly inspired Gabby's Christmas wish. No toys. No pretty dresses. Just a quiet, peaceful home.

That was when she saw the shadow pass across her bedroom window.

"Santa?" she uttered quietly, pressing her nose against the frigid glass.

She immediately spotted a tall, gaunt figure on the front lawn, cast in shadow. There was a flash of what looked like a red suit, and the silhouette of a beard, but that was where similarities to Santa ended.

The skeletal figure looked inhumanly tall, with odd-shaped limbs that stretched unnaturally. He dropped to the snow-covered ground and *slithered* toward her two-story house.

Gabby's initial delight had turned to fear. The reddish Santa-thing began to crawl up the side of the house like a spider...straight towards her bedroom window.

Backing away in horror, she watched as it began to ooze through the tiny space between the bottom sash and the sill. She'd always wondered how Santa entered homes without chimneys, and the answer was now clear. He poured through the slit-like bright red blood and reconstituted inside her room.

Inexplicably, the scream that had been building in her throat dissipated the moment he offered his disarming grin. In his eyes there seemed to be an understanding. As if he knew her pain intimately and was there to take it away.

She didn't flinch when he reached out with elongated fingers and placed them gently on her shoulder. Instinctively, she knew he wasn't going to hurt her.

This wasn't Santa, of course.

It was Satan.

With her mild dyslexia, Gabby occasionally reversed letters. And unbeknownst to her, the prayers' multiple references to "Old Nick" were definitely not the same as St. Nick.

Old Nick glanced down then, seemingly impressed by the ancient evocation symbol on the floor drawn with fresh, innocent blood. Gabby had prepared it exactly as the details of the prayer had instructed.

She had noticed many such symbols in her grandma's untitled book with the red, cloth cover. The text, however, remained indecipherable, as it was written in a different language.

In the center of the symbol were the bloodied remains of her beloved Squeaky, who had sacrificed his life just a short time ago. Gabby had hidden the small carpenter's ax she'd used in the back of the closet.

"You've done well, Gabby," said Old Nick.

She gathered her courage and said, "My parents are downstairs drinking wine and watching TV."

"Indeed," he grinned knowingly.

Gabby watched, awestruck, as his exceptionally long fingers sprouted black claws, like those of a fierce bird, right before her eyes.

A grin spread across the young girl's face. "Can I watch?"

Old Nick gave a rich, full-throated laugh and his eyes sparkled with delight. "You are a special one, aren't you?" He gestured for the door. "Lead the way, young lady."

Gabby felt special at that moment, and more importantly, she felt safe in his presence. Much like her closet sanctuary, she felt safer in the darkness. Perhaps she might help her new guardian more in the future and benefit from his continued protection.

Moments later, they headed downstairs to see Gabby's parents about her Christmas wish.

There would, of course, be terrible, anguished screams and blood-splattered walls. But by Christmas morning, Gabby would receive her wish of long-lasting peace at home.

Two-time Bram Stoker Award Finalist **Taylor Grant** *has spent the larger part of his career as a professional storyteller. His work has been seen on network television, the big screen, the stage, the Web, as well as in comic books, newspapers, national magazines, anthologies, and heard on the radio.*

As an author, Taylor has been published by Random House, Cemetery Dance, Crystal Lake Publishing and many more. His first collection, The Dark at the End of the Tunnel, *was nominated for a Bram Stoker Award.*

As a screenwriter, he has sold multiple feature film projects to studios such as Universal, Lionsgate Films, and Imagine Entertainment. His professional writing career began in children's entertainment, writing scripts and develop-

ing stories for such shows Beetlejuice, Mighty Morphin Power Rangers, *as well as* Monster Farm, *which he created for TV. He also wrote music videos for major artists that aired on MTV and VH1. His short films* The Vanished *and* Sticks and Stones *both received distribution through Sony, premiered at the prestigious Cannes Film Festival, and were picked up by SHORTS TV, which has over 100 million subscribers worldwide.*

He is currently Head of Global Animation at Wattpad WEBTOON Studios, where amongst many other things, he is a producer of the upcoming horror film Gremoryland, *alongside Roy Lee and Vertigo Entertainment (*The Ring, It Chapter 1 *and 2). As a WEBTOON creator, Taylor wrote and produced the #1 horror comic adaptation* Rot & Ruin *for WEBTOON, which now has over 13 million reads on the platform.*

THE END?

Not if you want to dive into more of Crystal Lake Publishing's Tales from the Darkest Depths!

Check out our amazing website and online store or download our latest catalog here.https://geni.us/CLPCatalog

Looking for award-winning Dark Fiction?
Download our latest catalog.

Includes our anthologies, novels, novellas, collections, poetry, non-fiction, and specialty projects.

TALES FROM THE DARKEST DEPTHS

We always have great new projects and content on the website to dive into, as well as a newsletter, behind the scenes options, social media platforms, our own dark fiction shared-world series and our very own webstore. Our webstore even has categories specifically for KU books, non-fiction, anthologies, and of course more novels and novellas.

Readers...

Thank you for reading this special print addition of Shallow Waters. We hope
you enjoyed this anthology.

If you have a moment, please review it at the store where you bought it.

Help other readers by telling them why you enjoyed this book. No need to
write an in-depth discussion. Even a single sentence will be greatly appreciated.
Reviews go a long way to helping a book sell, and is great for an author's career.
It'll also help us to continue publishing quality books.

Thank you again for taking the time to journey with Crystal Lake Publishing.

You will find links to all our social media platforms on our Linktree page.
https://linktr.ee/CrystalLakePublishing

Follow us on Amazon:

MISSION STATEMENT

Since its founding in August 2012, Crystal Lake Publishing has quickly become one of the world's leading publishers of Dark Fiction and Horror books in print, eBook, and audio formats.

While we strive to present only the highest quality fiction and entertainment, we also endeavour to support authors along their writing journey. We offer our time and experience in non-fiction projects, as well as author mentoring and services, at competitive prices.

With several Bram Stoker Award wins and many other wins and nominations (including the HWA's Specialty Press Award), Crystal Lake Publishing puts integrity, honor, and respect at the forefront of our publishing operations.

We strive for each book and outreach program we spearhead to not only entertain and touch or comment on issues that affect our readers, but also to strengthen and support the Dark Fiction field and its authors.

Not only do we find and publish authors we believe are destined for greatness, but we strive to work with men and women who endeavour to be decent human beings who care more for others than themselves, while still being hard working, driven, and passionate artists and storytellers.

Crystal Lake Publishing is and will always be a beacon of what passion and dedication, combined with overwhelming teamwork and respect, can accomplish. We endeavour to know each and every one of our readers, while building personal relationships with our authors, reviewers, bloggers, podcasters, bookstores, and libraries.

We will be as trustworthy, forthright, and transparent as any business can be, while also keeping most of the headaches away from our authors, since it's our job to solve the problems so they can stay in a creative mind. Which of course also means paying our authors.

We do not just publish books, we present to you worlds within your world, doors within your mind, from talented authors who sacrifice so much for a moment of your time.

There are some amazing small presses out there, and through collaboration and open forums we will continue to support other presses in the goal of helping authors and showing the world what quality small presses are capable of accomplishing. No one wins when a small press goes down, so we will always be there to support hardworking, legitimate presses and their authors. We don't see Crystal Lake as the best press out there, but we will always strive to be the best, strive to be the most interactive and grateful, and even blessed press around. No matter what happens over time, we will also take our mission very seriously while appreciating where we are and enjoying the journey.

What do we offer our authors that they can't do for themselves through self-publishing?

We are big supporters of self-publishing (especially hybrid publishing), if done with care, patience, and planning. However, not every author has the time or inclination to do market research, advertise, and set up book launch strategies. Although a lot of authors are successful in doing it all, strong small presses will always be there for the authors who just want to do what they do best: write.

What we offer is experience, industry knowledge, contacts and trust built up over years. And due to our strong brand and trusting fanbase, every Crystal Lake Publishing book comes with weight of respect. In time our fans begin to trust our judgment and will try a new author purely based on our support of said author.

With each launch we strive to fine-tune our approach, learn from our mistakes, and increase our reach. We continue to assure our authors that we're here for them and that we'll carry the weight of the launch and dealing with third parties while they focus on their strengths—be it writing, interviews, blogs, signings, etc.

We also offer several mentoring packages to authors that include knowledge and skills they can use in both traditional and self-publishing endeavours.

We look forward to launching many new careers.

This is what we believe in. What we stand for. This will be our legacy.

Welcome to Crystal Lake Publishing—Tales from the Darkest Depths.